PENGUIN BOOKS

LIGHT FROM HEAVEN

Jan Karon is the author of nine Mitford novels, *At Home in Mitford*; *A Light in the Window*; *These High, Green Hills*; *Out to Canaan*; *A New Song*; *A Common Life*; *In This Mountain*; *Shepherds Abiding*; and *Light from Heaven*, all available from Penguin. She is also the author of *The Mitford Bedside Companion*; *Jan Karon's Mitford Cookbook & Kitchen Reader*; *A Continual Feast*; *Patches of Godlight*; *The Mitford Snowmen: A Christmas Story*; *Esther's Gift*; and *The Trellis and the Seed*. Her children's books include *Miss Fannie's Hat*; *Jeremy: The Tale of an Honest Bunny*; *Violet Comes to Stay*; and *Violet Goes to the Country*.

www.mitfordbooks.com

Join the Mitford community online to share news, recipes, birthday greetings, and more, and to receive notes from Jan and special offers.

www.penguin.com

The Mitford Years

Light from Heaven

JAN KARON

Penguin Books

PENGUIN BOOKS
Published by the Penguin Group
Penguin Group (USA) Inc., 375 Hudson Street,
New York, New York 10014, U.S.A.
Penguin Group (Canada), 90 Eglinton Avenue East, Suite 700, Toronto, Ontario, Canada
M4P 2Y3 (a division of Pearson Penguin Canada Inc.) • Penguin Books Ltd, 80 Strand,
London WC2R 0RL, England • Penguin Ireland, 25 St Stephen's Green, Dublin 2, Ireland
(a division of Penguin Books Ltd) • Penguin Group (Australia), 250 Camberwell Road,
Camberwell, Victoria 3124, Australia (a division of Pearson Australia Group Pty Ltd) •
Penguin Books India Pvt Ltd, 11 Community Centre, Panchsheel Park, New Delhi –
110 017, India • Penguin Group (NZ), 67 Apollo Drive, Rosedale, North Shore 0632,
New Zealand (a division of Pearson New Zealand Ltd) • Penguin Books (South Africa)
(Pty) Ltd, 24 Sturdee Avenue, Rosebank, Johannesburg 2196, South Africa

Penguin Books Ltd, Registered Offices:
80 Strand, London WC2R 0RL, England

First published in in the United States of America by Viking Penguin,
a member of Penguin Group (USA) Inc. 2005
Published in Penguin Books 2008

5   7   9   10   8   6   4

Copyright © Jan Karon, 2005
Illustrations copyright © Penguin Group (USA) Inc., 2005
All rights reserved

"Let the Stable Still Astonish" by Leslie Leyland Fields, appearing in *Christmas: An Annual
Treasury* (Augsburg Fortress, Minneapolis, 1995). Reprinted
by permission of the author.

ISBN 0-670-03463-0 (hc.)
ISBN 978-0-14-311351-5 (large print pbk.)
CIP data available

Printed in the United States of America
Set in Adobe Bembo
Designed by Francesca Belanger

Illustrations by Donna Kae Nelson

For my sister and brothers,
Brenda Wilson Furman, Barry Dean Setzer,
and Phillip Randolph Setzer,
who helped me become better
than I might have been . . .

And in memory of Clarence Bush,
beloved younger brother of my grandmother
(Miss Fannie), who perished in World War I,
and all the brothers and sisters who have
given their lives in mortal conflict
and are lost to us forever.

Acknowledgments

James Davison Hunter; Colin Hunter; Kevin Coleman; Mac McClung; Ed Abernathy; Jessi Baker; Gloria Berberich; Brenda Hyson; Fr. Anthony Andres; Stewart Brown; Fr. Edwin Pippin; *Cook's Illustrated;* Robert Mares; Betty Pitts; Tanya Faidley; Alex Heath; Bobbie Dietz; Kathy Campbell; Melissa Wait.

Lacey Wood; Wayne Erbsen; Bill Watson; Carol Hill; *The Anglican Digest;* Mike Thacker; Cheryl Lewis; Rick Moore; Joel Valente; Bonnie Setzer; Johanna Farmer; Mrs. Scott Newton, deceased; Susan Cunningham; Brenda Furman; Goldie Stargell; Lillian Ballard; John (J. D.) Diven; Martha Sanusi; Tal Bonham; Royce Elliott; Jeff Pozniak; Judy Austin; Marcelle Morel; Wendell Winn Jr.; David Vander Meulen; Mary Ann Odom.

Dr. Paul Klas; Dr. August Sanusi; Dave Archer; Charlene Norris; Dr. Chris Grover;

Fr. Peter Way; Dr. Christopher Holstege; Candace Freeland.

Special thanks to: Bishop Keith Ackerman; Joann Ackerman; Brad Van Lear; Richard Rankin; Polly Hawkes.

Light from Heaven

If thou indeed derive thy light from Heaven,
Then, to the measure of that heaven-born light,
Shine, Poet! In thy place, and be content . . .

—WILLIAM WORDSWORTH

Contents

Light from Heaven

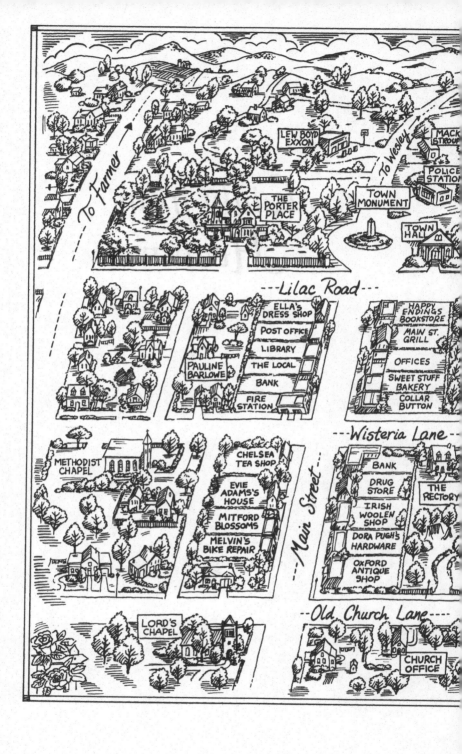

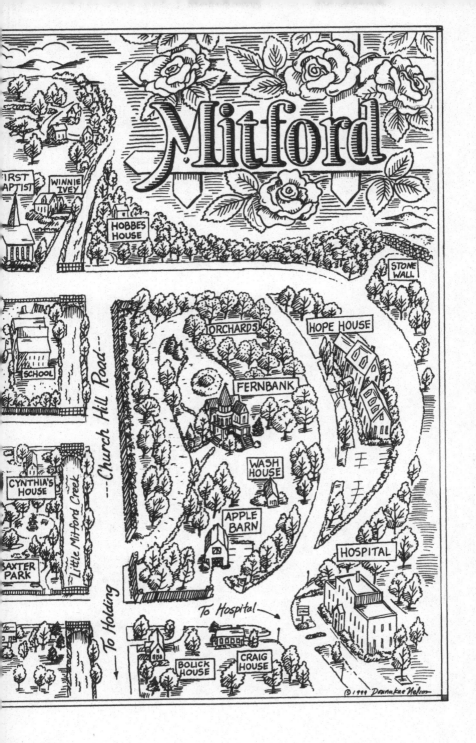

Mitford

FIRST BAPTIST

WINNIE IVEY

HOBBES HOUSE

STONE WALL

SCHOOL

ORCHARDS

HOPE HOUSE

FERNBANK

WASH HOUSE

CYNTHIA'S HOUSE

—Church Hill Road—

Little Mitford Creek

APPLE BARN

HOSPITAL

BAXTER PARK

To Holding

To Hospital

BOLICK HOUSE

CRAIG HOUSE

© 1999 Donnakae Nelson

CHAPTER ONE

A Winter Eden

The first flake landed on a blackberry bush in the creek bottom of Meadowgate Farm.

In the frozen hour before dawn, others found their mark on the mossy roof of the smoke-house; in a grove of laurel by the northwest pasture; on the handle of a hoe left propped against the garden fence.

Close by the pond in the sheep paddock, a buck, a doe, and two fawns stood motionless as an owl pushed off from the upper branches of a pine tree and sailed, silent and intent, to the ridge of the barn roof.

The owl hooted once, then twice.

As if summoned by its velveteen cry, the platinum moon broke suddenly from the clouds above the pond, transforming the water's surface into a gleaming lake of molten pearl.

Then, clouds sailed again over the face of the moon, and in the bitter darkness, snowflakes fell thick and fast, swirling as in a shaken globe.

It was twelve minutes after six o'clock when a gray light rose above the brow of Hogback Mountain, exposing an imprint of tractor tires that linked Meadowgate's hay barn to the cow pasture and sheep paddock. The imprints of work boots and dog paws were also traceable along the driveway to the barn, and back to the door of the farmhouse, where smoke puffed from the chimney and lamplight shone behind the kitchen windows.

From a tulip poplar at the northeast corner to the steel stake at the southwest, all hundred and thirty acres of Meadowgate Farm lay under a powdery blanket of March snow.

Cynthia Kavanagh stood in the warmth of the farmhouse kitchen in a chenille robe, and gazed out on the hushed landscape.

"It makes everything innocent again," she said. "A winter Eden."

At the pine table, Father Timothy Kavanagh leafed through his quote journal until he found the record he'd jotted down. "Unbelievable!

We've had snow one, two, three, four . . . this is the fifth time since Christmas Eve."

"Snow, snow, and more snow!"

"Not to mention dogs, dogs, and more dogs! It looks like somebody backed up to the door and dumped a truckload of canines in here."

Following his customary daylight romp, Barnabas, a Bouvier-wolfhound mix and his boon companion of ten years, was drowned in slumber on the hearth rug; Buckwheat, an English foxhound grown long in the tooth, had draped herself over the arm of the sofa; the Welsh corgi, aptly named Bodacious, snored in a wing chair she had long ago claimed as her own; and Luther, a recent, mixed-breed addition to the Meadowgate pack, had slung himself onto his bed in the corner, belly up. There was a collective odor of steam rising from sodden dog hair.

"Ugh!" said his wife, who was accustomed to steam rising off only one wet dog.

Father Tim looked up from the journal in which he was transcribing notes collected hither and yon. "So what are you doing today, Kavanagh?"

Cynthia mashed the plunger of the French coffee press. "I'm doing the sketch of Violet looking out the kitchen window to the barn, and I'm calling Puny to find out about the twins—they're days late, you know."

"Good idea. Expected around March fourth or fifth, and here it is the fourteenth. They'll be ready for kindergarten."

"And you must run to Mitford with the shopping list for Dooley's homecoming dinner tomorrow."

"Consider it done."

His heart beat faster at the thought of having their boy home for spring break, but the further thought of having nothing more to accomplish than a run to The Local was definitely discouraging. Heaven knows, there was hardly anything to do on the farm but rest, read, and walk four dogs; he'd scarcely struck a lick at a snake since arriving in mid-January. Willie Mullis, a full-timer who'd replaced the part-time Bo Davis, lived on the place and did all the odd jobs, feeding up and looking after livestock; Joyce Havner did the laundry and cleaning, as she'd done at Meadowgate for years; Blake Eddistoe ran the vet clinic, only a few yards from the farmhouse door, with consummate efficiency; there was even someone to bush hog and cut hay when the season rolled around.

In truth, it seemed his main occupation since

coming to farm-sit for the Owens was waiting to hear from his bishop, Stuart Cullen, who had e-mailed him before Christmas.

<Heads up:

<I will almost certainly have something for you early next year. As you might expect, it isn't anything fancy, and God knows, it will be a challenge. Yet I admit I'm patently envious.

<Can't say more at this time, but will be in touch after the holy days, and we shall see what's what (I do recall, by the way, that you're spending next year at the Owens' farm, and this would not be a conflict).

He had scratched his head throughout the month of January, trying to reckon what the challenge might be. In February, he'd called Stuart, attempting to gouge it out of him, but Stuart had asked for another couple of weeks to get the plan together before he spilled the beans.

Now, here they were in the middle of March, and not a word.

"You're sighing, Timothy."

"Wondering when Stuart will get off the pot."

"He's retiring in June *and* consecrating the cathedral—altogether, a great deal to say grace over. You'll hear soon, dearest."

She handed him a mug of black coffee, which he took with gratitude.

So here he sat, retired from nearly four decades of active ministry as a priest, toasting himself by an open fire with his good-humored and companionable wife of seven years, and situated in what he believed to be the most breathtakingly beautiful countryside in America.

Why bother, after all, about some "challenge" that may or may not be coming. Hadn't he had challenges enough to last him a lifetime?

His wife, on the other hand, was ever drumming up a challenge. During their year at the farm, conveniently located twenty minutes from Mitford, she'd decided to accomplish three lifetime goals: learn needlepoint, make perfect oven fries, and read *War and Peace*.

"So how's it coming with *War and Peace*?"

"I despise telling you this, but I haven't opened it *once*. I'm reading a charming old book called *Mrs. Miniver.*"

"And the fries?"

"Since Dooley comes tomorrow, I'll be conducting my next experiment—to see whether soaking the potatoes in ice water will make them crispier. And I'm definitely using peanut oil this time."

"I'll peel and cut," he said. He hadn't seen any activity around the needlepoint plan, so he declined to mention it.

"Pathetic," she said, reading his mind. "I'm all thumbs. Learning from a book is not the way to do it. I've decided to let Olivia tutor me, if she has a free day now and then. Besides, having lunch with someone who also wears eye shadow might be fun."

"I'm definitely a dud in the eye shadow department."

She thumped into the wing chair opposite him and took a sip from her coffee mug. "And what about you, dearest? Have you accomplished all your lifetime goals?"

Oddly, the question stung him. "I suppose I haven't thought about it." Maybe he hadn't wanted to think about having any further goals.

He closed his eyes and leaned his head against the back of the wing chair. "I believe if I were charged with having a goal, it would be to live without fretting—to live more fully in the moment, not always huffing about as I've done in recent years . . . to live humbly—and appreciatively—with whatever God furnishes."

He reflected for a moment and raised his head and looked at her. "Yes. That would be my goal."

"But aren't you doing that?"

"No. I feel obligated to *get out there,* to open myself to some new and worthwhile service. I've been a bump on a log these last weeks."

"It's OK to be a bump on a log once in a while. 'Be still,' He tells us, 'and know that I am God.' We must learn to wait on Him, Timothy. All those years of preaching and celebrating, and doing the interim at Whitecap—what a lovely legacy God allowed you to have there; and ministering to Louella and Miss Sadie and Hélène Pringle and Morris Love and George Gaynor and Edith Mallory and the Leepers . . ." She took a deep breath. "On and on, an entire community, for heaven's sake, not to mention volunteering at the Children's Hospital and rounding up Dooley's little sister and brothers . . ."

"One brother still missing," he said, "and what have I done about it?"

"There may be nothing you can do about it. There's absolutely nothing to go on, no leads of any kind. Maybe God alone can do something about it. Perhaps Kenny is God's job."

The fire crackled on the hearth; the dogs snored.

His wife had just preached him a sermon, and it was one he needed to hear. He had a mate who knew precisely what was what, especially when he didn't.

"'Let us then be up and doing,'" he quoted from Longfellow, "'with a heart for any fate!' Where's the grocery list?"

"In my head at present, but let's get it out." She opened the small drawer in the lamp table and removed her notebook and pen.

"Steak!" She scribbled. "Same old cut?"

"Same old, same old. New York strip." This would be no Lenten fast, but a Lenten feast for a starving college boy who was seldom home.

"Russet potatoes," she said, continuing the litany.

"Always best for fries." His blood would soon get up for this cookathon, even if he couldn't eat much on the menu. While some theologians construed St. Paul's thorn to be any one of a variety of alarming dysfunctions, he'd been convinced for years that it was the same blasted affliction he'd ended up with—diabetes.

"Pie crusts," she said, scribbling on. "Oh, rats. For the life of me, I can't remember all the ingredients for his chocolate pie, and of course, I didn't bring my recipe box."

"I never liked the recipe we use," he said, suddenly confessional.

"You're not supposed to even touch chocolate pie, Timothy, so what difference does it make? Dooley loves it; it isn't half bad, really."

"It needs something."

"Like what?"

"Something more . . . you know."

"Whipped cream!"

His wife loved whipped cream; with the slenderest of excuses, she would slather it on anything.

"Not whipped cream. Something more like . . ." He threw up his hands; his culinary imagination had lately flown south.

"Meringue, then."

"Meringue!" he said, slapping his leg. "That's it!"

She bolted from her chair and trotted to the kitchen counter. "Marge's recipe box . . . I was thumbing through it the other day and I vaguely remember . . . Let's see . . . Onions in Cream Sauce, Penne Pasta with Lump Crabmeat, that sounds good. . . ."

"Keep going."

"Pie!"

"Bingo."

"Buttermilk Pie . . . Vinegar Pie . . . Fresh Coconut . . ."

"Mark that one!"

"Egg Custard . . . Fresh Peach . . . Deep-Dish Apple . . ."

"Enough," he said. "I'm only human."

"Here it is. Chocolate Pie with Meringue."

"Finish that list, Kavanagh, and I'm out of here."

Ha! He'd denied himself as sternly as one of the Desert Fathers these last weeks; he would have the tiniest sliver of that pie, or else . . .

"I know what you're thinking," she said.

He pulled on his jacket and foraged in the pockets for his knit cap, and kissed her warm mouth.

"You always know what I'm thinking," he said.

His hand was on the doorknob when the phone rang.

"Do try to find a haircut while you're in town," she said, picking up the receiver. "You've got that John-the-Baptist look again. Hello! Meadowgate Farm."

He watched her pause, listening, then grin from ear to ear.

"Thanks for calling, Joe Joe. That's wonderful! Congratulations! Give Puny our love. I'll be over on Thursday. Timothy's headed into Mitford now, I'm sure he'll stop by."

"*So?*" he asked, excited as a kid.

"Boys! Weighing in at fifteen pounds total! Thomas and . . ." She paused, and looked all-knowing.

"*And?*"

"Thomas and *Timothy!*"

"No!"

"Yes! One named for Puny's grandfather and one named for you. Now there are two little boys in this world who're named for you, and I hope you realize that people don't go around naming little boys for a bump on a log."

Boys! And because Puny's father was long deceased, he would be their granpaw, just as he was granpaw to Puny and Joe Joe's twin girls.

His entire chest felt suffused with a warm and radiating light.

He turned onto the state road, which had already been scraped for the school buses, and headed south past the Baptist church and its snow-covered brush arbor. He glanced at the wayside pulpit, which was changed weekly.

IF LOVING GOD WERE A CRIME, WOULD YOU BE IN JAIL?

Getting around was a piece of cake. The heavens had given them only a couple of inches, and in a farm truck built like a tank, he felt safe and thoroughly above it all.

Patently envious. Patently envious. What could a bigwig bishop, albeit his oldest friend, envy in a country parson? There it was again, the tape running in a loop and promising to work his mind into a lather.

"I roll this whole mystery over to You, Lord," he said aloud, "and thank You for this day!"

In truth, the whole day belonged to him. He would stop by the hospital to see Puny and her new brood; he would run over to Hope House and visit Louella; he would make a noon stop at Lew Boyd's Exxon where the Turkey Club was lately convening; he would have a chin-wag with Avis at The Local. . . .

As for getting a haircut, he had no intention of trusting his balding head to Fancy Skinner ever again, period; Joe Ivy had retired from cutting hair and wanted nothing more to do with such a trade; trooping to the barber shop in Wesley would take too much time. So, no, indeed, absolutely not, there would be no hair-cut on this trip into civilization.

The sun broke through leaden clouds and flooded the countryside with a welcome light.

"Yee hah!" he shouted against the consider-able din of the truck engine.

Why had he felt so bereft and grumpy only a half hour before, when he was now beginning to feel like a new man?

He switched on the radio to the blast of a country music station; it was golden oldies time.

"*I bought th' shoes that just walked out on me. . . .*" someone sang. He sang along, hardly caring that he didn't know the words.

"Country come to town!" he whooped as he drove into Mitford.

Roaring past the Exxon station, he blew the horn twice, just to let the general public know he'd arrived.

He bent and kissed her forehead.

"Well done," he said, a lump in his throat. Two sets of twins! May God have mercy. . . .

"They're whoppers," she said, smiling up at him.

His so-called house help of ten years, and the one whom he loved like a daughter, lay worn but beaming in the hospital bed.

He took her hand, feeling the rough palm that had come from years of scrubbing, polishing, cooking, washing, ironing, and generally making his life and Cynthia's far simpler, not to mention indisputably brighter.

"Thank you for naming one of your fine boys after this old parson."

"We won't call 'im by th' fancy name. It'll jis' be Timmy."

"Timmy. I always liked it when Mother called me Timmy."

"Timmy an' Tommy," she said, proudly.

"Timmy and Tommy and Sissy and Sassy."

"You'll be the *boys'* granpaw, too," she said, in case he hadn't considered this.

"It'll be an honor to be their granpaw."

"Father?"

Since he'd officiated at her wedding several years ago, she had taken to calling him by his priestly title in a way that subtly claimed him as her true father. He never failed to note this. Blast, if he wasn't about to bawl like baby. "Yes, my dear?"

"I sure do love you and Cynthy."

There they came, rolling down his cheeks like a veritable gulley washer. . . .

"And we sure do love you back," he croaked.

"So, how's the food at Hope House these days?"

He sat on the footstool by Louella's rocking chair, feeling roughly eight or ten years old, as he always had in the presence of Miss Sadie and Louella.

"Oh, honey, some time it's good, some time it ain't fit for slop." He noted that Louella said *ain't* now that Miss Sadie, who forbade its use, had passed on. "You take th' soup—th' menu has th' same ol' soup on it every day, day after day, long as I been here." She looked thoroughly disgusted.

"What soup is that?"

"Soup du jour! If they cain't come up with more'n one soup in this high-dollar outfit, I ain't messin' with it."

"Aha," he said.

"My granmaw, Big Mama, said soup was for sick people, anyway, an' I ain't sick an' ain't plannin' to be."

"That's the spirit."

Louella rocked on. The warm room, the lowering clouds beyond the window, and the faint drone of the shopping network made him drowsy; his eyelids drooped. . . .

Louella suddenly stopped rocking. "I been meanin' to ask—what you doin' 'bout Miss Sadie's money?"

He snapped to attention. "What money is that?"

"Don't you remember? I tol' you 'bout th' money she hid in that ol' car."

"Old car," he said, clueless.

"In that ol' Plymouth automobile she had."
Louella appeared positively vexed with him.

"Louella, I don't have any idea what you
mean."

"Your mem'ry must be goin', honey."

"Why don't you tell me everything, from the
beginning."

"Seem like I called you up an' tol' you, but
maybe I dreamed it. Do you ever dream somethin' so real you think it happened?"

"I do."

"A while before she passed, Miss Sadie got
mad 'bout th' market fallin' off. You know she
made good money in that market."

"Yes, ma'am, she did." Hadn't she left Dooley Barlowe a cool million plus at her passing?
This extraordinary fact, however, was not yet
known to Dooley.

"She say, 'Look here, Louella, I'm goin' to
put this little dab where those jack legs at th'
market can't lose it.' I say, 'Miss Sadie, where
you goin' to put it, under yo' *mattress*?' She say,
'Don't be foolish, I'm goin' to put it in my car
an' lock it up.' She'd quit drivin' an' her car was
up on blocks in th' garage. She say, 'Now don't
you let me forget it's in there.'"

"And?" he asked.

"An' I went an' let 'er forget it was in there!"

The 1958 Plymouth had been sitting for several years in the garage behind Fernbank, Miss Sadie's old home on the hill above Mitford. Fernbank was now owned by Andrew Gregory, Mitford's mayor, his Italian wife, Anna, and his brother-in-law, Tony.

"Well, it probably wasn't much," he said, reassuring.

"Wadn't *much?* It mos' certainly *was* much. It was nine thousand dollars!"

"*Nine thousand dollars?*" He was floored.

"Don't holler," she instructed. "You don't know who might be listenin'."

"You're sure of that amount, Louella?"

"*Sure,* I'm sure! Miss Sadie an' me, we count it out in hun'erd dollar bills. How many hun'erd dollar bills would that be? I forget."

"Umm, that would be ninety bills."

"Yessir, honey, it was ninety, it took us 'til way up in th' day to count them hun'erds out, 'cause ever' time we counted 'em out, Miss Sadie made us start all over an' count 'em out *ag'in!*"

"Good idea," he said, not knowing what else to say.

"We got a rubber band and put it aroun' all them bills, an' took out a big envelope and whopped 'em in there, an' I licked th' flap and sealed it up tight as Dick's hat band, so nothin' would fall out.

"She say t' me, 'Louella, you th' best frien' I ever had, but you cain't go down there with me, this is between me an' th' Lord.'

"Then she struck out to th' garage, an' when she come back, she was proud as a pup wit' two tails.

"I say, 'Miss Sadie, where you put that money in case you pass?' She say, 'I ain't goin' t' pass any time soon, don't worry about it. Sometime later she mention that money; we was livin' at Miss Olivia's ol' house. She say she ought to go get it out of where she put it, but th' market was still real bad.

"Then, we both plumb forgot.

"Th' other day I was settin' in this rockin' chair watchin' th' soaps an' it come to me like a lightnin' strike. I said, oh, *law*! Somethin' bad goin' to happen to Miss Sadie's money, an' Miss Sadie, she'll be *hoppin'* mad."

He was dumbfounded by this strange turn of events. As far as what might be done about it, his mind felt oddly pickled.

Louella's immense bosom heaved with a sense of the urgent mission to be carried forth; she leaned toward him and lowered her voice.

"So," she said, "what you goin' t' do 'bout Miss Sadie's money?"

On the way to Main Street, he zoomed by their yellow house on Wisteria Lane and found it looking spic, not to mention downright span. Harley's general supervision of its welfare made it possible to spend this carefree year at Meadowgate.

He threw up his hand and waved.

"We'll be back!" he shouted.

He wheeled into Lew Boyd's Exxon, still occasionally referred to as the Esso station, and saw the Turkey Club sprawled in plastic deck chairs inside the front window. The lineup included J. C. Hogan, longtime *Mitford Muse* editor; Mule Skinner, semiretired realtor; and Percy Mosely, former proprietor of the now-defunct Main Street Grill.

He'd been hanging out with this bunch for eighteen or twenty years, and it had been a rude awakening when Percy and Velma packed it in last Christmas Eve, vacating a building that quickly became a discount shoe store. Currently occupying the spot where the club's rear booth had stood was a rack of women's pumps, sizes eight to ten.

"Hooboy!" Mule stood and saluted. "Here comes our Los Angelees movie producer."

"Who, me?"

"Pretty soon, you'll be whippin' that back in a ponytail an' wearin' a earring."

Father Tim suddenly felt his hair flowing over his shoulders like a medieval mantle.

"Come on, leave 'im alone," said Percy. "He's livin' out in th' boonies, he don't have to slick up like we do."

"If you call that slicked up, I'm a monkey's uncle."

"How long're you stuck out there in th' sticks?" asked Percy.

"Hal and Marge will be living in France for a year, so . . . roughly nine more months. But we don't feel stuck, we like it."

"I lived in th' country when I was comin' up," said Percy, "an' it like to killed me. They ain't nothin' but work on a farm. Haul this, fix that, hoe this, feed that. If it ain't chickens, it's feathers."

"About time you showed up, buddyroe, my fish san'wich is goin' south." J.C. rooted around in his overstuffed briefcase and came up with something wrapped in recycled foil.

Mule sniffed the air. "How long has that thing been in there?"

"Seven o'clock this morning."

"You're not goin' to *eat* it?"

"Why not? Th' temperature's just a couple degrees above freezin'."

Father Tim noted that the editor's aftershave should effectively mask any offensive odors within, loosely, a city block.

"What'd you bring?" Mule asked Percy.

"Last night's honey-baked pork chop on a sesame-seed roll with lettuce, mayo, and a side of chips."

"Man!" said Mule. He expected that anybody who'd owned the Grill for forty-odd years would show up with a great lunch, but nothing like this. He peered into his own paper sack.

"So, what is it?" asked J.C., hammering down on the fish sandwich.

"I can't believe it." Mule appeared disconsolate. "Fancy's got me on some hoo-doo diet again."

"Why is your wife packin' your lunch? You're a big boy, pack your own bloomin' lunch."

Mule examined the contents of the Ziploc bag. "A sweet potato," he said, devastated. "With no butter."

"A sweet potato?" Percy eyed the pathetic offering with disbelief. "What kind of diet is that?"

Mule slumped in his chair. "I can't eat a sweet potato; no way can I eat a sweet potato. I feel trembly, I had breakfast at six-thirty and now it's way past twelve."

"What'd she give you for breakfast? A turnip?"

"Hard-boiled eggs. I hate hard-boiled eggs; they give me gas."

"So, Percy," said Father Tim, unwrapping a ham and cheese on white from the vending machine, "see what you did by going out of business? Left us all high and dry."

"Yeah," said Mule. "I was happy with things th' way they were."

J.C. gobbled the remaining half of his sandwich in one bite. "Ah guss nobar hurrbowwissonor . . ."

"Don't talk with your mouth full," snapped Mule, who was digging in his pockets for vending machine change.

J.C. swallowed the whole affair, and knocked back a half can of Sprite. "I guess you turkeys didn't hear the latest about th' Witch of th' North."

"Witch of th' *South*," said Percy, recognizing the nickname, albeit incorrect, for his much-despised former landlord.

"Turns out she said her first clearly understandable word since that big crack on th' head in September."

"Money!" exclaimed Percy.

"What about money?"

"Money had to be th' first word out of that back-stabbin', hardhearted, penny-pinchin' . . ."

"Now, Percy," said Father Tim.

J.C. glared at the assembly. "Do you want to hear th' dadgum story or not?"

"Say on," commanded Father Tim.

"Ed Coffey was in town yesterday, haulin' stuff out of her carriage house up at Clear Day to take down to her Florida place. He said that right before he left, she was sittin' in her wheelchair at th' window, lookin' at birds, and she motioned him to come over. . . ."

Mule looked disgusted. "If brains were dynamite, Ed Coffey wouldn't have enough to blow his nose!"

"Then, she motioned 'im to come *closer*. . . ."

The Turkey Club sat forward.

"Ed said instead of all that word salad she'd been talking, she spoke up as good as anybody. . . ."

"What'd she *say*, dadgummit?" Percy's pork chop was stuck in his gullet; if there was anything he disliked, it was the way some people had to be th' bride at every weddin' and th' corpse at every funeral.

"Yessir, he said he was standin' right there when it rolled out, slick as grease."

"You already *told* us that, you goofball. What was it she *said*?"

J.C. wiped his perspiring forehead with a wadded-up paper towel. "Get off my bumper," he snapped at Percy.

The *Muse* editor sat back in the plastic chair and looked once more at the eager assembly. "She said God."

"God?" Percy and Mule exclaimed in unison.

"No way!" Mule shook his head. "No way Edith Mallory would've said God, unless she was tryin' to say th' word that used to get my butt whipped when I was little."

"Right," said Percy. "No way."

Yes, thought Father Tim. Yes!

He stopped by the grease pit where Harley Welch was lying on his back under a crew-cab truck.

"Harley!" He squatted down and peered at his old friend.

"Rev'ren', is that you?"

"What's left of me. How's it going?"

"Goin' good if I can git this U joint worked offa here. When's our boy comin' home?"

"Tomorrow. We'll catch up with you in a day or two. Did you hear about the twins?"

"Yessir, hit's th' big town news. Spittin' image of th' ol' mayor, they say."

He laughed. "I guess Lace is coming in?"

"Yessir, she's wrote me a time or two lately; you know she got that big scholarship."

"I heard. That's wonderful! By the way, when is the last time you worked on Miss Sadie's car?"

"Oh, law, that's goin' too far back f'r m' feeble mind. Let's see, didn't she pass in th' spring?"

"She did."

"I worked on it sometime before she passed, she was still drivin'. I remember she rolled in here one mornin', I had to change out 'er clutch. Miss Sadie was bad t' ride 'er clutch."

"Do you know if it's still parked in the garage up at Fernbank?"

"I don't know if he's sold it. They was some talk Mr. Gregory was goin' to restore it. . . . George Gaynor worked on it a day or two, maybe. I cain't hardly recall."

"You pushing along all right with Miss Pringle?" Hélène Pringle was the piano teacher who rented his house in Mitford, and Harley was his old buddy who lived in the basement.

"Let's jis' say I've heered more piana music than I ever knowed was wrote."

Father Tim laughed. "Come out to the sticks and see us, will you?"

"I will," said Harley. "I'll bring you'uns a pan of m' brownies."

"I'll hold you to it."

"How's Miss Cynthy?"

"Couldn't be better." He stood, hearing the creaking of his knees. "Got to put the chairs in the wagon, as my grandmother used to say, and run to The Local. Regards to Miss Pringle!"

He walked to the truck, whistling a tune he'd heard on the radio.

There was nothing like a visit to Mitford to get a man's spirits up and running.

He blew through the door of one of his favorite Mitford haunts, the bell jingling behind him.

"'I love the smell of book ink in the morning!'" he called out, quoting Umberto Eco.

"Father Tim!" Hope Winchester turned from the shelf where she was stocking biographies. "We've missed you!"

"And I, you. How are you, Hope?"

She lifted her left hand to his gaze.

"Man!" he said, quoting Dooley Barlowe.

"It was his grandmother Murphy's. Scott is at

a chaplain's retreat this week, he gave it to me before he left."

"One knee or two?"

"Two!"

"Good fellow!" He still felt a sap for having done a mere one knee with his then neighbor.

He gave Hope a heartfelt hug. "*Felicitaciones! Mazel tov!*"

"*Muchas gracias.* Umm. *Obrigado!*"

They laughed easily together. He thought he'd never seen the owner of Happy Endings Bookstore looking more radiant.

"I have a list," he said, hauling it from the breast pocket of his jacket.

"Your lists have helped Happy Endings stay afloat. Thank you a thousand times. Oh, my, that's a long one."

"It's been a long time since I came in. Tell me, how is Louise liking Mitford?"

"I'll be right back," she said. She hurried to the foot of the stairs and called up for her sister, recently moved from their deceased mother's home place.

Louise came down the stairs at once, fixing her eyes on her feet. Hope took her sister by the arm and trotted her over.

"Father Tim, this is my sister, Louise Winchester."

With some difficulty, Louise raised her eyes and met his gaze. "So happy . . ." she said.

Hope smiled. "Louise is shy."

"I find shyness a very attractive characteristic. It's as scarce these days as hens' teeth."

He took Louise's hand, finding her somehow prettier than her sister, with a mane of chestnut hair and inquisitive green eyes.

"Louise, we're happy to have you among us, you'll make a difference, I know. May God bless you to find your way here, and prosper you in all you do."

He was delighted by her seemingly involuntary, albeit slight, curtsy.

"Father Tim wondered how you like living in Mitford."

A slow flush came to her cheeks. "It feels like . . . home."

"Louise is working wonders with our mail-order business and has organized everything from A to Z."

"Well done, Louise!" He felt suddenly proud, as if she were one of his own.

"Here's Father Tim's list. We have only three of the nine. Could you order the others today?"

"Just regular shipping," he said, noting that Margaret Ann, the bookstore cat, was giving his pant legs a good coating of fur. "I'm about to be covered up, and not much time to read."

"Pleased to meet . . ." said Louise.

By George, she did it again! If push came to shove, Emma Newland could get a curtsy demo right here on Main Street.

"Any plans?" he asked Hope.

"We'd like to talk with you about that; we're thinking October, when the leaves change. Would you marry us, Father?"

"I will!" he vowed.

"Though we attend Lord's Chapel, we're hoping to find a little mountain church somewhere. Something . . ." She hesitated, thoughtful.

"Something soulful and charming?"

"Why, yes!"

"Completely unpretentious, with a magnificent view?"

"That's it!"

"I'll put my mind to it," he said.

He told her about the hospital staff that was blown away by its patient's delivery of a second set of twins; how the boys looked strong, healthy, and uncommonly like their paternal great-grandmother and Mitford's former mayor, Esther Cunningham; how Louella had apprised him of nine thousand dollars that she thought was hidden in Miss Sadie's car, and that so far, he had no clue what to do about it.

He reported that the snow on the roads was freezing fast; that Edith Mallory had spoken an intelligible, not to mention extraordinary, word for the first time since her grave head injury seven months ago; that J.C. Hogan was wearing aftershave again, for whatever this piece of news was worth; that Avis had given him a considerable bit of advice about perfecting oven fries; that Hope Winchester had an engagement ring and wanted him to marry them; that Louise Winchester promised to be a fine addition to Mitford; and last but certainly not least, that he'd seen a crocus blooming in the snow, *hallelujah*.

He was positively exhausted from the whole deal, both the doing of it and the talking about it; he felt as if he'd trekked to another planet and back again.

"Good heavens," said his wife, "I'm worn out just *listening*."

And how had her day gone?

Joyce Havner had called in sick.

Violet, the aging model for the cat books his wife was famous for writing and illustrating, had brought a dead mouse into the kitchen.

A pot of soup had boiled over on the stove while she did the watercolor sketch of Violet gazing out the window.

She had handed off the sketch to the UPS driver at one o'clock sharp; it was on its way to her editor in New York.

Olivia Harper had called, and Lace was arriving from UVA tomorrow.

"That's it?" he asked.

"Don't get high and mighty with me, Reverend, just because you've gone to the big city and bagged all the news, and your wife stayed home, barefoot."

He laughed. "Missed you."

"Missed you back," she said, laughing with him.

In the farmhouse library, an e-mail from Father Tim's former secretary, Emma Newland, joined the queue.

<Dear Fr Tim

<Last year, you told me to buy a black coat to go with my good navy dress for the trip to England.

<To wear the dress, I was supposed to lose ten pounds. But now the trip is only weeks away

and I've gained fourteen!!#)!!* Don't mention this to a soul.

<Since there's no way I'm going to lose twenty-four pounds by June, I'll have to buy a new dress to go with my black coat.

<So should I buy navy like I'd planned to wear all along? Or should I buy black, which will go with everything?

<Love to all.

<P.S. Advise ASAP, sales start next week.

<P.P.S. Harold no longer forced to take own toilet paper to post office, economy clearly on upturn.

They had prayed their Lenten prayer, eaten their modest supper, and made the pie—which would doubtless improve by an overnight repose in the refrigerator.

Now, they drew close by the fire, to the sound of a lashing March wind; she with *Mrs. Miniver* and he with *The Choice of Books,* a late-nineteenth-century volume he'd found in their bedroom. He was vastly relieved that she'd made no more mention of his hair, what was left of it.

"Listen to this, Timothy."

Cynthia adjusted her glasses, squinting at the fine print. "'It's as important to marry the right life as it is the right person.'"

"Aha! Never thought of it that way."

"I considered that very thing when I married you."

"Whether I was the right person?"

"Whether it would be the right life," she said.

"And?"

"And it is. It's perfect for me."

His wife, who preferred to read dead authors, put her head down again.

"How dead, exactly, must they be?" he had once asked.

"Not *very* dead; I usually draw the line at the thirties and forties, before the mayhem began setting in like a worm. So . . . moderately dead, I would say."

He tossed a small log onto the waning fire; it hissed and spit from the light powder of snow that had blown into the wood box by the door. A shutter on the pantry window made a rattling sound that was oddly consoling.

"And here's something else," she said.

"'This was the cream of marriage, this nightly turning out of the day's pocketful of memories, this deft, habitual sharing of two pairs of eyes, two pairs of ears. It gave you, in a sense, almost a double life: though never, on the other hand, quite a single one.'"

He nodded slowly, feeling a surge of happiness.

"Yes," he said, meaning it. *"Yes!"*

CHAPTER TWO

The Vicar

He awoke from a dream in which he felt a frantic impulse to deliver Russell Jacks's bi-monthly treat of livermush.

Russell had watched for his visits at the door of Betty Craig's little house, as eager as any boy for his two weeks' worth of livermush sandwiches on white loaf bread with mayo. But Russell Jacks was dead and gone, never again to entertain a hankering for "poor man's pâté."

Miss Sadie, about whom he often dreamed, was also gone. And then there was Absalom Greer: "Gone to glory!" as the old preacher might have said.

Gone . . .

The thought of loss gave him a hollow feeling.

He wasn't, however, afraid of dying; he knew where he was going. Of course, he wasn't going there because he had been "good," however nominally, but because he had long ago committed his heart to God, made known through the One who had died in order that he, Timothy Kavanagh, might have eternal life.

Strange. The anomaly of livermush seemed far odder than the extraordinary fact that Jesus Christ had chosen to sacrifice Himself for a small-town parson.

He would be seventy in June, a truth that he considered often these days. Seventy! He had no ability to effectively process this fact; it was beyond belief. But no, growing older hadn't made him fearful of death—hadn't Thomas Edison said, "It is very beautiful over there!" and Cotton Mather, he'd always liked Mather's last words: "Is this dying? Is this all? Is this what I feared when I prayed against a hard death? Oh, I can bear this! I can bear it!"

What he feared, instead, was leaving some crucial work undone, thereby failing to complete his mortal mission. This fear had nagged him for much of his life as both an active and now-retired priest.

It brightened his spirit, then, to remember that Dooley was asleep in the next room, his own mortal mission to be hammered out.

What if God hadn't sent Russell Jacks's eleven-year-old grandson to his door, like some precious special delivery that must be opened quickly and handled carefully, lest it perish? Indeed, in the ten years since Dooley had become his charge, he'd learned to love him as his own flesh.

As might be expected, some said that he'd "saved" Dooley's life. The truth was, Dooley more likely saved his. At the age of sixtysomething, he had gone from an inward-looking bachelor to an outward-striving father. And then, of course, Cynthia had moved in next door. A double miracle if ever there was one.

Lord, he prayed, *thank You for Your continued grace. Help me fulfill Your plan for my life; give me a heart to hear Your voice. . . . And please, if You would do the same for Dooley . . .*

He rolled toward his wife, slipped his arm around her, and felt the deep, drowning mystery of sleep come upon him.

After the Morning Office, he prayed with Cynthia, then came to the kitchen and went about the business of laying the fire.

He squatted on the hearth and placed a loose network of cedar kindling in the still-warm grate above the coals. After adding three sticks of well-seasoned oak and striking a match to the fatwood, he watched the flames lick up, and listened eagerly to the crackle and snap of the cedar.

He stood then, content, warming his backside until Cynthia joined him in her favorite, albeit threadbare, robe, to begin their team effort over breakfast.

"So tell me the truth about the oven fries," she said, buttering the toast.

"Good. Very good," he said, poaching the eggs.

"I'm looking for outstanding!" she said, pouring the juice. "Next time I'll brine the water."

"Reading *War and Peace* would be simpler," he said, mashing the plunger on the French press.

They sat and ate by the fire, receiving its benediction.

"Does he seem taller to you?" she asked.

"Six-two."

"When do you think you might tell him?"

"I've never enjoyed hauling around secrets. But something tells me to wait."

"I've always trusted you to know when the time is right." She sipped her coffee. "His Jeep is a mess; he needs a car."

"Agreed."

"You could use money from the trust to buy him a car. . . . You wouldn't have to reveal the extent of Miss Sadie's gift until you're ready."

"I've been considering that."

"I feel he should have something he really wants, not another used vehicle with someone else's troubles thrown in."

"What if he wants a BMW?"

"Lace has one. He might like one, too."

"BMWs are fast."

"I think he would be responsible."

"I mean *really* fast."

"Timothy, I love the little wrinkle that pops between your eyebrows when you worry. It's sort of . . . cute."

Cute! He'd never understood why others didn't fret about the things that plagued him. Not only were BMWs fast, they cost more than some people's houses; such a high-dollar car could give Dooley the big head; plus, the other students might hate his guts. . . .

His wife leaned her head to one side and blasted him with the cornflower blue of her eyes. " 'Taste and see that the Lord is good,' dearest, 'happy are they who trust in Him.' "

"Preaching to me again, Kavanagh?"

"Psalm thirty-four," she said, smiling at her husband.

He blew through the kitchen door from the woodpile, an icy wind at his back.

"I have some good news and some bad news," she said.

"The bad first." He trotted to the hearth, Barnabas at his heels.

"Joyce won't be coming again for several months. Blockages in her arteries, she'll need stents. The doctor says she shouldn't be cleaning houses at her age."

"Ah." He lowered the wood onto the hearth. "I'm sorry to hear it. I'll deliver a baked ham; we'll keep her in our prayers."

"Ready for the good news?"

"Always."

"James just called. Everyone loved the watercolor of Violet looking out the window at the snow. I did it for a little mailing piece, and now they'd like to have twelve watercolors of Violet's life in the country—for a wall calendar.

"Since I'm not writing a book these days, I thought it might be a wonderful idea. I'd give all royalties to the Children's Hospital."

"That's a new wing on the building right there!"

"I didn't give James an answer, yet; I wanted to see how you feel about it. I know you love it that I haven't slaved over a drawing board since we came to Meadowgate. We've had such a lovely time out here in the sticks, with nothing pulling at us."

He took off his jacket and tossed it on the window seat. "I want what you want, and I mean it." He did mean it—even though he lost her for long intervals when she was working on a book. But this wasn't a book.

"I'd like to do it," she said. "I think it would be fun. Liberating, somehow."

He sat in the wing chair and pulled her into his lap. "Violet chasing the guineas?"

"Wonderful! And how about Violet in the barn loft where we found the bantam nest?"

"Violet stuck in the chinaberry tree by the chicken coop!"

"Perfect!" she said. "Violet sunning herself at the smokehouse! Or better yet, perched on the roof of the smokehouse, peering out at the mountains."

"Remember the time I had to fetch her down from your rooftop? While you went off to the country club to do the tango with Andrew Gregory?"

"The rhumba," she said.

"So, how many months do we have so far?"

"January, February, March, April."

"Terrific. Do it. Piece of cake."

She smooched the top of his head. "It's a dream come true, really. Doing watercolors, living in the country in a wonderful old house on a beautiful farm, without any responsibilities . . ."

"Walking the dogs," he said, continuing the litany, "reading aloud by the fire . . ."

"Hey." Dooley stood in the doorway, in pajama bottoms and a tattered University of Georgia sweatshirt. He stretched and yawned hugely.

"Hey, yourself," crowed Cynthia. "It's twelve o'clock, you big lug."

"Man, I never saw so many dogs piled on one bed, I had to get up and sleep on the couch in the library." Barnabas shambled to Dooley, who gave him a good scratch behind the ear. "Hey, buddy, you're in the doghouse for rootin' me out last night."

Cynthia trotted to the refrigerator and opened the door. "Breakfast or lunch?"

"Pie!" said Dooley.

"It's Marge," she whispered as he came in from the library. "Yes, Marge, I'm sorry, too. The doctor said she mustn't even think of coming back for several months. . . .

"Oh, no, I'm sure Timothy and I can keep

the place straightened up, certainly nothing like Joyce has always done, but . . .

"Really, no, you mustn't . . .

"But we couldn't . . .

"The Flower Girls? They clean and wash windows and cook—the whole nine yards?

"I'm sure we won't need any help, though. It's just the two of us.

"Of course, yes, everything is lovely here. Lots and lots of snow since you left, but today should be bright, and warmer. Dooley's here, I know he'd want me to send his love. How is Rebecca Jane? Speaking French? Yes, static on our end, too, very hard to hear . . .

"The Flower Girls, yes. The number is in your little red book? But only if things get desperate, which I can't imagine . . .

"Love to Hal and Rebecca Jane, I think I'm losing you. . . .

"*Oui, bon soir, ma cherie!*"

As he took his jacket off the peg, he heard Dooley's size twelves on the stairs.

"Taking the dogs for a walk; how about coming along?"

"Sure. Then I'm checking the clinic to see what Blake has goin' on."

Dooley and Blake Eddistoe, Hal's junior vet, had differing ideas about the practice of veterinary medicine. While Dooley preferred using more natural, noninvasive methods whenever possible, Blake inclined toward aggressive programs of drug treatment. No doubt Blake's philosophy had worked, as he was well liked by Hal, whose four decades of experience wasn't exactly chopped liver. In any case, Dooley and Blake would be working together this summer, and Father Tim prayed that the old, sore issues between the two would be resolved.

They huffed to the driveway and hooked a right toward the barn, passing Willie Mullis's little house. From the kennel, Willie's beagles loosed a fervent hue and cry as the two men and the farm dogs trooped north into a stinging wind.

"Let's cut by the tractor shed into that little field by the sheep," said Father Tim. "I haven't explored over there."

Hoary pasture grass crackled under their feet; their breath formed clouds upon the air.

"I really like this place," said Dooley.

"It's your second home. Remember the first time we came out here, and Goosedown Owen bucked you off in the hog slop?"

Dooley laughed as they headed toward the

woods, crunching through random patches of lingering snow. Beyond the fence, fourteen Dorset sheep lay under the run-in shed, chewing their cud.

"Do you and Cynthia like it?" asked Dooley.

"We feel like we're on vacation, actually. But that can be . . . sort of a problem. . . ."

"What kind of problem?"

He felt a certain joy that Dooley was interested.

"I suppose I feel trifling sometimes. I'm used to being *out there,* doing what God called me to do."

"Can't you be out there . . . out here?"

"I suppose I can, but . . ."

Dooley looked at him, his blue eyes piercing.

"But I've been waiting for my marching orders, you might say. Bishop Cullen has something for me, but I haven't heard anything yet."

"You will," said Dooley. He threw a stick for Bodacious. "Yo, Bo!"

"I will?"

"Yessir. People really need what you have to give."

Father Tim pulled his knit cap over his ears. "Which is what?"

"God," said Dooley. "You give people God."

He felt moved by this, and genuinely contrite.

Why had he been whining? He could get out there without the bishop's seal of approval. What was he waiting for? His heart suddenly lifted up.

"Thanks, son, for your encouragement." He grinned at the handsome, freckled boy who had come into his life—and changed it utterly.

Dooley studied him for a moment. "Umm, your hair is really long."

"Yes, true." And he didn't have a clue what to do about it. He'd been barbered by everybody from an erstwhile house painter to a former Graceland security guard to a crazy woman in capri pants, and nothing ever seemed to work out for the long haul.

"Can Sammy come up and stay awhile this summer?"

"Of course! Absolutely." Dooley's younger brother Sammy had disappeared with his father years ago. And though Sammy had at last been found, he refused to leave the unemployed, alcoholic Clyde Barlowe, alias Jaybird Johnson, with whom he lived in a trailer that had no phone or postal delivery. To make things more complex, Sammy was forced to visit Dooley and his Mitford siblings on the sly—never a good thing.

Dooley walked with his head down. "I think a lot about Kenny."

"God knows exactly where he is, and one day, I believe He'll send him to us."

"Do you really believe that, or . . ."

"Or what?"

"Or is it something you think you're supposed to say because you're a priest?"

"I really believe it. Have you forgotten our deal? The one we made before Christmas last year?"

"I guess I forgot."

"We'll keep thanking God for His providence in giving us Poo and Jessie and Sammy, and praying and *expecting* Him to lead us to Kenny."

A small light returned to Dooley's eyes.

"High five," said Father Tim. The smack of their palms was crisp and clear on the frozen air.

"So! What kind of vehicle would you like to have?" *Lord, have mercy . . .*

"A pickup."

"Ah!" His breath released like air from a tire.

"Short bed. Crew cab. CD player. Leather seats. Tilt wheel. Cruise control . . ." Dooley shot a sidelong glance at Father Tim to see how this was going down.

"No MG? No Mercedes?"

"For old people."

"No BMW?"

"Too hot."

He laughed, relieved, as they walked on. "I didn't know there was such a thing as too hot for a college student."

"It's not cool to be too hot," said Dooley.

Over there, between the oaks, a path leading into the woods . . . a grand possibility for a springtime walk, thought Father Tim.

"What do you suppose this truck would cost?"

"Maybe thirty thousand."

That's what he'd paid for his two-bedroom house in Alabama when he was a curate all those years ago.

Dooley shoved his hands deeper into the fleece-lined pockets of his school jacket. "Six cylinders. Sliding rear window. Electronic shifter . . ."

"Sounds like you've done your homework. Anything else?"

"Red."

Father Tim laughed. "Color of your head," he said, voicing their old joke.

They rounded the bend by a copse of trees, where the dogs burrowed their noses into the pungent leaf mold beneath the snow.

"Are you planning to, like, buy me one?"

"We definitely need to get you a good, safe

vehicle. So . . ." His voice trailed off as they walked.

He had memorized most of the letter Miss Sadie's attorney had delivered to him after she died.

As you know, I have given a lot of money to human institutions, and I would like to give something to a human individual for a change.

I have prayed about this and so has Louella, and God has given us the go-ahead.

I am leaving Mama's money to Dooley.

We think he has what it takes to be somebody. You know that Papa was never educated, and look what he became with no help at all. And Willard—look what he made of himself without any help from another soul.

Father, having no help can be a good thing. But having help can be even better—if the character is strong. I believe you are helping Dooley develop the kind of character that will go far in this world, and so the money is his when he reaches the age of twenty-one.

(I am old-fashioned, and believe that eighteen is far too young to receive an inheritance.)

I have put one and a quarter million dollars where it will grow and have made provisions to complete his preparatory education. When he is eighteen, the income from the trust will help send him through college.

I am depending on you never to mention this to him until he is old enough to bear it with dignity. I am also depending on you to stick with him, Father, through thick and thin, just as you've done all along.

Miss Sadie's letter was mildly confusing—though the money was legally Dooley's at the age of twenty-one, he was not to know about it until he could bear the responsibility with dignity.

They stopped to unlatch the gate.

"So?" asked Dooley. "You said 'so.' You're starin' a hole through me."

"So, *yes*! We need to do something. But why a truck? What are you planning to haul around?"

"I'll just be breakin' it in for when I get out of vet school. By then, it'll be totally right for haulin' around a bunch of mangy ol' mutts like this crowd." Dooley threw another stick. "Git it, girl!"

Son, I have something important to tell you. When the time comes, you'll be able to buy your own building, have your own practice, and drive around in a brand-new truck, or even two . . . Why didn't he tell him right now, as they stood in the stinging cold by the gate? Holding this enormous secret inside felt as if he'd swallowed a watermelon.

"I don't like riding in Lace's car all the time."

"Is that her idea?"

Dooley shrugged. "She likes my Jeep. But her car is warm in th' winter and cool in th' summer, and since th' passenger door won't open in th' Jeep, she has to go in my side or . . . crawl through th' window."

Dooley flushed to the very roots of his red hair. This was definitely an embarrassment to him, and Father Tim was beginning to feel a shame of his own.

"OK." He gave his boy a clap on the shoulder. "We'll deal with it."

"Soon?"

"Soon. Before you go back to school."

Dooley beamed. But Father Tim saw in his eyes the faintest flicker of doubt and suspicion; it was a glimpse of the old Dooley who had been betrayed again and again.

"Tracy? Tim Kavanagh here," he said to the trustee handling Dooley's account. "Just wondering what our bottom line is these days—the after-tax value.

"I'll hold. Sure. Thanks."

He was taking a swig of tea when Tracy came back to the phone and gave him the numbers.

"Holy smoke!" He nearly spit the tea across the kitchen.

One million seven hundred and twenty-five thousand dollars.

"Well done!" he said, meaning it.

A strong wind keened around the farmhouse; they might have been crossing the Atlantic in a gale for all the rattling and groaning of hundred-year-old rafters and floorboards.

His wife lay next to him, peaceful as any lamb, while he tossed and turned and tried to settle his wayward imagination.

Winding mountain roads in both Georgia *and* North Carolina, the volume on the CD player cranked to the max, the cab and even the bed filled with his friends, six cylinders of torque under the hood; worst case scenario, Dooley, with little or no sleep, headed down the mountain on cruise control . . .

"Timothy!" said his wife, reading his mind.

"Right!" he said, reading hers.

He turned over and buried his face in the pillow.

He'd been thinking. . . . What, after all, was so wrong with hanging loose, as he'd done these last few weeks? Wasn't it the first time in his life, for Pete's sake, that he'd ever *hung loose*? Why couldn't he take one year after having served nearly forty? Why did he feel like a heel for not rising at five o'clock sharp as he'd done for decades and setting forth on his mount to joust among the rest of the common horde?

Hadn't he dreamed for years of doing this very thing? Hadn't he hankered for time to loll around, gabbing with his best friend and soul mate, reading whatever came to hand, walking in the frozen woods, watching *60 Minutes* and even an occasional Turner Classic movie? And so what if he flipped over to the cooking channel once in a while, what was wrong with that? *Nothing!*

"Timothy!"

"Don't let the bedbugs bite."

Indeed, if such a sum were stashed in Miss Sadie's '58 Plymouth, he'd have to keep mum about it or the news would spread through Mitford like a virus.

He dialed the restaurant at Fernbank, looking for Andrew.

Andrew's Italian brother-in-law and Lucera chef, Tony, answered.

"Andrew is buying for Oxford Antique in England, and be gone for three weeks."

"Well, then. I'll call in three weeks. Just wondering, Tony—is Miss Sadie's old Plymouth still in the garage?"

"On blocks. Andrew had work on it, something here, something there. He says to use it in the Fourth of July parade."

"Wonderful idea! It'll bring back fond memories to see that great tank on the street again. So how is business at the high country's finest restaurant?"

"Slammed! I hope you and Cynthia will come see us soon. You always be our guest. Andrew says Fernbank would not be . . . belonging to us without the help from you."

"We'll drive in one evening and paint the town red! Give our warm regards to your lovely sister, I'll speak with Andrew when he returns. Ciao!"

So the car was still there. But what about the nine thousand dollars?

Not a word from on high.

If Absalom Greer were alive today, he'd be

hunkered over the wheel of his old Ford sedan, faithfully burning up the back roads to his little handfuls, as he'd called the small churches scattered through the coves. And what was he, Timothy Kavanagh, hunkered over? A volume of English poets.

He stuck the bookmark between the pages and got up and paced to the window seat and gazed out to the snow melting off the smokehouse roof.

. . . *It isn't anything fancy, and God knows, it will be a challenge.*

He turned and paced to the kitchen door, pulled back the curtain, and looked toward the barn without seeing.

And now Cynthia had this terrific new project to get behind, and what did he have to get behind?

Four dogs and an armload of firewood.

"Three," said Willie Mullis.

Willie stood at the kitchen door, bareheaded and mournful, holding forth a battered fedora containing the day's egg inventory.

"Three's all we need," said Father Tim, reaching into the hat. "We thank you. Think the laying will pick up come spring?"

"Yessir."

"Good! Think we'll be having any more snow?"

"Nossir."

"Your arthritis coming along a little better?"

"Yessir."

"Looks like a nice, warm day. The temperature could soar into the high sixties, don't you think?"

"Yessir."

"Need any help at the barn?"

"Nossir."

"If you do, just give me a call."

"Yessir."

He put the brown eggs into a bowl on the table, observing them with satisfaction. With a little grated cheese, a tot of cream, a smidgen of onion . . .

"Was that Willie?" asked his wife, coming into the kitchen.

"Three eggs," he said, pointing. "The laying will, of course, pick up come spring; we won't be having any more snow; the temperature will probably be in the high sixties today; and his arthritis is improving."

"My goodness," she said, "*I* never get that sort of information from Willlie. He's a perfect chatterbox with you."

March 19. He turned the page on the Owens' desk calendar.

Dooley was spending a couple of nights in town with his blood family and taking Lace to a movie in Wesley. Then he and Dooley would hie down the mountain to Holding where truck prices, according to Lew Boyd, were competitive. While in Holding, they'd try to hook up with Sammy.

In the meantime, he was plenty disgusted with his bishop and even more disgusted with himself. He had determined to go forth and do something, even if it was wrong.

First, he would call on his old friend and back-country soup-kitchen boss, Homeless Hobbes, who had moved to this neck of the woods when the Creek was developed into a mall. Maybe he could give Homeless a hand with his soup ministry.

Then he'd drop in on Lottie Greer, Absalom's elderly sister, who lived up the road in the rear of a country store Absalom built in his youth. Dooley wouldn't mind if he took Miss Lottie a piece of his chocolate pie. . . .

"Bloom where you're planted!" he muttered to himself, quoting a bumper sticker. Ah, but

Wordsworth had had a far better way of putting it.

"If thou, *indeed*, Timothy, derive thy *light* from *Heaven* . . ." He walked to the coat pegs and took down his jacket.

"'*Then*,'" he bawled in a voice designed to reach the uttermost pew,"'. . . to the *measure* of that heaven-born light . . .'" He pulled on his jacket, shoved his stocking feet into his outdoor boots, and rummaged for his gloves. . . .

"'*Shine, Preacher! In thy place,* and be *content!*'"

"What on earth are you *doing*?" asked Cynthia, coming in from the hall.

He felt his cheeks grow warm. "Preaching myself a sermon!"

"You were rattling the windows."

"Yes, well . . ."

"It's the snow," she said, commiserating. "Three months of snow, certain to be followed by two weeks of slush."

"Listen to this, it's coming back and I can't waste it. He's talking of stars here.

"*. . . Though half a sphere be conscious of*
   their brightness,
Are yet of no diviner origin,
No purer essence, than the one that burns,

Like an untended watch-fire on the ridge
Of some dark mountain; or than those which
    seem
Humbly to hang, like twinkling winter
    lamps,
Among the branches of the leafless trees. . . ."

"Untended watch-fire," she mused. "Twin-kling winter lamps. Nice!"

He heaved a sigh and thumped onto the stool by the door.

"I need a job," he said.

"And I need you to have one, dearest. Oh, brother, do I ever."

He was backing the farm truck onto the drive when Cynthia ran from the kitchen and waved him to a stop.

He rolled the window down.

"It's Stuart!" she called.

He trotted up the walk, his heart pumping.

"Timothy, Stuart here, with unending apologies for the long delay. I could go on and on, but—to make a long story short . . .

"How would you like to be a vicar?"

CHAPTER THREE

Faithful Remnant

He found Cynthia in the laundry room.

"I'm so happy for you!" She planted a glad kiss on his cheek.

"And I'm happy for you," he said. "After all, this gets me out of your hair."

She laughed. "But I love having you in my hair. Speaking of hair . . ."

"Let's don't."

"So tell me, darling—what *is* a vicar? I come from the Presbyterian side, you know." She stuffed their jeans and denim shirts into the washing machine.

"A vicar is the priest of a church that isn't a parish church."

"So you're still a priest!" In went the laundry powder.

"Absolutely!"

"Do we still call you Father?"

"You do! Only a couple of things change, really. . . . First, the money."

"There's the rub."

"I'll get a stipend, a mere dab. But not to worry, Kavanagh, I have big bucks set aside for our jaunt to Ireland next year.

"Now, here's the good part—I won't have to mix it up with a vestry."

"Hallelujah!"

"Let's see what else we can stumble upon." He went to the kitchen bookcase and thumbed through one of the many tomes he'd toted to the farm, and returned to the laundry room.

"'Vicar: A parish priest appointed by a bishop, to exercise limited jurisdiction in a particular town or district of a diocese.' Here's another:'A bishop's assistant in charge of a church or mission.'

"And finally," he said, "'A clergyman in charge of a chapel.'"

She cranked the knob to "On.""That's quite enough to be in charge of, if you ask me."

"Especially as Holy Trinity has stood empty for nearly forty years."

His heart pounded as he contemplated such a thing. Empty for forty years! Why on earth would Stuart have been "patently envious" of such a prospect? Just getting the mice and squirrels out would be a job of vast proportion—and then, to fill it with people from Lord knows where . . .

"You look dubious," she said, folding towels.

"Not dubious. Dumbfounded!" He closed the book and put it under his arm. "And scared silly, to tell the plain truth."

"Remember, sweetheart, what James Hudson Taylor said; you've quoted it to me as I plunged into many a Violet book. 'There are three stages in the work of God: impossible, difficult, done.'"

Of all things! he thought. *Of all things . . .*

"Let me pray for you."

She took his hand in hers, and he had at once the sure and consoling knowledge that her touch was a lifeline, one thrown out to him by God as directly as if He were present in the room—which, of course, He was.

They recited the Lenten devotion in unison.

"'. . . Now as we come to the setting of the sun, and our eyes behold the vesper light, we sing your praises, O God: Father, Son, and Holy Spirit. . . .'"

He asked the blessing then, and they looked at each other for a moment across the pine table.

"I'm thankful for you," he said, "beyond words."

The dogs snored, the fire crackled, the clock struck seven.

She leaned her head to one side and smiled at him. "Here we sit, under the dome of a winter sky, two people facing the unknown, holding hands across the table in a room lighted by a single candle and a fire on the hearth. I find it all too wondrous, Timothy, and I feel the greatest peace about your new calling; He has called you to come up higher."

He knew she was right. No matter about mice and squirrels, or even, God forbid, snakes; he knew she was right.

He breathed easily, then did something he couldn't remember doing for a while. He leaned back in the chair and felt the tension release. "Ahhh," he said.

"Amen!" she replied with feeling.

After conferring with Cynthia, he went to the library.

<My dear Emma,

<Buy the black.

<Add red scarf.

<Yours in Him.

<Fr. Tim

Though he had no key to let himself in, he was off at dawn to see Holy Trinity, nicknamed Little Trinity due to its seating capacity of a mere forty souls.

No matter what obstacles lay ahead, he would roll them over on God and let Him do the managing; as for himself, he would pitch in head first, give it his all, and let the Enemy take the hindmost.

He would still wear his collar and vestments; he would still celebrate the liturgy and perform all other the offices of a priest. So indeed, hardly anything would change.

He shifted the truck into second gear for the incline, heading west. And so what if things did change?

The thought gave him a kind of buzz, as if something carbonated had been released into his system.

He glanced at Barnabas, who sat on the passenger seat looking fixedly ahead. "Vicar!" he said, tasting the word. "What do you think?"

Cynthia called him dearest; his cousin's wife called him Teds; as a boy he'd been called Slick, more's the pity; his mother had often called him Timmy; Dooley called him Dad; one and all called him Father; and now he'd collected yet another appellation, one derived, appropriately, from *vicarious*.

He made the sharp curves neatly, sticking tight to the shoulder. Some people in these parts enjoyed driving in the middle of the road, a risky affinity explained to him at the Farmer post office. "We pay taxes on both sides," said Merle Hoff, whose property bordered Meadowgate to the north.

First thing to be done was call a locksmith, he'd take care of that when he got back to the farm. And who would he call to sweep out the place and patch the roof and mend the chimney and replace any rotten floorboards, and generally make things right? He'd cross that bridge when he got to it.

Stuart said his coadjutor had planned to come and look over the situation at Holy Trinity, but circumstances had intervened, and they knew almost nothing of the details. In truth, the consecration of the cathedral, Stuart's retirement ceremony, and the consecration of the new bishop were all scheduled to happen in a single day, a fact that had every soul at diocesan headquarters upside down and backward, not to mention beside themselves and altogether witless.

Stuart had thus turned the entire Holy Trinity caboodle over to him. It was to be Tim Kavanagh's baby, lock, stock, and barrel; in other words, check it out, go to work, and get it done. According to Stuart, someone who'd anonymously given a cool million to help build the new cathedral also had a special interest in seeing Holy Trinity revived, and had pitched in an extra twenty-five thousand toward that end.

Further, Holy Trinity was to withhold all offerings from the diocesan assessment, to help fund physical improvements and local outreach programs.

"You're absolutely the one for the job," Stuart told him. "The fact that you currently live within shouting distance of the church had nothing to do with my decision—though it makes things convenient for my new vicar, I should think!

"You know my unbounded esteem for you, Timothy. I have no intention of prattling on about it and giving you the big head, except to say you're among the single finest *pastors*—please read my meaning here—that I've had the privilege to serve with."

"You're more than gracious," he'd replied. "But I must tell you I've promised to take Cynthia to Ireland next year for two or three months. I've been a bump on a log far too long and I must keep my promise."

"Can you give our arrangement one year?"

"Just that, I'm afraid."

"To quote you, Timothy, 'Consider it done.' You get Holy Trinity up and running, and we'll send in a curate for the long haul."

He didn't ask what, exactly, made his bishop feel so all-fired, patently envious.

He estimated he'd climbed several hundred feet along the winding track, which was in fairly rough condition. Some of the ruts were as deep as watering troughs.

Always a trick to keep a steep dirt roadway from washing . . .

It was still a winter landscape, though the minutest of leaf buds were visible. Glancing left into the barren woods, he occasionally caught a glimpse of mountains, a sight that never failed to compel his spirit. On the right, endless upland meadows with vast outcroppings of stone . . .

The road leveled off for a mile or two, then ended abruptly at a bold stream. He was relieved to see that the track continued on the other side. "A ford!" he explained to Barnabas. He hadn't seen a ford in years.

He drove the truck carefully through the high waters created by snowmelt from the mountaintop and checked his watch. If the directions from Willie Mullis were right, he should be close. As he left the stream behind, the trees began to form an arch above the lane; light filtered through interlocking branches and danced on the hood of the truck.

At an ancient white oak, the road curved sharply and he saw it—a white, shingled building with a bell tower, resting on a stone foundation and facing west.

But this wasn't what he'd expected, not at all.

Though the church sat with its back to visitors, it was obvious that the building and grounds were tended, even tidy. Nothing about it spoke of decline or disrepair.

His eyes searched the green tin roof and the tall window at the rear. Both appeared to be in decent order.

Was it indeed Holy Trinity? The weathered, hand-painted sign in what he construed to have been the parking lot confirmed that it was.

He turned off the ignition and reached over and opened the truck door for Barnabas, then jumped down himself. He felt at once the sharp sting of fresh mountain air in his lungs.

From where he stood, he could see sunlight warming the mountaintops, but the larger view was obscured by a low stone wall that ran in front of the church.

"Come on, buddy!"

He trotted alongside the church with a surge of excitement, as if he'd never before seen a rising sun illumine the hills beneath.

Good Lord!

Beyond the wall, it appeared that the whole of Creation opened itself to him. An ocean of the world's oldest mountains rolled away on their journey to the west, green upon green, and in the great distance, blue upon blue. Small lakes of mist collected in the hollows; a poker-red sun cast its light upon the ridges and hog-backs as it ascended above the trees behind him.

He crossed himself, exultant.

He might have been standing at the top of the world, with every fret and horror far beneath him; indeed, he might have been standing on hallowed ground . . .

But of course, he *was* standing on hallowed ground.

He turned and faced the church. Through open double doors and a shallow narthex, light gleamed in upon the pews.

"Barnabas! Is this a dream?"

He hurried up the three stone steps and entered the narthex.

The smell was incense to him, redolent of old wood and evergreen, of mist and stone and leaf mold, of the whole amphitheater of nature in which Holy Trinity had been set over a century ago.

He moved into the nave and bowed deeply toward the wooden cross above the altar, to the source of joy that had come upon him so unexpectedly.

And he'd expected the worst!

In truth, the pine floor was swept; no cobwebs draped themselves from the rafters; even the windows looked respectably clean.

He scratched Barnabas behind an ear, amazed and overcome.

So this is what God had for him.

He turned to the communion rail, and ran his hand along the wood. Oak. Golden and deeply grained. He rubbed the wood with his thumb, musing and solemn, then dropped to his knees on the bare floor and lowered his head against the rail. Barnabas sat down beside him.

Lord, thank You for preparing me in every way to be all that You desire for this mission, and for making good Your purpose for this call. Show me how to discern the needs here, and how to fulfill them to Your glory and honor.

He continued aloud, "Bless the memory of all those who have gathered in these pews, and the lives of those who will gather here again."

Barnabas leaned against the vicar's shoulder.

"I am Thine, O Lord. Show me Thy ways, teach me Thy paths, lead me in Thy truth and teach me.

"In the name of the Father, and of the Son, and of the Holy Spirit. Amen."

He raised his head and looked at the play of sunlight flooding through the open doors behind him. Where was the one who had opened the church? And why was it prepared for a congregation that hadn't yet been found?

He rose and gazed around him at the bead board walls, the ceiling supported by pine beams, the windows that welcomed trees and sky into the small room . . .

"Hello!" he shouted.

He stood in the single aisle with his back to the altar, looking across the pews and out to the mountains, green upon blue upon purple in the shifting morning light . . .

Shine, Preacher! In thy place, and be content!

His scalp prickled with anticipation and the honest cold of a spring morning at four thousand feet.

After glancing about for any evidence of prayer books or hymnals, which he didn't spy, he trotted along the aisle and down the steps and cupped his hands to his mouth and shouted again, "Hello!"

But there was only an echo, and the call of a male cardinal on the bough of a pine near the open door.

He and Barnabas bounded into the kitchen where Cynthia had set up her watercolor paraphernalia at the north-facing windows.

"Timothy?" She seemed oddly surprised at the sight of him. "You look years younger! What is it?"

He thumped onto the window seat. "You're not going to believe this," he said.

He told Dooley where the truck was coming from—namely, the generosity of Miss Sadie Baxter's heart and purse; he asked the trustee how to channel the funds to the dealer; and he had a final phone seminar on how to get off the lot without being scalped.

"Ask 'em to pick up th' freight charges."

"Aha." He could do that.

"An' don't kick th' tires; they don't nobody do that n'more."

So went Lew's bottom-line summation of how to buy a truck.

But of course, there was no truck to buy. Dooley's list of optional features required that such a vehicle be ordered from the factory, and the wait would be four months.

"How about three months?" he asked, hoping to appear no-nonsense.

"Four months," said the salesman.

He expected Dooley to settle for fewer options and go for a truck they could drive off the lot.

No deal.

Dooley smoked over the available blue model that offered several options he was looking for and made his studied pronouncement. "I'll wait for red."

"Which red do you want?" asked the salesman, who was sporting considerably more aftershave than J. C. Hogan. "If I was you, I'd go for th' Impulse Red Pearl, that's your metallic an' all, an' a real nice low-key maroon. You take

that Radiant Red, it's a whole lot more notice-
able to th' *po*lice."

"Definitely Impulse Red!" blurted Father
Tim. "Sorry, son. That's your call entirely."

Dooley grinned. "Impulse Red. That's what I
was going to say."

He was proud of his boy. Dooley's willing-
ness to wait for what he really wanted was, in
his opinion, a definite mark of character.

Miss Sadie would approve.

They trotted along the block of Holding's
Main Street where Sammy was best-known.
Though Dooley had sent his brother a general
delivery letter, saying he'd meet him at the drugstore this morning, the clerk said she hadn't
seen Sammy in a few weeks.

It must have been early February, she told
them; she was putting valentines in the card rack
when he came in and bought a Snickers bar.

"How did he look?" Dooley wanted to know.
"Was he sick or anything?"

"Oh, no," she said. "He was just his usual self,
said he was going to get a haircut."

Dooley and Father Tim glanced at each
other. Sammy was proud of cutting his own
hair.

"How much is a haircut in Holding?" asked Dooley.

"I think it's eight dollars. My husband, Wayne, died two years ago and I don't keep up anymore."

When they hit the sidewalk, Dooley frowned. "I wrote and told him I was coming home, an' I wondered why I didn't hear back."

Dooley kicked at the post of the street sign with the toe of his sneaker. "Seems like if he had eight bucks, he wouldn't spend it on a haircut."

"Let's hit the barber shop," said Father Tim.

The barber looked up from one of his two chairs. "Sammy! You look like you're preachin' a funeral, boy. Where'd you get them duds?"

"My name is Dooley; Sammy's my little brother. Has he been here lately?"

The barber blinked his eyes vigorously, as if to clear his vision. "Not since I cut his hair back in, oh, sometime in February, I believe it was. I've seen 'im around town since he was a pup, but that was th' first time I ever cut 'is hair."

"What did you cut his hair for?"

The barber looked puzzled. "Because he asked me to."

"I mean, was he going someplace special or . . . ?"

"Said he might be takin' a bus somewhere. I

don't recall where. You sure are th' spit-dang image of one another." The barber squinted at Dooley. "Maybe he's a hair taller."

"Two inches," said Dooley. "Who else in town would know about Sammy?"

"Don't have a clue. He makes th' rounds of th' drugstore and th' pool hall. I seen you already go in th' drugstore. I know he goes to th' post office some; then once in a while he drops by here to see what's goin' on."

They trekked to the pool hall and post office, then out to the river, where they tried to find Lon Burtie, the Vietnam vet who had taken a supportive interest in Sammy's welfare. Lon would definitely know where Sammy was. But Lon wasn't home.

They left a note stuck behind the metal grid of Lon's screen door, asking Lon to have Sammy call Dooley at the farm.

ASAP. Collect.

No truck and no little brother.
They drove up the mountain, silent.

"I'm taking you to see a sunset."
"I love sunsets!"
". . . in the pickup truck."

She pulled on her fleece jacket with the hood. "I love pickup trucks."

He laughed. "What don't you love, Kavanagh?"

"Twenty-five-watt bulbs in reading lamps, cats that throw up on the rug after devouring a mouse, age spots . . ."

"The usual," he said.

"Just look!" She showed him the backs of her hands.

"Freckles," he said. "Trust me."

He was positively light-headed at the thought of sitting on the stone wall with Cynthia, the one with whom he most wanted to share this extraordinary view. And next, of course, Dooley—he'd bring Dooley up here on his long summer break. And Puny and the grans, the whole caboodle . . .

"I'll help you in every way," she said as they bumped across the creek and up the lane on the other side. "Just please don't make me do spaghetti suppers."

"Holy Trinity isn't a spaghetti supper kind of place."

"What kind of place is it?"

"You'll see."

They sat on the wall and held hands, marveling.

"And this is only a *spring* sunset," she said. "Just wait 'til fall! How will we bear such beauty?"

He was glad the church door was locked; he wouldn't wish to divide the joy of the spectacle before them.

They walked to the truck, hand in hand in the gathering dusk.

"So what kind of place do you think it is?" he asked.

She looked at him, happy and expectant. "A dinner-on-the-grounds kind of place!"

"Bingo!" exclaimed the vicar.

In a cold, driving rain, he met the locksmith at Holy Trinity, where he saw no sign of anyone else. Indeed, the door was again locked.

The smith hunkered over the escutcheon while Father Tim attempted to fend off the rain with an umbrella.

"No way can I make a key for this sucker. Th' lock case must've been put on when George Washin'ton cut down th' cherry tree. I ain't got equipment t' handle makin' a key like this."

"So what can we do?"

"Change th' lock. Ain't nothin' else'll work."

"Today? Now?"

"Have to go back to town an' get what I need, I can meet you here tomorrow mornin' around eight, eight-thirty."

"So be it," he said. "But try to find something with an antique finish, nothing brassy."

On the way to the farm, he realized he didn't feel right about this idea.

Whoever was accustomed to taking such tender care of Holy Trinity would be locked out; indeed, he would be the interloper, not they.

He called the locksmith at home and left a message.

"Buster, this is Tim Kavanagh. Don't go up to Holy Trinity in the morning, I'd like to hold off a few days. Hope this is no inconvenience. I'll be in touch."

In the meantime, how was he supposed to hook up with whoever had appointed themselves Holy Trinity's sexton?

The answer that presented itself was simple, if not altogether mindless. He would leave a note.

Dear Friend, he wrote on a piece of Meadowgate Farm stationery, *May our Lord bless you generously for your concern for Holy Trinity's welfare. You have done a splendid job!*

Bishop Stuart Cullen has appointed me vicar of Holy Trinity, with a vision toward the revival of a flourishing local congregation.

To this end, I must have a key made. Unfortunately, my locksmith is not equipped to make a key for such a very old lock, and we are required, perforce, to have the lock changed.

If you would kindly call me at the number below, I would enjoy discussing this and other details of HT's impending renewal with you.

In Him Who loved us first,

He penned his name with the sign of the cross.

Father Timothy A. Kavanagh ✝

He tossed the roll of Scotch tape that he'd use to affix the note to the door into the truck.

He looked up. *Red sky at morning, sailor take warning . . .*

There was no red sky this morning, so perhaps there would be no weather to ruin his scribbled communiqué.

Leaving Barnabas asleep, he hauled west along the valley floor, then up the winding mountain road and across the still-bold creek through the tunnel of budding trees and around the bend by the oak and into the parking lot.

Twelve point six miles. Twenty-one point nine minutes.

He hurried to the church, and found the doors open. Ha! He wouldn't have to tape the note, after all.

"Hello!" His excitement mounted as he stepped into the nave.

"Hello!" he called again.

No answer.

"Blast!"

He spied the rope hanging to the right of the door and gave it a yank.

In the steeple above his head, the bell thunked pathetically. This would take a mightier pull than he'd thought . . .

Bong!

There, by George! He grabbed the rope more tightly still and gave another hard pull.

Bong!

The sound pealed forth across the great bowl of the gorge and returned to him, shimmering and lovely.

Bong!

He didn't have a hundred years to get this job done, he had 'til next April, and no time to lollygag.

Bong!

He was getting the hang of it now.

Bong!

The rope shot up, he clung on and pulled it again; the sound rang out. . . .

Bong!

Maybe this would round up the mysterious sexton. In any case, it was a darned good way to warm up on a cold morning.

Bong!

Enough.

He wiped his perspiring forehead with a handkerchief. Right up there with chopping wood . . .

He strode along the aisle and peered to either side of the altar for a light switch, found one, and flipped it. Aha! A small chandelier with three bulbs illumined the nave, albeit weakly. And over there to the left, a door. He'd missed that earlier. Should be the sacristy. . . .

Locked. The smith would have a prosperous time of it up here.

He darted along the aisle and down the steps, and checked out the north side of the church. No outside door into the locked room. . . .

And no toilet, of course. That would have been typical of the old mission churches. They'd have to bring in a Porta John.

He returned to the nave and took a note-book and pen from his jacket pocket, and sat in the front pew on the epistle side.

He'd need to order prayer books and hymnals and, of course, kneelers. The kneelers didn't have to be anything stitched in gold by an ECW crowd, he'd seen a catalog with a Naugahyde number that was going for around fifty bucks. A chalice and paten . . . fair linen . . . a couple of vases for altar flowers . . .

Ha! Of course! A pulpit! Pretty important piece of business, a pulpit. And a lectern for the lessons . . .

He paused in his scribbling and gazed at the chandelier. How in the dickens would anyone be able to read by that pitiful wattage? On a rainy or overcast day, they'd all need pocket flashlights!

What else? Communion bread, which he or Cynthia could bake from the recipe he'd cobbled together as a curate. A basin and water jug for the sacristy . . .

This was like setting up housekeeping. Where most priests would be given a fine building loaded with top-of-the-line accoutrements, he'd be starting from scratch.

Starting from scratch! Had a nice ring, once one got over the shock of it.

And music . . . what could be done about music? Maybe a sign at the post office would reel in a free piano. Then again, probably not. Perhaps he'd try to drum up a piano in Mitford . . .

In the meantime, he'd leave notices at the post office and country store, announcing that Holy Trinity would soon be open for business, as it were, and then, he'd call the county agent who'd probably help get the word out.

Though all that was well and good, the real key would be home visitation, no two ways about it. After Dooley left for school on Saturday, he'd hop right to it.

He looked around the nave toward the spot on the north wall where a stovepipe had once funneled smoke onto frigid winter air. He expected they'd need a stove again, for he saw no returns or vents that suggested Holy Trinity had been upfitted in the heating department. In any case, they'd cross that bridge when they came to it.

His mind wandered to Lord's Chapel, and the choir of twentyplus well-rehearsed voices, and Richard hammering away at the pipe organ, all of it making his hair stand on end, Sunday after Sunday. And the stained glass windows, set into the chestnut walls of the nave and sanctuary like rare jewels . . . Jesus in the turquoise pool beneath the descending dove and St. John in his loincloth, looking blasted out of his earthly senses by the wondrous appearance of the Divine Son of God, not to mention his own cousin. . . .

He remembered being worn from weeks of attention to endless dozens of details, only to experience once more the exultation of processing with the choir and congregation from the frozen churchyard into the warm nave, from Lent into Easter, all voices joined with that of a trumpet in the glorious hymn he'd loved since a boy.

> *Jesus Christ is risen today*
> *Al . . . le . . . lu . . . ia!*
> *Our triumphant holy day,*
> *Al . . . le . . . lu . . . ia!*

He was startled to find himself standing in the hush of Holy Trinity, as if awakened from a dream.

He glanced at his notes. Yes! Home visitation.

But where did people *live* up here, anyway? He didn't recall seeing houses on this side of the creek. A few on the other side maybe. Maybe.

He sighed. Stuart had said this would be a challenge, so why was he surprised? He bowed his head and closed his eyes and lifted his palms in silent supplication. *Lord!*

"Father?"

He startled. "Yes?"

A woman, cast into silhouette by the strong morning light at her back, stood in the door-way.

She moved toward him, and though he couldn't discern her face, he was drawn at once to her and hurried to greet the one whom the bell had summoned. He observed that she was tall and quick, though bent and using a cane, and as she stepped into the light from the window above the altar, he saw that her counte-nance was radiant with feeling.

She smiled and extended her hand, and with deep humility, he took it, aware that it trembled slightly in his own.

"Father, I'm Agnes Merton—one of the last of the faithful remnant."

CHAPTER FOUR

Agnes

"Mrs. Merton, I'm Timothy Kavanagh."

"Please. Call me Agnes."

They shook hands slowly, as if there were all the time in the world.

"Bishop Cullen has asked me to be vicar of Holy Trinity."

"We've waited many years for you, Father Kavanagh. God is faithful. He told us He would send someone."

"And here I am," he said, still shaking her hand. "Agnes! I've always liked that name. Are you the one who's looked after this place so faithfully?"

"My son, Clarence, and I. For more than thirty years."

"Thirty years! Such an endeavor boggles the mind!"

"We do it a little at a time, Father. Week by week, year by year. To the honor and glory of the One Who loves us daily."

"An extraordinary act of devotion."

"I do only the small things now. It's Clarence who repaired and painted the roof, and replaced the rotten beams, and installed the windowpanes broken over the years. And so much more, of course. He is a fine and gifted son."

"I'd be grateful," he said, "if you'd tell me everything. I come to Holy Trinity as innocent as a babe. All I know is that I'm to get it up and running. And I find that you and your son have already done the worst, if not the best, of it!"

She smiled. "'A deed begun is a deed half done.'"

"Horace."

"Yes!"

They realized in the same instant that they were still clasping hands. They drew back, laughing.

"Please—let's sit, shall we?"

She carefully lowered herself onto the seat of the front pew, and propped her cane beside the armrest.

"Your cane. May I look?"

A finely detailed lamb for the handle above a polished brass ferule. "Very beautiful!"

"My son carved it. *Lamb* is said to be one of the Greek meanings for *Agnes.*"

"Ah, Agnes!" he said, thumping down beside her. "I'm thanking God for you already!"

"And I for you!"

Agnes Merton's white hair was drawn back into a knot and fastened with pins, though wisps had escaped around her face. It was a lively and intelligent face, he thought, with good, strong bones beneath finely lined skin as pale as the petals of a moonflower. Older than himself, perhaps late seventies, he reckoned, and while the long dress beneath her brown cardigan was faded and worn, her appearance smacked of a certain elegance.

In truth, she looked like someone he'd known all his life, but he couldn't think who it might be.

"It's a long story, Father."

"I have a long time to hear it." He checked his watch. "At least 'til five this evening when I must be home. Our boy is bringing his lovely consort to supper."

"You have a boy?" Her eyes brightened.

"A gift directly from God. Dooley was left on my doorstep when he was eleven, and just last month, he turned twenty-one."

"What would we do without our sons?"

"I can't imagine. He's among the great joys of my life. But I'll tell you more about Dooley later. This is your story."

"I've brought us a thermos of tea, Father. It's by the door, if you wouldn't mind. . . ."

"Hallelujah!" He rose and hurried up the aisle. A thermos of tea! Blessing upon blessing.

He hefted the basket and trotted back to their pew as happy as any child. A long story and a thermos of tea . . .

"Permit me," he said, unscrewing the cap while Agnes brought forth two stoneware mugs. As he poured, the spicy scent of sassafras and mint rose to lift his spirits.

"In times past," she said, "Holy Trinity has been broken into by vandals, and the bell rung to celebrate their devilry. When I heard the bell today, I felt at once an unspeakable joy." She was silent for a moment. "I knew our prayers had at last been answered."

He was uncommonly touched by this confession.

"And so I made tea." She smiled, warming her hands around the mug. "I suppose I should begin at the beginning?"

"Always a good idea."

"When I was twenty-six years old, I came to these mountains from Rangeley, Maine, under the auspices of the Domestic and Foreign Missionary Society of the Protestant Episcopal Church in the United States of America." She drew a breath. "What a mouthful! No wonder we adopted the nickname the Episcopal Church!

"I remember the proper name very well because I required myself to write it five hundred times, thinking it would help make me saintly! After college, I taught school, then took my training as a deaconess. I wished with all my heart to go forth and save the world.

"I had read about these mountains being the oldest on earth, and I'd read, too, about the terrible poverty here. Dorothea Lange and Doris Ulmann had both photographed families in Appalachia, and I found myself deeply moved and even tormented by the images they captured.

"I didn't know the One True Light at that time, Father, not at all, though I'd sworn my vows and professed my faith, and trained as a deaconess. Yet down from the woods of Maine I came, armed with the most extraordinary self-importance, and with the blessing, however grudging, of my father. I had lost my dear mother when I was fourteen, and so had no hand to guide me, which turned out in the end to contain its own benediction.

"Jessie Bennett came with me; she had also trained as a deaconess. The church in those days often sent two deaconesses to a mission. In addition to the circuit priest who came once a month, deaconesses lived in the community and ministered to the flock."

He sipped his hot tea, contented.

"The church built us a school, where Jessie and I taught and made our home—indeed, it became a true home for everyone along this ridge. We also nursed the sick and distributed food and clothing that were free to anyone who asked; we had regular Bible studies, and community suppers on the big trestle table that Moses McKinney built.

"In winter, of course, we kept the fireplace and cook stove going all day, which made the schoolhouse a snug place for our neighbors to gather on our long and frigid evenings. Some quilted; some played music; all told stories.

"And Christmas! Oh, how I wish you could have been here to see the old schoolhouse on Christmas Eve. Moses always cut a tree whose top touched our eleven-foot ceiling, and the parishioners came trooping in with their ornaments—pinecones and dried yarrow and life everlasting and scraps of ribbon and yarn and fruit and buttons and birds' nests—why, you never saw such a jumble on a tree, and yet we thought it the prettiest sight this broken world ever beheld.

"Jessie and I worked for months making gifts—we wanted everyone on the ridge to find a remembrance, however modest, under that majestic tree."

He found himself thoroughly enchanted.

"The priest came to us on Christmas Day only once every four years, so the services were usually up to Jessie and myself. I remember always wanting to read the Epistle from Titus, 'The grace of God that bringeth salvation hath appeared to all men. . . .'"

Agnes Merton's face was wreathed with smiles.

"It was a happy time for Jessie and me, and for Little Bertie."

"Little Bertie?"

"Bertie was Jessie's niece. Jessie's sister and brother-in-law had perished in a boating accident, and Jessie became Bertie's legal guardian. Oh, she was the merriest child you'd ever wish to see! Such bright, happy eyes, and a great chatterbox with everyone, including perfect strangers.

"Though Jessie and I worked hard to gain everyone's trust, it was Bertie's way with people that brought them out, and their children with them, so that in time, all of us became family, all of us who lived then in this world above the clouds.

"We arrived here in September, having survived the long journey from Maine, and learned there had been serious floods.

"There we were, motoring up these narrow mountain tracks in a Buick Town Car, which my father had given the church as a charitable contribution! We had all our possessions in that old automobile, and oh, my, we were a sight for sore eyes. Pots and pans rattling about, and a baby cradle and steamer trunk lashed on top.

"Wilson's Creek was so swollen, it was running like a river, and we couldn't ford it. We lived in our car for two days, waiting for the water to subside. Then, one of the neighbors found us, and took us to their home. They fed us heartily and insisted we sleep in their bed while they slept on hardback chairs pushed together.

"Over the years, there have been bridges over Wilson's Creek. One of steel, Father. Steel, mind you! And the floods came and washed them all downstream, never to be seen again. The plain truth is, many of those left up here don't really want a bridge. Most of us use the one at McClellanville, two miles upstream.

"In any case, a lot of families have gone to live in Mitford or Wesley or Johnson City—adding yet another blow to the mission churches. Shifting demographics, they call it. Young people leave, old people die . . ."

"Roads get washed away," he said, "bridges disappear downstream." He lifted the thermos. "Agnes?"

"Please, Father. Thank you."

He refilled both their mugs as the light slanted through the windows, and the cardinal sang in his bush by the door. "Should I call you Deaconess Merton or Deaconess Agnes?"

"Please. Call me Agnes."

"And you may certainly call me Tim."

"No, indeed, Father, I have never called a priest by his first name, and never shall."

They lifted their cups in amused agreement.

"I won't forget that dark night, on the eve of yet another fearsome storm, when we drove up at last to our rude little cabin, where we lived before the schoolhouse was built.

"We made our beds and ate our supper by the light of a lantern—there was no electric here until 1954—and lay down, frightened out of our wits. It didn't seem an adventure anymore for two educated girls from Maine; it was suddenly a very real and terrifying scrape we'd gotten ourselves into.

"I remember the great shadows that flickered on the walls, cast by the lamp light. And the bats, Father, it was dreadful! The bats flew about our heads and swooped around the room, and then the storm rolled in upon us and we believed our time had come."

She took a long, reflective draft of her tea. "Have you tasted sassafras before?"

"I have. I'm a Mississippi country boy."

"It comes from a bush behind the schoolhouse, and the mint grows wild on the banks."

"The schoolhouse is still standing, then!"

"Oh, yes. Like a rock, and just a short walk through the rhododendron grove. It's been our home for many years. It was purchased from the Domestic and Foreign Missionary Society of the Protestant Episcopal Church in the United States of America."

They laughed easily together.

"In all the years I've lived here, I can't remember a rain so torrential, nor winds so fierce. The wind tore the roof off the cabin and flung it into the trees, and all the heavens opened above our heads.

"The rain came down with great force, beating upon us like hailstones, and because the lantern had been doused at once, we were thrown into utter darkness."

Agnes gazed toward the altar as she spoke, as if she was viewing a film.

"I can't begin to express our dreadful fear. We were completely disoriented, and ran barefoot over the broken glass of the lantern globe. We left the cabin and tried to find our car, but couldn't—and through all this, I remember Little Bertie screaming with terror.

"I also remember crying out to God, and as I did, I realized for the first time that I didn't know Him at all, that I had never surrendered anything of myself to God. I had reserved my heart and my soul as my own."

She turned her gaze to the vicar.

"Jessie and I called our introduction to these mountains the Great Baptizing, and yet I had been baptized only upon my stubborn and willful head. It would be years, Father, before I knew the One True Baptism in my heart. You might say I grew into faith as a child grows into shoes bought too large."

"And Jessie?"

"Jessie used to say that before we came to the ridge, she had been on speaking terms with Him. But after the storm, He became her best friend. I'm sure He remained so for the rest of her days."

Agnes was pensive for a time, sipping her tea.

"I suppose you lost your wonderful automobile . . ."

"Indeed, God protected it! He knew how we would rely on it for years to come, and it rode through that dreadful storm with barely a scratch.

"My gracious," she said, suddenly contrite. "I'll wear you to a frazzle going on like this!"

"Can't be done. Not when there's a good story at hand!"

"I've talked far too much about Agnes Merton. What are your plans, Father, for Holy Trinity?"

"We'll have our hands full, getting things up to speed. I've just been making a list."

"A list!" She removed a pair of glasses from her sweater pocket. "And what's on it, may I ask?"

"Everything but the kitchen sink. A stove. A pulpit. A lectern. Fair linen. The whole nine yards. Kneelers. Prayer books. Hymnals . . ."

"Thirty-seven prayer books are on the shelves of our old school."

"You don't mean it!"

"Do you use the 1928?"

"I grew up on it, but haven't used it in years. I'm certainly willing, however." He'd long wanted to refresh his knowledge of the much-venerated 1928 edition of the Book of Common Prayer.

"And hymnals. We have forty-one of those."

"Forty-one!"

"They were bought only months before the church was closed; they're in lovely condition."

"Now, don't tell me you have a pulpit and a woodstove." He was jesting, of course.

"The pulpit is stored in our loft; Clarence waxes it every fall, to keep it from drying out in winter; he made it from oak off the mountain. And the stove is in our back room, which used to be the infirmary. It only needs oiling."

"Agnes . . ."

"Yes, Father?"

"Is this a dream?"

"It certainly seems a dream to me. There were times when Clarence and I had given up utterly, but God always encouraged us. It's hard to wait."

"Very hard."

"What are you waiting for, Father?"

He reflected, but only for a moment.

"For Kenny Barlowe to be found." God forbid that Sammy might be lost yet again.

"Kenny Barlowe. I'll commit to wait and pray with you."

"Thank you, Agnes. Now, look what you've

done. You've gone and made things easy for your new vicar."

Smiling, she put on her glasses, and peered at his open notebook. "What else is on your list?"

"Fair linen."

"In my bottom bureau drawer, wrapped in tissue paper. They say tissue keeps linen from yellowing."

"A thurible."

"I don't know what they'd think of that. We were always low church here."

"One less item to round up! As for getting our services under way, I believe the first Sunday in May would be realistic. That gives us time to collect ourselves."

Agnes appeared thoughtful.

"Where will they come from, Agnes?"

"I can't honestly say. Only three remain in these parts who know anything of the Anglican form of worship. Two are elderly, but wise and sweet, and still get about. They'll be so happy. And perhaps we'll get some of the Baptist flock from below the creek. Their church burned to the ground last Christmas, a terrible thing. Clarence will take 'round a note from me, and we shall see whom the Lord appoints to grace this nave."

Why did he suddenly feel like a child who had been rescued? Tears welled in his eyes.

"I feel very moved. Very . . . amazed." He wiped his eyes with his handkerchief. "And very grateful."

"Perhaps God has asked you to do something smaller than you're accustomed to doing. Or perhaps He's asked you to do something greater . . ."

He nodded.

". . . and thereby your wonder has been stirred."

Yes! His wonder.

"Let's walk over to the schoolhouse," she said. "I'll refill our thermos and find us a bite to eat."

"Agnes," he said, on impulse, "do you know anything about . . ." How could he possibly ask this?

"About what, Father?"

"Cutting hair?"

His wife leaned forward and squinted at him.

"Timothy! You've done it, at last! And I must say, it looks terrific!"

He sat beside her on the window seat, and put his arm around her and kissed her cheek.

"What is it, darling? You're grinning like the Cheshire cat."

"You're not going to believe this," he said.

He was interested to see they'd driven out from Mitford in the Jeep.

"I think she wanted to," Dooley told him, "because, you know, because of you all."

He saw her point. Lace Harper had her own sterling character traits.

He had stepped out to the front porch with Dooley, who was headed to the vet clinic to see Blake Eddistoe. Only yards away from their front steps, the lights of the clinic burned against the gathering dusk.

"No word from Sammy?"

"No, and I'm really worried. But I don't want to go down there; I don't want to see him."

It was his father, Clyde Barlowe, whom Dooley didn't wish to see.

"I'll drive down next week, maybe Buck and I could make the trip together. Don't worry. Keep praying the prayer that never fails."

Dooley shoved his hands in his jacket pockets and gazed at the porch floor. "About what you said at Christmas . . ."

"What was that?"

"I said I'd like to take your name, and you told me to think about it. I've thought about it."

Dooley raised his head and looked steadily at Father Tim.

"I want to take your name."

Father Tim was quiet for a time, moved by the reality of this proposal. "Have you spoken to your mother? Would we have her blessing?"

"Buck wants to adopt Poo and Jessie, so they'll be Leepers. I don't see why it would matter for me to be a . . . Kavanagh."

"Would you like Cynthia and me to adopt you? Or do you just want the name change?" He hadn't really wanted to ask this—what if he didn't like the answer?

Dooley spoke at once. "Adopt."

Wordless, Father Tim embraced the tall, intense young man who'd been given him so long ago, and held him close for a moment.

"Consider it done. I'll call Walter, and we'll go from there."

Dooley's voice was hoarse with feeling when he spoke at last. "One of our rams is down."

"What is it?"

"Rams can get stones and crystals in their urinary tract, and it's hard to pass a catheter in. I think Blake should treat it medically with antibiotics and anti-inflammatories and probably a change of diet, and the stones will dissolve and pass."

"What does Blake think?"

"I'm going down to find out."

"Son . . ."

"Yes, sir?"

"Give him our regards; we'll see him up here for supper on Monday."

Mind your temper, he wanted to say.

They heard the front door slam, and Dooley coming along the hall to the kitchen.

Father Tim saw the seething anger in his face.

"Blake's going to create a stoma bladder hole; it'll go directly through the stomach, which means the ram will urinate through the stomach like a ewe."

"What's the problem with that?" asked Father Tim.

"He'll dribble urine, he'll get a bad urine scald around that spot, and nobody will have time to take care of it. You have to wash the hole every day; nobody has time to do that . . ."

"Dinner is served," said Cynthia.

Dooley yanked Lace's chair away from the table, and held it for her.

"Let's take a deep breath, sit down, and enjoy our meal together," said Father Tim. "Then we can talk about the ram."

Cynthia passed the prayer book to Lace. "Lace, dear, will you read this Lenten prayer for us?"

A faint blush of color came to Lace's cheeks as she read in a firm, clear voice.

"Assist us mercifully with Thy help, O Lord God of our salvation; that we may enter with joy upon the meditation of those mighty acts, whereby Thou hast given unto us life and immortality, through Jesus Christ our Lord."

"Amen!" they exclaimed together.

Father Tim extended his left hand to Cynthia, and his right to Lace. They bowed their heads.

"Lord, we thank You for the great power of Your grace in all our lives. Thank You for Lace and Dooley whom we love and cherish, and for the bright futures You've set before them. Thank You for the gifts You've so generously given Lace, which assisted her in winning this fine scholarship. Thank You for Your gift to Dooley of a heart concerned for all Your creatures, great and small.

"Thank You for Cynthia, who lightens and enriches the spirits of everyone who knows her. And now, Lord, thank You for this bounteous meal of the things Dooley enjoys most, and which we enjoy with him. You are good, O

God, and You are faithful. Tenderize and soften our Lenten hearts, we pray, lest they grow brittle and break.

"In the name our Lord and Saviour, Jesus Christ, Amen."

"Amen!"

Steak, oven fries, and arugula dressed with a hint of orange and walnuts. He had checked his sugar, and not only would he have some of everything, he would also have a hot roll. What's more, he would butter it, hallelujah.

As the steak platter passed from Lace to Dooley, he felt Dooley's mood brighten. His own spirits brightened, as well.

"*Man!*" said Dooley, forking the steak he'd earlier chosen as it came from the butcher's paper.

Cynthia passed the potatoes, arrayed on a blue and white platter. "I've slaved over these fries," she confessed, "and I think, I hope, I pray I got it."

"Lace," said Father Tim, "give Dooley a run for his money, and have a few more." He was struck, as ever, by Lace's extraordinary beauty, and the soulful depths of her amber eyes.

He recalled their first meeting several years ago. Instead of taking the road to Miss Sadie's house, he'd cut through the massive grove of wild cinnamon ferns on the bank. Near the big oak, he'd come upon someone in a hat, digging ferns by their root balls and rustling them into a burlap sack.

He thought it a boy or young man until the culprit turned around in surprise. It was his first sight of Lace Harper, then Lacey Turner. He'd seen the fear in her eyes, and the fury, as he walked toward her.

"I'll knock you in th' head," she'd said, "if you lay hands on my sack. I don't care if you are a preacher."

He'd asked her to consider replanting what she had dug, but she stood her ground. Cinnamon ferns had a strong dollar value on the local digging market.

She had grabbed her sack and mattock and fled, bareheaded and barefoot, down the embankment.

But God had greater plans for Lace Turner than digging ferns.

This harshly abused and largely self-educated young woman had surrendered her life to Christ at a revival meeting conducted by Absalom Greer. Then, following the death of her mother, she'd been adopted by the town doctor and his wife, and was excelling in her studies at the University of Virginia.

Most people, he supposed, didn't believe that miracles still happen. Those people were wrong.

"I think you got it," said Dooley, hammering down on the fries.

"Crispier on the outside?" asked Cynthia.

"Yep."

"Softer on the inside? More golden in color?"

"Yes, ma'am."

"Dooley Barlowe! I can't believe you called me ma'am."

Lace laughed. "That's really good."

"I know I'm a Yankee, and such things aren't supposed to matter, but would you continue to call me ma'am? I love the sound of it."

Dooley laughed the cackling laugh that Father Tim loved to hear.

"How did you do it?" Lace asked the cook.

"Bottom line, it's the pan. I've been using a lightweight pan, which caused the fries to look very pale and boring. So Avis suggested I use a heavy pan, and there you have it—the heavier pan conducts heat more evenly, and gives this lovely golden crust into the bargain."

"Well done!" exclaimed Father Tim.

He decided not to be discouraged by what he occasionally saw in Lace's eyes when she looked at Dooley. Sometimes it was fear. Sometimes it was anger. Sometimes it was love.

If they chose to spend their lives together, it wouldn't be easy. Each had been required to survive violence, rejection, and the cancer of bitterness. To claim their survival, they had built walls that couldn't easily be taken down.

And yet, while all this pertained, he would choose to trust what he saw right now, at this moment—a flush of genuine happiness in his boy, and in the bright and beautiful girl who had come so profoundly into their lives.

"Let me share a thought with you," said the vicar. "George Macdonald wrote this: 'Man finds it hard to get what he wants, because he does not want the best. God finds it hard to give, because He would give the best and man will not take it.'

"God is giving us the best tonight, and we're taking it. Thanks be to God."

Dooley looked at him intently for a moment, then at Lace. "Yes, sir," he said, quietly.

When he opened the kitchen door to let the dogs out, he found the air warm, nearly balmy.

"Spring," sighed his wife. "I can't remember when I've yearned for it so."

"Lady Spring is lingering just over the mountain in her gown of moss and buttercups, and is definitely headed this way."

She laughed. "Thank you, Hessie Mayhew!"

"In the meantime, our small fire is a benediction." He sat in his chair and reached across the lamp table and took her hand.

"That was a great dinner, my love. Thank you."

"I didn't want to say anything at dinner, but the fries need work."

"Beating a dead horse, Kavanagh. The fries are nailed."

"We'll see," she said.

Though he was more than a dash on the weary side, he felt his heart lift up. "Dooley's ready to become a Kavanagh. I asked if he wanted the name only, or wanted us to adopt—I thought that should be clearly spoken between us."

"He wants us to adopt, doesn't he?"

"Yes. I told him to consider it done."

"This is a good thing. I'm so glad."

"I'll call Walter and see where we go from here."

"Tell them to come visit, they'd love a week in the country."

"Will do."

"Dooley is dear to my heart; I find him very brave."

"Brave in what way?"

"Going off to that fancy Virginia prep school, barely out of overalls, and making a way for himself, and now he's an earnest college student with plans for the future. Think of how it might have gone."

"I often think of it."

"He gave me the biggest hug when they left; he's hardly ever done that without prompting. And he said yes, *ma'am!*"

They sat looking at the fire, amazed and satisfied.

"By the way," he said, "now that the fries are coming along, I suppose you're on to reading *War and Peace?*"

"Oh, phoo. I should never have set such an impetuous goal. I *need* to do it. I *should* do it. And over and again, I've *tried* to do it. But Timothy . . ."

"Yes?"

"I *can't* do it."

"Give it up," he said. "Life's too short."

She leaned her head against the wing of her chair and looked at him with a certain tenderness. "Thank you, sweetheart, I needed that. Why don't you read to us? A psalm would be the finest of nightcaps."

"I'll have to find my glasses," he said, springing up. How good to have a mate to whom a psalm was the finest of nightcaps!

"The kids were wonderful to help clean up," she said. "Lace is a joy."

"And to think she received almost all her education from a bookmobile. I never fail to find that wondrous. Mind-boggling!"

"We're being very good, don't you think, by not plotting their future together? We did that for a while, and it isn't fair to them—or to us, for that matter."

"I agree," he said. "We'll continue to keep our hands off and pray the prayer that never fails."

Cynthia curled deeper into the chair and yawned hugely. "Oh, please, it is so past my bedtime, and I must get up early and work on February."

He ran his hand along the top of the refrigerator. Not there. "You're done with January so soon?"

"A breeze. It scares me. I can't imagine the drawing is any good at all if it took only three days. That has never, *ever* happened to me before."

"I don't suppose your lowly husband could have a look." Ah! Perched on his head, for heaven's sake.

"If you really want to."

"Of course I want to. Very much." His wife had always been oddly unforthcoming about her work. "Let's have a look in the morning when the light is good." He sat down and opened his worn King James to the psalms.

"Which service are we attending tomorrow?" she asked. "Nine o'clock or eleven?"

"Let's not go to St. Paul's." He was surprised by the thought of quite another prospect. "Let's go up to Holy Trinity."

"Yes! I love that idea!"

"I'll take the communion kit," he said.

"And I'll pack a picnic lunch."

"Stick in one of those small loaves you baked last week."

"Perfect!"

He wouldn't mention it to his enthusiastic consort, but he would also take his purple Lenten vestments—it would be a dress rehearsal, in a manner of speaking.

As he tucked his Book of Common Prayer into the picnic basket the following morning, he was mildly astonished at his excitement. Indeed, he felt as if he were somehow going home.

CHAPTER FIVE

Loaves and Fishes

As on the previous evening, temperatures were unseasonably warm, a sign that the callow and unknowing might consider a promise of early spring.

However, no one living in the vicinity of Meadowgate and its highland neighbors to the west would be so easily duped. Hadn't the worst blizzard of the last century come in late March, and some of their deepest snows in May? And hadn't they been betrayed since time immemorial by countless false springs that wrecked their hopes with a killing frost?

Nonetheless, the common blue violet was everywhere pushing through damp leaf mold, while its near cousin, *viola rafinesquii,* sprinkled its bloom among the new grass of upland pastures. Also coming along smartly, if one looked with interest, was the pink and blue henbit, so named for being a sworn favorite of chickens during the Scottish-Irish settlement of the highlands.

"I can feel it," said Cynthia, as they drove through the overarching canopy of trees.

He shifted the truck into third gear for the two-mile flat stretch. "What can you feel?"

"The whole aliveness of everything, the sense that something is *going on*." She shivered with pleasure.

Something was going on, indeed; he felt it, too.

When they arrived at a quarter 'til ten, they found a pickup truck eaten to the chassis by rust and a 1982 Dodge sedan in the park-ing lot.

He also found the church doors open wide—and, to his amazement, several people sitting here and there among the pews. As Cynthia stayed behind to spread a cloth on the stone wall, he stood awkwardly in the doorway, holding his vestment bag aloft.

He realized his mouth was agape, and shut it promptly. He experienced a moment of panic, as if he'd known to be prepared and had somehow forgotten. Every head turned.

"Father Kavanagh!"

Agnes stood up from the front pew and, leaning on her cane, met him in the aisle. "They all heard the bell yesterday, and thought it might be announcing a ten o'clock service, as in the old days. Clarence and I walked over for our own service this morning, and . . . here we all are!"

Agnes was flushed with surprise.

"Yes! Well! My goodness!" He looked toward his astonished wife, who had appeared in the doorway. "I'm Father Timothy Kavanagh, and this is my wife, Cynthia, and . . ."

He took a deep breath. ". . . and you were absolutely right, there *is* a service today at Holy Trinity, and what a glorious morning for it! Have you seen the mist rising from the hollows? The way the trees are budding out? And thank you for coming, may God bless you for coming!"

He was babbling like a brook, his vestment bag still held aloft so his alb and chasuble wouldn't drag the floor.

"Morning Prayer or Holy Communion?" Agnes asked.

"Ah." His head was swimming. "Communion! We have bread and wine, not much wine, but enough to go around."

Cynthia hurried down the aisle with the picnic basket, stuck it on the seat of a pew, and relieved him of the vestment bag. "I'll help you vest."

"Will Mrs. Kavanagh be chalice bearer?"

"Oh, no, I'm only certified to sit in a pew!"

"Agnes," he said, "will you?"

She hesitated briefly. "I will."

"Granny!" cried a young voice. "I got t' pee!"

An elderly woman and boy jostled by them, hurried up the aisle, and made a hasty exit to the laurel grove.

"Candles?" he asked Agnes.

"On the altar."

"Is the sacristy unlocked?"

"I'm sorry, no."

"I don't suppose we have a crucifer?"

"Clarence is here. He knows what to do."

"Good! Ask him to bring the cross and meet me outside. I'll vest under the maple. Could someone pull the bell? Bread and wine are in the basket, with a chalice."

He snatched his prayer book from the basket, thrust it at Agnes, and dashed up the aisle and out the front door with Cynthia, his vestment bag flapping in the breeze.

Thank goodness he'd declined to bring Barnabas. His good dog would be sprinting along at the head of this wild processional, barking like a maniac, and wouldn't that be a sight for sore eyes?

Clarence was a large man, perhaps in his early forties, with a reddish beard, a balding head, and a shy smile. He wore overalls with a plaid shirt and faded suit jacket, and held in both hands a cross roughly made of wood, still bearing its husk of bark.

"Clarence, God bless you! You lead and I'll follow."

He might have been a young curate, for all the pounding of his heart. He prayed fervently and glanced at his watch.

Ten o'clock sharp.

The bell tolled four times, ringing out into the great amphitheater of coves and hollows.

As Clarence lifted the cross, the grand-mother and boy scurried from the path and fell in behind the crucifer. Then, up the steps they went, their new vicar bringing up the rear.

In the few minutes it had taken him to robe, Agnes had lighted the candles, spread the altar with a simple fair linen, and opened the 1928 prayer book to the Order for Holy Communion.

He had a moment of something like cold fear at the absence of his familiar 1979 version. But as the older version was all they had for the four, five, six—he counted hastily—seven congregants, there was no looking back.

He was convinced he would croak like a frog when he opened his mouth; stress had always done an odd job on his voice.

Then he saw his wife beaming at him from the front pew—She Who Loved Surprises should have enough to last her for a month of Sundays—and he miraculously relaxed, as if something in him were melting.

He felt suddenly like a balloon that had been cut free to rise and float, unfettered, above all that had ever plagued or constrained him.

He helped Agnes kneel by the altar on the bare pine floor.

"The blood of our Lord Jesus Christ, which was shed for thee, Agnes, preserve thy body and soul unto everlasting life."

The old and familiar words came flowing back, easy and full of grace.

"Drink this in remembrance that Christ's blood was shed for thee, and be thankful."

At the conclusion of the service, he found himself distinctly moved by the bowed heads before him, and the view that swept his gaze full hundreds of miles to the west.

"The peace of God, which passeth all understanding, keep your hearts and minds in the knowledge and love of God, and of his Son Jesus Christ our Lord: And the blessing of God Almighty, the Father, the Son, and the Holy Ghost, be amongst you, and remain with you always."

"Amen!"

"Brothers and sisters," he said, as the congregants rose to leave, "please join Cynthia and me for a simple meal on the stone wall." The idea had come to him quite out of the blue.

"It's a picnic made for two, but God intended it for eight, which reminds me of the old table grace, 'Heavenly Father, bless us and keep us all alive; there's ten of us for dinner and not enough for five!'

"He has given us loaves and fishes this morning, that we might celebrate the beginning of our journey as a congregation, and offer thanks for a marvelous new chapter in the life of Holy Trinity.

"Now, let us go forth to do the work that He has given us to do."

Three voices responded. "Thanks be to God!"

As he moved along the aisle in his purple Lenten vestments, he sensed in his soul the definite quickening of Easter.

"We started bringing things over yesterday evening," Agnes said. "Twelve prayer books, the fair linen, and the old alms basin, and look how we had need of them all! Mr. Cowper made it perfectly clear that God works in mysterious ways."

"So clear that many think his line of verse to be Holy Writ! Tell me, is it uncomfortable for you to kneel—I mean, with the cane, I thought . . ."

"It is uncomfortable, but I shall kneel as long as I'm able—and as long as you'll help me up again!"

He mingled with Agnes and the visitors as Cynthia unpacked the basket at the stone wall. "And where has Clarence got to? He was a dab hand at the candles, not to mention carrying the cross and passing the basin . . ."

"He's gone back to the house for a bit. He's extremely shy; this is the most activity we've had at Holy Trinity in a very long time."

Cynthia set out two thick sandwiches of sliced roast chicken on whole wheat, and cut them into eight pieces. Then she withdrew from the basket a jar of Lew Boyd's bread-and-butter pickles and a chunk of white cheddar . . .

Walking with her cane, Agnes approached the wall. "Is there something I might do to help, Mrs. Kavanagh?"

"Will you please call me Cynthia?"

"Cynthia. That was my paternal grandmother's name. And you'll call me Agnes."

"Agnes, what would we have done without you and Clarence?"

"You would have done perfectly well! May I introduce you to Granny Meaders and her grandson, Rooter?"

"Hey," said Rooter, "can I have that 'un?"

"That one what?" asked Cynthia.

"That piece of sam'wich you jis' cut."

"That would be the biggest one."

"Yeah. That 'un."

"Well, I suppose since you're the youngest, and still growing, you need it most."

"An' I'll have me some of them cookies, too."

"There's no sugar in these cookies."

"Pfaw. I ain't eatin' 'em, then."

"Granny," Cynthia held out her hand. "I'm pleased to meet you."

"Hit's nice t' meet you'uns. We was baptized at th' church what burnt down Christmas Eve. Hit was th' wars."

"The wars?"

"The wires," said Agnes. "They were old. They say the church will be rebuilt, but farther down, in the valley."

"Shall I call you Granny?" asked Cynthia.

"Ever'body does, honey."

"Please take a napkin and I'll pile on what we have. Would you like a pickle?"

"Are they sweet? My stomach cain't hardly tolerate sour."

"Yes, ma'am, they're sweet. And here's a cookie, and a slice of apple and a bit of cheese . . ."

"I cain't hardly chew nothin'."

"She can *gum* it t' death!" said Rooter, proud of such a skill.

". . . and of course, we have a lovely thermos of raspberry tea, but only two drinking cups. Rats in a poke!"

"What's 'at you jis' said?"

"I said, 'rats in a poke.'"

"Is that cussin'?"

"Well, sort of, I suppose."

"'At ain't what I say when I cuss."

"Yes, but you could say 'rats in a poke' and get lots more attention than those words you're alluding to. I mean, no one pays any attention to that old stuff anymore."

"I got it licked about y'r tea. You'n th' preacher could drink out one of them cups, me'n Granny could drink out th' other'n."

"What about everyone else?"

"Ol' Robert he could drink after me'n Granny, an' Mr. Goodnight, he could drink out of th' lid of that bottle y' got there."

"Rooter," said Agnes, "run along that path to the little house—not the big one, the little one, and ask Clarence for eight paper cups. If he's not there, look over the sink at the back door. Eight! Run!"

Rooter ran.

His grandmother grinned, revealing pink gums. "Hit's good y' didn't need n'more, he cain't hardly count past ten."

"Thank goodness I put these in!" Cynthia withdrew yet another comestible from the basket. "I packed for a celebration, and I was right!" She peeled away the foil and displayed two small apple fritters. "They'll slice perfectly into eight small bites."

"Lloyd Goodnight, this is Mrs. Kavanagh."

"We welcome you, ma'am." Lloyd Goodnight extended his large, rough hand.

"Lloyd came to this church as an infant."

"I was baptized in Wilson's Creek down yonder. An' I was twelve year old when they closed th' church. They wadn't nobody around to come n'more, 'cept my mama and daddy, an' then we moved offa th' mountain. I come back home to th' ridge last year."

Lloyd Goodnight looked pleased about his homecoming.

Cynthia served the pie onto napkins. "Did you enjoy the service this morning?"

"Oh, yes, ma'am, I did. It was me that pulled th' bell." Lloyd drew himself up, beaming.

"And well done, I must say!"

"I could've went on pullin', but seem like we was all ready to get goin'."

Cynthia laughed.

"I've missed our old church. I carried th' cross when I was a boy, an' done a lot of what Clarence done today. I can still hear th' priest say, 'Let us pray f'r th' whole state of Christ's church.' I thought that was a mighty big thing, to pray f'r th' whole state of th' church across all th' whole wide world."

"Yes," said Cynthia. "It is a mighty big thing. And we still need it in a mighty big way."

"We have Robert Prichard over there," said Agnes. "Robert, will you come and greet Mrs. Kavanagh?"

Robert, who had sat on the back row and hadn't come to the rail for communion, was leaning against a tree, looking upon the gathering with an expressionless face. He was tall and lean, and wore a short-sleeve shirt that revealed numerous tattoos.

He took his time walking over. "Hey," he said, putting his hands in the back pockets of his jeans.

"Hey, yourself," said Cynthia.

Rooter ran up, breathless, and surrendered the cups. *"Here!"*

"Thank you, Rooter." Cynthia lined up the cups on top of the wall. "I believe we'll each have a half cup to the very drop. Agnes, will you pour?"

"I didn't hardly know what t' say in y'alls meetin'," confessed Granny Meaders.

"Hit was all wrote down," said Rooter. "Plain as day."

"Them words was too little f'r me t' half see."

Cynthia was digging slices of pickle from the jar and putting one on top of each sandwich. "I didn't hear you speak up, Mister Rooter."

"I ain't a-goin' t' read out loud in front of nobody."

"He was held back two year in 'is grades," said Granny.

"An' I ain't a-goin' back t' that school after I git done in August, neither."

"Where d'you think you're a-goin'?" asked Granny.

"T' hell an' back before I go down th' mountain in a *bus*, I can tell y' that."

Cynthia held forth a laden napkin. "Robert . . ."

Robert took it, wordless.

"I hope you'uns don't mind me wearin' m' bedroom slippers," said Granny. As everyone peered at her open-toed slippers, she wiggled her digits beneath wool socks. "I cain't hardly wear reg'lar shoes n'more, my feet swells s'bad."

Cynthia nodded. "I understand perfectly!"

"I ain't never seen a preacher in a dress," said Rooter. "How come 'e was wearin' a dress?"

Now disrobed, Father Tim strolled into the midst of the party in his favorite gray suit. "Let's thank the good Lord for our loaves and fishes! Shall we wait for Clarence?"

"He wouldn't want us to wait," said Agnes. "I'm sure he'll come along in a while."

But Clarence didn't come along.

"Senior dry food only," said Blake Eddistoe. "This fella's been living too high."

"I figured it might come to this."

"We need to get about seven pounds off his frame. Hip dysplasia is aggravated by weight gain, and of course the extra weight isn't good for his heart. I believe you said he's what, ten, eleven?"

"He was young when he came to me; I don't know his age exactly, but yes, I figure eleven years."

"More romps in the pasture wouldn't hurt the old boy."

"Wouldn't hurt this old boy, either," said the vicar, who hadn't a clue where he'd find time to romp in a pasture.

<No time to blab.

<Bought black dress, got crud, dropped seven pounds.

<Harold says it was fluid.

<Dress now too large. Was on sale so can't take back. Cost of alteration out the kazoo, so refuse to do.

<Will lose seventeen pounds and wear my good navy.

<Pray for me.

<Love to all,

<Emma

<Do you bow or curtsy if you meet the Queen?

"Adele's been promoted," said J.C. "You'll read about it in th' *Muse* tomorrow."

He thought J.C. looked oddly dejected.

"Promoted to what?" asked Mule.

"From corporal to sergeant."

"Congratulations!" said Father Tim. "We're proud with you."

J.C. ducked his head and fumbled with his overstuffed briefcase, which sat beside him on a dinette chair salvaged from a Mitford dumpster.

"Are they promotin' her nine millimeter, too?" In Mule's opinion, women shouldn't be allowed to become police officers, much less tote heavy metal around in a holster.

"She's not carryin' a nine millimeter anymore," snapped J.C. "She's carryin' a forty-caliber H and K."

"You don't have t' bite my head off."

"So what else is new?" asked Percy.

"Gene Bolick's not doing so hot," said J.C.

"Th' tumor's too deep in there to operate, and the medication's not working like it should."

Mule peered into his lunch sack. "Uh oh. What in th' dickens . . ."

"Don't even start that mess," said Percy. "I don't want t' hear it." Percy unwrapped the foil from his wedge of lasagna, and removed a plastic fork from his shirt pocket.

"Lasagna!" marveled Mule, peering over the top of his glasses. "What'd you bring?" he asked Father Tim.

"Chicken sandwich on whole wheat with low-fat mayo and a couple of bread and butter pickles."

Mule looked into the recesses of his paper bag and sighed deeply.

"We thank the Lord for this nourishment!" said Father Tim.

"Amen!" Percy forthwith hammered down on last night's leftovers. "Lew needs to get 'im a microwave in this place. Hey, Lew, why don't you put in a microwave?"

Lew walked in from the garage, wiping his hands on a rag.

"Put in your own bloomin' microwave. I ain't runnin' a restaurant, in case you didn't notice."

"Lookit," said Percy, "we buy drinks, we buy

Nabs, we fill up with gas an' whatnot—it'd be an investment in keepin' us as reg'lars."

"Yeah, well, these turkeys was all reg'lars up at your place, an' look what happened, you went out of b'iness!"

Everybody had a good laugh, except J.C., who was staring at his unopened cup of yogurt.

"Thanks again for the Christmas pickles, Lew," said Father Tim. "I believe this is the recipe that inspired Earlene to kiss you on the mouth when you won the blue ribbon."

Lew blushed. "Yessir, that's th' recipe, all right."

"When is Earlene moving down to Mitford?"

"September!" said Lew. "Lock, stock, and barrel."

"An' don't forget Mama," said Mule. "Lock, stock, barrel, and Mama."

Lew ignored this reference to his mother-in-law, who was moving from Tennessee with his once-secret wife. "How's your new church comin' along, Father?"

"We had our first service yesterday, I'm happy to say."

"Great!" said Mule. "How many?"

"Including yours truly? Eight."

Mule removed a see-through plastic container from the bag. "Mighty low numbers."

"Numbers aren't everything," said the vicar.

"Who give you that haircut?" asked Mule. "Pretty sporty lookin'."

"A woman who lives above the clouds across a creek without a bridge."

Percy stared at him blankly. "No wonder it gets s' long between cuttin's," he said.

"So, J.C., any more news of Edith Mallory?"

"I hear she said *God* again and was tryin' to add another word."

"How'd you hear that?" asked Percy.

"Ed Coffey."

Mule looked offended. "Why were you talkin' to that low-life bum? You just talked to 'im th' other day."

"None of your business."

"Thank you very much." Mule snapped off the lid. "Oh, *law!*"

Percy looked the other way. "Don't tell us what it is, we don't *care* what it is."

"What is it?" asked Father Tim.

"I'll be darned if I know. Lookit." Mule displayed the item for all to inspect.

"That makes yogurt look like pheasant under glass," said J.C.

"It's brown," said Percy. "Or is it dark green? My glasses ain't doin' too good."

Father Tim peered closely. "Dark green."

"Call 'er up and ask what it is," said Percy. "I'd give a half-dollar to have it identified."

Father Tim searched his pants pocket for a couple of quarters. "I'll give the other half."

"I usually don't call Fancy at th' shop, but for a dollar . . ."

J.C. pointed to the wall. "There's th' phone."

"Yeah, but if I use th' phone, which costs a quarter, I don't get but seventy-five cents out of th' deal."

"It's seventy-five cents you didn't have," counseled Father Tim.

"Right. OK."

Mule dialed.

"Fancy, baby? Got a minute? What's this you packed for my lunch?"

Long silence.

"You don't mean it. I declare, that's th' way it goes, all right."

More silence. The members of the Turkey Club sat forward on their chairs.

"What color was it before?"

Further silence.

"It's not th' first time somebody threatened to sue you over a hair deal. It ain't goin' to happen, so don't worry about it. Right. Right. I love you, too."

"You call your wife *baby*?" J.C. appeared mildly stricken by this revelation. "You tell 'er you *love* 'er in front of God and everybody?"

"Wait a minute, wait a minute," said Percy. "We're gettin' off track here. What is that mess she packed you for lunch?"

"Dadgum," said Mule. "She forgot to say, an' I ain't spendin' another quarter."

"You're losing all around on this deal," said Father Tim. "Canceled out your dollar, and invested a quarter of your own money."

"Shoot," said Mule. "I quit. I guess I ought t' just eat th' thing an' get it over with, I'm half starved."

"Who's suing Fancy this time?" asked J.C.

"What do you mean, *this* time? There's only been one other time," said Mule, offended.

"So that was that time, and this is this time."

"You said it like somebody's suin' 'er *all* th' time."

"Lord help us," said Percy. "Your blood sugar's shot, you need nourishment. Get you a pack of Nabs out of th' machine, and hush *up*, for Pete's sake." If Velma Mosely was here, she'd knock Mule Skinner in the head once and for all. How they'd dealt with ornery, hard-to-please Grill customers for more than forty years was way, *way* more than he'd ever understand.

"Smell it," said Mule, trying to hand off the plastic container to Father Tim.

"No, thanks."

Mule gazed into the container. "I think it's guacamole." He fished around in his lunch bag for a plastic fork and gave the thing a poke. "*Ha!* You'll be sorry you bad-mouthed this little number. It's guacamole over roasted chicken!"

J.C. stood up and grabbed his briefcase. "I'm outta here."

"Where you goin? You ain't even touched your yogurt."

"I'm headed down to th' dadblame tea shop with th' women. *Sayonara, hasta la vista,* and see you in th' funny papers."

"Man," said Mule, as J.C. blew through the door.

"His aftershave nearly gassed me," said Percy. "Prop th' door open, get a little air circulatin' in here. What's 'is problem, anyway?"

Father Tim didn't comment, but he thought he recognized J.C.'s problem as one he'd formerly had himself.

On the way to Hope House, he mused on Edith Mallory, for whom he often prayed, even when he didn't want to.

He couldn't imagine having all logical thought blasted to smithereens. The childhood memory of running his hand into the grain bin at the hardware store came to mind. Tens of thousands of grains of corn, all looking and feeling alike, and all silken to his touch—what if he'd been searching for one particular grain in the bin, as Edith was searching for a particular word in the great sea of random words turned loose in her mind?

Lord, he prayed, *help her find the next word. And the next, and the next . . .*

"Louella?"

Louella sat in her chair by the window, the television on mute.

"Miss Louella is sleepin'," whispered the nurse, who tiptoed in behind him. "She stayed up late last night watchin' the beauty pageant."

"Please tell her I stopped by and will stop again, will you?"

"Oh, yes, sir."

"How is she?" It had somehow astonished him to find her sleeping; he'd thought for a moment . . .

"Oh, she's well, very well. We had to get that little bladder infection treated, you know, that wasn't a good thing, but other than that, she's perky and has her appetite!"

After the nurse left, he stood by her chair and prayed for his friend and Miss Sadie's much-loved companion; he did not want to lose Louella.

He drove the Mustang from Hope House to Old Church Lane and turned right onto Main Street, where he parked in front of Dora Pugh's Hardware.

"Can you duplicate this?" he asked Dora.

"Now, Father, you know better than to ask me if I can do somethin'."

"Right, but can you?"

Dora cackled. "Of course I can. But where'd you find this thing? It looks like somethin' that dropped out of our town founder's saddlebag when he rode up th' mountain in 1846. Or was it 1864?"

With the new key on the sterling ring given him by Walter and Katherine, he walked at a clip to the Sweet Stuff Bakery and made a purchase. Using Winnie's phone, he also made a call to Esther Bolick, but there was no answer and no answering machine.

Afterward, he dashed to The Local and dropped off a shopping list that Avis would have ready for pickup before the trek home to Meadowgate.

With the still-warm paper bag sitting on the

passenger seat, he drove north on Main, made a left onto Lilac Road, and a right into the rear entrance of the Porter place, aka Mitford town museum.

He rapped on the backdoor, hard by a green plastic hanging basket containing the remnants of last summer's geranium, and heard a shuffling gait on the other side.

"Who is it?" squawked Miss Rose, throwing open the door.

She was barefoot, and wearing a chenille robe topped by a woolen Army jacket with several war medals displayed on the lapel.

"It's the preacher. I've come to visit!" He spoke loudly, and tried to sound cheerful, but truth be told, Miss Rose had always scared him half to death.

"Bill's laid up in bed."

"Is he sick?"

"I don't know; I haven't asked him."

"May I come in and sit with him?"

"We're not able to entertain company."

"I have a bag of doughnuts for the two of you, but I guess I'll just . . . *take them home and eat them myself.*" He'd never said anything so contrary to Miss Rose.

"Come in, come in!"

He thought the old woman looked less, but only a little less, fierce.

"And be quick about it," she commanded.

Still clutching the paper bag, he blew past Miss Rose and down the hall to the bedroom, which smelled strongly of urine.

Kneeling beside Uncle Billy's bed, he saw that his face appeared unnaturally puffy.

"I've brought you a doughnut, Uncle Billy. Still warm. Winnie sends her love."

"I'll be et f'r a tater"—Uncle Billy's breathing was labored—"if it ain't th' preacher." His eyes opened, then fluttered shut.

"Are you feeling all right?"

Uncle Billy coughed. "Sharp as a briar."

"Tell me what's going on."

His friend's hand was dry and fragile, a corn husk in winter.

"Uncle Billy, can you tell me what's going on?"

"I done tol' you," Uncle Billy whispered.

"Tell me again, if you will, I didn't quite hear it."

Uncle Billy's eyelids trembled.

Something was wrong. Very wrong.

He ran to the kitchen and tossed the bag of doughnuts on the table. "I'm calling an ambulance."

"You'll pay for it, then!" Miss Rose gave him a menacing look, grabbed the bag, and shuffled along the hall to the bathroom. He heard the lock click into place.

He tried the wall phone, but the line was dead, and he had no cell phone. Like it or not, he'd have to start carrying a cell phone with the rest of the common horde.

"I'll be back!" he shouted.

He ran across the side yard and ducked through the bushes and sprinted across the street in front of the monument and raced up the steps of the town hall and through the lobby and into the mayor's office where the receptionist was reading *People* magazine.

"Get an ambulance out to the Porter place," he said, gasping for breath. "It's Uncle Billy."

CHAPTER SIX

Above the Clouds

"Congestive heart failure," said Hoppy.

"His heart isn't pumping normally, but the medications are working; we're getting the fluid off. I think he can pull through this."

"Thank God."

"He'll pee a bucket, which will help his breathing and get rid of the swelling. But what happens when he gets out of here? That's where the cheese gets binding. He'll need to restrict his salt intake, big time, and somebody needs to see that he gets a decent diet."

"That's a tough one. Miss Rose refuses to move up to Hope House and Uncle Billy won't leave without her. But—I'll do what I can. By the way, we loved seeing Lace."

"We loved seeing Dooley," said his old friend and overworked town doctor.

In the deeps of New Jersey, the answering service of his cousin Walter's law practice advised him that Mr. Kavanagh was next door at Starbucks and would be along any minute, leave a number.

He rang Dooley's mother, Pauline Leeper, in the dining room at Hope House, and asked if he could drop by later in the week.

"Is anything wrong?" He heard the anxiety in her voice.

"No, nothing wrong at all," he assured her. He felt certain Pauline would approve. In any case, Dooley was twenty-one, and fully able to make this decision without parental approval.

He dialed Betty Craig at the little house where Dooley's grandfather Russell Jacks had lived out his last years in a spare bedroom.

"Betty! It's . . ."

"Father Tim! I know your voice, an' I know why you're callin' me."

"Now, Betty . . ."

"You want me to go an' sit with Miss Rose while Uncle Billy's in th' hospital!"

What could he say? "Will you do it?"

Long, pondering silence. "My rates have gone up!" she blurted.

"Not a problem."

"It's *not*?"

Betty Craig, who had tried for several years to retire from registered nursing, was too kind to refuse outright this onerous opportunity.

"Not at all. In truth, you've been needing to raise your rates."

"I *have*?"

"Can you go over this morning and take care of the laundry and change the sheets and do a little cooking?"

"Well, but . . ."

"Why don't we raise your rate by twenty percent? Does that sound fair?"

"Oh, very fair."

"Whatever you need at The Local, put it on my account. Thank you, Betty, and of course, when Uncle Billy comes home, we'll need you to do all the good things you did last time he was sick. God bless you, you're an angel. Let me know your hours."

He hung up quickly, took a deep breath, and dialed again.

"Buck?"

". . . in a hole . . ." Static.

"Call me at the farm. You have my number?"

Static. "Down th' mountain . . ." Static. Dial tone.

He checked his e-mail.

Five messages.

He didn't have all day, he had to get up to Holy Trinity and meet with Agnes at . . . he looked at his watch . . . nine-thirty. Good. He had an hour.

He dialed.

"Hello?"

Babies howling.

"Puny! It's . . ."

"Hey, Father! Can you hear 'em bawlin'? Law, these boys is a *handful*."

"I'll bet."

"But I love 'em, we all love 'em! Got to go, Father, you never *seen* s' many dirty diapers. I never knowed boys make more dirty diapers than girls, did you ever hear that?"

"Never did. May I stop by in a few days?"

"Call me first, this house is upside down an' backwards, you should've seen me packin' Joe Joe's lunch this mornin', I put a stuffed bear in 'is lunch box and laid 'is sandwich on th' toy shelf. Guess I'll eat it myself.

"Oh, law, got to go." *Click.*

He pulled the keyboard toward him, and rolled up the sleeves of his flannel shirt.

<Subject: The Queen

<How to curtsy:

<One foot forward.

<Bend your knees.

<Lower your body.

<Your faithful servant

He selected a font. He clicked on a border. He chose a type size. He formatted the page. He scratched his head. He typed.

He hit "print" and ordered twenty-five copies, then saw how good they looked, and duplicated the first order.

He stuck the whole caboodle in a folder, and trotted to the kitchen, feeling upbeat. Though he was sales and service, not marketing, this effort nonetheless pleased him.

He swung by the window seat where the easel was up, the watercolors were out, and February was toeing the mark. "What do you think?" He stuck a flyer under her nose.

"I love it!"

"It could have been, um, more exciting copy. But in the end, I decided to keep it simple."

"Always the best approach!" She gave him a laudatory kiss.

What more did a man need in this world?

He blew by Green Valley Baptist Church and gave the wayside pulpit message two thumbs up.

COINCIDENCE IS WHEN GOD
CHOOSES TO REMAIN ANONYMOUS.

Agnes met him at the wall, where they stood looking down at clouds collected in the hollows after last night's rain. Then, carrying the tea basket, and the folder under his arm, he walked with her to the nave.

He saw it at once and drew in his breath.

"Beautiful!" he exclaimed, hurrying ahead of her to the pulpit placed on the gospel side of the aisle.

He smelled the familiar scent he associated only with churches and his mother's parlor; the pungent wax that had been rubbed so carefully into the oak would long after release its sweet savor upon the air.

She came behind him on her cane. "Clarence made it four years ago, when God renewed our conviction that He would send someone. It sat here only a short time, and then we took it to the schoolhouse where it would be safe."

The polished oak glowed in the light from the window above the altar. "Exquisite!" he said.

"He brought it over on Sunday evening, and with great joy, we installed it. Do you like where it's placed?"

"Couldn't like it better! What became of the original?"

"It was stolen many years ago. The vandals who did this were not thieves, but desecrators of another stripe."

She pointed to the initials rudely carved into the left side of the pulpit. "Just there . . . 'JC loves CM.' We were at first greatly distressed, then I realized what we might take it to signify: Jesus Christ loves Clarence Merton."

He laughed. "Lemons into lemonade, and gospel truth into the bargain! And look here! Such elaborate detailing. He did this, as well?"

"Yes, with the old carving tools given him long ago."

He ran his fingers over the tooled oak, tracing the path the knife had taken before him.

A crown of thorns. A heart. A dove. A dogwood blossom. And in the center of these, a cross.

"Agnes . . ." That's all he could find to say.

She was moved, proud. "Yes."

"Let's thank God!" Indeed, it was pray—or bust wide open.

He took her hand in both of his, and they bowed their heads.

"We praise You, Lord, we thank You, Lord, we bless You, Lord!

"Thank You for the marvel and mystery of this place, for these thirty remarkable years of devotion, for Your unceasing encouragement to the hearts and spirits of Your servants, Agnes and Clarence, for Your marvelous gifts to Clarence of resourcefulness and creativity, and for Your gift to them both of a mighty perseverance in faith and prayer.

"We thank You for this nave above the clouds in which Your holy name has been, and will continue to be, honored, praised, and glorified. Thank You for going ahead of us as we visit our neighbors, and cutting for each and every one a wide path to Holy Trinity. Draw whom You will to the tenderness of Your unconditional love, the sweetness of Your everlasting mercy, and the balm of Your unbounded forgiveness.

"In the name of the Father and of the Son and of the Holy Spirit."

"Amen," they said together.

"Well, then!" He felt ten feet tall, and growing. "I got the flyer done up; want to see it?"

"I do!"

He produced a copy from the folder. "And I brought tape so we can tape it to the door if someone's not home, and thumbtacks for power poles and fence posts."

"You've thought of everything!" she said, sharing his excitement.

Holy Trinity Episcopal Church
Wilson's Ridge
Est. 1899
Will reopen its doors
Sunday, May 1st
At ten o'clock in the morning
With the glad celebration of
Morning Prayer and the Order of
Holy Communion
Come one, come all

"'The Order of Holy Communion' should have gone on a line all its own," he confessed. "I didn't know how to set the thingamajig."

"It's just right," she said. "I like your border."

"Today, we can read the litany for Ash Wednesday, and finish our visitation list, and . . . what else?"

"I'll show you the cemetery."

"And in the morning, we'll set out first thing, if that's all right. I'll pick you up at ten o'clock?"

"I'll be ready," she said, happily, "with a thermos of tea."

"In the meantime, I'm mighty eager for the next installment of your story."

She looked tentative. "Do you really want to hear it? I'm not proud of all I'll be bound to tell you, Father."

"I want to hear it. Very much."

In the front pew, she took the mugs from the basket, and he unscrewed the cap from the thermos and poured the steaming tea.

Though the morning sun was warm on the flanks of the mountains, the nave was distinctly chilly. He kept his jacket on, and she had drawn her old cardigan closer about her thin frame.

"I'd also like to hear about everyone who came on Sunday. Rooter and his grandmother . . ."

"Granny isn't Rooter's blood grandmother. She was a neighbor who took him in as a baby when his parents abandoned him."

His heart felt the blow of that.

"Is there no end to it, Agnes?"

"No, Father, there isn't. The world is harsh and unforgiving, which is but one of the reasons you find me here today."

"Here?"

"On this ridge, seemingly so far from the cruelty that everywhere assaults us if we let it."

"And Clarence?"

"He's happy here, very happy; this is where Clarence finds himself. He has a workshop in our yard and creates lovely things from wood, which he sells to a man who travels around to the mountain shops." She lowered her eyes, modest. "Clarence has won many awards."

"Wonderful! I don't doubt it. And tell me about Robert."

"Robert was in prison for eleven years; he lives alone, just down the road."

He saw the quickening of sorrow in her countenance.

"Why was he in prison?"

"He's said to have killed a man."

"Do you know him well?"

"No one knows him well. Yet I believe him innocent. He pled innocence all along. The man he was convicted of killing was his grandfather."

"I see a great hunger in his eyes. Robert wants to know God."

"Yes. He does. Though he may not know or even imagine that he does. I sense that he's unbearably lonely."

He put his elbows on his knees and leaned forward in the pew and gazed without seeing at the pine floorboards. "And Lloyd?" He hoped for a brighter story about Lloyd.

"He's a good man. He, too, found the world hard, albeit instructive, and came home again, hoping to find all things golden, as in his boyhood." Agnes laughed softly. "Of course, he's been gravely disappointed!"

He sat up and leaned back, comfortable on the wooden pew seat. "I hope to go home again one day; it's been years since I visited Holly Springs in Mississippi. I think I'm afraid of . . . I'm not certain . . . finding it so changed, or worse, finding it all too familiar."

"I understand."

"But please, start where you left off. You and Jessie and Little Bertie endured the Great Baptizing. What happened then?"

She smiled and sipped her tea, inhaling the heady scent of sassafras, undiluted on this occasion by the common grace of mint.

"We found that we loved the people, and found also that we were loved by them. I came to understand that the people here weren't objects to which one does good, but true hearts whom I wanted more than anything to help.

"Jessie and I pled with the diocese to send

every thread of clothing they could collect, we even went to Asheville on two momentous occasions, to sound a special plea for winter coats and shoes. You can't imagine the want we found here in those days."

He smiled. "I was a young clergyman in the backwaters of Mississippi nearly forty years ago. So, I can imagine."

"I'm sure you've had long experience with all sorts of souls. Forgive my boldness, but perhaps one day you'll tell your story."

"Deal!" he said.

"We used our Buick Town Car to ferry people to the doctor, sometimes all the way to Holding. It took a full day to go to Holding and back, we often forded the creek well past dark."

"No doctor in Mitford?"

"Only on occasional days. Like a clergyman, he rode the circuit. And none of us cared for the sour old fellows in Wesley—they were twins, and both looked as if they'd eaten a bucket of green persimmons!

"But everyone loved our Buick. So many had never ridden in a car at all. They'd pile up in the backseat like taters in a basket, as Jessie used to say, and all clinging to the hand ropes for dear life. I think I was a very fast driver in those days, some said Miss Agnes just whipped around these back roads."

She laughed. "I remember there would be a knock on the door and two or three unwashed young 'uns saying 'Miss Agnes, can we set in your automobile?' And one winter night Jessie went out to put two squash pies in that cavernous trunk—which we also used for refrigeration—and there were three neighbor children dead asleep under our lap robe on the backseat. They'd come to spend the night in Miss Agnes's car! It was quite the thing to do for a year or two.

"Of course, not everyone in these parts enjoys the notion of automobiles. There are a few, even today, who don't fancy hurtling down the side of a mountain in a vehicle."

"I'm one of them, actually."

"Jubal Adderholt hasn't been off this ridge in fourteen years. He's someone I'd like us to visit tomorrow." She gazed away. "Perhaps . . ."

"Perhaps?"

"Perhaps we should be making our plan for visitation, instead of sitting here like turnips."

"Ten more minutes?"

She hesitated, then nodded her assent.

He thought a shadow passed over her face then, but perhaps he was mistaken.

"We know the roads today aren't always the best, but in those days, they were immeasurably worse. Touring a Buick Town Car around the poorest county in the state may sound adventurous or even romantic, but all that wear and tear took a great toll on everything from tires to engine.

"Not long ago, I asked an elderly lady what she'd found most remarkable in her long life. 'Men on the moon!' I thought she might say, but she looked at me with the firmest conviction and declared, 'Good roads, Agnes, good roads!'

"Parts were frightfully expensive then, as I hear they are today. We had parts shipped from Bangor, Maine, for several years, because we could trust the dealer; but as you know, far-fetched is dear-bought. I suppose it was a blessing, really, when our grand old automobile simply gave out, and we were forced to make a transition . . . to a truck. . . ."

She looked beyond the high window above the altar to the branches of an oak. He felt she'd forgotten he was there.

"Are you all right?"

She crossed herself. "Yes," she whispered. She turned then, and looked at him steadily.

"I know I'm going to tell you everything, Father; it simply must be done."

She glanced behind him, and he saw the

anxious expression of her face at once trans-
formed. "Clarence!"

He turned and saw Clarence's large frame
silhouetted in the doorway.

"I never got to speak more than a word to
him on Sunday. This is a blessing!" He rose
from the pew as Clarence came toward them
along the aisle.

"Clarence . . ." He extended his hand. "It
was a very happy pleasure to serve with you,
and I'm absolutely astonished at the beauty of
our pulpit."

Agnes used her hands in what Father Tim
recognized as sign language.

Clarence smiled with unmistakable happiness as he extended a large, calloused hand to
Father Tim. Then he signed to his mother, who
translated his greeting to the vicar.

"He says we have waited a long time. And he
rejoices that you have come."

Clarence closely observed his mother as she
spoke, and nodded in assent.

"My son is completely deaf, Father, nor can
he speak. His heart converses, instead."

"Look, Stuart, I know you're busy . . ."

"Not too busy to talk with you, old friend.
How's it going with Holy Trinity?"

"Did you know the building and grounds have been maintained for three decades by a woman and her son?"

"I didn't know it, actually, until after I e-mailed you in December. Then I decided not to mention what I found out, so you could discover it for yourself. Besides, I didn't know how much of what I heard was true. It sounded like some Appalachian folktale."

"It's no tale. And the woman, Agnes Merton, is a deaconess, a remnant of the old mission church deaconesses. I didn't know there were any left."

"A few, of course. One in Virginia, one or two in New England, maybe more, I don't know. It's a lost part of church history."

"Now I know why you said you were patently envious."

Stuart laughed. "Did I say that?"

"You did."

"And I am. You've never seen so much high muckety-muck as the trifold event of cathedral consecration, my retirement, and the installation of the new bishop. We're all just this side of stroke. And there you are on your untrammeled mountaintop, birds eating from your hand, mountain panthers lying curled at your feet . . ."

"Right. Precisely."

"Truth be told, you sound fifteen years younger, possibly twenty. Uh-oh, have to trot. Keep me posted. See you in June!"

"You're ever in my prayers."

"And you in mine. May He provide all you need for Holy Trinity."

"I can hardly believe what He's provided thus far. But I'll tell you everything another time. You and Martha must come here, you must."

"Perhaps next fall. After the consecration, we're headed to the islands for a month. I have no idea what I'll do with all that time."

"You'll figure it out," said the vicar.

A *month*? In the *islands*! He couldn't begin to imagine such a thing for himself. He knew only that he was glad to be where God had planted him—looking down upon the clouds, at roughly forty-five hundred feet above sea level.

<Do I put just <u>any</u> old foot forward, or one <u>particular</u> foot? **Be more specific!!!**

<How <u>much</u> bend in the knees?

<How <u>far</u> do I lower my body?

<And when I'm through acting like a monkey, can I <u>look her in the eye?</u>

<Surely she's not too stuck on herself to be looked in the eye???

<If she is, then who even needs to meet her in the first place?

<And think of all the old people who can't bend their knees. Are they robbed of the chance to meet Her Royal Highness???

The e-mail raved on at some length. Clearly, Emma was scared out of her wits about flying across the pond, and had gone ballistic.

Willie Mullis presented the contents of his hat. "Nine."

"Nine! How wonderful!" He took the egg bowl from the shelf above the coatrack. "Won't you step inside?"

"Nossir."

"I suppose the laying will pick up to—what do you think?"

He plucked the eggs from the hat and put them in the bowl. Four brown, five white. "To maybe a dozen a day?"

"Nineteen."

"Nineteen?"

"Yessir."

"A *day*?"

"Yessir."

"We have quite a few left from yesterday; would you like these back?"

"Nossir."

"Ah, well, then. Won't you help us out and take some all along?"

"Eggs gives me gas."

"I see. Care to come in for a cup of hot cocoa?"

"Nossir." Willie's eyes lowered to his boots, which had attracted a considerable bit of straw on the soles. "Been muckin' out th' stalls this mornin'."

"I see. Well, if you need help, let me know. And thank you, Willie, thank you."

"Yessir."

"I don't think he likes me," he told Cynthia.

"Phoo, darling. Everyone likes you."

"Now, now, Kavanagh. So, tell me—what are we to do with nineteen eggs a day?"

She sighed. "I have no idea. Quiches. Omelets. Egg salad. What did *Marge* do, for heaven's sake? She never said. I refuse to bake a cake, by the way, I have no time to bake a cake, so don't even *mention* baking a cake!"

"A cake? I would never mention such a thing."

His wife looked oddly pale and distraught.

"What is it, my girl?" He put his arm around her as she stood at the kitchen sink.

"For one thing, it's laundry! Where does it all come from? It multiplies like coat hangers in a closet! And then there's dusting and sweeping and cooking and shaking out the dog beds and emptying the dishwasher and working on the calendar and . . ."

"How's February coming?"

"Ugh. Not well. Not well at all. I got off light with January and I'm paying my dues with February."

"How can I help?"

"This house was so cozy and snug and even sort of *small* when Joyce was here, and now it's positively *huge*. That vacuum cleaner, whoever invented the thing should be put in *stocks.*"

"Come and sit down," he pled, tugging her away from the sink. "I'll do the laundry, leave it for me. And how about this, I'll start wearing my shirts three days instead of two. Plus, I'll make dinner tonight! How about omelets? Or a quiche, I could do a quiche . . ."

"And the fireplace," she said, thumping into the wing chair. "I don't know what's wrong with it, but every time there's a *breath* of wind, it starts blowing ashes all over the floor."

He couldn't bear to see his usually cheerful wife so frazzled and worn. Worse still, why hadn't he noticed before? Was he as blind as a bat or merely as dense as a rock?

Or both?

"I'll be in Holding a couple of days checkin' the job we're doin' with th' bank," said Buck. "I'll look up Lon Burtie, and see what's goin' on at Clyde Barlowe's trailer."

"Good. You're sure you don't need me?"

"Don't see why I would."

"How's business?"

"We're slammed," said Buck. "But no way am I complainin'."

A few years ago, Dooley's stepfather had asked God to turn his life around, and since then, he and Buck had worked together more than once to search for the missing siblings. In truth, a deep bond had grown between the vicar and the uncompromising job supervisor who'd overseen the construction of Hope House.

"Pauline said you called. Anything wrong?"

"Dooley wants to take the Kavanagh name." He felt mildly uncomfortable saying it. "I'd appreciate it if you'd let me speak with Pauline before you mention it. I plan to be at Hope House on Thursday."

"Cat's got m' tongue."

"Do you think she . . . how do you think she'll receive this?"

"Don't know. Could make 'er feel she's losin' one of 'er kids all over again. I've kept quiet about Sammy bein' missin'. Course, we don't know if he's missin'."

"True." He only knew he didn't feel encouraged about Sammy. His heart was heavy when he thought of the boy who looked enough like Dooley to be a twin, and who had a gift for turning rude wilderness into the miracle of a garden.

"How long does it *take* to get a cup of coffee at Starbucks?"

"For Pete's sake, I wasn't at Starbucks; I was in Atlanta for four days."

"Aha."

"I have the answering service from the netherworld," said Walter. "What's up, Cousin?"

"Dooley turned twenty-one in February. After what I hope is soulful consideration, he wants to take the Kavanagh name."

Walter laughed. "I like it when an Englishman opts for an Irish name. Probably happens at least once or twice a millennium. In any case, that's great news; I believe there's enough melancholy in your boy to make an admirably authentic Irishman. And hey, you'll be a dad! At the tender age of what—seventy?"

"Sixty-nine, if the legal stuff happens before June twenty-eighth."

"This is not my specialty, but I think it's going to be pretty simple, given that he's the age of majority. Let me look into it and get back to you."

"Soon, do you think?"

"A day or two, let's say no later than next Wednesday, max. How's your ravishing bride?"

"Wanting you and Katherine to join us on the farm this summer."

"And muck about with the sheep and cows? We'll talk about it, sounds great. So, what are you up to in your dotage?"

Dotage! He realized he absolutely loathed this word; he refused to be in a dotage—in any way, shape, or form.

He should never, ever, have gotten himself into this mess with Emma, he'd known better.

He hit "reply," and typed.

<Right foot.

<Little bend.

<Not far.

<Yours truly.

Someone was definitely sitting at the foot of their bed, on his side. He raised his head from the pillow.

Miss Sadie was barefoot and wearing a long, white nightdress.

Miss Sadie! His heart was in his throat. *I thought . . . I thought you were . . .*

Crossed over? I am!

Where are your shoes? You'll catch your death!

She giggled like a girl. *Too late!*

He thought it strange that she didn't look old at all, but extraordinarily young. Where had she been, and what had she been *doing* all this time?

He felt definitely cross with her. Why had she pretended to be dead, which had saddened them all so grievously, and broken Louella's heart? And had she stopped even once to think how homesick he'd been for her over the years? He was furious that he'd allowed himself to be so profoundly deceived.

When are you going to tell him, Father?

"When the time is right," he said, grumpy as a bear.

Cynthia rolled toward him and slung her arm across his chest. "What did you say?" she murmured.

Miss Sadie had been *right there,* as real as life! She'd been sitting there in the very *flesh*—after a fashion.

"Miss Sadie!" he said, thunderstruck.

"Oh," replied Cynthia, and resumed her whiffling, albeit companionable, snore.

CHAPTER SEVEN

Go Tell It

Agnes hung on to the strap as the truck jounced through a hole the size of a washtub.

"This was once a Cherokee trading path!"

"A trading path would have been a distinct improvement!" Indeed, the availability of the farm truck was providential; the Mustang would be chopped liver in his new parish.

Throughout the morning he'd been praying for Sammy, as he knew Cynthia would be. "Agnes, will you add another name to your prayers?"

"With pleasure."

"Sammy." He was surprised that his voice broke as he said the name.

"Clarence will pray, too."

"You know better than anyone that Clarence is clearly exceptional."

Her eyes brightened.

"How can I learn to speak with him?"

"I can teach you."

"Wonderful!"

"Clarence and I use American sign language, as we've done since he was a child. This includes finger spelling, or the ABCs, body movement—often referred to as gestural—signing, and facial expression. There's great dynamism in facial expression, which of course everyone uses; though in my opinion, the deaf employ it in more pronounced and interesting ways. The face of a deaf person can be very alive with expression."

He geared down for the steep decline. "Aren't there simple hand signs that express whole thoughts or sentences? Even complex concepts? I'm looking to begin with Sign Language 101."

"Here's one that's known universally; you can sign this tonight to your beautiful Cynthia."

She raised her right hand and, bending her middle fingers toward the palm, extended her little finger, forefinger, and thumb, and told him the meaning.

He'd once known this sign, but had quite forgotten it; it was lost knowledge come home to him when he needed it. He repeated her gesture with his left hand, feeling a piercing of happiness.

"Very good!" said Agnes. "It's a lovely bit of hand language to know if you never learn any other."

"What about signs for words only?"

He slowed the truck to a crawl as she held her hands, palms down, above her head, then opened them upward.

"Steeple!"

"Close. Heaven."

"Aha!"

"And this?"

She touched her shoulders lightly and moved her hands outward.

"Umm . . ." He wished to be clever, but couldn't.

"Angel."

"A very ecclesiastical language!"

"A very full and exciting and immediate language!" she said. "One more for today. It's what you are to us at Holy Trinity."

She formed a letter with her right hand, brushed her left arm twice, and placed her arms alongside her body.

"Beats me," he said.

"Shepherd!"

"This is hard."

"It is, in the beginning. And then, like any spoken language, you realize one day that your new language is coming together at last. One sign flows naturally into another; and suddenly, you're *communicating*.

"I remember the agony of learning that Clarence was deaf, and the hopelessness I felt; he was fourteen months old. Very little was known in those days about the deaf among us. I found several books in the library; every free moment was devoted to studying them—I signed to him without ceasing.

"It took time, Father. I came to think that perhaps sign language was all a lie, and my efforts would be utterly in vain. Then came a day I shall never forget, when my son began speaking to me, expressing his heart with his hands. He was four years old—I was filled with joy at the marvel of it."

Tears stood in her eyes; she looked out at the branches of trees swaying in the wind, then turned to him, smiling. "Now! Let's run through the alphabet as a sort of limbering-up exercise."

"I'd like that."

"You may not remember a whit of it afterward, but we can practice each time we meet. Here, then, is *A*."

"Good old *A*!"

She closed the fingers of her hand into a fist and rested her thumb against the forefinger.

He returned the gesture, excited as ever to be learning.

"Perfect! And this is *B*." She held the fingers of her hand straight up, and bent the thumb inward, against her palm.

"The earnest and forthcoming *B*!" he said, forming the gesture with his left hand.

She smiled. "You're a willing pupil for this old teacher."

"Agnes . . ." Dare he ask this? "I'm a southerner, born and bred, and let me say that I know better than to ask such a thing. If I offend, I plead your forgiveness in advance . . ."

She appeared dubious.

"Would you mind very much . . . that is . . . what is your age?"

"I will be eighty-seven in September."

"Extraordinary! You appear years younger!" In truth, he was dumbfounded. "Michelangelo was eighty-seven when he wrote '*Ancora imparo,*' or 'I am still learning.'"

"Learning has always been intoxicating to me, and to Clarence, I'm happy to say."

"Is it OK that you're . . . so far away from medical help?"

She laughed. "I've concluded that one can't get too far away from medical help! Clarence's best medicine is working with wood; my own reliable remedies are our garden and our books. However . . ."

She looked at him—somewhat mischievously, he thought. ". . . I must confess the use of yet another nostrum."

"Confess away!"

"I am utterly devoted to the crossword puzzle."

He laughed.

"Doing a crossword delays, I hope, the petrifaction of my poor brain, and also induces a peaceful slumber . . . if hoeing the garden hasn't already done the trick! But to answer your question, Father—I have a checkup and flu shot in Wesley every spring, and I trust God to continue His mercy and grace in our lives. And you, may I ask? How many years have you graced this earth?"

"I'll be seventy at the end of June. Seventy! It boggles the imagination."

"I'm reminded of something George Herbert

wrote, that lovely man. 'And now in age I bud again . . .' I sense that God has set you on a wonderful new course, that you're entering a kind of golden passage."

"A golden passage," he mused. "Thank you for that thought."

"As I continue to tell my story, I must plead your forgiveness in advance."

"I can't imagine what forgiveness you might want or need from me. But consider it done."

They bumped along the windswept road, finishing off their finger-spelling session with G.

"Do you sing, Agnes?"

"I can carry a tune, Father, but only in a bucket."

"I know it's a Christmas song, but I'm in the mood for 'Go Tell It on the Mountain.'"

"Written by Mr. John Work!"

"I must say you have a very wide-ranging mind."

"I was a librarian for a number of years."

"Here?"

"In Chicago."

"Then you left the mountains!"

"Yes. I can't say I remember all the verses; there are three, I believe."

"I can't remember them, either. What the heck, we'll sing the refrain twice. But don't make me sing alone, you'll regret it."

With the exception of his best friend who, fortunately, was also his wife, he found he was more comfortable with Agnes Merton than nearly anyone he'd ever known. God had sent this woman to him as surely as the angel was sent to Daniel in the lion's den.

"You lead and I'll follow," she said.

He threw back his head and hammered down.

> *"Go tell it on the mountain,*
> *Over the hills and everywhere*
> *Go tell it on the mountain*
> *That Jesus Christ is born . . .*
> *. . . Go tell it on the mountain*
> *That Jesus Christ is born."*

"By heaven, that felt good! Did I hear a little harmony there, Miss Agnes?"

The lines around her eyes crinkled when she smiled. "Only a little," she said.

A rising wind struck them a blow as they pulled into the yard of a cabin.

"Jubal Adderholt will not warm to us immediately."

He set a wooden stool, which he'd fetched from the Meadowgate barn, by the passenger door. "Grab on," he said, offering his hand. Agnes grasped his hand, carefully put one foot on the stool, then stepped to the ground with her cane, relieved.

"I *see* you'uns a-comin' on m' property! This here's *private* property!"

Their long-bearded, barefoot host had opened the door of his two-room cabin and peered across the yard at his visitors. Smoke puffed from the chimney and was snatched away by the wind.

"Mr. Adderholt! Good morning! We've brought you hot tea."

"Is that Miss Agnes?"

"It is!" she said, establishing a firm grip on her cane.

"I done run ye off I don' know how many times, an' ye keep a-comin' back!"

"And I will continue to do so, Mr. Adderholt."

"I never seed th' beat, a man can't have a minute to hisself. Who's that with ye? Are ye settin' th' law on me?"

"This is Father Timothy Kavanagh, our new vicar at Holy Trinity."

"Don't ye bring no God people in m' place, you're all th' God people I can swaller."

"We won't visit long, Mr. Adderholt."

"Keep advancing," she whispered to Father Tim.

"I'll set m' dogs on ye!"

"The tea is nice and hot for a chilly spring morning!"

"Dogs?" Father Tim whispered.

As they climbed the steps to the porch, Jubal's bearded face vanished from the doorway.

"He hasn't a dog to his name! It would be a desperate mongrel, indeed, who'd take up with Jubal Adderholt."

He thought Agnes looked positively delighted with the reception they were getting.

They stood a moment on the creaking floor-boards of the porch, which was stacked with split firewood. A profuse assemblage of squirrel tails had been nailed to the log walls, and even to the front door. The wind ruffled the hair of the tails.

"His collection extends around the cabin," Agnes said in a low voice. "It is, you might say, a fur-covered cabin."

"Good insulation for winter!"

Through the open door, appetizing cooking smells escaped into the air.

"We're coming in now, Mr. Adderholt!"

"I hain't here, I done jumped out th' winder."

She pushed the door open with her cane. "Good!" she said. "That's more tea for Father Kavanagh and myself."

"I'm naked as a jaybird!" Jubal threatened from the other room.

"Don't mind us, Mr. Adderholt; we've seen worse, I'm sure."

The cabin was close with heat; something simmered on the woodstove in an iron pot.

Agnes was removing the mugs and thermos from the basket when Jubal came into the room, wearing a thermal undershirt and pants held up by braces. He was stooped, with dark, bushy eyebrows and a mane of white hair that flowed into his long beard.

The old man peered angrily at Father Tim.

"Don't ye be a-tryin' t' save this ol' sinner, ye hear? An' don't be a-tryin' t' warsh m' feet, I warsh m' own dern feet, thank ye."

"That was the Baptist preacher who wanted to wash your feet, Mr. Adderholt." Agnes poured a mug of tea and handed it to Jubal.

"An' look what happened t' their church hall—hit burnt down." He took the steaming mug and sniffed its spicy aroma. "I done drunk up th' dried 'frass ye brought," he said, looking accusingly at Agnes.

"You know full well where to find more like it in your own woods."

"A man my age can't be hobblin' aroun' th' piney woods by hisself."

"Miss Martha is nearly ten years your senior, and still tilling up her garden every spring."

"Ye come t' pester me ag'in, did ye?"

"I did," said Agnes, half smiling at Jubal. "Pestering you keeps me young."

"How'd you git hooked up with that 'un?" Jubal shot a piercing look at Father Tim.

"I rang the bell up at Holy Trinity, and there she was."

"God he'p ye." Jubal took a long swallow of his hot tea, then another. Tears suddenly spilled down his cheeks. "Jis' like my ol' mam used t' make."

Uncertain how to respond to Jubal's show of feeling, the vicar looked around the room. Several pictures, cut from magazines, hung on the log walls; a spider had spun her web in a ceiling corner. "A comfortable place you have here."

Jubal wiped his eyes on his shirt sleeve. "Hain't room enough t' cuss a cat without gittin' fur in y'r teeth, but hit'll do. Long as you'uns're pushin' in on me like this, ye might as well set down."

Taking his cue from Agnes, Father Tim thumped onto the ancient sofa, from which a cloud of dust arose. Agnes sat in a caned chair by the woodstove, and Jubal lowered himself onto the sofa with the vicar, who consequently sneezed three times.

"Bless you!" said Agnes.

"Thank you," said Father Tim, whipping out his handkerchief. A thunderous blow of wind roared down the stove chimney, fanning the fire. "And how was your winter, Mr. Adderholt?"

"Call me Jubal. Only one as calls me mister is that 'un there. Winter was too dadblame long; hit was too dadblame cold; hit snowed too dadblame deep; an' I'm dern glad t' see it over with.

"Only good thing about winter was th' squirrels, don't ye know; they was nice and meaty. A while b'fore dinnertime, I like t' set on m' porch with m' twenty-two pump, hit's easy as takin' candy from a little young 'un. Blam! Square behin' th' front leg is where I git 'em at. I don't never shoot 'em in th' head; I like t' stew 'em whole an' suck out th' brains th' way m' granddaddy done."

Jubal settled back on the sofa and looked at the vicar. "I reckon ye knowed ye can't eat squirrel when th' weather turns hot."

"I don't believe I knowed—knew—that," said Father Tim.

"Hot weather, they git worms as burrows right down in th' skin. Hit's cold weather as makes squirrel good eatin'; I'll be cookin' squirrel on up into May. If you'uns'd like to stay an' eat a bite, I'm stewin' me one right now; goin' t' make me a few dumplin's with this 'un."

"Thank you," said the vicar, "but we'll be pushing on soon."

"Now you take turkeys, you got t' shoot a turkey in th' *head*, an' ye have t' be a mighty sharp shooter, 'cause they ain't much head *on* a turkey."

Father Tim glanced at Agnes to see how this information was going down. She was apparently unfazed.

"I git me a turkey ever' now an' ag'in; th' turkeys hain't as many this year as squirrels, seem like. Rabbits has fell off pretty sharp, too, but they'll be back. I'll plant me a row of cabbages ag'in, that'll bring 'em a-runnin'."

"I'll say!"

"They's some on th' ridge as eats whistle pig, but I don't mess with no whistle pig—too much grease. An' deer, hit's too much dadblame work t' dress out."

"Aha."

"Th' whole point to th' thing is, a man can live good if he's got a sharp eye an' a steady hand. Looky here at m' hand." Jubal held forth his wizened right hand.

"Steady!" said Father Tim, impressed.

"If a man's goin' t' keep a steady hand, he's got t' stay away from liquor. I've made it, I've hauled it, I've bootlegged it, but hit never got a-holt of me. When I was a boy, I got into a bad jug of shine, hit like t' kilt me. I never touched n' more of it."

"Dodged a bullet," said the vicar.

"I got m' eyesight, too; I'm as good a shot as you ever seed, an' me a-goin' on eighty-two year."

"Well done!"

"I hain't never put out m' eyes with readin' like some do. Nossir, I cain't read a lick an' never wanted to. Hit'd make me crazy as a bedbug t' have all them words a-swarmin' around in m' head like bees in a hive.

"On th' other side of th' dollar, I hain't got no teeth a'tall 'cept these jackleg choppers I put in when comp'ny comes." Jubal snatched the dentures from his mouth and tossed them into the seat of a badly worn recliner. "That's enough of that tribulation."

"Do you have family, Jubal? Brothers, sisters?"

"They was five of us, but only two a-livin'. We all come into th' world by way of a ol' granny woman who forded th' creek down yonder on a mule. She bornded young 'uns all over this ridge. Me, I costed m' daddy a chicken—plucked, singed, an' quartered was th' deal. Ol' Toby, he costed two rabbits, kilt an' dressed. Jahab costed . . ." Jubal looked at Agnes. "What'd I tell ye Jahab costed?"

"A laying hen," said Agnes.

"On an' on like 'at 'til hit come t' m' little sister, Romey, th' baby. She costed a pig."

"A pig!" exclaimed the vicar.

"Th' most we ever give f'r any of us young 'uns was 'at sow pig."

"Inflation."

Jubal drained his tea mug; another blow came down the chimney, huffing smoke into the room.

"Any children of your own? Did you ever marry?"

"Ol' Peter Punkin Eater is what they called me, I couldn't never keep a-holt of a wife. Had one, she took off with a crook a-sellin' lightnin' rods. Had another'n; she one day baked me a pie, hit was settin' on th' table with a note when I come in from th' saw mill at 'Lizbethton. My neighbor read it to me, hit said, 'Jubal, I'm gone an' don't look f'r me.'" Jubal sighed. "Th' last I ever seed of Ruthie Adderholt was 'at pie."

There was a ruminative silence.

"Hit was blueberry," said Jubal.

"Umm, what are you paying for shells these days?" Father Tim had no idea where such conversational fodder had come from; it appeared to have dropped from the sky.

"Too dadblame much, I can tell ye that. Let me show ye m' rifle, I've jis' cleaned 'er up. She's goin' on twenty year ol' an' as good a arn as th' day I got 'er."

Jubal's untied shoelaces dragged the floor as he shuffled to a gun rack and took his rifle down.

"Is she . . . loaded?" asked the vicar. He hadn't handled a gun since he was twelve and had nearly blown his foot off. No, indeed, he was no friend of firearms.

"Dadblame right, she's loaded. A man's got t' keep 'is gun loaded if 'e's t' keep his belly full."

Jubal presented his rifle, holding the stock in one hand and the barrel in the other. Father Tim touched the polished stock, tentative. "Aha!" he said, not knowing what else to say. "Well, Jubal, we'd best get moving. We came to invite you up to Holy Trinity when we reopen our doors the first Sunday in May."

"I hain't a-comin'."

"Just wanted to let you know you'd be mighty welcome; we'd be happy to have you join us."

Jubal glared at the vicar. "I don't b'lieve none of that church b'iness, all that dyin' on th' cross an' love y'r neighbor an' such as that. I hain't a-havin' it, an' if I've told 'er once, I've told 'er a hun'erd times." He shot a hard look at Agnes, who was collecting the mugs.

Jubal Adderholt, sporting a beard to his belt buckle and a loaded gun in his hand, was not, thought the vicar, a pretty sight.

They were getting into the truck when Jubal stuck his head out the door and bellowed at the top of his lungs.

"An' don't you'uns be a-prayin' f'r me, neither!"

They laughed their way through, and over, the potholes.

"Now, Father, confess. That squirrel in Jubal's cook pot was making you hungry as a bear."

"It was! I also confess I wouldn't want to rile Jubal Adderholt."

"He's completely harmless, of course, and always glad for company, though he pretends we're a nuisance. Rather like a child who wants to be held and loved, but chooses, instead, to pitch a fit."

Father Tim nodded; he'd seen many such Jubals in his years as a priest.

"He weeps each time I bring him tea. When he smells the sassafras, it reminds him of his mother; she was cooking on the hearth of their cabin when her clothes caught fire. Jubal got to her too late, and she burned to death. He was just a young boy, the only one of the seven children who heard her cries and tried to save her. The beard disguises the terrible burns on his face."

They were quiet for a time, bumping along a dirt track that had turned off a state road. He would, of course, pray for Jubal Adderholt, whether Jubal liked it or not.

"What," asked Father Tim, "is a whistle pig?"

She laughed. "A groundhog."

"I'll be darned."

"I've been meaning to tell you, by the way, that Holy Trinity hasn't been completely forgotten by the world. Over the years, a sentimental priest or two has been found peering in the windows, and occasionally we get picnickers. Or, once in a rare while, someone visits the cemetery and leaves flowers.

"Then there was the summer day an entire busload of tourists debarked below the creek. They were out to see historic churches, and climbed up the ridge to Holy Trinity. They had the best sort of time, and even took the lack of toilets with proper good cheer.

"It just happened to be the day I was conducting our annual Evening Prayer. You know we must hold one liturgical service a year, to remain under church ownership and off the tax rolls. Imagine our joy to have every pew filled." She looked at him, her face radiant.

"I think I can imagine!"

"It was one of the many ways God encouraged us over the years."

"Would today be a good time to pick up your story where you left off?"

She smoothed her dress over her knees, silent.

"Your venerable Buick had died, and you switched to a truck." He tried to imagine Agnes Merton whipping around these narrow, winding roads in a pickup truck.

Agnes didn't speak for some time, but looked out the window into the woods. A male cardinal swooped across the lane, a flash of scarlet against the still-leafless trees.

"I sometimes think," she said at last, "that God didn't fashion or fit me for the world. Perhaps I am a type of Desert Mother, transported to the oldest mountains in the world."

She grew quiet again, then turned and gave him one of her half smiles.

"I never thought much about marrying; my mission work was rewarding and often very exhausting. Jessie and I toiled hard, and her faith greatly overshadowed my own. I was laboring for the people; Jessie was laboring for God. She often recited something from St. Francis, which I committed to memory, so that we might encourage one another.

"'Keep a clear eye toward life's end. Do not forget your purpose and destiny as God's Creature. What you are in His sight is what you are and nothing more. Remember that when you leave this earth, you can take nothing you have received . . . but only what you have given; a full heart enriched by honest service, love, sacrifice and courage.'"

He recalled that he'd once preached on those words of the troubador, in a sermon titled "A Clear Eye."

"If one breaks this passage down, line by line," she said, "it is deeply instructive. For years, I believed in giving my life to honest service, love, sacrifice, and courage, without any need at all to trust my life to God. I had made a covenant with my head, but not with my heart.

"Quint Severs had given his heart to God long years before Jessie and Little Bertie and I came to the ridge. Quint was a wonderful mechanic for our Buick; he was completely self-taught, and had a natural gift for engines, for the way things worked in general. He always rendered his service to us as unto the Lord. He was an angel if ever there was one.

"But our truck was another matter. Oh, my, here we are at the sisters'; they're on our list for the last stop, but we could visit now instead of on the way home . . . if you'd like."

"Let's do it now," he said. "I can use more spontaneity in my life!"

"Pull in here, then. You can park by the old shed."

He saw an unpainted house with a sagging porch beside a pile of discarded mattresses, a refrigerator, and a variety of other abandoned household goods. All had been arranged in an orderly manner, and left to season beneath a blue tarpaulin stretched over four sapling poles. An orange and white cat perched on the side of an old watering trough, drinking. Neat stacks of used tires lay about the yard, punctuated by the ancient chassis of a tractor and a mélange of rusted oil drums. Overall, he found the spectacle oddly ceremonial in effect.

He parked by the shed, which leaned toward the truck as if it might come down upon the hood at any moment. "I've been thinking," he said, as he opened her door. "We need a Porta John for Holy Trinity."

"They won't bring a truck up these roads to pump it. It's the piney woods, Father, and no help for it."

"Ah, well!"

She gave him her amused half smile. "Don't fret. When we get under way, I'll open the schoolhouse to the congregation."

"But that's your home."

"It's His home," she said, stepping onto the stool, "and I'm sure He would approve."

"Necessity *is* the mother of invention," he said, grinning.

"We were *cradle* Episcopalians," Martha McKinney told him, "and very heartbroken to see our old church closed as if it was nothin' more than a gas station!"

They had assembled in the kitchen of the McKinney sisters, in the house their father had built "in nineteen-aught-two." Though the kitchen contained an electric range, the air was redolent with cooking smells from the pot on a wood cook stove.

If he'd thought Jubal's squirrel made his mouth water . . .

. . . and what was going on in the McKinney *oven*? Something was definitely going *on* in that oven; he suddenly had the appetite of a stevedore.

Martha removed her thick-lensed glasses. "In the end, there was nothin' to do but what we did," she said with finality.

She turned toward the window and held her glasses to the light. "Lard!" She gave the lenses a vigorous polish with the hem of her apron.

"And what was it you did?" He hoped he wasn't being overly nosey.

"We became Methodists!" confessed Martha.

"We became Methodists!" crowed her sister, Mary, who sat by the stove with her bare feet tucked onto the stretcher of the chair.

"Aha!"

"But we didn't really want to!" said Mary.

Martha gave her sister a stern look. "We *certainly* couldn't fall away to the *Baptists*! Needless to say, Father, I miss the liturgy!"

"She misses the liturgy!" said Mary.

Martha popped her glasses on again and looked him in the eye. "We need to get this show on the road. You like white meat or dark?"

Had their unexpected visit forced their hosts to share their meal? Would accepting be the thing to do or should they run along? What was the social code in this matter? The cold spring wind keened around the corners of the house; he looked at Agnes for guidance.

"Miss Martha," said Agnes, "we like anything that doesn't go over the fence last."

Chicken and dumplings in a mountain kitchen warmed by a zealous woodstove; the fragrance of strong coffee percolating on the back burner; Eastertide drawing nigh; and every grand possibility stretching ahead.

He was relishing the many wonders of his new parish, not the least of which were the sisters, one as round as the moon and shy, the other as tall as a corn shock and bold. Indeed, Martha McKinney appeared able to roof a house single-handedly, or possibly plow up forty acres with a mule.

"Mr. Adderholt," said Agnes, "was making squirrel stew when we stopped by."

Martha laughed. "Jubal Adderholt has helped himself to every squirrel in the county. They'll be a lost species if that old so-and-so keeps livin'. Five years ago Christmas, he promised to shoot me a squirrel, but I haven't seen hide nor hair of it!"

"I'll remind him," said Father Tim.

"Tell him to send two while he's at it, they're scant meat. You'll not see me wastin' a shell on a squirrel."

"You have a gun?" he asked.

"Of course I have a gun!"

"She has a gun," said Mary, wide-eyed.

"Oh, pshaw! Everybody on this ridge has a gun."

"Johnny had a gun," said Mary.

Having refused all offers of assistance, Martha was clearing dishes from the table as the orange and white cat devoured giblets from a saucer behind the stove.

"Miss Mary's Johnny once brought us tenderloin of bear," said Agnes. "Johnny was a lovely man who plowed our garden before Clarence was old enough to do it."

The younger sister smiled broadly, revealing a set of new dentures. "Of a day, me an' Johnny stayed out of one another's way," she confided to the vicar, "but of a e'enin', we come home an' jis' courted." She put her hand over her mouth and giggled.

"A good plan," he said, meaning it.

"We was married forty-two years."

"See there? A *very* good plan!"

Martha threw up her hands. "Don't mind her, she talks about Johnny all th' time!"

"I talk about Johnny all th' time," said Mary.

"Johnny was part Cherokee, his great-granddaddy was a medicine man. Did you know a Cherokee medicine man cain't doctor his own self? It was a rule. I'm a Chiltosky, but ever'body calls us th' McKinney sisters."

"Where in th' nation did I put my pot scrub?" asked Martha. "Sister, have you seen my pot scrub?"

"When he passed ten years ago, I left my place down th' road an' moved up with Sister."

"Yet another good plan, if you ask me. Miss Martha, your chicken and dumplings are the finest I've enjoyed in many years. Are you sure you aren't from Holly Springs, Mississippi?"

Martha scraped the remains of the pot into a bowl. "Born and raised on this ridge, and never left it except to go to college at Connelly Springs. Then I moved back to the home place and taught fifth grade for forty years in the valley.

"I had to go off this ridge every day of th' school week, in every kind of weather you'd want to name. Walked a mile to th' creek, then trotted across on a log, or pulled my shoes off and waded through—whatever it took. I did everything but swing over on a vine!"

Martha had a good laugh over this, as did the rest of the assembly.

"I'd meet Portman Henshaw who was a bank clerk in Holding, and ride as far as Granite Springs, where he dropped me at the school door. Every single year, I had to get permission from his wife, Miss Hettie, to ride with him. I had to ask her in a formal note the first of January, and the answer always came back in a note toted to me by her poor, hen-pecked husband.

"'Dear Mrs. Henshaw,' was my petition, 'I would be beholden to you if I could ride to school and back with Mr. Henshaw this year. Thank you in advance. Yours sincerely.' I would always send two quarts of string beans with that note and a jar of strawberry jam.

"In a flash, here'd come her little jot, added to the bottom of mine, and not a word in longhand! She printed like a second grader! 'Dear Miss McKinney, You may ride to school with Mr. Henshaw if you do not keep him waiting at the creek. Please don't track mud on the floorboards. Yours sincerely.' At the end of the year, I always sent a bushel of potatoes with four jars of butter beans and five one-dollar bills, which I thought was a gracious plenty since he was goin' that way anyhow."

Mary nodded in agreement. "He was goin' that way anyhow."

"Portman drove a Ford in the beginning;

I always liked a Ford, but over the years, we went through five or six different buggies, one being a Pontiac."

Martha shook her head, disapproving. "I don't know what possessed Portman Henshaw to buy that Pontiac. Agnes, do you remember that Pontiac?"

"I do. Dark green, with slipcovers sewn by Miss Hettie."

"I missed thirty-three days of school over that bloomin' Pontiac. It was a lemon if I ever saw one, and I still had to send over a basket of rations and five hard-earned dollars."

Martha poured Agnes a cup of coffee from the battered pot on the stove.

"Anyhow, I rode with Portman 'til he retired, then I tried hitchin' a ride with every Tom, Dick, and Harry who had a wheel, but it never worked, so I up an' retired, too. It was either that or buy my own buggy, and I didn't want to fool with it!"

"How do you ladies shop for food and get to church?" asked the vicar.

"Portman's oldest boy, Thomas, took over where his daddy left off; he hauls us food shoppin' once a week. I'm goin' to leave him that tractor in th' yard when I pass, it's an antique. He'll get good money for that tractor.

"Then there's Agnes's boy, Clarence, he takes

us around every chance he gets; I'm leavin' him that waterin' trough to soak his grapevine in. Course, I put in a big garden every year; it keeps us goin' pretty strong if we miss a week or two down at Winn Dixie, and Sister and I still go blackberryin' . . ."

Martha opened the oven door, and a furnace of heat blasted the small kitchen. Father Tim realized he was on the edge of his chair with anticipation.

Wearing a pair of long-used oven mitts, Martha removed a cobbler, still bubbling in its crockery dish and, with evident pride, thumped it onto an overturned skillet on the table. "Picked the first week of August an' all th' chiggers removed free of charge."

He had the impulse to cross himself.

"As for church . . ." Martha dug into the steaming blackberry cobbler with a wooden spoon, "we walk if we have to. For goodness' sakes, it's only two miles." Out of respect for clergy, Martha passed the first serving to Father Tim, who handed it off to Agnes.

"Two *miles*?" Hadn't Agnes said that Miss Martha was Jubal's senior by a decade?

"Keeps us hale!" declared Martha. "Besides, somebody always brings us home."

Mary nodded. "Somebody always brings us home!"

Had he checked his sugar this morning? He couldn't recall. *Lord* . . .

Agnes inhaled the fragrant steam rising from her coffee cup. "Miss Martha, won't you take your apron off and sit down with us?"

"Oh, law, no, I never take my apron off!" said Martha.

"She never takes her apron off!" said Mary.

Father Tim noted that the woodstove had lent a rosy flush to every cheek.

"Miss Martha, Miss Mary, it's time we told you why we came. We feel we have some very good news."

"Well, now!" exclaimed Martha. "I like good news!"

"She likes good news!" said Mary, showing her dentures to good effect.

Thumb up, forefinger out, the remaining three fingers tucked into the palm.

"This," said Agnes, "is *L*. And that—is Donny Luster's trailer. You'll notice I don't tell you much about your new parishioners beforehand; it seems best to let you form your own impressions. I'll just say that Donny is a most remarkable young man."

"Spotless," he said, peering around as he

parked beside a pickup truck. "Someone is proud to live here."

Agnes looked for a moment at her hands, lying palms up in her lap. "Father, I must say what I have to say . . . now. It can't wait any longer."

She lifted her head and looked at him; he saw the firm resolve in her eyes.

"The longer I hesitate, the more I dread my confession."

"You needn't confess anything to me."

"It's important that it be done. Then I shall be free to tell you in peace the rest of my story, which is also Holy Trinity's story."

Behind the trailer, early afternoon light sparkled on upland pasture where a small herd of cows grazed.

Agnes crossed herself as she told him what must be spoken.

"I never married," she said.

"I'm five."

Sissie Gleason held up as many fingers.

"Five!" exclaimed the vicar. "I remember being five!"

It was merely a flash of memory, like a sliver of celluloid carved from a lengthy documentary. His mother was pushing him on the tree swing behind their house in Holly Springs. It was the day before his fifth birthday, and she was singing the song he would never forget as long as he lived.

> *Baby Bye, here's a fly,*
> *Let us watch him you and I . . .*

"I'm not a baby!" he shouted.

"Is that so? I did forget for a moment, but only a very tiny moment!"

He thought his mother the most beautiful woman in the world . . .

"I'm five!" he shouted again, flying toward a perfectly blue sky. The soles of his bare feet pushed against silken summer air.

"You have a whole day left before you're five! I want this day to go on and on and . . ."

"It's good to be five," he said, stooping down to look into the solemn eyes of the child with tangled hair. In the corner of the room, a TV hawked the wares of a shopping network.

"I was this many b'fore." She held up four fingers. "How many are you?"

He raised both hands and extended his fingers seven times.

She observed this lengthy communication. "That's too many."

"Darn right," he said, creaking upward on resistant legs.

"What's 'at roun' your neck?"

"My tab collar."

"What's it f'r?"

"It marks me as a preacher, a priest. It lets people know I'm someone they can come to, confide in, pray with."

"And this," Agnes told him, "is Dovey Gleason, Sissie's mother and Donny's sister."

He bent over the bed where Dovey lay, and looked into another pair of brown and solemn eyes. "Dovey." He took her hand and instinctively held it in both of his.

"Dovey," he said again; the name seemed an odd comfort to him. "May I pray for you?" He knew nothing about her except what he saw in her eyes.

"Yes," she whispered.

He sat in the chair beside her. "Dear God and loving Father, Creator of all that is, seen and unseen, we thank You for Your presence in this home, at this bedside, and in the heart of Your child, Dovey. Give us eyes to see Your goodness in her suffering, give us faith to thank You for her healing, give us love to strengthen us as we wait. In the name of the Father, and of the Son, and of the Holy Spirit, Amen."

"Amen," said Agnes.

"Amen," whispered Dovey.

When he looked up, he saw Donny Luster standing at the foot of the bed. "Amen," said Donny. "Miss Agnes, how you?"

"Very well, Donny, thank you. Please meet Father Timothy Kavanagh." The thin, blond young man leaned toward him and they shook hands.

"Very pleased to meet you, Donny. I've been called to be the vicar at Holy Trinity."

"That's good. We was startin' to get shed of all our churches around here, what our'n burnin' down an' your'n closed up."

"What is Dovey's illness?"

"We don't know, ain't found nobody that knows. I've took 'er to Wesley and Holdin' both. They're treatin' 'er for depression, but they's some as thinks it was a tick bite."

"How long . . . ?"

"She's been down th' last four, five months, an' wadn't feelin' too good way b'fore that."

"She cain't do nothin'," said Sissie. "Sometime she cain't git up, she pees in th' bed."

Donny gave Sissie a sharp look. "You hush up, little miss."

Father Tim continued to hold Dovey's hand. "I saw some fine-looking cows on the hill. They're yours, Donny?"

"Yeah, I run a few head now an' then."

"Very nice place you have here. Slick as a whistle. May I ask what do you do?"

"He does *ever'thing!*" said Sissie.

"Is that right?"

"Cookin' . . ."

"That's a good thing to do."

". . . washin' dishes, cleanin' up th' whole place."

"Ah."

"Takin' care of me an' Mama."

"The best of things to do!"

"I got a loggin' b'iness," said Donny. "I do a little drywall on th' side, an' cut hay in th' valley."

"An' he plays th' fiddle an' all them things hangin' on th' wall." Sissie looked proud.

Only now did he see that the wall leading into the next room was hung with musical instruments.

"That 'n's a guitar." Sissie pointed. "That 'n's a banjer. That 'n . . . what's that 'n, Donny? I f'rgit."

"Dulcimore. But he don't want t' hear that mess."

"Yes, I do. You play all those instruments?"

"Yeah."

"How did you learn?"

"Come natural," Dovey whispered.

"He plays th' jaw harp, too," said Sissie.

"Sissie," said her mother, "please hush."

"I'm jis' *talkin'*, Mama."

Donny sat on the foot of the bed. "Mine an' Dovey's granpaw was a picker, he was th' best in this county an' ever' where else; he taught me t' play anything with a string on it. I started out when I was nine year old, playin' 'at ol' washtub base settin' yonder."

"Where do you play?"

Sissie clambered onto the bed. "He plays at churches an' camp meetin's, ain't that right, Donny?" Sissie crawled over and patted her mother's cheek. "Donny, he preaches, too."

"Preaches?"

Donny's face colored. "Don't worry, I ain't no competition for a real preacher!"

"This beats all. Logging, cooking, cleaning, making hay, playing music, preaching . . ."

"A Renaissance man!" said Agnes, looking pleased.

Dovey lifted her head from the pillow. "Sissie, bring m' pitcher, m' cup's right here."

Sissie scrambled off the bed and went to the sink and fetched a pitcher. "It ain't got much in it."

"Fill it up," said Dovey. "I got t' take m' medicine."

Sissie trotted back with the pitcher and set

it on the bed table." 'At pitcher was her mama's.
Mamaw Ruby give Mama a whole set of dishes
when she was little. She uses 'em ever' day,
won't use nothin' else."

"All cracked an' chipped," said Donny, disapproving. "They need t' be th'owed out."

"They was *Mama's,*" Dovey said fiercely.

Sissie bounced on the bed. "Turn on y'r
record player, Donny!"

"They don't want t' hear that; now, hush up."

"Hit'll play anything," Sissie informed the
vicar. "Donny he likes th' Monroe Brothers.
He tries t' sing like 'em."

"See that switch over yonder? You're lookin'
t' git wore out, an' I don't mean maybe."

"Would you play something for us?" asked
Father Tim. "Would you mind?"

"He don't mind," said Sissie.

Donny looked at his sister. "If Dovey'll sing
with me."

"I cain't, Donny, I cain't sing now."

"Yes, you can, Dovey; you know you can.
Come on an' try."

Donny went to the wall and studied it a
moment, then took down a guitar.

" 'What Would You Give,' Dovey." He pulled
a stool to the foot of the bed and propped his
foot on a rung.

"I don' know if I can, Donny . . ."

"Sure you can." He turned the pegs, tuning. "Come on, now. Jis' a little on th' chorus, I'll do th' verses."

Donny Luster strummed the guitar and began to sing. His voice was clear, and plaintive.

"Brother afar from your Savior today
Risking your soul for the things that decay
Oh, if today God should call you away
What would you give in exchange for your soul?
What would you give . . ."

Still holding the vicar's hand, Dovey sang, her voice trembling, "In exchange . . ."

"What would you give . . ."

"In exchange," she sang again.

"Oh, if today God should call you away . . ."

The brother and sister finished the refrain together. ". . . What would give in exchange for your soul?"

"That's good, Dovey. One more time."

"Mercy is callin', won't you give heed
Must th' dear Savior still tenderly plead
Risk not your soul, it is precious indeed
What would give in exchange for your soul?
What would you give . . ."

Waiting for Dovey to respond, Donny sang the line again. "What would you give . . ."

"I cain't, Donny."

Father Tim turned to Dovey and saw the tears on her cheeks.

Sissie patted her mother's arm. "It's OK, Mama. Donny, stop makin' Mama sing if she don't want to!"

"I'm sorry," said Father Tim. "I shouldn't have asked."

"It ain't your fault," said Donny. He turned from the bed, angry, and hung the guitar on the wall, then looked at Dovey as he pulled on his jacket. "I come in t' tell you Granny'll be here in a little bit; I won't git home 'til after dark. You 'n' Sissie have y'r dinner, I done eat."

"I'll walk out with you," said Father Tim, as Donny headed for the door.

Donny went to his truck, ignoring the vicar.

"Donny . . ." Preaching and meddling were often accused of being one and the same, thought Father Tim, but so be it.

Donny turned around, tears swimming in his eyes. "She could git well if she tried."

"I can see she has no strength to sing; I'm sure she'd sing if she could."

Donny covered his face with his hands. "Oh, God!" he said, sobbing.

Though she'd never received the Eucharist, Dovey, who'd been baptized at the age of eleven, had been pleased to take it. As vicar of Holy Trinity, he determined never to make a home visit without his communion kit.

On their way back to the ridge, he told Agnes how the strain had affected Donny Luster.

"He's convinced it's depression and thinks she can get over it at will. When she doesn't feel like singing, he's angry and discouraged. And needless to say, he's working himself to death. Is there a husband?"

"He left three years ago; Donny moved Dovey and Sissie to his place when she became so ill. Granny comes some days when Rooter is in school, and Clarence occasionally drops me off when he goes to Wesley."

He felt a weight on his heart.

"How does Granny help?"

"Mainly, she keeps Dovey and Sissie company, and helps Dovey eat her midday meal."

"Thank God for Granny."

"Granny's a gem. Her grandfather came here when the government would give a man all the property he could walk around in a day—if he

built a house on it. The old house is still standing, but just barely. Lloyd Goodnight and a few
others have done what they can, but it's a mere
bandage on the critically wounded."

They drove for a time, silent.

"Did Donny tell you their mother is in
prison?" asked Agnes.

"What for?"

"Killing their father."

"No," he said, stricken. "When did it happen?"

"Dovey was sixteen; Donny was going
on ten."

"How old is he now?" Twenty-five or
twenty-six would be his guess, though in a way
he looked older.

"Seventeen."

He had no words. Words would not suffice.

As he walked Agnes to her door, he stopped
and struck his forehead.

"I can't believe my forgetfulness! We've visited around the livelong day, and failed to give
out a single flyer."

"Perhaps . . ."

"Perhaps?"

Agnes looked resolved. "Perhaps it's just as
well."

"Why is that?"

"Is it possible that the flyer announced the wrong date, Father? I've prayed mightily about this, and here is what I propose. Let's not wait until May. So many need what God is eager to give at Holy Trinity. Let's open our doors to one and to all . . . on Easter morning."

"Easter morning? But that's only three days away."

Though worn from their trot over hill and dale, her eyes sparkled with feeling. "'Every noble work is at first impossible.'"

"Thomas Carlyle," he said, suddenly grumpy.

Flowers, music, communion wine, kneelers—he mentally ticked off the items on his list, which was, in his opinion, on the huge side, not to mention a homily with meat on the bone. . . . An Easter service couldn't be thrown together like some hilltop picnic, for heaven's sake . . .

"For heaven's sake!" he blurted.

"Your lovely flyers won't be wasted at all. We'll mark through the old date and put in the new, and Clarence will deliver them around."

He took a deep breath.

"Shall we do it, Father?"

She had waited forty years; who was he to wait 'til May?

"Yes," he said, suddenly beaming at his deaconess. "Yes! Absolutely!"

He felt as if he'd left Meadowgate days, even weeks, ago. It had been a long trek, and somewhere in his mortal frame, he felt every pothole.

Yet when he saw Cynthia at her drawing board by the window, he saw her, somehow, with new eyes. She turned and looked at him, smiling, and his weariness vanished. He went to her and put his hand on her shoulder.

"I'm happy to be home," he said, nuzzling the top of her head with his cheek. "Get dressed, we're going out to dinner. At Lucera!"

"Out to *dinner*? At *Lucera*? In *Lent*?"

"I need to start courting you again."

She gazed up at him, happy. "I didn't realize you'd stopped."

He made the sign Agnes had shown him.

"I love you, too!" she said.

"How'd you know that?"

"When I taught Sunday School, the children and I learned it."

She pointed to the fireplace, and the ashes that lay about the hearth, then rolled her eyes heavenward and shrugged and threw up her hands.

Now *there* was gestural and facial for you.

He sat on the side of the bed and watched her pluck pink curlers from her hair, as she'd done on the day of their September wedding.

What a day that had been, with his bride-to-be locked in her bathroom in a chenille robe the age of his English boxwoods, while the organist at Lord's Chapel hammered down for dear life and the choir checked their watches.

Chances are, half the congregation supposed she'd skipped town rather than exchange vows with their bachelor priest. Though to a man, his parishioners were known to adore him, they couldn't imagine that anyone else actually would.

Alarmed by her uncharacteristic lateness, he'd run all the way to the yellow house in his dress shoes and tuxedo, liberated her from the bathroom, waited in a panic as she dressed in five minutes flat, then raced back to Lord's Chapel, his fiancée huffing at his side in high heels, and covering the distance with flabbergasting speed.

"Why you didn't fall and break your neck . . ." he mused aloud.

"What on earth are you talking about?"

"Our wedding day. I was just thinking of our wedding day, and how you plucked the curlers out of your hair like so many chicken feathers; they were raining around us—and then the Talladega thing we did to church; you were flying, Kavanagh!"

She laughed as she spritzed herself with the stuff that turned the room into an arbor of wisteria.

Perhaps it was the memory of that day in September, or the relief of coming home after a long and productive sojurn among his new parish—or both.

Whatever it was, he realized he was happier than he remembered being in a long time.

Before they left for Mitford, he popped into the library. Wind shuddered along the tin roof as he checked phone messages.

"Father, Buck here. Lon Burtie don't have a clue where Sammy is. He says Clyde Barlowe cut out a few weeks ago, an' he thinks Sammy saw his chance an' took off. Lon said he gave it a couple of weeks to see if Sammy turned up, but he was ready to call us when I called him. He said Sammy had been talkin' about goin' out on his own. Th' only thing worries Lon is that Sammy tells Lon everything, an' Sammy up an' left without sayin' a word. I went around to th' drugstore, th' poolroom, th' usual, but no-body's seen 'im. I'm wonderin' if we should get the police in on this. Give me a call." *Beep.*

"Tim, it's your one and only cousin. Piece of cake. All you do is file a petition with the cir-cuit court. The name issue is separate from the issue of adoption, but both can be filed on the same petition. Fortunately, he's twenty-one—makes things a whale of a lot simpler, and no parental assent of any kind is required. The pro-cedure basically terminates their right to the biological child.

"So you're on your way, buddy, and congrat-ulations. I'm personally delighted that the family name, however tattered or torn, will be perpet-uated. Happy Easter, and love to Cynthia." *Beep.*

"Father Tim! It's Emma! Gene's back in th' hospital an' not doin' too good, you need to go see Esther if you can catch 'er at home. She's a basket case."

Emma was apparently eating something known for its high-performance crunch.

"Th' wind's been blowin' up a storm all day. If you're out in it, I hope you've got your head covered up. I read where bald-headed people get sick twice as fast as people with hair."

Slurping something through a straw . . .

"Somebody said the queen goes to her

country place in May, so I'm over even *thinkin'* about runnin' into her, which I'm glad of since I nearly broke my neck tryin' to curtsy by your directions."

More crunching . . .

"Anyway, ten weeks to go and I'm out of here. Say hey to Cynthia, I hope y'all aren't turnin' into a bunch of *hayseeds.* Ha-ha."

Agitated barking . . .

"Oh, hush up! That was Father Tim, you remember him. No, no, get down, you wouldn't like pork rinds. Too salty. You'd drink a gallon of water and wee wee in th' closet, because I'm *definitely* not runnin' you down th' driveway in *this* wind . . ." *Beep.*

The fatigue returned, but he was going through with their dinner at Lucera, and no two ways about it.

When they opened the front door, it nearly blew off the hinges. He shut it at once. "Holy smoke!"

He wife looked at him, imploring. "Dearest— let's don't go."

She leaned her head to one side, smiling. "You can court me at home, can't you?"

"Oh, boy," he said, vastly relieved. "Can I ever."

CHAPTER EIGHT

This Dark Hour

He and Cynthia read Evening Prayer from the 1928, and before turning off the bedside lamp, he entered a quote by Will Rogers in his journal: *Go out on a limb—that's where the fruit is.*

That would preach . . .

He peered at the other scribbling he'd done on the back of an old receipt from The Local.

"And it will come to the question of how much fire you have in your belly." Directly beneath the first entry, he jotted this wisdom by Oliver Wendell Holmes, then turned to a blank page and gazed at it for a time, pensive.

Mr. Dooley Kavanagh, he wrote.

With some wonder, he considered what he had penned, then wrote again.

Dr. Dooley Kavanagh.

"Look," he said to Cynthia.

She raised her head and saw what he'd written, and smiled.

"Yes," she said. "Yes!"

He was on his feet before he realized what he was doing. A terrible crash somewhere below, dogs barking their brains out . . .

Cynthia sat up in bed. "Good Lord!"

"I'm going downstairs," he said, pulling on his robe.

The smell of ashes and wood smoke, the infernal howling of the wind . . .

He raced into the hall and turned on the light above the landing and flew down the steps, Barnabas at his heels. It was something in the kitchen; he heard a loud crumbling sound, then a tremendous *thunk* against the side of the house that rattled the shutters. *Lord, not the old oak . . .*

He snapped on the light at the kitchen door.

The room was clouded with the dust of ashes; rubble lay on the hearth and about the floor. Mortar, soot, broken bricks . . . he took a handkerchief from his robe pocket and held it over his nose, dumbfounded.

Bodacious clung to the sofa; the other dogs crowded to the perimeter of the debris, barking wildly at the intrusion.

"It's the chimney," he said as Cynthia came into the room. "I heard something hit the side of the house. Stay by the sink, who knows what else may come down. I'll go out and look."

The gale was from the northwest; he had to push hard against the door to open it.

Roughly half the brick chimney had collapsed in the wind; he saw the jagged outline against the first light of Maundy Thursday.

Willie had installed a piece of plywood over the fireplace opening to keep soot from continuing to come in; but it was too little too late. The wind continued to thrum down the hollow until Willie at last rounded up the plywood and the hole was covered. Particles of ash hung in the air.

Her forehead streaked with soot, Cynthia sat across the table, looking red-eyed and disconsolate.

He held his hand over his warm coffee mug to keep the stuff from sifting into it. "Willie knows a brick mason, he said he'd try to get him out here today or the first of next week.

The chimney is more than a century old, so no wonder."

She put her head in her hands. "Ugh."

"Willie gave me the name of the company that insures all the buildings on the place, I'll call them as soon as their office opens. When they come out, Willie can show them around if I'm not here. And, of course, I'll need to talk with Hal, let him know . . ."

"I don't want to trouble Marge about cleaning the house," she said. "We're adults, we need to figure out what to do. It's all over the place; it's on everything, even the furniture and windowsills upstairs. And there's no way I can ask Puny to come out and help do this."

"Didn't Marge give you the name of a cleaning service when you talked last time?"

"The Flower Girls!" His wife's face was instantly brighter. "She said to look in her red phone book."

Cynthia flew to the bookcase, and hauled the book down. "D, E, F . . . Fagan, Flanagan, Flemming . . . Flower! Flower Girls, Pansy. What time is it?" She coughed mightily.

"May be a tad early. It's only six-thirty."

"Working women are up at six-thirty!" she announced, snatching the handset from the hook.

He had to get to Mitford today. Agnes and Clarence weren't, after all, some ecclesiastical retail complex in which he might find all that was needed for the Easter service. According to Agnes, she was down to a few candle stubs, and not a drop of communion wine on hand.

He would check Mitford Blossoms for Easter lilies, dash to The Local for wine and candles, then swoop by the yellow house and pick up his Easter vestments.

He made a hasty list and tucked it into his jacket pocket. He also needed to visit Uncle Billy, Esther Bolick, and Louella. He would run up and see Louella after he met with Pauline. He phoned Hope House and asked them to tell Pauline, now their dining room manager, that he hoped to see her before the big push at noon.

Puny and the twins . . . that visit would have to wait 'til after Easter.

He rubbed his sandpapered eyes and checked his watch. If he played his cards right, he'd have a half hour to noodle with the Turkey Club, and hit the vending machine for nourishment.

The wind had died down, thanks be to God. But he felt like a heel for running out on his wife. Though they'd cleaned up the floor and wiped off the table, the kitchen was a disaster. Fortunately, her work on the easel had been draped with a cloth that she put on each evening like a cover on a birdcage.

"Don't worry about me," she had said. "You have your work to do and I have mine. I'll manage the inside if you and Willie will take care of the outside." She sneezed mightily. "Do not, I repeat, do *not,* expect me to manage a crew of brick masons."

"You have my word."

He had wiped her forehead with his handkerchief and made the sign. She signed back, and he gave her a heartfelt, albeit guilt-stricken, hug.

He'd talked to Buck last night; they had prayed together on the phone that Sammy would turn up, safe and sound. Buck said Lon Burtie had been to the Barlowe trailer and looked in the windows. Nothing appeared suspicious.

Lon had asked around about Clyde Barlowe's whereabouts and a couple of people claimed he'd gone off with Cate Turner, who was Lace Harper's father and Clyde's long-time drinking buddy.

In the end, the question was the same: Should the police be notified?

Father Tim, Cynthia, Agnes, and Clarence would be working at the church on Saturday, giving it a complete cleaning, and readying it for Sunday morning. Thus the only time he could get down to Holding with Buck was tomorrow, Friday. They agreed they'd meet at eight o'clock at Lew Boyd's Exxon, and head down the mountain to the Holding police station.

He and Cynthia had further agreed to have their own Maundy Thursday service this evening in the ash-blasted kitchen—a fitting setting.

As for the paperwork on the adoption/name change, he'd be in touch with his attorney next week, and by the time Dooley came home for the summer, he would walk in the door as a Kavanagh.

Esther wasn't at home, but he left a note at the patio door, and a box of chocolates that he'd picked up at the pharmacy.

It was a pathetic offering; his heart was wrenched for Gene and Esther, whom he'd known as friends and parishioners for twenty years. He looked at the patio and thought how many steaks had been grilled and song birds fed and geraniums watered, and no one, not even once, thinking of inoperable brain tumors.

Tears sprang to her eyes.

"I think it's wonderful," said Pauline Leeper. "I know he'll feel proud to carry your name."

"He'll always spend time with you and Buck and Poo and Jessie when he comes home; you'll always be his family."

"Yes, sir." She took a Kleenex from her uniform pocket and wiped her eyes. "I'll be lookin' a mess," she said, laughing.

He felt awkward and disconsolate. "Thank you for your understanding. You're a fine and caring soul, Pauline."

"By th' grace of God is th' only way that could happen," she said, tears streaming down her cheeks.

"What you doin' 'bout Miss Sadie's money?"

Clearly, he'd been mistaken to think Louella forgetful.

"I'm waiting for the owner of the car to come home so we can talk about it. I can't search the Plymouth without his permission."

Louella looked skeptical of this modus operandi, and returned her attention to the box of sugar-free candy he'd toted along.

"What's that? I cain't half see. I'm lookin' for somethin' wit' nuts."

"Nougat."

"No nougat. What's that 'un right there?"

"Umm." He was salivating. "Dark chocolate."

"Here, honey," she said, holding forth the box. "Fin' me somethin' wit' nuts."

He took the sugar-free dark chocolate for himself. Not bad. But not good, either. "What do you think Miss Sadie would have us do with the money if we find it?"

"Give it to th' Lord!"

"We'll definitely do that. But do you think she'd like something specific? The Lord's Chapel roof is perfectly fine, thanks to her. The expansion was paid for long ago. Hope House is running in the black. . . ."

"I think we should pray about it. That's what Miss Sadie an' I always do when she givin' money. I 'member how we prayed 'bout th' money she give your boy. Whew, law! When Miss Sadie wrote that down, that was more aughts than I ever seen behind a number! What's he doin' with it, anyway?"

"He doesn't know he has it. I haven't told him."

"What you waitin' for? Th' creek t' rise?"

"I'm not sure."

"Child, I'm glad nobody ever give me a million dollars; it would've been my ruination."

"You think so?"

"This 'un an' that 'un would have took it off of me like takin' candy from a baby. No, honey, I never liked to fool with money."

"Here," he said. "This whole row has nuts."

Louella gave him a fond look. "Ever' time you come t' see me, I feel like Miss Sadie in th' room. You an' her was *close,* honey."

"I dreamed about her the other night."

"How'd she look?"

"She looked young! I was amazed to see her looking so well!" He remembered the dream as if it had been a visit.

Louella winced.

"What is it?"

"This ol' shoulder be actin' up ag'in. Hurtin' me all night."

"Let me have a go at it," he said.

He got off the low stool where he always sat when he visited, and touched her shoulder. "Here?"

"No, honey, that ain't th' place. Move up a

little to th' lef'. . . . . That's right. On up a little more."

"Right here?"

"Right there! Oh, mercy, that's sore as a boil, don't rub too hard."

Nurse Herman stuck her head in the door.

"I'm next in line after Miss Louella!" she said, grinning.

He stepped along the hall to Ben Isaac Berman's comfortable room.

Ben Isaac nearly always kept his door open, and was nearly always listening to classical music. The offering of the moment was definitely Mozart . . . possibly the Divertimento no. 10 in F Major, but only possibly.

He knocked on the open door. "Ben Isaac?"

"Here, Father, right here! Come in, come in."

The tall, handsome old man appeared, using a cane and dressed in a coat and tie with dark trousers.

"Ben Isaac! You're dressed fit to kill."

Ben Isaac leaned toward the vicar, and spoke in a low voice. "I have a nice woman friend, Father."

Father Tim shook his hand vigorously. "I'm

happy to hear it! That changes everything, doesn't it?"

"It certainly does. We're walking down to lunch together in half an hour."

"And where does this fortunate lady live?"

Ben Isaac's eyes gleamed as he pointed to the wall and whispered. "Right next door."

"Right next door is the very place I found my wonderful wife!"

The old man chuckled. "Oh, my," he said. "Oh, my."

He popped into the chaplain's office, glad to see Scott Murphy, who had been a literal Godsend to Hope House—not to mention the Kavanaghs' favorite bookseller.

"Congratulations!" he said, embracing his friend.

"Thank you, thank you, Father. And thanks for agreeing to officiate at our wedding."

"The pleasure is all mine," he said, meaning it. "We're having our first service at Holy Trinity on Easter morning at ten o'clock. Wish you could come up."

"My service is also at ten. But we'll definitely come another Sunday. What's the driving time?"

"Fifteen or twenty minutes to the farm, then about fifteen or twenty to the ridge. You could come for coffee and follow us up." He checked his watch. "Got to get moving. . . ."

"Any advice before you go?"

"For . . . ?"

"For being engaged? I've never done this before."

Father Tim laughed. "You don't want any advice from me. I nearly botched the whole thing. No, wait, here's my advice; it's what I'd have done if I'd had sense: Thank God continually for His kind favor. And send flowers before you mess up, as well as afterward."

Scott grinned. "Consider it done," he said. "And umm, there's something on your left cheek. Looks like . . ."

The vicar reached up and rubbed his cheek.

"Soot," he said. "But you don't want to know."

"Blast! A dollar fifty for a pack of Nabs and a Diet Coke," he told J.C. "The trouble is, we remember when a pack of Nabs was a nickel."

"I don't go as far back as th' nickel," snapped J.C.

"Oh, excuse me, I forgot your extreme youth places you in the dime category."

"Fifteen cents," said J.C., hammering down on something unidentifiable.

"When pigs fly," said the vicar. He thought the *Muse* editor looked as if he'd tossed and turned all night—in his clothes. "So where's Mule? Where's Percy?"

"Percy's gettin' a colonoscopy. Mule's takin' Fancy to lunch in Wesley."

The vicar thought he'd rather have the colonoscopy. "Let me ask you something," he said, popping the tab on his Coke.

"Ask away."

"What's eating you?"

J.C. frowned and held up the remains of a sandwich. "I'm eatin' *it*."

"Come on, be straight with me."

He'd never messed in J. C. Hogan's business, with the possible exception of the time J.C. was courting Adele and, in both his and Mule's opinions, doing it all wrong.

J.C. rewrapped his sandwich and stuffed it in his briefcase. "Adele got a promotion."

"Right. And a new gun. You told us."

"She got a raise."

"That's good."

"She got a new hairdo."

"Aha."

"She's gettin' a new squad car."

"Oh, boy."

There was a long silence. Father Tim watched a fly crawl up the inside of Lew's front window; a horn blew in the grease pit; Lew came in to ring up a gas sale.

When Lew left, J.C. looked at Father Tim, obviously miserable.

"An' she got a new partner."

Bingo. "Driving partner, I take it."

"Right."

"So, look. I'm out of here in ten minutes. Let me ask you something. What are you doing about all this? Wasting time thinking Adele's sweet on somebody else? Trying to figure out what she's up to? Worrying that you aren't number one anymore?"

"Yeah," said J.C.

"So a lot of good things are happening for Adele. Have you congratulated her?"

"No."

"Unbelievable! Sent her flowers?"

"That's not my style."

"Told her she's the best? Kissed her when you came home? Kissed her when *she* came home?"

"That hasn't got anything to do with anything."

"It has everything to do with everything, buddyroe. I remember what you did for Adele when you were courting. You took a couple of pork chops over to her house. And you did *that* only one time! This is serious business, J.C., and once again, you're giving it the old pork chop routine—which never cured anything; never has, never will."

"You're preachin' me a sermon."

"You've got that right. When you have a terrific wife like I have a terrific wife, you can't diddledaddle around. How long since you took Adele out to dinner? How long since you courted this woman? Your wife is going places. Are you going places with her?"

No response.

"I believe I know Adele pretty well, she works her tail off to make Mitford a better place to live, plus she does all she can to keep you straight. You need to be rubbin' her feet at night, takin' her a cup of coffee in th' mornin'. . . ." He was lapsing into his Mississippi vernacular.

The editor's face was as red as a parboiled beet. "*Rubbin' her feet?* Are you out of your cotton-pickin' *mind?*"

"OK, OK, somewhere between pork chops and a foot rub is where this thing needs to fall. But let me tell you, a new aftershave won't cut it. And bein' too high and mighty to get excited about her success definitely won't cut it. You got to court this woman, and you got to get a *move* on."

"I got to court her *again*?"

"The way you courted her the first time was so triflin', it didn't even *count*. You got to court Adele like *this* is the first time."

"I should never have said pee-turkey to you." J.C. slammed his briefcase shut.

"And I'm sayin' all this to *you* because I think the world of Adele, and dadgummit, buddy, I love you." Good grief, he'd never said such a thing to J. C. Hogan in his life.

"Over and over again, I acted the fool with Cynthia, and let me tell you, that is a very dangerous thing to do." He remembered being unfairly jealous of her editor, threatened by her success, and desperately afraid of losing all that God had given him. "Do you love Adele?"

"Yeah," said J.C. "Big time."

"Did you take your vows seriously when I married the two of you?"

"I did."

"The way I see it, you don't have any time to lose. You need to get yourself down to the police station and walk in there . . ." He looked at his watch. "I saw her patrol car in the parkin' lot a few minutes ago—walk in there and . . ."

"And what?"

He had preached himself into a lather. And what, indeed? J.C. was sitting on the edge of his chair.

"Say you're turning yourself in for bein' a fool."

"Come on! Don't be a horse's behind."

"Ask her to sign out early tonight, tell her you have plans."

"What kind of plans?"

"My meddlin' ends right there." Father Tim wadded up the wrapper from the Nabs and tossed it in the trash bucket. "You'll have to figure that out for yourself."

He'd forgotten to ask J.C. if he knew anything more about Edith Mallory. He prayed for her faithfully and thought of her often—trying to imagine her urgent search for the connecting word among what Jubal had likened to the swarming of bees.

And what if the first word she had expressed with such feeling was lost again?

God, she had said! On the day she'd locked him in the room with herself at Kinloch, she had no heart for God, not in the least.

He didn't want her to lose that word; it was

imperative that she be able to hold on to that word.

Hold on, Edith! he thought, as he removed the key from the ignition in the town museum driveway.

Betty Craig looked done in.

"How is he?"

"Not a bit good."

"And Miss Rose?"

"Th' meanest ol' woman that ever drew breath, Father, an' that's all there is to it."

"What's going on?"

"He's jis' goin' down; he won't hardly eat nothin', an' you know he loves my cookin'. He wanted chicken an' dumplin's, but just sucked some of th' broth out of a spoon."

"Does he need to go back to the hospital?"

"I think he does."

"Pulse?"

"Weak."

"Where's Miss Rose?"

"In th' bathroom, grinnin' at 'erself in th' mirror last time I looked. She's jis' wicked!"

"Not wicked. Sick. It's a terrible disease, and hardly any money's ever spent to learn more about it."

"What ought we t' do?"

"I'll call Hoppy. Should I go in?"

"I think you should. You're always good medicine for people."

"I don't know about that," he said, meaning it. J. C. Hogan had been ready to knock him upside the head.

He stood by the bed, silent, gazing upon the man who had caused so many to laugh for so long . . .

Without opening his eyes, Uncle Billy held up his hand and Father Tim took it. "Is that . . . th' preacher?"

"It is, Uncle Billy." He had a knot in his throat the size of a golf ball, honored to be recognized merely by his touch.

How many sickbeds had he visited in his lifetime? His own mother's had been the most wrenching, and this one, this bedside, seemed oddly similar. He realized it was because Bill Watson was more than a cherished friend, more than a long-time parishioner—he was family.

"Let me pray for you," he said.

"That'd be good."

But when he knelt to do it, he found he couldn't speak for the tears.

He pulled into the Meadowgate driveway with seven potted lilies crowded onto the passenger seat and floorboard, and saw the green pickup truck parked in the pull-over.

The odor of ashes and creosote greeted him as soon as he hit the back steps.

"Darling, look who's come to see us. Pansy Flower, this is my husband, Father Tim Kavanagh."

"Pleased," said Pansy, who did a miniature bob. The curtsy hadn't gone the way of the milk wagon, after all. Indeed, it was cropping up all over the place—a regular comeback!

"Pansy of the famed Flower Girls! I'm happy to meet you, Pansy."

"Pansy's telling me about her large and very talented family," said Cynthia.

"Ten young 'uns! Eight girls, two boys. None dead. I myself personally am th' baby."

"Aha!"

"Iris, Lily, Rose, Arbutus, Delphinium, we call 'er Del," Pansy totted them up on her fingers. "Vi'let. Daisy. Jack in the Pulpit, we call 'im Jack. An' Sweet William, we call 'im Billy."

Father Tim observed that she positively beamed during this pronouncement.

"Let's see, now. Iris is the one who sews?"

Cynthia had her notebook and pen at the ready.

"No'm. Iris irons. 'Cept she can't do much right now, she's got corp'ral tunnel."

"So. Iris irons. *Lily* sews."

"No'm, it's Rose that sews. Lily cooks for parties."

"And Arbutus?"

"She don't do nothin'. She married Junior Bentley an' lives in a brick house."

Tuckered, he sought the solace of his wing chair and avoided looking at the plywood.

"A brick house?"

"Yes, ma'am. On th' new bypass across from Red Pig Barbecue. With two screen porches."

"So let me make sure I understand. I call Rose if I need sewing, Iris if I need ironing, and Lily when I give the Christmas party."

"Yes, ma'am. Oh, an' we forgot to talk about Daisy, she's twenty-two, an' works with Jack an' Billy killin' hogs."

"Killing hogs!"

"Yes, ma'am, from October to March, they kill hogs ever' Saturday an' make sausage. It's available in links, patties, or bulk."

He thought his wife looked a tad on the pale side. "Please, just write it all down," she said, transferring the notepad to Pansy.

"Don't you want to know 'bout Vi'let?"

Cynthia thumped into a chair at the pine table. "Of course! Have a seat, Pansy, and tell me everything."

"Vi'let works of a week, an' sings country music for parties on Saturday night."

"The parties that Lily caters?"

"Yes, ma'am, they hire out as a team. Barbecue an' fried catfish is Lily's specials; she serves that with cole slaw, hush puppies, an' homemade tater tots. Or if it's fried chicken you want, she does coleslaw, mashed taters, an' biscuits. Vi'let, she sings jis' like Loretta Lynn, an' plays th' guitar."

He caught himself nodding off.

"Her an' Lily charges by th' head. Twenty dollars a head for cookin' an' singin'."

"What if someone wants cooking and no singing?"

"They don't work that way; you have to take th' whole package. An' no Sundays 'less it's a church party. For a church party, Vi'let sings gospel an' they give a ten-percent discount. But they don't get much church b'iness."

"I suppose not; church people like to do their own singing."

"Yes, ma'am, an' their own cookin' in many cases."

"Well, Pansy, what I really need is someone to *clean*. As you can see, this dreadful mess can't wait 'til the cows come home. I need someone tomorrow morning, bright and early. Doesn't anyone in the family *clean*?"

"Oh, yes, ma'am! 'Cept for Arbutus who married Junior Bentley an' lives in a brick house, we *all* clean."

"Thank the Lord!"

"But for cleanin', we rotate."

"Rotate?"

"Yes, ma'am, you don't git the' same one twice runnin'. It goes like this—Lily comes Monday, Rose comes Tuesday, I come Wednesday, Del comes Thursday, Iris . . . no, wait, I think it's Rose as comes Monday an' Lily as comes Tuesday. Oh, shoot, I can't remember all that mess; it's too confusin'. You let us work that out."

"Happy to," said his wife, who appeared ready for a nap.

The cross stood in the center of the bare pine table, draped in purple.

Cold air, and with it a noxious sift of creosote, flowed down the broken chimney and seeped around the plywood into the kitchen.

Though Cynthia had done what she could to freshen things up, the malodorous smell permeated the room.

It was a time in the church year that always moved and jolted him. He'd sat in many a church on this night, with only candles lighting the nave, sorrowing over His suffering and death, keeping watch for His resurrection. Indeed, he'd never known any way to receive the authentic joy of Easter without entering into this dark hour.

His feelings were stirred by the clear and shining voice of his wife as she read from the first Epistle to the believers at Corinth.

"'I have received of the Lord that which also I delivered unto you, That the Lord Jesus the same night in which he was betrayed took bread; and when he had given thanks, he brake it, and said, Take, eat: this is my body, which is broken for you: this do in remembrance of me. After the same manner also he took the cup, when he had supped, saying, This cup is the new testament in my blood: this do ye, as oft as ye drink it, in remembrance of me. For as often as ye eat this bread, and drink this cup, ye do shew the Lord's death till he come.'"

He pulled the candlestick closer and read aloud from the Gospels of Luke and John in the old prayer book.

"'. . . Then said Jesus, Father, forgive them; for they know not what they do. And they parted his raiment, and cast lots. . . .

"'Now before the feast of the passover, when Jesus knew that his hour was come that he should depart out of this world unto the Father, having loved his own which were in the world, he loved them unto the end. And supper being ended . . .'"

He thought he heard a knock somewhere but couldn't be certain. "Did you hear something?"

It came again, louder this time, at the backdoor. "Willie!" he said, leaving the table. "It must be important."

He switched on the light and opened the door, but saw no one. "Willie? Is that you?"

A tall, thin figure stepped into the porch light.

"It's m-me. S-S-Sammy."

CHAPTER NINE

Keeping the Feast

On the morning of Good Friday, a mild, nearly balmy breeze blew into the valley.

Relishing the liberty of a short-sleeve shirt, Father Tim stood outside the laundry room with a brick mason who nursed a plug of tobacco in his jaw and surveyed the damage.

"Back then, they laid their chimney stacks one brick thick."

"That's not good, I take it."

"Was then; ain't now. It's a wonder it ain't fell in before. Out here, see, y'r storms come mostly from th' west, th' side y'r chimney's on. All that wet blowin' in collects in y'r mortar, then when y'r freezes come, th' mortar *contracts;* y' know what I mean?"

"I do."

"Swells up, freezes, swells up, freezes. Pretty soon, comes loose, falls out, big gale blows, down she goes."

"Got it."

Throughout the house, the ancient window sashes had been forced open to let in drafts of spring air, and sweeten the bitter smell of wood ash. Father Tim heard the drone of several vacuum cleaners operating simultaneously on bare wood floors, in concert with the rumble of a supersize clothes dryer and the agitation of a washing machine.

The mason shot a stream of tobacco juice into a camellia bush. "Busy place," he said to the vicar.

A serious contingent of Flower Girls had reported for duty, and according to the look on his wife's face only moments earlier, Father Tim determined that all was right with the world.

He sat with Sammy on the back steps, taking a break.

"Thanks, buddy."

Sammy nodded with a short, self-conscious jerk of his head.

They'd piled the debris collected behind the plywood into a couple of wheelbarrows. As transferring the detritus from the barrow to the truck bed would be too labor intensive, they'd huffed the heavy barrows to the farm dump beyond the root cellar.

"We're glad you're here," said Father Tim. "You're safe with us."

Another jerk of the head.

Déjà vu, thought the vicar. These porch steps were exactly where he'd sat with Dooley on their first visit to the farm all those years ago.

"How did you get here?"

Sammy raised the thumb of his right hand.

"How did you know where we are?"

"Asked at th' gas station in Mitford, they all knowed."

"Dooley and I looked for you in Holding. He was pretty worried when we couldn't find you."

"Yeah."

"What happened?"

"I w-w-wanted t' git out on m' own; I w-wanted to make it on m' own, like D-Dooley."

"Dooley didn't make it on his own."

A guinea streaked by, with another in hot pursuit. It was mating season at Meadowgate.

"For that matter," said Father Tim, "I didn't make it on my own, either. We can't make it on our own; we need each other. Why didn't you tell Lon?"

"I wanted t' sh-show 'im I could do it without no help. I didn't have n-nobody t' talk to."

"You have somebody now. Dooley. Poo. Jessie. Buck." Mentioning Sammy's mother wouldn't be a good thing; Sammy bitterly resented the wrong she had done all her children. "Cynthia. Barnabas. Me." He put his hand on Sammy's shoulder, and felt him flinch. He also felt the bone beneath the skin.

"I got me a job at a n-nursery. Lasted th-th-three weeks."

"Didn't work out, then."

"They said I s-stole money. I didn't do it; it was a f-fat boy done it."

"We may have a paying job for you right here, if you're interested. After all, if we're going to have tomato sandwiches, we've got to have tomatoes. I'm pretty good with roses, but don't know much about tomatoes."

A light flickered in the boy's eyes. "I can grow t'maters, big time."

"I'll bet you can."

"C-cukes, squash, melon, pole beans, all 'at."

"Okra?" He was a fool for okra.

"I ain't never g-growed okra but I could do it."

"Any plans to go back to your father?"

"I ain't n-never goin' back. He pulled a gun on me, made me set still without hardly b-breathin', said if I moved he'd blow m' brains out. He was b-bad drunk. After while, he passed out an' I run. I slep' that night in' the neighbor's garage an' kep' goin' 'til I c-come t' M-Morganton. I found a nurs'ry an' got a job."

"Where did you stay?"

"I slep' in th' sh-shed where they kep' th' clay pots an' all. I hope him an' C-Cate Turner is burnin' in hell right now."

There was a long silence; only the squawking of the guineas, the call of a bird.

"What became of your beautiful garden?" Father Tim remembered the garden Sammy had created in "a waste place," as the Bible sometimes put it; its loveliness had brought tears to his eyes.

Sammy shrugged. "It'll g-grow over an' no-body'll know it was there."

"Any idea where you want to go from here?"

"Don't know where I'd s-stay at."

"Cynthia and I talked about it; we'd like you to stay with us for a while. But we have a few house rules."

Better lay it out upfront.

"No smoking. No cussing. Keep your room

in order. If you leave, let us know where you're going. Curfew—eleven o'clock."

Sammy watched the guineas disappear around the smokehouse. The old scar on his face reddened.

"Did you hear me, son?"

"Y-yeah."

"Interested?"

Sammy nodded. "Yeah."

"How long since you were in school?"

"I ain't been t' school since eighth grade, an' I ain't goin' back, neither."

"How old are you?"

"S-s-sixteen."

"When did you turn sixteen?"

Sammy shot him an aggrieved look.

"If you're going to stay with us, and I hope you will, I need to know the score."

"Last month."

"March, then."

"Yeah. Th' fourteenth."

In North Carolina, it was legally permissible to drop out of school at the age of sixteen. While that may not be the best of rulings, Father Tim was relieved; if they had to force Sammy to go to school, Sammy might be lost to them forever.

Father Tim sniffed the air; a wondrous aroma was wending its way through the kitchen door and out to the porch . . .

It had a been a long time since Sammy had wolfed down his supper last night and crashed on Annie's bed without removing his clothes.

"That muffin we had a while ago is history. Let's go in and have some breakfast."

Sammy shot to his feet; a grin tried to spread across his face. The vicar noted that Sammy caught it before it got very far. In any case, it was sunlight breaking through leaden clouds.

Good Friday was a fast day, and though Cynthia later vowed she'd asked for something "very simple," Lily-who-cooks-for-parties had done herself proud.

Cheese grits, bacon, fried apples, scrambled eggs, drop biscuits, and cream gravy sat in bowls and platters on the pine table. She had also fried up half the sausage she'd toted as a gift from the sausage-making operation, and set out two jars of jam from the farm coffers.

His wife trotted in from the laundry room and gasped. "Is this a *dream*?"

"Hallelujah and three amens!" said the vicar. He'd better call the Mitford Hospital and reserve a room. "What do you say, Sammy?"

Sammy appeared dumbfounded, unable to reply.

Lily was already elbow-deep in a sinkful of hot, soapy water, giving the pots and pans a thorough what for. She giggled. "Better not carry on like 'at 'til you see if it's any good."

The vicar pulled out a chair for his marveling wife. "We hear by the grapevine that you sing like Loretta Lynn!"

"Oh, no, sir, that's Vi'let as sings like Loretta. If I was t' sing a'tall, which I don't, I'd sing more like Dolly."

"Aha. And thank you for the sausage, Lily. A very thoughtful gift!"

"It's th' mild, not th' hot; we didn't think you'uns looked th' hot 'n' spicy type."

"Very thoughtful!" he said. How could he eat such a feast when his commitment was to fast?

"Anyhow, it ain't from me; it's from Daisy. Daisy does sausage. I don't have *nothin'* to do with *sausage* makin'! No, sir, it's way too messy. I'll *never* make no *sausage* . . ."

"I believe Lily is the one who also sews, dear."

"Oh, no ma'am, that's Rose as sews. I'm not facilitated to do nothin' but cook an' clean."

"Let's pray," he said.

Worn, they sat in the library by a waning fire. Sammy was watching a billiards competition on the TV in his room; Violet was curled on the lap of her mistress; the farm dogs snored in their accustomed places in the kitchen. Peace like a river . . .

"Let me read to us," he said. He believed his homily was nailed; the rest was up to the Holy Spirit.

He thumbed through the little volume of Longfellow's poems that he'd found among Marge's many books, and read from "Endymion."

"... *O drooping souls, whose destinies*
Are fraught with fear and pain,
Ye shall be loved again!

No one is so accursed by fate,
No one so utterly desolate,
But some heart, though unknown,
Responds unto his own.

Responds, as if with unseen wings,
An angel touched its quivering strings;
And whispers, in its song,
'Where hast thou stayed so long?' ..."

"Do you believe with Mr. Longfellow," she

asked, "that no one is so accursed by fate but some heart responds to his own?"

"I do believe it. It's true for Dooley, and for Lace. It was true for Buck and Pauline . . ." He could go on and on. "It was true for us."

"For so many years I thought that no heart, however known or unknown, would ever respond to my own. I never dreamed of this happiness with you. And for you to read aloud to me is such a lavish gift; it's above all I could ever ask or think."

"Do you remember the time you came down to my study?" he asked. "It was in the middle of the night, and I was walking through the valley . . . you read the hundred and third psalm to me. I was so happy to see you, I felt I'd been rescued from drowning; your voice meant everything to me."

They sat for a time, gazing at the crimson embers beneath the grate.

"Mother read to me," he mused, "but not for entertainment. It was purely instructional, bless her soul! But I had Peggy, as you know. Peggy couldn't read, but she told me stories. Lengthy, complex, wonderful stories of her childhood in the backcountry of Mississippi. Then, when I learned to read, I read to her."

"I'm trying to remember—when did you see her last?"

"I was ten when she disappeared. Just vanished. I was stricken." Where did she go? He never knew . . .

He suddenly felt again the old sorrow, as if a door had opened somewhere, spilling a grim light into the corridor.

His truest friend had simply never come back to his mother's kitchen, to cook with her and make her laugh; to slip him a forbidden sweet, and listen to his cares as if they were actually important.

After she'd gone, he often rode his bike down the narrow lane, and entered her cold cabin and called her name. The cabin looked as if she'd simply walked away and would soon return—a dress still hung on a nail, an apron was thrown over the back of a chair, wood for a cook fire had been brought in and placed by the hearth.

His mother, whom he believed to know everything, had appeared to know nothing about Peggy's disappearance. More than once, he'd trekked to the barn—what if she'd been gathering eggs in the loft, and fallen through the rotten boards? For months, he looked for her on the streets of Holly Springs, and once went to her church on Wednesday night and stood in the road to see whether she came.

It occurred to him as he sat here, more than a half century later, that he'd looked for Peggy for most of his life. Or more truly, he'd looked for her particular warmth. In the divided, often-cold household of his childhood, Peggy's warmth had ignited in him a kind of fire to love and be loved.

He gazed at his wife with quiet amazement. "I never thought of it before," he said.

"What have you never thought before?"

"You remind me of Peggy."

She leaned her head to one side and smiled. "I'm proud to remind you of Peggy," she said. "Why don't we go up now, darling—to clean sheets and swept corners?"

She took his hand and led him along the stairs, and once again he felt the happiness of these last weeks. He would do something wonderful for his wife one day. He'd do all in his power to give back what she had so generously given him.

He opened his eyes and looked out the window near their bed. In the cold first light, the distant tree line appeared rimmed with platinum.

"Are you awake?"

"I am."

He rolled over and kissed her on the cheek. "He is risen!"

"He is risen, indeed!"

"Alleluia!" As ever on Easter morning, a certain heaviness departed his spirit.

"I'm excited about our first real service at Holy Trinity," she said. "Wait, I take that back. Last Sunday was wonderfully real."

"I like the way you think; you'll always be my deacon." He slid out of bed. "I'll start the coffee; the ham's ready to pop in the oven just before we leave."

"I'll make breakfast for Sammy and me. Are you having toast?"

"Just toast. And a little butter." While a priest typically fasted before the Eucharist, his blasted diabetes wanted mollycoddling.

They made the sign to each other; it had become their new private liturgy.

Father Tim pushed open the door to the room where the Owens' daughter Annie had lived until she finished college. Her years in the foreign service had kept her away from home for long periods, but soon, she'd be moving to Asheville, a fact that thrilled not only the Owens, but himself, as well.

Barnabas bounded in and stood by the bed, wagging his tail.

"Sammy! Good morning! Time to get up, son."

"What's g-goin' on?"

"A blessed Easter to you! We're off to church in an hour or so, breakfast on the table in twenty minutes."

"Church?" Sammy sat up in bed, wearing one of Dooley's left-behind sweatshirts. "I ain't goin' t' no ch-church."

"We talked about it last night."

"Y-yeah, but I didn't s-s-say I'd g-go."

"House rule. We go to church as a family."

"That rule wadn't on th' l-list you give me b'fore."

"I'm sorry. I took that rule for granted and failed to mention it. Please get up now and have some breakfast."

"Quit *breathin'* on me!" he heard Sammy say to Barnabas, who caught up with his master on the stairs.

He realized again that he'd never enjoyed making anybody do anything. But enjoyment wasn't necessarily what it was all about when a lost boy comes under your roof. It had often been tough sledding with Dooley, and it could be tough sledding again.

Lord, he prayed, *thank you for being on the sled . . .*

They were early, yet four vehicles were already parked in the lot.

As he blew through the door with Barnabas at his heels, he checked his mental list. Pew bulletins on the top shelf by the bell rope. Juice and cups and a tin of cookies on the bottom shelf. Bread and wine in the sacristy; his white vestments hanging behind the door. Lilies in front of the altar, the snowy fair linen laid on, floors swept clean, windows shining . . .

Yesterday's housekeeping detail with Sammy and Cynthia and Lloyd and the Mertons had been one of the highlights of his priesthood.

Buzzed with excitement, he marshaled his troops.

"Miss Martha, do you sing?"

"Real loud!" announced Mary.

"Good! That's what we need this morning. Open up those pipes, ladies.

"Kavanagh, I'm depending on you, as well."

"You know perfectly well I was given an eye, not an ear!"

"No excuses! Lloyd, do you sing?"

"Tenor. But can't read music t' save my life."

"Not a problem, we're using the old hymns. And there's a visitor! Welcome to Holy Trinity! Happy Easter! Do you sing?"

"It'll set y'r dog t' barkin'," declared Sparkle Foster.

"Set him to barking, then. We're here to celebrate!" He hurried toward the sacristy, calling over his shoulder: "Christ being raised from the dead dieth no more!"

Cynthia smiled at the early comers. "My husband is always like this at Easter," she said.

His wife, a gift from God.

Sammy Barlowe, a gift from God.

His eyes roved the pews.

Agnes Merton, Clarence Merton, gifts from God . . .

Robert Prichard . . . yes, a gift from God . . .

Every saint has a past, the sixteenth-century poet had said, *and every sinner has a future.* And all because of what He did for love.

"Christ our Passover is sacrificed for us: therefore let us keep the feast. Not with old leaven neither with the leaven of malice and wickedness; but with the unleavened bread of sincerity and truth . . ."

"As it was in the beginning, is now, and ever shall be, world without end . . ."

The old words seemed somehow reborn, as his spirit stepped forth to embrace his new parish.

They gathered in the churchyard, close by the stone wall.

How many souls had gathered at this wall in the life of Holy Trinity, and looked out to clear skies and dark alike? One thing the vicar knew for certain, there wouldn't be many Easter morns as glorious as this.

A soft, impressionist light bathed every ridge; the still-bare trees, seemingly grim and resolute only days ago, appeared relieved and hopeful; for the first time, he noticed buds on the rhododendron.

Barnabas sprawled atop the wall, eyeing all comers.

"'At's th' biggest dern dog I ever seen in m' life," said Rooter. "Is 'e a bitin' dog?"

"Not so far," said Father Tim.

"I don' want t' be eat up by no dog."

"Shouldn't be a problem; he had breakfast before we left."

He stood with Cynthia and Agnes by the

wall, dispensing cartons of eggs. Sissie Gleason was first in line, holding fast to Granny's hand.

Sissie looked up at Father Tim. "Was God here t'day?"

"He was!" said the vicar. "And is."

Sissie raised one foot in the air. "I wanted 'im t' see m' new shoes."

"Ain't them th' prettiest little yeller shoes you ever laid eyes on?" asked Granny.

"They are!" Cynthia agreed. "I'd love a pair exactly like them."

Sissie peered into the carton of eggs. "They ain't colored," she said. "They ain't fit t' hide."

"Take them home and boil them hard," said Cynthia, "then color them with your Magic Markers and hide them to your heart's content. Do you have Magic Markers?"

"What is Magi Markers?"

"I'll bring you some next Sunday. Do you read?"

"Nope. I ain't in school yet."

"I'll bring you a book," said Cynthia. "It has lots of pictures. Kiss your mother for us."

Father Tim squatted to Sissie's level. "Thank you for coming, Sissie. Tell your Uncle Donny he'd sure be welcome to join us. And tell your mother she's in our prayers."

"Sparkle Foster," said the fortyish woman,

shaking Cynthia's hand. "I do hair in th' valley, pleased to meet you. An' this is my husband, Wayne."

"Sparkle! Wayne! A blessed Easter to you!"

"Same to y'all. This is sure a different kind of church for us. I was raised Holiness, Wayne was raised Baptist."

"I was raised t' *shout*," said Wayne, setting the record straight, "but *fell away* to th' Baptists."

Cynthia handed off a carton to the red-haired Sparkle, who appeared touched by the gesture. "Why, thank you, how nice. Other than it bein' Easter, is there a special meanin' to givin' eggs away at church?"

"There is, actually! Our hens lay faster than we can use up the proceeds! Where did you get your wonderful name?"

Sparkle laughed. "My granmaw got it out of th' funny papers."

"Very creative of your granmaw! We're happy to have you and hope you'll come again."

"I don't know if we can keep up with th' way y'all do things."

Wayne nodded, clearly in agreement.

"We need to have some lessons on the prayer book," said the vicar. "Would be good for everybody. What about a covered dish next Sunday? Followed by a discussion on how we do things?" In his new parish, there would be no slacking; it was fish or cut bait.

"Great idea!" boomed Martha McKinney, moving up in line. "I'll bring my German chocolate cake."

"She'll bring her German choc'late cake," said Mary, clearly thrilled by the prospect.

"Miss Martha, Miss Mary, He is risen!"

"He is risen, indeed!" they recited in unison.

Martha received their dozen with obvious gratitude. "We used to be covered up with eggs, everybody and his brother kept chickens! But today, there's hardly a soul who'll keep a chicken."

"They run out in th' road," said Mary. "That's why."

Father Tim indicated the open doors and the crowd milling about in the churchyard. "Well, ladies, what do you think?"

Tears brimmed in Martha's eyes. "It's the best thing that's happened on this ridge in more years than I can count. I was so excited, I was up half th' night!"

"We was *both* up half th' night!" said Mary.

"A blessed Easter to you!" He hugged Miss Mary, while Cynthia hugged Miss Martha. Teamwork!

"Lloyd!" The vicar clasped the hand of the

other cradle Episcopalian in their midst. "He is risen!"

"He is risen, indeed!" said Lloyd, who received his dozen with a big grin. "Come summer, I'll keep you an' Miz Kavanagh in corn. I grow Silver Queen."

"Our sworn favorite! I meant to ask you yesterday what you do with your time now that you've moved home."

"I was in th' contractin' bi'ness a good many years, workin' as a brick mason. I'm what you call semiretired, but I still lay a little brick now an' again."

"Look how the Lord works! I'm just getting estimates on a chimney that blew down in the wind. Quite a mess. Care to give us a price? We're in th' valley, Dr. Owen's place."

"Glad to. Happy to! I know right where you're at."

"Tuesday morning, first thing?"

"You can count on it."

"A blessed Easter to you, Granny. Fresh from the nest."

"Rooter'll have th' whole bunch et up b'fore you can say jackrabbit."

Rooter took the eggs. "We wouldn't mind gittin' some more when you'uns have 'em," said Rooter.

"What d'you say?" prompted Granny.

"Thank you'uns."

"You're welcome," said the vicar, giving Rooter a clap on the shoulder.

Rooter made a face. "I ain't never heerd none of them songs you'un's sing."

Father Tim heard Agnes chuckle.

"Come again next Sunday," he said, "and we'll have some more songs you never heard! But guess what?"

"What?"

"You and Granny keep coming, and one day, you'll start recognizing the words and the tunes, and next thing you know . . ."

Rooter grinned. "I might keep a-comin', but I won't be a-singin', I c'n tell y' that." He turned to Agnes. "I'd like t' say somethin' to Clarence. Can you show me some of them hand words y'all do?"

"What would you like to say?"

"How you doin', man?"

"Step over here and I'll show you," said Agnes.

"And by the way," said Father Tim, "I'd like to see Clarence's work, myself. When it's convenient."

"Consider it done!" said Agnes, borrowing his line.

"Robert . . . for you. A blessed Easter!"

Robert took the carton without speaking, his head lowered. When he looked up, Father Tim felt his very soul pierced. In Robert Prichard's eyes was a look of utter desolation.

Father Tim spontaneously embraced him. "He is risen!" he whispered, hoarse with feeling.

The cookies had vanished, as had the juice, when Rooter ran back to Agnes.

"I done it! What else can I say to 'im?"

"What else would you like to say?"

"I want t' know how he makes all them things in 'is little house. Them bears an' deer an' all, an' them bowls, I want t' know how 'e makes them bowls. I don't see how he done 'at."

"Watch," said Agnes.

She made a sign. "Can you do this?"

"Yeah." He did it.

"That means *how.* Can you make this sign?"

"Yeah."

"That means *do.* Now here's the rest of your question: *this? How do this?*"

Rooter watched intently, duplicating the last sign.

"I done it right, didn' I?"

"You did it perfectly! Here comes the hard part; let's do them all in a row now. How . . . do . . . this?"

Father Tim looked on. This boy was quick.

"I done it ag'in!"

"Yes, you did. How amazing."

"I'll be et f'r a tater!" said Granny, marveling.

Agnes brushed a wisp of hair from her forehead. "Let's go over it once more."

They went over it once more.

"Now, run find Clarence!"

Rooter started to race away, then turned back. "Don't he talk none a'tall?"

"None at all."

"How'd he learn to make them things?"

"God taught him."

"I ain't believin' that. You cain't see God."

"God put the gift to carve wood in Clarence's heart and mind and hands. Clarence touches the wood and knows things that most of us can't know."

Rooter sighed. "Now I done forgot what I learnt."

"Look here." She made the signs, and he mimicked them without fault.

"Hurry, now! Run!"

Rooter ran.

"Ain't he a catbird?" said Granny.

They were pulling out of the church lot as Lloyd was getting into his pickup.

"What would you think," he asked Cynthia, "about setting another plate for Easter dinner?"

"I would think it's a wonderful idea."

He leaned out the window of the Mustang and shouted. "Lloyd!"

"Yessir?"

"Do you like ham and corn pudding and hot rolls and green beans?"

With Lloyd following behind, he steered the Mustang down the gravel road toward the creek, still intoxicated by the scent of beeswax, old wood, lemon oil, lilies . . .

He wanted to remember the happiness of this day for a very long time.

"How's it going back there, Sammy?" A quick glance in the rearview mirror . . .

Just as Sammy had maintained his distance from the parishioners, he was giving wide berth to his companion on the backseat.

After Lloyd had gone home to the ridge, he sat with Cynthia in the library and totted the numbers.

Not counting his good dog, Holy Trinity had expanded from seven parishioners to fourteen.

Though numbers weren't everything, he was mighty impressed with their rate of growth, which was a whopping 100 percent.

"One hundred percent!" he announced to his wife. "In the space of a single week, mind you."

"Let the megachurches top that," she said.

Willie Mullis was living up to something Father Tim's grandmother used to say of the overharried—he looked like he was sent for and couldn't go.

"Triplets."

"Triplets?"

"Two ewes an' a ram. All hale."

"Wonderful! Thanks for the report." It was nine o'clock at night, for Pete's sake, he didn't know if he could handle another lifetime event today. "Want to step in for some hot chocolate? It's chilly this evening."

Willie frowned. Why would anybody want

to waste time drinking hot chocolate when they could come to the barn and witness something that didn't happen every day of the week? Twins were pretty common. But triplets? He shook his head, disgusted with town people in general.

As Willie turned to leave, Father Tim felt Violet wrapping herself around his ankles. Suddenly, the proverbial lightbulb switched on. He looked at his wife; she looked at him.

"Violet and the triplets!" they whooped.

"I'll grab my sketchbook!"

"Get Sammy while you're at it!" he said. "I'll get a flashlight. Hey, Willie! Wait up, we're coming!"

Before he could round up the flashlight and don his boots, his wife had commandeered Sammy, raced to the coatrack by the door, found her wool socks and pulled them on, shoved her feet into her boots, stuffed her pajama bottoms therein, drawn her barn jacket on over her chenille robe, crammed a knit hat on her head, and was out the door with Sammy and Barnabas at her heels, the screen door slapping behind.

Lambs on long, wobbly legs.

If there was ever a sight to restore one's hope, it was a lamb.

His wife was sitting in the straw of the triplets' lambing pen, sketching her brains out while two of the newborns suckled with good appetite. Sammy looked on from outside the pen, awed.

"This, I presume," he said to Cynthia, "knocks out March."

"March, and possibly even April," she said.

Willie came in with a bottle. "I had t' pull that 'un yonder. 'E's not takin' dinner from 'is mama, an' I got t' go look about th' rest of th' lot." Willie gave Father Tim a meaningful look.

"You want me to . . . umm . . ."

"Yessir."

The vicar took the bottle and sat in the straw beside Barnabas. "Hand him over here, get me started. I'm new at this."

Willie picked up the lamb and forked it over; it was wet and sticky from the birth sac, and its iodine-treated umbilical cord was still bloody.

With a little coaxing, the lamb found the nipple of the bottle and nursed with surprising energy.

Father Tim leaned back against the boards of the lambing pen, grinning. His new barn jacket had at last been broken in.

"Close up the house," said Hal. "You don't need the aggravation of a chimney being rebuilt under your noses. Willie can look after things."

"No, no, we'd like to stay on. I confess we've gotten pretty comfortable here and we're looking forward to spending the summer with Dooley. We hope we have years yet to be at home in Mitford."

"Whatever suits you, old friend. Glad to hear Sammy showed up; that's four out of five, thanks be to God!"

As the usual static came on the line, Father Tim hung up, relieved.

Somehow, he and Cynthia had gotten rooted into Meadowgate like turnips; yanking it all up and moving back to Wisteria Lane would be a job of no mean proportion. Besides, he wanted to watch the lambs grow up, and eat okra and tomatoes from the alluvial soil of a valley garden.

"Okra!" he said aloud, rhapsodic.

His wife stopped squinting at her sketchbook and squinted at him. *"Okra?"*

"Fried, whenever possible."

"Certainly not stewed!" she said, meaning it.

During a light spring rain on Wednesday, the UPS driver screeched into the driveway and, unable to summon anyone to the backdoor of the farmhouse, used a dolly to transport twenty boxes to the rear steps. Seeing no way around the onerous task of off-loading them onto the porch, he sighed deeply and went to work.

Holy Trinity's kneelers had arrived.

Shortly afterward, the driver of a competitive delivery service huffed a weighty carton onto the front porch and sprinted to the truck before anyone could ask him to set it in the front hall.

Holy Trinity's candles, Host box, altar vases, chalice, paten, hymn board, and altar sticks had reached their destination.

CHAPTER TEN

So Shall Ye Reap

Twins.

A single.

A single.

Twins.

A single.

Twins.

Twins.

A single.

At Meadowgate Farm, lambs were arriving as frequently as flights into Atlanta.

As if fitted with coils, they sprang around the barn and over the pasture, doing what the English long ago defined as *gamboling*.

"Also known as *frisking*," said his wife, hunkered down with a camera.

"How many rolls so far?"

"Only eleven."

"Ah yes, but shooting them is one thing, and having them developed is another."

"In my calling, dearest, all tax deductible!"

Satisfied ewes lay about the greening pasture in fleecy mounds, chewing their cud. Here and there, a mistaken lamb gave a ewe's udder a great, upheaving nudge and was scolded off to its own mother.

It was the time of year at Meadowgate when cars and trucks slowed along the state road. Whole families occasionally piled out of their vehicles to stand at the fence and marvel.

Father Tim threw up his hand to Willie, who was heading down the pasture with his walking stick. Willie waved back.

Using her zoom lens, Cynthia shot several frames of their good shepherd, who, due to the lambing and calving season, was looking decidedly overworked. Indeed, in the Meadowgate pasture to the north, four calves had recently been born, with six more expected.

"He needs the help of a wife, poor soul."

"He has the neighbor boy," said Father Tim.

"Yes, but does the neighbor boy have a hot meal on the table when Willie straggles in from the barn?"

"You have a point."

"We'll send him an apple pie. I found two in the freezer, I'll pop both in the oven this afternoon; the kitchen will smell wonderful."

"One for Willie and one for Sammy?"

"Precisely. You and I will feast merely on the aroma."

"Works for me," he said.

He looked up and saw something moving at a pace along the brow of the hill. Guineas. The entire flock. Chasing madly after something white . . . aha!

"Kavanagh, remember one of the calendar pictures we talked about—Violet chasing the guineas?"

"I'm planning that for the September page."

The caravan raced down the hill at breakneck speed and disappeared around the barn.

"You may need to revise it slightly."

Even with the attentions of the Mitford Hospital staff, Uncle Billy Watson wasn't improving. Now stuck with cooking for Miss Rose and checking on her three times daily, Betty Craig was desperate; and no, there was no opening at Hope House until . . . "well, you know," said the director of admissions.

Though he hadn't the faintest idea what to do, he felt he must do something.

"Lloyd," he said, shaking the rough, ham-sized hand of the low-bidding mason. "Welcome to Meadowgate."

"I'll take care of some prep work today, an' startin' tomorrow I'll have a helper. We'll do you a good job," said Lloyd.

Unlike some poor saps who were promised such a thing by a contractor, the vicar was relieved to know he could take Lloyd's promise as the gospel truth.

"Let's play a game," he said to his wife.

"I love games!"

"What don't you love, Kavanagh?"

"Jeans without Lycra, lug soles on barn shoes, age spots . . ."

"Ditto."

"And," she continued, "any sitcom more recent than *M★A★S★H*."

"So. Let's say someone was working with you in the house two days a week. Now that you have the calendar to contend with, would that bother you?"

"Not if they did their work and let me do mine. Why?"

"End of game," he said.

"Who won?"

"We both won," he said. "Trust me."

"Lily?" he whispered into the phone.

"Who *is* this?"

"It's Father Tim," he said, still whispering.

"Why are you *whisperin'*?"

"I don't want my wife to hear."

"Why, shame on you! I've heard of preachers like you!"

"Wait, no! It's nothing like that. I'm trying to hire you to help Mrs. Kavanagh. It's sort of a surprise."

Skeptical silence.

"Two days a week," he said.

"Doin' what?"

"Cooking and cleaning."

"For how many?"

"Three. This summer, there'll be four."

"I cain't take any Saturday work; that's when I do parties."

"Of course."

"An' no Friday work, that's when I get *ready* t' do a party."

"Fine. Fine."

"An' no Monday work, that's when I get *over* doin' a party."

"Ah." He sat down.

"Sometimes I'd have to send Del or even Vi'let in m' place."

"I thought Violet was married to somebody in a brick house and . . ."

"That's Arbutus."

"Of course."

"Del can't cook t' save 'er life, but mama says she cleans like a Turk."

"Like a Turk . . . what does that mean, exactly?"

"Upends y'r chairs on y'r table; pulls th' furniture out from th' walls; beats y'r rugs with a paddle. Don't miss a trick."

He was having a sinking spell. "Can you come?"

"I guess I ought t' tell you Vi'let sings as she works. I hope you don't mind singin'. She's very popular with ever'body."

"I'm sure!"

"Lite Country, she calls it."

"Can you *do* it?"

"When would I start?"

"Immediately. Right away. Tomorrow."

"How long would this job last?"

"'Til sometime in January, when the owners of Meadowgate return."

"I have reg'lars, y' know. I'd have t' make other arrangements, which can be a heap of trouble."

"I understand," he said. "And by the way, Mrs. Kavanagh . . ."

"She tol' me to call 'er Cynthia."

"Cynthia . . . needs a lot of concentration to do her work. She can't be disturbed."

Long pause. Background music from a radio . . .

"I jis' prayed about it," said Lily, "but I didn't get a answer. Zip. Zero."

"How long do you think it might take . . . to get an answer?"

"You oughta know better'n me, you're th' preacher."

He sighed; Puny Bradshaw Guthrie had spoiled him for all others. "Why don't we just . . . talk later?" A brilliant idea.

"Wait a minute, wait a minute, I think I'm gettin' a answer. Hold on."

Longer pause. The deejay was singing along.

"I can do it!" she whooped. "Ever' Wednesday an' Thursday!"

"Wonderful! Terrific!"

"I'll be there Wednesday mornin' at eight

o'clock. I bring m' own cleanin' rags an' sweet tea, an' I have a allergy to cats so I'll be wearin' a mask."

"A mask. Right. Anything else?"

"I sign out at three o'clock, sharp."

"Perfect."

She giggled. "You can stop whisperin' now."

"It's all yours," he told Sammy.

He stood inside the rusted gate with Sammy and surveyed the sun-bathed vegetable garden. Marge once said this patch of ground had been continuously worked for more than a century, with cow, sheep, and chicken manure, at least during their tenure, being the principal fertilizers.

"That g-green stuff's asparagus."

Sammy lowered the bill on his ball cap, as his eyes roved the ruin of winter. He picked up a faded seed packet. "Beets was here. Maybe c-c-carrots an' onions over there."

"Pole beans grew on that trellis," said Father Tim. "I picked a hatful two years ago."

"Prob'ly t-taters here." Sammy kicked at the mounded earth. "An' t'maters over yonder."

"Think we'll have any room for squash?"

"What kind?" asked Sammy.

"Yellow."

"Yep. How 'bout watermelons?"

"I don't know. Can you grow watermelons in the mountains? I believe they need sandy soil."

"You c'n g-git sand at a nurs'ry."

"That's the spirit! As ye sow, so shall ye reap!"

"I'd put c-corn in here, 'bout f-four or five rows. And put y'r okra in next to th' c-corn."

"How do you know all this?"

"I learned it offa Lon; he g-grows ever'thing he eats. If we're goin' t' git seeds an' plants an' all, we need t' b-bust ass."

"We'll make a run to Wesley tomorrow." Sammy's arms were definitely longer than the sleeves in Dooley's sweat shirt. They'd hit the department store while they were at it, and a haircut wouldn't hurt matters, either.

"About the fertilizer. Mrs. Owen says they use sheep, cow, and chicken manure."

"That'll work."

"The problem is—you have to collect it."

"You mean—git it out of th' f-field?"

"Right."

"Is it rotted?"

"I don't know. You'll need to work with Willie on that. A good wheelbarrow, a pitchfork, a shovel, and you're in business."

Sammy adjusted his ball cap.

"Can you use a tiller?"

"I don' know; I ain't never used one."

He clapped Sammy on the back. "I'll show you."

Two robins swooped across the garden. The emerging leaves of a fence-climbing trumpet vine trembled in the morning breeze.

Though Sammy seldom allowed his face to register his feelings, his eyes weren't under such strict command. Father Tim saw that this garden would be more than food for their table; it would be food for Sammy Barlowe's soul.

<Flash!

<Somebody told me you can go online—and search the entire federal prison system for the name of a prisoner. As soon as I figure out how to do it, I'll get right on it. Seems like we should try this. Do you know if his real name is Kenneth or should I just type in Kenny?

<As for the state system, you have to do a search state by state. With forty-eight states, or is it fifty-two, I might need help on this deal.

<Decided to wear pumps I already have. Black. Will need to get them stretched, my feet must have grown while I wasn't looking, haha. Travel is a royal pain in the youknowwhat.

<I haven't seen you in a coon's age. Happy Easter to you and Cynthia. Call me. Love, Emma.

• • •

<Emma,

<He is risen!

<Have at it! I feel encouraged. Hope you don't find KB in this particular circumstance, but then again, the point is to find him.

<Sammy here with us. Showed up at our door, thanks be to God! Taller than Dooley, though five years younger.

<Will call later in week if don't hear from you first. New parish up and running. Cynthia painting twelve scenes for Violet wall calendar. Fifteen lambs born to date. Four calves.

<Kenneth. Middle name Russell. Remember there's an e in Barlowe.

<Grateful for all you've done in past to help round up those missing. Dropping off a dozen

eggs this week at Lew Boyd's for you to pick up. Will leave in his cool box.

<A blessed Eastertide!

<Fifty states.

"Willie, how's it going?"

Willie held out two egg cartons. "Fourteen. This here carton's five short."

"Just fourteen?" He'd promised a dozen to Emma, a dozen to Percy, a dozen to Esther . . .

"The hens must be on strike."

"Looks like."

"They're on their laying mash?"

"Same as ever."

"Snakes?"

"Too early."

"Right. Well! I'm town folk, you know. Thank you, Willie. Anything new at the barn?"

"Two singles."

"Almost done, then."

"Yessir. An' thank y'r missus f'r th' pie. I et it at one settin'."

"Good! My wife will love hearing that!"

He hated to give away less than a full carton. Percy would have to wait.

With Andrew's cordial permission, he and Sammy dug through the Plymouth looking for, as he told Sammy, a manila envelope. At scarcely more than four feet tall, and weighing less than ninety pounds, Miss Sadie wouldn't have had the strength to pull the lower seat out and stash something behind it, but they pulled it out anyway.

They felt around behind the dashboard; they looked in the glove compartment; they examined the roof liner as best as they could without removing it. They opened the trunk and rifled through a rusted green toolbox, they looked under the floor mats, and even inspected the ashtrays.

"You c-couldn't git a big envelope in them little bitty ashtrays," said Sammy.

"True!" he agreed.

Their labors, he knew, were rudimentary. All the places they looked would have been the places Miss Sadie could easily access, but Miss Sadie was no dummy. She wouldn't have hidden nine thousand dollars where any Tom, Dick, or Harry could stumble across it.

He remembered George Gaynor talking about the jewels hidden in the oil pan of a Packard, but Miss Sadie, for all her savvy, was not the oil pan type.

"Nothing," he said to Andrew, who was looking his usual trim and urbane self, while lamenting the downward spiral of the dollar and the upward spiral of the pound.

"We probably shouldn't mention this to anyone," he suggested to Andrew.

"I agree completely."

"Tony said you may be having it restored?"

"I looked into it a few months ago. Something nostalgic for the Independence Day parades! However, at several thousand dollars to bring it into mint condition, and the economy in its present state . . ."

"Indeed. How's business at the Oxford?"

"Slow. The good stuff is harder and harder to find. How's life in the country?"

"Slow," he said, chuckling.

"Law, lookit how you've growed!"

"J. C. Hogan, Percy Mosely, Mule Skinner, Lew Boyd—meet Sammy Barlowe, Dooley's brother."

"No way!" said Percy. "I took 'im for Dooley."

"Set down, set down," said Lew, clapping Sammy on the back. "Let me treat you to a Coke an' a pack of Nabs."

"I'll kick in a bag of chips," said Mule. "You want sour cream or barbecue?"

"B-barbecue," said Sammy.

"I thought we'd have lunch in Wesley," said Father Tim.

"Don't go over there an' fling your money around." Percy dropped a half dollar in the slot of the vending machine. "Keep y'r b'iness at home is what I always told my customers."

A Moon Pie thunked into view; Percy handed it off to Sammy. "On me!"

Father Tim eyed the Moon Pie with some disdain. "We were going to the all-you-can-eat salad bar in Wesley."

Percy rolled his eyes. "This boy don't need a salad bar, he needs somethin' to put *meat* on 'is bones! Ain't that right, Sammy?"

"They got another word out of Edith Mallory." Conversation froze; J.C. looked around at the assembly, relishing his moment.

"Spit it out, buddyroe."

"Said she rolled into 'er breakfast room th' other mornin', looked her people dead in th' eye, an' said . . ." J.C. leaned back in his plastic chair and milked the pause.

"He's doin' it again," said Mule. "Come on, dadgummit."

"An' said . . . 'God *is*.'"

"God is what?" asked Percy.

J.C. shrugged. "That was it. All she wrote."

"Could have been a complete sentence," said Father Tim. For Edith Mallory, those two words alone would be an astonishing affirmation.

"Prob'ly tryin' to say God is one mean so-an'-so for droppin' a ceilin' on 'er head. Who knows? Who *cares*?" Percy's estimation of his former landlady was decidedly on the low side. "How's that little church comin' along?"

"Growing! Attendance is up one hundred percent."

"No way," said Mule.

"I'll be dogged," said Percy.

"They ain't got a t-toilet," said Sammy. "Have t' use th' b-bushes."

Hee haws, thigh slapping, general hilarity.

Lew Boyd stepped in from the grease pit.

"That's what I like to see at Lew Boyd's Exxon," he said. "People enjoyin' theirselves."

They schlepped the whole caboodle into the kitchen until it could be sorted through tomorrow morning: seeds, seedlings, seed pots, planting mix, an English garden spade, a set of tiller tines, fifty pounds of organic fertilizer, four sport shirts, four T-shirts, a sweatshirt with a hood, two pairs of khaki pants, two pairs of jeans, a dozen pairs of socks, tennis shoes, a V-neck sweater, a windbreaker, two packages of underwear, a case of Cheerwine, and, in readiness for Lily's visit tomorrow, four sacks of groceries.

He'd dropped Emma's eggs at Lew's; left a dozen in Esther's screen door with a note; gone by to see Uncle Billy, who was sleeping; and stopped on the highway for a sack of burger combos, which they devoured to the last fry before leaving the town limits. As for Sammy's haircut, no cigar.

He was killed, and so was Sammy. At eight o'clock, they dragged up the stairs to bed, maxed to the gills.

"*Lily?*" he said, opening the back door.

"No, sir, it's Delphinium, you c'n call me Del. Glad to meet you." The tall, well-built woman gripped his hand in an iron clasp— was that one of his knuckles breaking?— and swept by him with a bucketful of cleaning rags.

Del who pulls furniture out from walls! Who upends chairs on tables! Who beats rugs . . . "But I thought Lily . . ."

"Lily's sick as a dog. Puking!" said Del. "Want t' show me what you'uns need done?"

He didn't know how Del would go down with his wife; Cynthia may not like the furniture pulled out and the rugs beaten.

"I've got a surprise," he told Cynthia as she came along the hall to the kitchen.

"You're white as a sheet."

"You may not like it."

"Of course I'll like it; I love surprises."

"It was supposed to be Lily," he whispered.

"Supposed to be Lily?"

"But it's Del."

"Del?"

"She pulls furniture out from the walls and can't cook to save her life."

"Timothy, why are you whispering? And what are you talking about?"

He threw up his hands, stricken. "I hired Lily to help you, but she's puking and sent Del."

"One of the Flower Girls! Is she in the kitchen?"

"She's very tall," he said.

He came out the backdoor at a trot, and not a minute too soon. Del had just whipped on a head rag and was ready to roll.

"Lloyd, how long do you think you'll be with us?"

"You know we've got t' tear th' rest of y'r chimney down t' where it goes t' two-brick wide. We'll be layin' two-brick wide all th' way to th' top this time."

"Right."

"Then you'll have t' get y'r flue put in." Lloyd gazed at the sky. "If th' weather holds like this, which it won't, prob'ly take about six weeks."

"I've been meaning to ask—can all your work be done from the outside? I'm sure my wife is hoping as much."

"'Fraid not. Once we get goin', there'll be a good bit of in an' out."

He positively roared out of the driveway and onto the state road.

The new wayside pulpit message went by him in a blur.

"Thirty-eight across; the clue is baloney," said Agnes. Her glasses sat near the tip of her nose as she pored over the folded newspaper with great concentration. "Thirteen letters."

They'd had their signing lesson, and were on

to the crossword as they bumped along on their visitation rounds.

"What do you have so far?"

She told him.

"Umm." He'd never been good at the cross-word, especially if he couldn't look at the blasted thing. Nonetheless, he wanted to be helpful. "Remind me again about twenty-four down."

"Claim on property. Four letters. Starts with *L*."

"Lien!" he said.

"Of course! That gives us an *N* in thirty-eight across! Now we're getting somewhere."

"I'd like to stop and say hello to Jubal. What do you think?"

"Important business to tend to," she said, tapping the crossword with her pen. "I'll sit in the truck."

"God people's always a-*harryin'* me." Though Jubal looked fierce, he opened the door wider.

Father Tim eased across the threshold. "Brought you a dozen eggs." There was a mighty aroma of something cooking . . .

Jubal took the carton, suspicious, and lifted the lid. "I'll be dogged!" The old man's eyes brightened. "Brown Betties is what we called 'em when I was comin' up. I thank ye."

"You're mighty welcome."

"Don't be a-tryin' t' weasel in on me, now. Preachers are bad t' weasel in on a man."

"Hope you enjoy them!"

"They'll go good with th' 'coon I shot last e'nin'. That's him a-cookin'."

"Coon?" He realized he was backing over the threshold.

"A whopper."

"Aha!"

"I once boughted a coon dog, but hit turned out a possum dog."

"Got to scurry, Jubal."

Jubal squinted at him. "You ain't up here t' git a bridge put o'er th' creek, are ye?"

"I hadn't given it any thought."

"We don't want ary bridge o'er th' creek; they'd be people a-swarmin' ever' whichaway. Nossir, we don't want no bridges an' don't ye be a-tryin' t' give us none."

"You can count on me!"

He stepped off the porch into the yard. "I'll drop in again if you don't mind, bring you some more Brown Betties." *You're in my prayers,* he almost said, but caught himself. "By the way, anytime you have a spare squirrel or two, Miss Martha said she'd sure like to have a couple."

Jubal's eyes narrowed. "Tell 'at ol' woman t' shoot 'er own dadgone squirrel!"

"Come to think of it, I believe she might swap you a pie, or maybe a batch of cookies still warm from the oven."

Jubal's jaw dropped.

"Take care of yourself, now!"

He hastened to the truck, his face about to bust from grinning.

"Miss Agnes, we might be working this puzzle 'til Judgment Day. We only have three letters in thirty-eight across."

"It'll be finished tonight!" she said, confident. "But I'd covet getting at least two more letters in thirty-eight across before we part. By the way, if there's time after church on Sunday, will you and Cynthia come and see Clarence's work?"

"We'd be honored."

"He's just gotten the biggest order he's ever had. It will require a great deal of him for many months."

"I'll pray for God to supply all his needs."

"So many boys to pray for," she said.

"And girls," he said, turning into Donny Luster's yard.

"You're wearing your yellow shoes!" said Father Tim.

"Mama says I c'n wear 'em one day b'sides Sunday. I picked t'day."

"They're mighty nice and shiny."

She bent low over her shoes, admiring. "I c'n near about see m'self; Donny he rubbed 'em with a biscuit."

"With a biscuit?"

"Mama says they's lard in a biscuit; hit makes shoes shiny."

"I'll remember that! That's a very handy tip."

"Mamaw Ruby teached Mama t' use a biscuit."

He sat in the chair beside the bed and took Dovey's hand; Agnes eased herself into a rocking chair.

"How is your mother, Dovey? Do you hear from her?"

Sissie stood by the bed and patted her mother's arm. "She'll be a-cryin' if you talk about Mamaw Ruby."

"Crying can be good," said Father Tim.

Tears ran along Dovey's cheeks and onto the pillow. "She's doin' fine," Dovey whispered. "She's turnin' fifty-two th' last of May."

"Mamaw Ruby teaches 'bout Jesus in th' prison house."

"Please hush, Sissie, an' let our comp'ny talk."

"I'd like to write her, if you'll give me her address."

"Sissie, git me Mama's address, an' bring th' medicine in m' cup."

Sissie trotted to the front of the trailer.

"Mama didn't go t' kill Daddy," said Dovey. "He'd beat 'er since we was little, an' she never done nothin' about it. Then he went t' beatin' me. She'd never picked up a gun in 'er life, but she took 'is twelve-gauge an' . . ."

She turned her head away from him. "Mama didn't go t' do it. He was beatin' me so bad . . ."

"I understand," he said. Perhaps he did; perhaps he didn't.

"Miss Martha, I have a confession to make."

"It's about time *clergy* started confessin'; I read th' newspapers, you know."

"Well, we don't want to go there, do we?"

"Certainly not in my house!" she said, affronted by the whole notion.

"I asked Jubal about sending you and Miss Mary a couple of squirrels."

"An' th' ol' so-an'-so refused."

Try as he might, he couldn't keep from grinning. "He did. Said let Miss Martha shoot her own."

To his glad surprise, Martha McKinney hooted with laughter.

"Now here's my confession," he said. "I told him I thought . . . I thought you might bake him a pie. You know—in exchange."

Miss Martha looked thunderstruck. He had stepped in it, big time.

She folded her arms across her ample bosom and looked down at him from on high. She was a mighty oak; he was a worm.

"Or, maybe"—he was back-pedaling, and no help for it—"a few cookies?"

Lower than a worm.

"A biscuit or two?"

"*Meddlin'*! If there's anything I can't tolerate, it's meddlin'! I spied evidence of this hopeless affliction when I first laid eyes on you!"

It was true. He was the worst meddler in the world. He bowed his head, resigned to this ineffable flaw in his character.

"Look!" said Miss Mary. "He's a-prayin'."

"He'd better be prayin'!"

He heard Agnes chuckling, Miss Mary giggling.

He looked up, as one about to be beheaded.

Miss Martha was as red in the face as a turkey gobbler, trying to hold back her laughter.

"You tell th' old dirt dauber I'll bake him a

blackberry pie, but if you ever go an' do such a thing again, I'll . . ."

"You'll . . . ?"

"I'll give you th' rollin' pin an' let you bake your own bloomin' pie!"

"Yes, *ma'am!*" he said, thankful to be among the living.

He'd known he wouldn't be at home, but he left a note and a carton of eggs on a shelf beside the door.

> *Dear Robert,*
> *There's more where these came from.*
> *We hope to see you at Holy Trinity on Sunday. Afterward is the Covered Dish, but no need to bring anything, we'll have a gracious plenty.*
> *Your friend in Christ,*
> Fr Kavanagh †

He'd fretted about the covered dish deal. Should he let Robert off the hook because he lived alone and probably didn't cook, or should he allow him to step up to the plate with the rest of the parish? In any case, the vicar would be bringing a ham; Lily would be baking a cake; his wife would be making enough potato salad for the Roman legions; and all would be well.

"Thank you," said Agnes when he returned to the truck.

He looked at her, curious, but didn't ask her meaning.

"How can I find Robert during the day?"

"He has an automotive repair shop in Lambert, about ten miles away. I haven't been there in years. Lloyd would know how to find it."

"I'd like to make a call soon. Want to come along?"

"I believe just the two of you would be best."

"Why did you thank me just now?"

She appeared oddly moved. "For meddling," she said.

The other people on their list hadn't been at home. At every stop, they left a new flyer, and inserted quite a few into roadside mailboxes.

Arriving at Meadowgate a little before three, he sat on the top step of the back porch, removed his brown loafer, and shook out what felt like a piece of driveway gravel. Through the screen door he heard Del and Cynthia talking.

"I seen y'r white cat at th' smokehouse."

"That's Violet. She was sunning herself."

"I'd keep 'er in if I was you."

"Why is that?"

"Bear."

"Bear?"

"Spotted one crossin' th' road th' other mornin'." Long silence, the rattle of a lid against a pot. "Then there's bobcat an' coyote."

"Certainly not!"

"Oh, yes, ma'am. Th' coyotes used t' didn' mess around these parts, but now they've come over th' mountain and sometimes carries off little animals, don't you know."

He heard his wife's sharp intake of breath.

"Course, I guess you heard 'bout th' painters."

"The painters?"

"*Wild* painters. They mostly live in th' mountains, but some has seen 'em in th' valley."

"What on earth is a wild painter?"

"A cat. Like in Africa, but diff'rent. They say they're extinct, but they ain't. You ought t' hear 'em scream. I ain't never heard 'em scream, but my brother Jack has. He said th' only way t' keep a painter from tearin' y' t' pieces is if you shuck off your clothes while you're runnin' an' drop a piece at a time. That gives 'em somethin' t' stop an' chew on so you can git away."

"Anything else I should know?"

"Hawks."

"Hawks?"

"Yes, ma'am. They've been known t' carry off little animals that cain't hardly fight back."

Bolting from the kitchen and slamming the screen door behind her, his wife nearly mowed him down on her way to the smokehouse.

"Fourteen," said Willie.

"Again?"

"Nineteen lambs, seven calves, fourteen eggs." Willie gave him one of his very rare grins. "Farmin' these days is all about numbers, ain't it?"

Though he dreaded the answer, the question had to be asked.

"How did Del do?"

"Absolutely *towering* strength. Have never seen her *equal*. Was a *blur* the livelong day."

"But how did she do?"

"I'm so *grateful,* darling, that you pulled all this together. It was *wonderful* of you."

"But?"

"If Del comes again, I'm leaving."

"I was afraid of that."

"Yanking up rugs, hauling them to the clothesline, beating them within an inch of their lives . . ."

He decided not to comment.

". . . screeching furniture across the floor, up on the stepladder polishing ceiling fixtures, scrubbing the countertops like there's no tomorrow . . ." His wife looked pale. "And *then* . . ."

"And then?"

". . . scaring the daylights out of me about bears and coyotes and an absolute *zoo* of creatures prowling around out there, including something called *wild painters.*"

"Panthers," he said.

"Panthers?"

"Local people say painter for panther."

He decided the timing wasn't right to mention that once Lloyd and his helper got going, there'd be—how had Lloyd put it?—a good bit of in and out.

CHAPTER ELEVEN

A Clean Heart

<No Kenneth or Kenny Barlowe in fed system.

<Absolutely cannot look into state systems right now, am up to kazoo.

<Snickers has ear infection, drops three x a day. <u>You should check Barnabas's ears on a regular basis.</u>

<Harold down with flu and home from P>O>. Don't feel so rosy myself. Remember to wear something on your head, it is still flu season big time.

<Going to Atlanta to see Catherine!!! for two weeks!!! Pray for Harold and Snickers who are helpless without Yours Truly.

<Can you <u>believe</u> what's going on in the Queen's family? Pray for her while you're at it.

<Emma

<P.S. Gene Bolick transferred from Charlotte to Mitford Hosp., better get over there.

•   •   •

<Dear Father Tim and Cynthia,

<We wanted to tell you the glad news about Morris Love.

<He has been invited to play the organ at St. John's Cathedral in New York City!

<We are overjoyed. There is talk of a bus trip from our own little St. John's. Otis will help underwrite. June 14. Let us know if you can possibly meet us in New York, we would be thrilled to death!

<Little Timothy growing like a weed. All here would love to see his namesake again.

<We pray faithfully for Sammy and Kenny, as you asked.

<With love as ever from Sam and Marian

•   •   •

<Dear Sam and Marian:

<To God be the glory, great things He hath done!

<Sammy arrived at our back door, we are taking things slowly. Continue him in your prayers. Kenny still unaccounted for. My new mountain parish a great blessing to Cynthia and me.

<We hope to see you after my year's tenure here.

<With great love and appreciation from both of us.

<Fr. Tim

• • •

<Hey, Dad—

<When are you going to get a cell phone?

<Dooley

• • •

<Hey, Buddy!

<When you get your truck.

<Love, Dad

• • •

<I'll program it for you.

<Tell Sammy I'll call him tonight.

<I hope things are working out.

•   •   •

<Things are working out.

<We look forward to our time together this summer.

<Sammy is going to load us up with okra.

•   •   •

<I pass.

•   •   •

<Dear Timothy,

<So here we are in our dotage, and, after years of busting rocks with the big guys, we find ourselves Priests of the Hindmost. You in a church with no facilities, much less a crank organ, and me in no church at all, reliant merely upon two trustworthy feet (now sporting a veritable array of bunions) and a truck with an engine older than the Bill of Rights. What on earth did we do—or fail to do? How have we offended?

<Just talking to hear my brain rattle, of course.
I must say I love this farflung mission work
better than all those years of coddling, and
being coddled by, the lukewarm. Forgive me!

<Come now, are you really above the clouds?
We are beneath a waterfall! The great pounding
and bellow of this fall is a godly tongue that I
cannot interpret with the mind, but somehow
understand with the heart.

<When the three of us first encamped here in a
four-room cabin, I thought the almighty roar of
it might drive me mad as a hatter (why are
hatters mad, anyway?). Now, if I'm away for a
day or two, as is the occasional case, I miss it
heartily!

<I was downhearted that you and Cynthia
weren't able to join this marvelous ministry—
Timothy, on my life, you would love it—but
then, I am happy that He has flung you out into
your own backyard, to accomplish His odd and
peculiar business.

<Perhaps when we are old and gray (I am
gray, but have thus far refused to be old),
we might sit by a fire in wing chairs (what

is it about the wing chair that seems so consoling?) and smoke a pipe and talk of the adventures with which He so generously endowed us in this short and wondrous life.

<Remember Abner? The boy who sent you that marvelous ark tableau which he carved without any training or example? He has surrendered his life to Christ, and I must tell you he is the finest of evangelists when we go calling around these hills and hollers. What a grand being he is, and has yet to become, in our Lord.

<In closing, I charge you with the task of <u>improving the frequency of your communications</u>! And for heaven's sake, as always, SEND MONEY.

Fr Harry

While he found e-mail pretty exciting stuff, snail mail continued to exert its charms—one of which was the required afternoon jaunt to the mailbox.

He read George Gaynor's handwritten letter as he trekked up the driveway, a biting April wind at his back.

Dear Father,

After all these years, I've discovered my niche. My job as Chaplain to the inmates of this somewhat remote prison is definitely what God has long prepared me for. Indeed, I believe my prison term was spiritual boot camp for what I'm doing today . . . proving once again what Paul told us in his second letter to the Thessalonians—in everything . . .

Have heard the good news from Hope and Scott. I plan to attend the wedding, and look forward to seeing you and Cynthia and Harley. It will be the first wedding, other than my own mistaken affair, that I've been part of since college. Best Man! Until I entered into relationship with Christ during the long sabbatical in your church attic, I was most assuredly Worst Man. His grace continues to astound and humble me.

Had a line from Pete Jamison, we keep in touch. I'll never forget your two-for-one deal. He is growing in faith, though beset, like most of us, with advancing one step and falling back two.

Hope says you've been given a mountain church that was closed for decades, and asked to get it going ASAP. You, Father, are the very one for such a call. He has girded you with strength,

*he has made your feet like hinds' feet, and set
you upon high places.*

Write when you can, mail is manna.

In His mercy,

George

It was the farm dogs' grooming day at the
kennel, thus only he and Barnabas answered
the knock at the door.

"It's me!" Lily announced. "I'm b–a–ack!"

"Thanks be to God!" he said. "I didn't know
who to expect, but I knew you wouldn't let me
down."

"Oh, nossir, I don't let people down if I can
he'p it."

"Are you recovered?"

"Good as new, didn't last hardly twenty-four
hours. Went th'ough me like seed corn th'ough
a goose."

Lily refrigerated her bottle of sweet tea,
stuffed her purse into the old pie safe, and put
on what appeared to be a nurse's mask. "Did
Del do you'uns a good job?"

He opted for strict diplomacy. "Better than
good!"

"She wore you'uns out, is what I'm guessin'.
Del wears us *all* out, bless 'er heart, but this

floor won't need scrubbin' for a month of Sundays!"

Violet trotted from under the kitchen table and wound herself around Lily's ankles.

"See there? Never fails. Ever' cat in creation rubs theirself ag'in' me. Shoo! Git! An' *stay* git!"

"Cynthia suggests you see what's on hand and cook whatever you think best. With the thought that there's a diabetic in the house." He hated saying it.

Lily tied on an apron. "No problem. My husband's got diabetes."

He felt oddly glad to hear of another poor sap who suffered this odious tribulation.

"They had t' cut off four of 'is toes."

"Good heavens!"

"But don't worry," she assured him, "it wadn't my cookin' that done it."

He and Willie sat on pallets of fresh straw, each giving a hungry lamb its bottle.

"Ever had a wife, Willie?"

"Had one."

"Ah."

"Gone t' glory. Th' best of th' lot. No replacement."

"I'm sorry. Want to eat with us tonight? We've got a fancy cook working today."

"Don't believe so, thank y'."

Father Tim stood, creaking in the knees, the hip joints, and the greater portion of the lower back. He wondered if he'd ever grow used to such dilapidation. . . .

"We'll send something over. Whether you need it or not."

There was Willie's grin again. "I'd be beholden."

"How'd it go?" he asked.

"Terrific! She's wonderful! Lovely meals in the freezer, the cake is beautiful, and I sent Sammy over to Willie's with a meat loaf."

"Not my old recipe, I devoutly hope."

"*Absolutely* not!" She laughed. "She even wanted to bake your ham for Sunday, but I said you insist on baking your own."

She peered at him. "Did you just sigh?"

"I've been thinking—I haven't been much of a granpaw lately."

"You've been busy being much of a vicar. Puny understands; we talked today. The girls are working hard in school, the boys are eating like dockhands, Joe Joe's working the night shift, and she's worn to a frazzle—precisely the way it always is with a houseful of tots.

Though heaven knows, I can't speak from experience."

"You always wanted children. . . ."

"Yes." She was silent for a time. "And now I have Dooley!" she said, brighter. "And Sammy—for as long as God gives him to us."

"How is it with you and Sammy?"

"It may be a long wait. Remember how long it took with Dooley?"

"I do."

"But I have time to wait."

"You're the best of the lot, Kavanagh."

"Thank you."

"No replacement," he said.

He pondered their talk as he walked Barnabas through the old horse pasture. As for how long Sammy would be with them—that was definitely God's department. In any case, a summer on the farm with his brother would be a very good thing.

They would simply take it as it comes, and go from there.

On Friday evening at Holy Trinity, sheets of rain lashed the windows, rattling the panes in their fragile mullions. On the lower branches of the rhododendron behind the stone wall, a male cardinal bent his crested head beneath his wing and waited out the storm with his mate.

Down the road and around the bend, 129 squirrel tails nailed to the logs of Jubal Adderholt's cabin whipped wildly in the blowing rain; smoke pouring from the chimney was snatched by the wind and driven hard toward the east where Donny Luster's double-wide was stationed.

Inside the trailer, images of a revolving sapphire necklace broke into colored blocks on the television screen; moments later, the screen went black. In the darkened front room, an unfiltered Camel burned down in the ashtray as Donny Luster sat looking out the window, seeing nothing. In their bedroom, Dovey and Sissie Gleason slept as close as spoons in a drawer, oblivious to the shuddering of the trailer on its pad of concrete blocks.

Two miles to the northwest, in the well-stocked yard of the McKinney sisters, the old watering trough filled up, overflowed, and ran into a ditch worn by years of overspill. On the porch, the orange and white cat hunkered under an ancient washing machine covered with a flapping tarp.

A half mile to the west, Robert Prichard's TV antenna was torn off the roof and flung into a stand of rotting rabbit hutches. It was briefly trapped among the hutches, then hurled down the slope behind the two-room house. It landed near a pile of stones dug from the black soil more than a century ago by someone wanting a corn patch, and came to rest on a maverick narcissus in full bloom.

Scornful of calendar dates or seasonal punctuality, spring was announcing its approach on the blue mountain ridges above the green river valley.

He hurried down the stairs, mindful of the honking of Canada geese flying over the house to the farm pond.

"Alleluia!" he said, struck by the scene in the kitchen window. The sill was lined with blue Mason jars of tulips: crimson, purple, buttery yellow, pink with splashes of lime green.

"They began opening this morning, I'm painting them like mad." His wife, who sat on her stool at the easel by the window, had a fetching daub of red on her chin. "Be off with you, Father, your deacon is busy at her own calling."

"Sammy's getting his seed in pots down at

the shed. Thought I'd blow in to see him, then I'm off to Holy Trinity. Agnes and I need to get our act together for teaching the prayer book. Also need to figure out what to do about our covered dish if the rain keeps up."

"The Weather Channel says rain through Saturday. But in case it's wrong, there's a folding table in the furnace room. I think it would fit behind the back pews."

"Brilliant! I'll schlep it up there today, in case."

"The Lord be with you, dearest!" She squinted at the stroke of color she was brushing onto the paper.

"And also with you!"

Nothing like a good, sound, liturgical send-off, he thought, noting a new spring in his step.

His mackintosh hung, dripping, on a nail as he stood and watched Sammy deftly tuck seeds into the black potting medium.

"'Is here's t'maters."

"How many plants will we put in?"

"I figure eight."

"There'll be you, Dooley, Willie, Blake, Cynthia, and myself, and we all like tomatoes. Will eight plants be enough?"

"Way enough. This here's p-peppers. An' 'at's eggplant. I s-sure ain't eatin' it, but Cynthia said you'uns do."

"What about cucumbers and squash?"

"Th' seed goes right in th' ground."

"Thank God for Lon Burtie. And for you, Sammy."

"You know I got t' bring all 'is stuff to th' house an' keep a grow light on it. Th' f-furnace room would work. Got t' have light 'n' heat."

"You're a wonder," he said, meaning it.

Sammy shrugged.

"What do you remember about Kenny?"

Sammy recited the liturgy of the Barlowe family. "Mama give 'im away f'r a g-gallon of whisky."

"Anything else?"

"Dooley said th' man that took 'im was n-named Ed Sikes."

"Dooley thinks Kenny would be eighteen."

"Kenny's t-two years older'n me. So, y-y-yeah."

"Anything special about his looks? Does he look like you and Dooley and Poo?"

"He l-l-looks more like . . . you know."

"Your dad."

"But he has hair like us."

"What else?"

"He's sh–shorter'n me."

The vicar chuckled. "Who isn't?"

"He's got a big ol' m–mole on 'is face . . ." Sammy thought. "On 'is left cheek. An' 'e's got a big ol' m–mole on 'is back, too. He'd m–make me scratch 'is back an' said he'd whip me good if I scratched 'is m–mole—but he didn't mean it, he was jis' jivin'."

"You know what I believe?"

"What?"

"I believe Kenny will find us, or we'll find him. I'm actually expecting that. But in the end, I have to let it all go to God; it's really His job."

"He ain't doin' too g–good, if y' ask m–me."

"Consider this. The Bible tells us that two sparrows once sold for a penny. Yet, one of them shall not fall to the ground without His knowing—and caring. If He cares about a sparrow, I'm inclined to believe He cares about me—and you—even more. How many hairs are on your head?"

Sammy made a face; he shrugged.

"God knows how many. Jesus says so, Himself—'The very hairs of your head are all numbered.'"

"I ain't believin' 'at."

"Here's the deal. He made you. He cares

about you. He loves you. He wants the best for you." Father Tim was quiet for moment; this was a lot to take in, even, sometimes, for himself.

"And because of all that, He even has a plan for you, for your life. That's why we can trust Him to do what's best when we pray the prayer that never fails."

"Wh-what prayer is 'at?"

"Thy will be done."

Squawking, the guineas chased each other around the barn in their annual zeal to make keets.

"You mean jis' let 'im do whatever 'e w-wants t' do?" Sammy was plenty irritated by the idea.

"That's it. Whatever He wants to do. Because what He wants to do is what's best for you. He can't do things any other way—that's how He's wired, you might say."

"Wh-what if I'd ask 'im t' f-find Kenny?"

"He knows exactly where Kenny is, of course."

"If 'e's s' good an' all, s-seems like 'e'd s-send 'im on."

"While we're at it, let's not forget what He's already done—we've got Dooley; we found Jessie; we found Poo. We found you."

He remembered his first sight of Sammy Barlowe, walking along a creek bed, his red hair a coronet of fire in the afternoon light.

"Four out of five, Sammy. Four out of five! Seems to me God has been very hard at work on the Barlowe case."

Sammy tore open a package of seeds. "I ain't prayin' nothin'. I tried it one time; I didn' g-git what I'd call a answer."

"It may not be the answer you're hoping for, but you can count on it to be the right answer."

Sammy looked at him, his eyes hard. "I ain't goin' t' do it."

"That's OK," said Father Tim. "I'll do it. And Cynthia. And Dooley." And Emma, he thought, and Buck and Pauline and Marian and Sam and Agnes and Clarence . . .

They had set up the table and covered it with a rose-colored cloth, which gave an uplifting new look to the small nave.

"We'll leave it there, rain or shine!" said the vicar. "Put our pew bulletins on it, and maybe a few books—start a lending library!"

"And won't a vase of tulips look lovely on that old cloth? Jessie and I used it at the schoolhouse; it's lain in a drawer these many years." She looked around the simple room with pleasure. "It's no venerable edifice with a Norman tower and stained glasswork, but it's wonderful, isn't it, Father?"

"It is, Agnes!" Indeed, he was ardently proud of Holy Trinity, though to some in his calling, it would be a mere crumb, an offense . . .

"Ready for a cup of tea?"

"More than ready."

The rain drummed steadily on the tin roof as Agnes withdrew the thermos from the basket, set two mugs on the seat of the front pew, and filled them with the steaming tea.

"I've been praying about it, Father, and I'm ready to tell you the rest of my story. If you're ready to hear it."

"Agnes, Agnes! Surely you jest." Rain on a tin roof. The smell of evergreens and leaf mold, beeswax and lemon polish. All that and a story, too. "Your Town Car had given out," he said, leaning back with the warm mug, "and you bought a truck."

She sat beside him, inhaling the scent of the tea.

"I'm afraid we'd tried to make a sow's ear out of a silk purse! Our old Town Car was a pathetic sight when we finally sold it! It went for forty dollars to a family who removed the interior fittings and used it for a storage unit. In their front yard, I might add! Years later, they began stringing it with Christmas lights—it became quite a tradition in these hills."

He chuckled. He could picture it as clearly as if he'd seen it with his own eyes.

"Quint Severs had never worked on trucks, so he sent me to a man who did. Rumor had it that he was something of a genius with all things mechanical; gifted, in a way. Unfortunately, our truck gave us many problems—we sometimes found ourselves as impoverished as our parishioners.

"I refused to ask my father for money; it was imperative to both Jessie and me that we depend upon the Lord for His providence. We were the poorest diocese in the state, and there was no reliable stream of funds coming from Asheville.

"Our new mechanic worked wonders. It was as if he'd joined our team, and was as eager as we to keep the truck going so we could ferry people to the doctor and the hospital—even to school."

Agnes looked up to the window above the altar. "Ah, Father . . ."

She turned to him and he saw, perhaps for the first time, the full span of years in her countenance. "I feel I should make a very long story short.

"I fell in love for the first time. With a man who was not a believer, and indeed, had ways about him which were . . ."

He watched her select her words with some care.

". . . coarse and cruel.

"We became . . . intimate. What can I say to you to defend my behavior? Nothing. I lost my head; I lost my heart. I was forty-five years old."

Agnes sat with her cup in her hands, as if turned to marble. Rain darkened the windows.

"I was devastated, of course, when I learned that I was . . ."

Agnes Merton was of another world and time, in which such truths were scarcely uttered.

"I understand," he said.

"John Newton wrote, 'Guilt has untuned my voice; the serpent's sin-envenomed sting has poisoned all my joys.'

"I could barely function. I felt that everything I stood for, everything I had done in His service, had come to less than nothing. I kept it from Jessie for as long as I possibly could, but my great distress could not be hidden. She demanded that I tell her everything. The news was in many ways as crushing to her as to me.

"She could not forgive me, Father.

"In the midst of all this, I was deeply concerned about my age. In those days, a woman in her forties was likely to be at risk in . . . bearing a child. And then we learned that the church and schoolhouse would soon be closed. No funds were available to keep them open.

"The world quite literally crashed around us; I felt myself wholly responsible before God. I had failed Jessie and Little Bertie. I had failed this parish. And certainly I had failed the Savior. As church doors closed throughout these mountains, I even believed I had caused God to punish the church for my sins. That was nonsense, of course, but then I was beset by every guilt imaginable. I became the dry bones of Ezekiel's field, with no one to prophesy His mercy and grace."

She sipped her tea. "The fifty-first psalm. Do you know it well, Father?"

"Well, indeed. During a dark hour in my own life, I learned to recite it from memory."

"Could we say it now?"

Together, they spoke the words of the psalmist.

"Have mercy on me, O God, according to your
    loving kindness;
In your great compassion, blot out my offenses.
Wash me through and through from my
    wickedness
And cleanse me from my sin.
For I know my transgressions, and my sin is
    ever before me.
Against you only have I sinned . . ."

Above the gorge, the clouds began to lift; a
shaft of sunlight shone upon the ridge.

"For behold, you look for truth deep within me,
And will make me understand wisdom
    secretly.
Purge me from my sin, and I shall be pure;
Wash me, and I shall be clean indeed.
Make me hear of joy and gladness,
That the body you have broken may rejoice.
Hide your face from my sins
And blot out my iniquities.
Create in me a clean heart, O God.
And renew a right spirit within me . . ."

"During that long Lenten season," she said,
"those words were ever on my lips. What I
couldn't know then, is that He did all that I im-

plored Him to do. But much time would pass before I could accept His love and forgiveness.

"My father knew how happy I'd been here. And when the diocese closed this and so many other church properties, he insisted on buying the schoolhouse for me, and the attached hundred acres.

"This posed yet another bitter conflict. I didn't wish to remain on the ridge; I wished to flee this place forever. Yet I couldn't refuse such a generous gift. I supposed that I might one day sell it, and be given the grace to forget all that had happened here.

"Jessie took Little Bertie and went back to her family. She was given a mission church in the west. The parting was almost unbearable—Jessie's coldness toward me, and Little Bertie clinging to me as to life itself."

He prayed for her silently as she paused, waiting to go on.

"I remembered hearing of a woman in Chicago who took in young women who . . .

"Grace Monroe was willing to take me in. I locked up the schoolhouse and asked Quint to watch over it. The truck was sold. I never spoke of my condition to . . . the father, and certainly not to my own father.

"I arrived in Chicago with three hundred and seventy-four dollars and a box of clothing.

"Grace was elderly and I was the last to enjoy the privilege of her wonderful compassion. I cooked for her and dusted her antique porcelains, and made myself as useful as I knew how.

"When Clarence was born, she asked us to stay. She loved Clarence very tenderly; when he was yet a tot, she taught him to be gentle with all that he touched.

"She began this patient instruction by giving him a rare piece of early Staffordshire, a milkmaid with a brown cow. She taught him to lift the piece with great care and dust beneath it.

"Over and over again, he did this under her watchful eye, with never a chip or a crack, Father, and he was but a toddler!

"All that love pouring into him is today poured out into his beautiful bowls and animals and walking canes."

"Cynthia and I look forward to seeing his work on Sunday."

"Have I worn you thin?" she asked, looking worn herself.

"Never. But perhaps we should save the rest of your story for another time. I feel this has taxed you."

"It taxes me still further to withhold it. Yes, there is more. Much more. But now we must talk about our teaching on Sunday! Thank you, Father, for hearing me. Your compassion is a great gift."

He signed the three words he'd signed to Cynthia that morning.

Her eyes brimmed with tears of relief as she signed them back.

CHAPTER TWELVE

Covered Dish

The contributions of early arrivals had been placed on the rose-colored cloth.

In the center of the table, Miss Martha's German chocolate cake was displayed on a footed stand next to Lily's three-layer triumph. Also present were Lloyd's foil-covered baked beans, Cynthia's potato salad made from Puny's recipe, Father Tim's scandal to the Baptists—a baked ham with bourbon sauce, Agnes's macaroni and cheese, and Granny's stuffed eggs.

"Granny," said the vicar, "how are stuffed eggs different from deviled?"

"Th' diff'rence is, I don't *call* 'em deviled," Granny declared. "They's enough devilment in this world."

"Amen!" he said.

At the far end of the folding table, the vicar's surprise gift stood tall and gleaming, perking into the air an aroma fondly cherished in church halls everywhere.

"French roast," he told Lloyd, tapping the percolator. "Freshly ground. Full bore."

"Hallelujah!" said Lloyd, who didn't think much of church coffee, generally speaking.

Sammy had cut an armload of budding branches from the surrounding woods, and delivered them to Cynthia for a table arrangement. Removing himself from the fray, the vicar trooped into the churchyard to greet new arrivals and contemplate the view with Granny. A chill wind had followed the long rain; the ocean of mountains shone clear, bright, and greening.

"Robert! Good morning to you!"

Robert wiped his right hand on his pant leg before shaking.

"Thank y' f'r th' eggs, I didn' bring nothin' f'r th' dinner."

"No need, we have plenty. Can you sing, Robert?"

"Ain't never tried."

"Try today! We've got to crank up the singing around here, to help keep us warm. Just

get in behind me and go for it. I'm not much
to listen to, but I can keep us on key at any rate.

"Sparkle! You're the very breath of spring."

"Yeller, blue, green, purple, an' pink, topped
off by a fleece jacket! If anybody's havin' a
tacky party today, I want to be th' winner!"

"Where's Wayne?"

"Down on his back, rollin' around under a
piece of junk he calls a car."

"Tell him to get up here, we need his fine
baritone."

"If Wayne Foster ever shows 'is face up here
ag'in, I'll drop over. He didn' know doodley-
squat about what was goin' on last Sunday. He
thought your kneelers was somethin' to prop
his feet up on."

"A good many Episcopalians think the same!
What is that heavenly aroma?"

Sparkle held forth her foil-covered contribution. "Meat loaf!" she declared. "My mama's
recipe. You will flat out *die* when you taste it."

"A terrible price to pay, but count me in."

As Agnes stepped outside to deposit a daddy
longlegs on a patch of moss, they saw Rooter
coming at a trot from the laurels.

"Which reminds me," Agnes told the vicar.
"The schoolhouse facilities are open; you may
wish to make an announcement."

"Looky here, Miss Agnes."

Rooter signed to Agnes, the first and second fingers of his right hand gesturing toward his eyes.

"Why, Rooter Hicks!" she said, clearly pleased.

"Y' know what I jis' said?" he asked the vicar.

"Not a clue."

"I said, 'See y' later, man.'"

"How did you learn that?" asked Agnes.

"I seen it in a book."

"A book!"

"At th' lib'ary at school. They got a whole lot of books on hand talkin'. With *pictures.* Looky here ag'in," he said, slightly curling four fingers, extending his thumb, and making a motion at his chin. "You know what 'at's sayin'?" he asked Agnes.

"You're saying 'Watch!'"

"Yeah. I'm goin' t' use 'at 'un when I want t' watch Clarence work on 'is bowls an' all."

"You're smart as a whip!"

"I ain't smart," said Rooter, offended.

"Quick, then," she declared. "You're very quick. And in any case," Agnes signed her words as she spoke, "I'm tickled pink."

"I'm goin' t' learn s'more of 'at stuff. I brung one of them books home."

"He don't like t' bring books home," said Granny. "Seein' as it must be special, I looked in it m'self."

"Well done!" said the vicar.

"But I couldn' make hide n'r hair of it."

Rooter's eyes brightened. "I'll teach y'!"

Father Tim sat down on the wall. "I've got an idea, Rooter. What if we put you in charge of teaching the congregation one simple hand sign every Sunday? Something everyone can do. That way, we'll all learn how to talk with Clarence."

Rooter looked astounded. "Y' mean stand up in front of all 'em people an' do what I jis' done?"

"Yes. Don't you think so, Agnes?"

"I do!"

"Next Sunday, you could teach 'How are you doing, man'—which you already know."

"Yep." Rooter signed what the vicar had said.

"The following Sunday, you could teach 'See you later, man.' And so on. Would that work for you?"

"I ain't standin' up in front of no people. No way."

"Why not?" asked Father Tim.

"'Cause . . ."—Rooter made a face—"'Cause they'd look at me."

"Right. Looking at you is the way they'd learn to talk to Clarence. Right now, the only people who talk to Clarence are his mother . . . and you. And maybe me . . . but only a little. Three people."

Rooter pondered this, then looked up at Agnes.

"You'd have t' do it with me."

"I'd be honored," she said. "Come now, it's time for worship."

The vicar saw his patient and affable crucifer waiting for him with the hand-carved cross. He signed the three words to Clarence, who grinned broadly and signed back. To Lloyd, standing by to ring the bell, he gave a thumbs-up.

Bong . . .

Bong . . .

Bong . . .

The sound shimmered out from the tower, across the gorge and dappled ridges.

Processing behind the cross to the altar, he realized he was missing Sissie.

"Thirty minutes," he said, checking his watch, "and you're on your way.

"Thanks to everyone who prepared nourishment for today's table of fellowship. I've had more than my share of such holy meals, and must tell you that today's offering was as good as it gets.

"I'd also like to thank those who enjoyed what was prepared and said so—that's an important contribution in itself, as any cook can tell you.

"Agnes informs me that this was Holy Trinity's first official dinner on the grounds in . . . how many years do you think, Rooter?"

"A hundred!"

"Good guess, Rooter. Miss Martha?"

"Forty-three years!"

"Forty-three years! And isn't it wondrous, that at the time of His blessed resurrection, Holy Trinity should also rise out of death into new life? Alleluia! Or, as Granny might say, hallelujah!"

Startled by unexpected recognition, Granny involuntarily lifted her hand and waved at the vicar.

"I grew up, primarily, in the Baptist Church, and love that pronunciation as well. However you say it—and both ways are correct—it feels good to again utter that glorious word of praise. And speaking of words . . .

"This morning, the Baptists, Methodists, Lutherans, and Presbyterians worshipped in a *sanctuary.* You worshipped this morning in a *nave,* and you entered the nave through a *narthex.*

"I see that Lloyd and Robert are sitting on the *gospel* side. And Agnes and the rest of you are sitting on the *epistle* side.

"These and other unique words—and traditions—make us a little different at Holy Trinity. Before Agnes and I talk next Sunday about our prayer book and, for example, the great help you'll find in the *rubrics,* we'll talk to-day about this building, God's house—which I believe we'll all come to love as a true home . . ."

"This is his treasure, Father."

In the dark, cool interior of the woodworking shop, Clarence reverently lifted the lid of the burnished mahogany chest, and revealed the contents of early handmade tools. The vicar caught his breath.

"W-wow," said Sammy.

"Ditto!" said Cynthia.

Clarence signed to them as Agnes spoke the interpretation.

"When Mama and I lived in Chicago, I went to a school for the deaf. I took a woodworking class and that's when I knew I wanted to work wood for the rest of my life."

Father Tim noted the unmistakable joy on the face of his crucifer.

"A really old man used to come and teach us special skills, like hand-carving a bowl instead of turning it on a lathe. He was ninety-four, and had this tool chest which he would bring to the shop for the students to look at. We couldn't touch any of the tools. But I really wanted to."

Clarence removed a tool from the chest and handed it to Sammy. He handed another to Cynthia and one to Father Tim.

"The man's name was George Monk, and the chest had come down in his family of woodworkers from Sheffield, England. Somehow Mr. Monk thought I was pretty good at woodworking, and one day after everybody had left the shop, he let me take all the tools from the box and handle them. He talked about how they were used, and told me he thought I was . . ."

Clarence dropped his eyes to the chest, awkward.

"Gifted!" Agnes explained. "He said Clarence was gifted."

His face flushed, Clarence signed again. "Mr. Monk didn't have any children," Agnes interpreted, "and when he died, the lawyer came over with the chest. I was eleven years old, it was the most important thing that ever happened to me."

Clarence appeared moved by this memory.

"Mr. Monk said it was better than any tool chest he'd seen in museums," explained Agnes. "We were deeply touched by his gesture of love and trust. Clarence says you're holding a gouge, Father. Cynthia, that is a socket chisel . . . do you see the maker's mark, John Green, just there? Sammy, that's a brad awl."

Clarence signed to Sammy.

"It was used to bore pilot holes for nails. The handle is mahogany, the ferrule is beech. The handle feels really nice in the hand; it was probably used by four different woodworkers before Mr. Monk inherited it."

Sammy pointed. "W-what's 'at?"

Agnes's fingers flew as she signed both questions and answers.

"A homemade brace or bitstock, it's for drilling holes."

"Do you use all 'is s-stuff when you work?"

"I used a lot of these tools on the pulpit, and on Mama's walking stick."

Father Tim was struck by the experience of Clarence's woodworking shop; it was like nothing he'd never seen. Every tool hung in its place with others of its kind, including an assortment of bench planes, braces, hollows, and rounds; wooden shelves held bread trays and dough bowls of buckeye and poplar. A broom stood propped against a caned chair on a swept pine floor. In the corner, afternoon light slanted onto a mysterious wooden contraption with a grave and solemn dignity.

Agnes leaned on her cane. "And over there is some of the lovely work inspired by Mr. Monk's influence."

They turned to the rear wall where walking canes with carved handles hung in rows. Beneath the canes, a menagerie of carved animals was crowded onto a trestle table.

The vicar picked up a black bear and held it in a shaft of light. He turned it this way and that, entranced. In truth, he'd never seen a bear—until now.

"Clarence has made a gift for each of you," said Agnes.

Clarence began handing the gifts around.

"For you, Father, a Gee-haw Whimmy Diddle. The Cherokee used it as a lie detector; Clarence will show you how to work it. For you, Cynthia, a Flipper Dinger, one tries to get the ball in the basket—and for you, Sammy, a Limber Jack who'll dance on his board 'til the cows come home. We hope these old mountain toys will be a great lot of fun."

Cynthia was beaming. "I'm having fun just hearing the names!"

As he left the churchyard, Father Tim took Agnes's hand, his heart infused with a kind of joy he hadn't known in years.

"You and Rooter teaching sign language, the pair of us teaching the prayer book . . . why, we'll be a regular university up here!"

"'And now in age I bud again,'" she said, quoting their mutually well-favored poet.

"'I once more smell the dew and rain!'" he responded. "By the way, what was thirty-eight across? Baloney was the clue, as I recall."

"Utter nonsense!"

"*That* would be a good clue for what the church is sometimes known to advocate."

Agnes's ironic smile couldn't be suppressed. "Surely you don't dwell on that bitter subject."

"Certainly not!" he said, grinning.

"Shall we take Sissie her Magic Markers and Violet books?" asked Cynthia as they clambered into the truck.

He looked at Sammy, who was wedged between Cynthia and the passenger door. "Will your seeds sprout without you, buddy?"

"Yeah. N-no problem."

Soon, he'd have to do with Sammy what he'd done with Dooley: begin the long and arduous trial of changing *yeah* into *yes, sir* and *yes, ma'am* and *no* into *no, sir* and *no, ma'am*. Such instruction had led to a battle royal with Dooley Barlowe, but for all the pain and aggravation on both their parts, the seed had sprouted and come to flower. Truth was, he should have discussed this with Sammy at the beginning . . .

"Consider it done!" he told his wife, turning left instead of right off the church lane.

"Did you talk Sparkle out of her grandmother's recipe?"

"Right here," he said, patting his jacket pocket. He would never put oatmeal in meat loaf again. No, indeed. Life was way too short.

Sissie answered the door in a T-shirt, pajama bottoms, and her yellow shoes. Her eyes were reddened and puffy.

"Mama's sleepin'," she said. "Granny's here t' make 'er eat, but she won't eat nothin'."

"You remember Cynthia." His wife didn't like formal titles; she was Cynthia to one and all.

"Hey," said Sissie, looking miserable.

"Hey, yourself. I brought you the books I promised." She handed Sissie copies of *Violet Comes to Stay* and *Violet Goes to the Country.*

Sissie studied the covers, silent.

"And here's your Magic Markers."

Sissie took the box, fretful. "I don' know what *is* Magi Markers."

"Where's Donny?" asked Father Tim.

"We don' know where 'e's at. Donny's drinkin'."

Preachers had the right, as it were, to drop by unannounced, but pressing to be invited in was another matter.

He and Cynthia looked at each other.

"Why don't you ask Sammy to wait for us," she said. "Perhaps he'd like to look for Indian pipes in the woods. And give me a few minutes with Dovey and Granny before you come in."

"You got t' eat, Mama."

"I don' want to, Sissie."

"You got to! Granny says you'll die if y' don't."

"Nossir," Granny argued. "I didn' say nothin' 'bout dyin'. I said she cain't live if she don't eat."

Sissie put her fists on her hips. "'At's th' same as dyin'!"

Sissie stomped to the bed. "Looky here, Mama, I'm goin' t' dance f'r you, OK? Turn y'r head an' look over here, I'm dancin' f'r you in m' yeller shoes. I'm dancin' f'r you, Mama! Please *eat*!"

"Come, Sissie." Father Tim held his arms out to her, and she came and sat on his lap, reluctant. "Dovey, there are some things we have to do whether we want to or not. You must take some nourishment."

"Bring me m' plate an' all, then."

"Hit's green beans an' mashed taters," said Sissie. "An' what else, Granny?"

"A little stew beef cooked plenty done, with some tasty broth."

"What's 'em red things?"

"Beets."

"She don' like beets."

Granny looked firm. "Beets is got *arn*. She needs arn if she's goin' t' git out of that bed."

Sissie jumped off his lap and took the plate from Granny.

"Arn, Mama, you need *arn,*" she said, proffering the plate.

"Help me up, then."

Cynthia helped Dovey sit up, and rearranged the pillows behind her. "After you eat, I'd like to brush your hair and help you change your pajamas. Would you like that?"

"Yes, ma'am."

"We'll send Father Tim outside. Will you drink some water?"

"Yes, ma'am, thank you. An' I need m' medicine. You can put water in m' pitcher if y' don't mind."

Cynthia went to the sink with the transferware pitcher, Sissie following with instructions.

"You got t' hold th' bottom real good, th' handle's been broke off an' pasted back two times. Mama's had it since she was little, an' all 'er pretty dishes, too. Her whole set's got a castle on it, with cows in th' yard an' a river, but it's near about all broke an' pasted back. Mamaw Ruby give it to 'er, Mama said maybe I could have it when I'm big."

"I wisht you'd take this young 'un on y'r rounds sometime," Granny told the vicar. "She never gits out t' hardly do nothin', stays pent up here like a bunny in a cage."

"Sissie, how would you like to come with Agnes and me one day—on our rounds?"

"What's y'r rounds?"

"We visit people. And talk. You like to talk."

"Oh, Lord help," said Granny. "She never hushes up!"

"Look!" said Sissie. "Mama took a bite! She's chewin'!"

He stepped outside with Granny where they found Rooter examining a worm crawling on his pant leg. They thumped down in plastic chairs that had seen more than a little weather.

"Where was you at?" Granny asked Rooter.

"You said don't come in, so I went up th' road an' found 'is worm."

"Well, don't set on it an' mess up y'r britches." Granny looked around at the small company, pleased with another chance to socialize. "We can watch th' cars go by!"

Though unable to find Indian pipes, Sammy staggered from the woods with a more valuable find. He thunked a large rock into the truck bed. "Hit'll catch th' garden gate when it swings back."

"Well done! Come and sit with us, buddy; we'll be going soon."

Sammy pulled up a chair next to Rooter, nodding to Granny.

"Did you'uns know Donny's mama shot 'is daddy?" Rooter asked the vicar. The worm traveled up his forearm.

"We know."

"Kilt 'im dead. An' I reckon y' know Robert kilt 'is granpaw? He was in jail a long time; Granny says longer'n I been alive."

"Don' talk about that awful mess," said Granny.

"Did you see him do it?" Father Tim asked Rooter.

Rooter picked the worm off his arm and studied it in his palm. "I wadn't alive when he done it."

"How do you know he did it?"

"Ol' Fred what lives in th' school bus said Robert done it, sure as fire. Ol' Fred's got voices in 'is head; he talks t' people that ain't even there."

"Have you been down to that school bus?" Granny looked fierce. "You know good 'n' well you ain't s'posed t' go down t' that school bus."

"You cain't whip me f'r doin' it, 'cause you cain't catch me."

"I'll have th' preacher here whip y' f'r me."

"No ma'am, I'm not in the whipping business. Let me ask you, Rooter, did Fred say he saw it happen?"

"He said he never seen it happen, but he was walkin' by on th' road an' heerd Robert an' 'is granpaw fightin', said he heered 'is granpaw holler out Robert's name."

"Did Fred testify in court, Granny? Do you know?"

"I don't keep up with trash, hit's hard enough keepin' up with decent people." Granny reached over and snatched Rooter by the hair of his head.

"Oww!" said Rooter.

"I'll ow y' worser'n this if y' go down there ag'in." Granny continued to grip a handful of Rooter's hair. "D'you hear me?"

Rooter looked at Sammy and Father Tim, abashed.

"Do you hear her, son?"

"I hear ye," he said to Granny.

If he'd spent the morning on the mountaintop, he now found himself in the valley, both literally and figuratively. He was spent.

He leaned back in the library wing chair across from his wife and closed his eyes.

They should have Sammy's little brother and sister out one weekend. He could pick them up in town, they'd relish seeing the lambs and chickens. Sammy needed the solace of blood kin. Try as he and Cynthia might, they couldn't give him that.

"How many eggs today?" asked his wife, yawning hugely.

He yawned back. "Same. Fourteen."

"They'll be stacking up in the fridge again, please take some on your rounds this week," she said. "Miss Martha must have used her full dozen in that German chocolate cake. And what a cake!"

"Don't talk about it," he said. He could have sworn Martha McKinney had baked a magnet into it, the way it had drawn him to the table time and again. By sheer grace alone, he'd managed to keep his distance, though he'd enjoyed a few crumbs of Lily's, in case she asked for an opinion.

"I don't think Dovey's problem is depression," she said.

"What do you think it is?" He'd walked through a deep vale of his own, and though he hadn't stayed in bed, he had darn well wanted to.

"It's a hunch, really. I feel her problem has its taproot in the physical or physiological. Perhaps the depression comes because her ailment isn't healing."

He pondered this, weary in every part. "How about a little nightcap?"

The dogs were snoring, Sammy was on the phone having his almost-nightly talk with Dooley . . .

"That would be perfect," she said. "Why don't *I* read to us?"

He willingly forked over the book. "This is

from 'Michael,' a wonderful poem by Words-
worth. It reminds me of the view from Holy
Trinity. Now that I've rediscovered the poem,
I'll always imagine sheep among the rocks.
Take it from where my thumb was."

Violet leapt into Cynthia's lap and settled
herself, as her mistress adjusted her glasses and
read:

"*The pastoral mountains front you, face to
      face,
But, courage! For around that boisterous brook
The mountains have all opened out
      themselves,
And made a hidden valley of their own.
No habitation can be seen; but they
Who journey thither find themselves alone
With a few sheep, with rocks and stones, and
      kites
That overhead are sailing in the sky.
It is in truth an utter solitude . . .*"

She looked at the fireplace where the plywood had been removed, and a ladder inserted
into the chimney. She noted the soot and cin-
ders that had fallen onto the hearth since Lily
vacuumed, and considered what Lloyd and his
helper said they'd be doing first thing Monday

morning. Then she looked at her husband, who had fallen asleep with his glasses pushed onto his head.

"Utter solitude, dearest!" She spoke as if he were wide awake. "Can you even imagine such a thing?"

He didn't know what to make of the decidedly attractive woman standing at their back door. She was wearing a blond wig or his nickname wasn't Slick Kavanagh—not to mention cowboy boots with pointed toes and an outfit with fringe that was definitely in motion.

"Hi! I'm Vi'let," she said, giving him a huge smile.

"Violet! I was expecting Lily."

"Oh, shoot, Lily's *ever*'body's fav'rite."

All well and good, he wanted to say, except she rarely shows up. How does she get to *be* everybody's favorite?

"She said she'll roll in at nine-thirty, on the dot. Her van had a flat tire; she had to call th' gas station 'cause her husband's in Hick'ry gettin' 'is heads ground. Since I was comin' this way, she asked me t' stop an' tell you; she don't carry a cell phone, you know. Can you imagine not carryin' a cell phone in t'day's fast-paced world?"

He could imagine it, actually.

"I'm on m' cell phone day an' *night,* seems like. How 'bout you?"

"I don't have a cell phone."

Her blue eyes appeared suddenly larger. "I ain't b'lievin' that!"

"But," he said, grumpy, "I'm going to *get* a cell phone."

"When?"

"In July."

"I'll help you program it when I do a fill-in for Lily. Well, got to fly; I'm on th' radio at twelve o'clock."

"On the radio?"

"Singin'." So saying, she began to sing. "'Delta Dawn, what's that flower you have on? . . .'"

He heard an odd noise, something like a small trumpet played by a small person.

"Oops, m' cell phone, there it goes! What'd I tell you?" She clattered down the steps. "High Country Lite, ten-forty on your dial! Have a great day! Hey, this is Vi'let, who's this . . . ?"

He noted that Lloyd and his helper stood transfixed, their mouths open.

"I always make up any time I miss!" Lily shouted as he came into the kitchen. Their erstwhile housekeeper trundled the vacuum cleaner across the wooden floor as his wife sat at her easel and appeared ready to jump out the window.

"Right," he shouted back. "Glad you made it safely!"

He noted that someone was in the fireplace, he saw work boots on the rung of the ladder that disappeared into the throat of the firebox.

"I'm out of here, Kavanagh. Off to see Lottie Greer and Homeless Hobbes. It's a visit way overdue. Need to pick up a couple of things for our hard-working gardener, and while I'm at it, Lloyd said he could use a trowel; his trusty blade just separated from its handle after twenty-five years. Think of that!"

"Got his money's worth!" said his wife, looking stoic.

"Three of the kneelers came in with loose seams in the Naugahyde, and have to be returned; thought I'd drop those at UPS. And Blake can't leave today, he's found foot rot in several ewes, which is bad business; I told him I'd pick up the treatment he needs at the vet in Wesley. And if there's time, I might pop over to Mitford and see Gene and Uncle Billy. Of course, I'd also like to get up to Lambert and look in on Robert Prichard . . ."

"Dearest."

"Yes?"

"You're in a lather."

He knew he was out of breath but he hadn't figured out why.

"Come with me," she said, taking him by the arm.

They trooped onto the porch and down the steps.

"Where are we going?" he asked.

"*Away!* Away from the charming *tap, tap, tap* of the trowels now *inside* the chimney and beneath my very nose! *Away* from the tormenting thunder of the vacuum cleaner, and poor Lily's thousand apologies for disappointing us yet again, and two laundry baskets piled to the ceiling with Sammy's muddy gardening clothes . . ."

Conciliatory, he let himself be dragged along like a sack of potatoes.

"*Away* from mounds of dog hair," she raved on, "and white cats who insist on running out of doors to be eaten by wild painters! *Away* from the commerce of calendars, and lambs that look like dogs in woolly pajamas and must be painted again and again, and most *especially* . . ."

They were trekking toward the sheep pasture, lickety-split, as if on the lam from some criminal act.

". . . away from a new deadline just foisted upon yours truly, which makes me furious with my obdurate, slave-driving, pinheaded editor! *Away!*"

"But away to where?"

"I have no idea. *None.* Furthermore, I don't even *want* an idea."

"Aha."

"Then again," she said, out of breath, "if I were to *get* an idea, it might be something like this. Away to peace. Away to solitude. Away to laughter!"

She stopped suddenly and sat in the grass.

He sat down beside her. "You're beautiful when you're angry." He'd read that line in a comic book when he was a boy. He'd always thought it a great line.

She burst into laughter and lay back in the grass.

"You've been going at a trot yourself, Timothy, just like you always did at Lord's Chapel and Whitecap. Even when you don't have a church, you go at a trot. It's the way you're wired, sweetheart. I'm not wired that way in the least, yet I find myself being swept along by the trot at which everyone else is going!"

He didn't want to race away when his wife was venting a dash of exasperation; she never raced away when he vented his. However, Miss Lottie wouldn't be around forever . . .

"Ireland next year," he said, patting her hand. "And Whitecap, for a long visit."

She sat up. "But it all seems a century away. Besides, we need something sweet and simple right now. Something . . . uncomplicated."

"Like our clergy retreats of yore?"

"Exactly! I mean, look over there . . . at that lovely little path leading into the woods. Wouldn't it be fun to 'journey thither,' as Mr. Wordsworth said, and explore it to the end?"

"I remember seeing that path when Dooley was home."

"I love the way the old fence is falling down on either side of the path, and vines are growing up the posts. There must have been a gate there—and think of the wonderful beds of moss we'd find along the creek. The creek does run into those woods, doesn't it?"

"I don't know."

"Timothy, we're living in the country like two bumps on a log. And I have no idea what to do about it!"

"I haven't seen Miss Lottie in more than a year. She's ninety, you know."

"Of course you must go." She stood up and brushed off her pants. "And I must call New York and thrash over this wrenching new production schedule, and get the drawing ready for FedEx by eleven o'clock, and decide what sort of pie Lily should bake today, and . . ."

"Cherry!" He creaked to a standing position. "Ask her to bake cherry and I'll kiss your ring."

"You big lug," she said. "Consider it done."

She kissed his cheek, then drew back and looked at him, sobered. "Forgive me. We have so much to be thankful for, yet I allow the vagaries of this good life to overwhelm me. You never seem to be overwhelmed."

"I can't believe that you've lived with me for nearly eight years, and can say that with a straight face."

"All right, then. But you handle it better."

"You handle it just fine, Kavanagh. Our Lord, Himself, had to get away from the vagaries of life. We'll explore the path next week. Let's set aside some time just for that."

"I'll bring the picnic basket," she said.

He felt his grin spreading. "And I'll bring the blanket."

After knocking on the door of her life-estate quarters at the back of the Greer general store, he inquired of the storekeeper.

"Miss Greer went out with a neighbor about an hour ago."

"Then she's still getting around!" Thank God he hadn't come too late.

"You bet."

"Her cat?"

"Gone to glory, as she says. Eighteen years old, that cat was!"

"I'll be darned. Well. Tim Kavanagh."

"Judd Baker from California. Me an' my wife, Cindy, bought this place a year ago, and decided to keep the Greer name. What do you think?"

He looked around. Definitely not the old store where he and Absalom had robbed the drink box and talked a blue streak; not the old store where he and Absalom had sat in the back rooms and eaten Miss Lottie's mashed potatoes and lamb with homemade mint jelly; and certainly not the store where a young Absalom had seen the choir of angels . . .

"Good! Oh, yes, very good. But . . ." He sighed without meaning to.

"But different," said the storekeeper, nodding wisely.

Homeless Hobbes wasn't at home, either.

His old confidant and one-man soup kitchen had relocated himself from a hut at the Creek to a small, white house by the side of a gravel road. A note of greeting was tacked on the wood surround of the screen door.

Dear Friend,

This is God's house. In my absence, you are welcome to sit on the porch and rest a while and drink from the tap to the right of the steps. In any case, I shall return at four o'clock on the afternoon of the 23rd. God bless you.

H. Hobbes

He penned a note of his own and stuck it in the mailbox attached to the porch railing.

Dear Homeless:

Once again, you have refused to live up to your name, and have got yourself a very fine dwelling!

I think of you often, and miss our conversations on what Jefferson called "antediluvian topics." I'm living down the road a piece and pastoring Holy Trinity on the crest of Wilson's

Ridge. Ten o'clock each Sunday morning. How I would relish seeing your face!

   In His great mercy,
   T. Kavanagh †

Here's one for you, my book-loving friend—by François Mauriac:

"If you would tell me the heart of a man, tell me not what he reads but what he rereads."

   Amen.

During his years as a priest, he'd gazed into countless pairs of eyes—some reflecting Christ's own love; many more guarded, or angry and distrustful. He read in Robert Prichard's eyes something he couldn't absolutely define. But there was hunger, certainly. Pleading, yes. And a terrible grief that was wrenching to look upon.

He gestured toward the faded lettering above the grease-pit door: Prichard Enterprises. "This is yours, then? Well done!"

Robert took a rag from his pocket and used it before he shook the vicar's hand.

"Thought I'd drop by and say hello. Beautiful country out here." Across the road from the auto shop, he saw the great swell of mountains rolling away to the west.

"I wanted to say we're glad to have you at Holy Trinity. Each and every one of our little handful is a blessing."

The vicar watched Robert continue to wipe his hands on the rag, uncertain. A visit from a parson often threw people off kilter.

"I'd like to see your shop, if you have time to show it."

"They ain't much t' see. I got a rack, a pit, no big deal."

"Looks like a vending machine over there. May I treat you to a cold drink? It's warming up today."

"I got t' git this Chevy van out of here by two o'clock. But yeah, that'd be OK. We can set over yonder." Robert jerked a thumb toward a bench under a stand of scrub pine.

"Sounds good. What'll you have?"

"Cheerwine."

The machine produced a Cheerwine, then he punched a button for a diet drink—he'd learned his lesson well.

They walked across the worn asphalt to the bench, and sat down. There was an awkward silence; Robert looked at him, defensive.

"I didn' do it, if that's what y're here about."

He would risk something by digging in, but he'd prayed about it, and here was his opening, plain as day. "I want to tell you that I don't believe you did it."

A squirrel raced up the tree behind them. Robert didn't respond to this declaration but toyed with his drink can.

"I ain't never talked about it much; it scares people t' think about it, 'specially when they think I done it."

"It took courage for you to come to Holy Trinity."

"Yeah."

"Can you tell me what happened?"

A muscle moved in Robert's jaw.

"Hit's hard. Hit's hard t' talk about."

"Let's just visit, then."

"Naw." Robert released his breath, as if he'd held it a long time. "I'll tell you.

"Me'n Paw had fought twicet. Both times about money. He'd borry off of me, then not pay it back. Said he didn't have no mem'ry of borryin' off of me. Th' last time was five hundred dollars I'd saved f'r a truck, you cain't hardly git t' work up here if you ain't got wheels.

"I went over to he'p 'im dress out a deer, an' had m' good deer knife on me; I'd carved m' initials on th' handle, R.P. After we skinned th' deer—it was a young 'un an' didn't take too long—I laid m' knife up on th' shelf in th' shed. Th' shed was right by th' house. Then we went in th' house t' git th' washtub. We was goin' t' load th' meat in it an' carry it out to th' smokehouse.

"Hit'd got t' rainin' pretty hard, an' Paw told me t' poke up th' fire, an' we set around f'r a little while. Paw he was drinkin', which was usual.

"I remember lookin' out th' winder an' seen somebody walk past. I couldn't see who it was f'r the rain, but it was a man wearin' some kind of a hat. I said looks like they's somebody out there, so 'e took 'is gun an' went out an' come back soaked to th' skin, said they ain't nobody out there, you've been a-drinkin.'

"I'd been drinkin', but he'd been drinkin' a lot worser. I said when're you goin' t' pay back m' money, he said they won't nothin' t' pay back. He said he was m' granpaw, he was blood, an' blood don't have t' pay back. We got t' hollerin', an' he hit me pretty hard with a iron skillet. I knowed if I didn't git out of there, I'd knock 'is head off."

Robert looked at the vicar. "So I run.

"I took off for th' house. Then I remembered m' knife layin' up on th' shelf; I'd give thirty dollars f'r that knife."

Robert was folding his grease rag into a small square.

"Th' rain had slacked off when I headed back, an' when I got to th' shed, I heard somebody holler, 'Hush up talkin'.' Plus a word I ain't goin' t' say in front of a preacher.

"Then I heard Paw holler out, it was a sound you don't never want t' hear ag'in.

"Hit scared me s' bad, I didn't go in th' shed, I run back home. Th' next day, th' phone started ringin' at m' mama's house, people sayin' Paw had been killed. I reckon I must be stupid, I never thought they'd come after me. Th' sheriff an' two men come about dinnertime. Whoever it was had used my knife, but th' only fingerprints on it was mine.

"Th' sheriff seen th' place Paw hit me with th' skillet; hit was black an' blue an' swole up bad. I was a goner from th' minute they took me out of th' house.

"I don't mind tellin' y' that a time or two, I'd prayed for Paw t' die. Many a night I laid awake hatin' 'is guts f'r how he treated ever'body. But somehow . . ." The muscle clenched in Robert's jaw.

Father Tim waited.

"Somehow, I guess I . . . kind of loved 'im."

Robert put his head in his hand, weeping.

"If I'd've went back in there instead of runnin', I might could've saved 'im."

If he, Timothy Kavanagh, had hung in with his father at the end, instead of running . . .

He sat with Robert Prichard for what seemed a long time, praying silently. Then they got up and walked back to the shop.

"What about Fred who lives in the school bus?"

Robert frowned. "What about 'im?"

"Did he testify in court?"

"Said he heard me fightin' with Paw."

"How well did you know him?"

"I didn't hardly know 'im a'tall. He moved 'is bus down in there a couple of months b'fore it all happened. I heard Paw mention 'is name a time or two; maybe I met 'im on th' road, but I never knowed him t' speak of."

"Thank you for your trust, Robert. It means a lot to me. You're faithfully in my prayers."

"Thank y'."

"And I want to say again that I believe you."

"One or two does, maybe. Most don't. I guess it don't matter."

"It matters," said Father Tim. "It matters."

CHAPTER THIRTEEN

Flying the Coop

"Father?"

He glanced at the clock: four a.m.

"Can you come?"

"I'm on my way."

Though he'd been called out in the middle of the night only a dozen or so times in his priesthood, he resolutely adhered to a common practice of fire chiefs—he kept a shirt and pair of pants at the ready, and his shoes and socks by the bed.

He was entering the town limits when he realized he'd just blown past a Mitford police officer.

No need to be surprised, he thought, when he saw the blue light in his rearview mirror.

The officer stooped down to peer in the window. "You were haulin'."

Clearly, Rodney Underwood had begun hiring people twelve years old and under.

"I was, officer. I'm sorry." He adjusted his tab collar, to make sure the officer noticed he was clergy. "It's Uncle Billy." To his surprise, tears suddenly streamed down his cheeks.

"Uncle Billy?"

"One of the most important people in Mitford. He's dying; Dr. Harper called me to come."

"Don't let it happen again."

"Certainly not."

The young turk shook his head, as if greatly mystified.

"I don' know what it is about preachers. All y'all seem t' have a lead foot."

In his room at Mitford Hospital, Uncle Billy tried to recollect whichaway th' lawyer joke started off. Was th' lawyer a-drivin' down th' road when he hit a groundhog, or was he a-walkin' down th' road? An' was it a groundhog or was it a sow pig?

His joke tellin' days was givin' out, that's all they was to it.

He looked at the ceiling, which appeared to be thick with lowering clouds, and with something like geese flying south.

Winter must be a-comin'. Seem like winter done come a week or two ago, and here it was a-comin' ag'in, hit was enough t' rattle a man's brains th' way things kep' a-changin'.

He shivered suddenly and pulled the covers to his chin.

Snow clouds, that's what they was! Hit's goin' t' come a big snow or worser yet, a gulley-washin' rain.

Bill Watson! What are you yammering about?

He hadn't opened his trap, as far as he knowed. Out of the corner of his eye, he could see her settin' up in th' bed next t' his 'un, lookin' like a witch on a broom.

Did you say it's going to snow?

He lay as still as a buck in hunting season, and pressed his lips together so no words could escape.

Are you talking to yourself or to me, Bill Watson?

No, dadgummit, I ain't a-talkin' t' you, I ain't said a word t' you! Lord knows, you've fretted me 'til I'm wore to a nubbin. Now, *lay down!*

He squeezed his eyes shut even tighter, in case they popped open and she saw that he was awake.

In a little bit, he'd try an' git his mind back t' th' joke about th' lawyer, maybe he'd stir up a laugh or two if anybody come a-knockin' on th' door, like maybe Preacher Kavanagh.

He breathed easier, then, and opened his eyes and gazed again at the ceiling. The geese had disappeared.

Gone south!

Hush my mouth? squawked his wife.

He felt a chill go up his spine; he reckoned 'is wife was *a-readin' 'is mind*!

He'd never heered of such a low trick as that!

Lord have mercy, they was no end to it.

He didn't know when he realized he was passing up through a cloud, like a feather floating upward on a mild breeze.

There was light ahead, and the cloud felt like his toaster oven set on low, just nice and warm, as it was a long time ago in his mama's arms.

He kept his eyes squeezed shut so he wouldn't see the ceiling coming at him, then reckoned he must have floated right through it, as easy as you please.

The light was getting stronger now. He found it odd that it didn't hurt his eyes one bit; indeed, it felt good, like it was making his worn-out eyes brand-new . . .

Uncle Billy felt a hand close over his own. It was a touch that seemed familiar somehow . . .

The Almighty and merciful Lord . . .

Now, he was in the topmost branches of an apple tree, throwing apples down to his little sister, Maisie, and over yonder was his mama, waiting for him . . .

. . . grant thee pardon and remission of thy sins . . .

It seemed the words came from a very great distance . . .

He knew only that he was happy, very happy; his heart was about to burst. He tried to utter some word that would express the joy . . .

". . . and the grace and comfort of the Holy Spirit," said Father Tim. "Amen."

His voice sounded hollow in the empty room.

The following morning, Mitford learned that two of their own had been taken in the night.

William Benfield Watson had died in his sleep with a smile on his face, and in so doing, had attained the chief aim of every soul who desired a peaceful passing.

Less than an hour later, Gene Bolick died of the causal effects of an inoperable brain tumor. His wife, Esther, worn beyond telling, had left the hospital only a short time earlier at the insistence of the nursing staff.

It was Nurse Herman who stood at Gene's bedside when he spoke his last words.

"Tell Esther . . ."

Nurse Herman leaned down to hear his hoarse whisper.

". . . to pay the power bill."

Nurse Herman didn't know whether to share with Esther these pragmatic sentiments; the bereft widow might have hoped for something more.

Yet her greater concern was that Esther's power might, indeed, be shut off—not a good thing with so many family and friends dropping by.

Thus, with the blessing of Dr. Harper, she recited these last words to Esther, and was vastly relieved when the grieving and exhausted widow thanked her for the reminder.

"Are you sure that's all he said?" Esther mopped her eyes with a wadded-up section of hospital toilet paper.

As ardently as Nurse Herman wanted to report something truly heartwarming, the truth was the truth. "Yes, ma'am, that's all."

Indeed, she had long kept a memorized selection of made-up last words to offer a bereaved family—but only if absolutely, positively necessary.

In this case, *Tell Esther I love her* would have been very nice, though basic.

Tell Esther I appreciate all the years she devoted herself to my happiness would be more flowery, but not completely believable, as Mr. Bolick hadn't been the flowery type.

Tell Esther I'll see her in heaven would be tricky, as it was sometimes impossible to figure who was going to heaven and who was going to the other place.

And then there was her personal favorite: *Tell Esther she was the light of my life.*

She had heard of people saying amazing things as they passed. She would never forget being told in seventh grade what Thomas Edison had said: "It is very beautiful over there."

That sort of remark was comforting to those left behind; she wished dying patients would say things like that more often.

In any case, she had told Esther the plain truth and, happy to have these odd last words off her chest, reported further that Mr. Bolick had looked peaceful, very peaceful, and had not struggled at the end.

Willie handed the carton over the threshold. "Twelve."

"Twelve? Pretty big drop."

"Don't know what's got into 'em."

Willie had a lot to say grace over these days. Maybe it hadn't occurred to him to do it. So he'd do it himself.

Trekking across the yard with a plastic bag of cabbage leaves and apple peelings, he looked toward the vegetable patch. Sammy was trundling a wheelbarrow through the gate.

"Good job, *Sammy!*" he shouted, pumping his fist into the air. Sammy nodded, intent on his work. The vicar recalled that payday was right around the corner; that would bring a smile to their young gardener's face.

He lifted the latch and let himself into the hen house. Two on the roosting poles. One on a nest. Another pecking in the mash trough.

Four.

He went out, hooked the latch, and peered into the fenced lot.

Six. Eight. Ten. Twelve, thirteen. Chickens weren't much at holding still to be counted. Blast. Six. Eight. Ten. Eleven. Twelve.

Twelve.

Had he counted right?

He counted again.

Twelve.

Strange, he thought. Mystifying.

He opened the bag and tossed cabbage leaves into the lot; the hens scampered after them, gleeful. One by one, the remaining four exited by the opening in the side of the house and flew down the ramp as the shower of apple peelings fell through the wire at the top of the lot.

"Chick, chick, chick!" he called. That was how Peggy had taught him to gather the chickens when he was a boy. He remembered letting himself into the lot, unafraid of the rooster, and squatting down to look the whole caboodle in the eye.

What did chickens think? Were they stupid like some people said? They didn't seem stupid, but they did seem nervous. Did they know about dumplings, about the things that were going to happen to them? How did God get eggs into chickens?

At the conclusion of this scientific investigation, Peggy discovered he was crawling with lice. They were in his hair, in his clothes . . .

"Run to the washhouse!" said his horrified mother, "and wait for Peggy and me."

It was, in his opinion, a bitter remedy; he could remember the smell to this day. Sulfur!

Stuffing the empty bag in his pocket, he

struck out for the barn, where Willie was giving a lamb its bottle.

"I just went to the henhouse and counted. Didn't you say we had nineteen?"

Willie looked perplexed. "Yes, sir, I counted 'em m'self on New Year's Day."

"I counted twice. We've got twelve."

Willie looked shocked, then perplexed. "But that don't make no sense. I ain't seen any dead when I feed up."

Father Tim squatted next to Willie. "Any way they could be getting out? Flying the coop?"

"That little house is tight as a drum. No way out, no way in. An' I been looking aroun' th' fence t' see if anything's been diggin' under. Ain't nothin' diggin' under."

"So it couldn't be a mink?"

"We'd find feathers. Worser'n 'at, we'd hear th' uproar. When a fox or mink gits in a henhouse, chickens go t' squawkin'. They ain't no way anything could get in there without unlatchin' th' door like . . . like me'n you." This thought appeared to give Willie a bad turn.

"Should I leave the farm dogs out tonight?"

"Y'r farm dogs won't sleep out, they're inside dogs now. Miz Owen's done ruined 'em. Anyhow, all but one of 'em's too dadgone old t' do much barkin'."

"What about your dogs?"

"I don't let m' dogs run at night. We got coyote, y' know."

"So I've heard. Could anybody get by your kennel without stirring your dogs?"

"I guess if they was smart enough an' quiet enough, they could. At night, it ain't too hard f'r somebody t' slip in on chickens without 'em squawkin'. You can lift one off of th' roost pretty easy if you know how t' handle it."

"Do you know the neighbors?"

"Not t' speak of. Once in a while, I see a neighbor or two at Kirby's Store. But don' look like nobody'd steal chickens this day an' time."

"Right," said Father Tim, "all a man has to do is run to Wesley; he can get one already dressed for less than a buck and a half a pound." He shook his head, pondering. "So, how's this little fella coming along?"

Willie came as close to beaming as Father Tim had seen. "He'll be strappin'."

"Good. Keep your eyes peeled," said the vicar.

"Will do," said the shepherd, still looking perplexed.

"Have you ever noticed, Father, the peculiar surnames of certain clergy? When I first came here, Father Church was our priest, and I read an article recently by Father Paradise."

He chuckled. "In my time, I've known a Father Divine, a Bishop Steeple . . . oh, and a Bishop Bell. Old Bishop Bell! A force to be reckoned with! And let's see, there was Father Cross in Alabama. Wallace Cross, as I recall."

"What do you make of it?" she asked.

He laughed heartily. "I've never known what to make of it!"

They bumped along on their way to pick up Sissie. A day of stinging cold, though with bright sun and clear skies. Agnes huddled on the passenger side in a heavy, albeit threadbare, coat.

"Well, then, we'd best move along to more important considerations. What am I saying, Father?" Agnes signed something familiar, then something puzzling and strange. Their lessons for the week had begun.

"Law, look who's here! Sister, come see who's callin' on us!"

Miss Mary shuffled into the parlor, her cheeks flushed from the stove.

"It's Miss Sissie Gleason in her Sunday-go-to-meetin' shoes!" announced Miss Martha.

Miss Mary clapped her hands. "Oh, my

mercy! It's Miss Sissie Gleason in 'er Sunday-go-t'-meetin' shoes!"

Proud, Sissie stuck up one foot and then the other.

"And us without a crumb in th' house!" Miss Martha looked stricken. "Well, come in, come in, we'll find something sweet in th' painted cabinet; we always do."

"No, ma'am," he said, "we didn't come to eat, we came to make a delivery and see your smiling faces. Then we'll be on our way."

"You don't turn up at th' McKinney sisters without puttin' your feet under th' table. Come in th' kitchen where it's warm! This part of th' house has been closed off for five years, it's a morgue in here!"

"Five!" said Sissie. "That's how many I am!"

Miss Martha was herding them along like so many sheep, no matter how he and Agnes might protest. Truth be told, he was happy to be herded into the sisters' kitchen where they received a salutatory blast of oak-fired heat.

"Ladies, Cynthia estimates you used up your dozen for that splendid cake. Here's a replacement."

"Look at that! An answer to prayer if I ever saw one. Less than ten minutes ago, I said, Lord, there's nobody to carry us to the store for eggs and we're plumb out!"

"Plumb *out,*" affirmed Miss Mary.

"We can carry you to the store," he said. "Glad to."

"Where on earth would we all ride?" Miss Martha asked. "One of us would have to be tied on top, and it wouldn't be me!"

"It wouldn' be me!" piped Miss Mary.

"It wouldn' be me, neither!" announced Sissie, who was, nonetheless, intrigued by the idea.

"I'll be staying behind to poke up the fire," said Agnes, "so it wouldn't be me."

"And it absolutely, *positively* wouldn't be me," said the vicar. "I'm driving!"

They all had a good laugh.

"Thomas will carry us on Friday," declared Miss Martha, "which leaves us free to enjoy the afternoon. Got your tillin' done, Father?"

"Sammy just got the patch cleaned up and the rotted manure down; tilling is right around the corner. How about you?"

"I'm not putting in a garden this year. Too much bloomin' work!"

Miss Mary nodded furiously. "Too much bloomin' work!"

"Where's y'r painted cab'net at?"

"Now, Sissie," said Father Tim.

"It's in this little room right here behind the stove." Miss Martha opened the door, revealing a dark, unheated space with bead board walls and canned goods on shelves lined with oilcloth. "It's right back here; come on, don't fall over that tub of potatoes. I'll just switch on th' lightbulb."

He and Agnes had made their way to the door and saw the painted cabinet at the end of the small room.

Miss Martha pointed to it with pride. "Walnut off th' home place. Our papa made it, bless his soul."

"An' our mama painted it," said Miss Mary. "Bless hers, too!"

"Beautiful!" exclaimed Agnes.

"Papa was mighty grieved to see walnut painted over, I can tell you that! But he loved our dear mother, and the paint made it doubly precious in the end.

"See the cow on the right-hand door? That was mama's cow when she was growing up. Its name was Flower, she did this from memory. And over here's our house, the very one you're standing in. And here on the other door is Papa's bird dog, Ol' Mack, and his favorite wagon team."

"A treasure," said Father Tim. "Wonderfully executed!"

"What's in it?" demanded Sissie.

"Never mind that, young lady, pay attention while I tell you what's on it.

"Right here on the top drawer is Wilson's Creek; see it winding through the mountains? And over here's our little dog, Tater."

Sissie peered at the image of the spotted dog. "Does he live in th' house? I want t' see 'im."

"Tater passed on," said Miss Martha. "Fifty years ago this June."

"Johnny had a dog; its name was President Roosevelt, we called 'im Teddy . . ."

"Now! Bottom drawer, here's Miss Agnes's schoolhouse with the old bell—and over here by th' knob is . . . what's this, Sissie Gleason?"

"Th' church me'n' Granny goes to!"

"Yes! Holy Trinity. With a shake roof, before they put on the green tin."

"A gem!" said the vicar.

Sissie stomped her foot, impatient. "What's *in* y'r cab'net?"

"You stomp that foot again, miss, and you'll never lay eyes on what's in this cabinet. You hear me?" Miss Martha was ten feet tall.

"Yeah."

"Yes, *ma'am,*" instructed Miss Martha.

"Yes, ma'am, what's in y'r cab'net, *please!*"

Miss Martha looked at the vicar and sighed. "It's the squeakin' wheel that gets the grease," she said, opening the cabinet door.

"Oh, law! Enough apple butter to sink a ship! But no biscuit to put it on."

She closed the door and opened a drawer.

"Why, look here, Sister, I forgot about the cookies I baked on Saturday! Nice and chewy; oatmeal with raisin! I'd forget my head if it wasn't tied on. Sister, set out five glasses, we'll want milk with these cookies."

Oatmeal with raisin! His favorite!

He lingered with Miss Martha as her sister walked with Agnes and Sissie to the truck.

"What do you know about Donny?"

"The finest boy you'd ever want to meet, but a drinking problem. They say he doesn't drink right along, but, how do they say it? In binges. And no wonder, if you ask me."

"Did you know Robert Prichard's grandfather?"

"Everybody knew Cleve Prichard, and there's not a soul on this ridge that misses th' low-down sonofagun!"

"That's plain talking."

"He was nothin' but trouble. Only two people showed up at his funeral. Agnes Merton was one, because he used to work on her truck, and I can't recollect the other. You know

Robert says he didn't do it, and to tell the truth, I believe him!"

"I believe him, also."

"Some say a convicted murderer oughtn't to be in church."

"Who says that?"

"I've already spoken a wicked thing against the dead, and I'll not go tattlin' into the bargain!"

"What made Cleve Prichard low-down, as you say?"

"Gambling and drugs! Bringing lowlife into our little holler! Corrupting our young! Running that hateful homemade!"

"People still make whiskey?"

"They certainly do; it's not ancient history in *these* hills. But to be fair, I'll say this about Cleve Prichard—he didn't start out mean and no-account. He was a hard worker, and was making a good name for himself, but he was weak-minded and fell in with the wrong crowd."

The truck horn blared. Sissie, no doubt.

"Full of herself!" Miss Martha declared. "Dangles her participles! Needs a firm hand!"

Leanna Millwright was home, as were her seven sick and coughing children. She took a flyer and asked the vicar to drop by another day.

Rankin Cooper was looking for two cows that had gotten loose from the pasture; Mr. Cooper met the truck in the road as they slowed to turn into his driveway. He was a lapsed Baptist, he said, but a God-fearing Christian, and would consider visiting Holy Trinity if he could talk his wife into it, which he seriously doubted, as she stemmed from Methodists.

They left leaflets with everyone, and resupplied the store at the bridge. He was pleased that the owner, Hank Triplett, remembered him from a former visit.

"The little church on the ridge is up and running," the vicar told the several customers. "We welcome one and all!"

"It's th' church me 'n' Granny goes to," Sissie announced. "They always got cookies, an' sometimes they got *cake!*" She lifted one foot in case anyone wanted a closer look at her yellow shoes.

As they walked to the truck, Sissie reached up and took his hand.

"I like helpin' you'uns out," she said.

"Where is Donny today?" he asked Sissie as they drove along the road to the trailer.

"He's loggin'."

He didn't want to ask if he was still drinking. If he was working, he assumed things had settled down. God knows, drinking and logging would be a lethal combination.

"I'd like to talk to your mother in private."

"What's in private?"

"Just the two of us. Agnes?"

"We'll sit in the lawn chairs and work the puzzle," said Agnes.

"I've been thinking," he said. "I think forty-four across may be *heliotrope*."

"Of course! Father, you're a genius."

"What's a genius?" asked Sissie.

Wordless, Dovey offered her hand to him. He took it and held it in both of his. "Feeling any stronger?"

"I keep thinkin' I will be, but I ain't."

"I'd like to take you to see my friend, Doctor Harper, in Mitford."

"No, sir, I ain't goin' to another doctor."

"Do you want to get well?"

"More'n anything." Tears escaped along her cheeks. "I jis' need time for th' medicine t' work."

"You've been taking it a few months, Donny says."

"I don't want to go back ag'in. They was pokin' holes all over me an' drawin' blood. I one time fainted and would've fell out of th' chair but th' nurse grabbed ahold of me."

"Sissie needs you."

She withdrew her hand and stared at the ceiling.

"It may be hard to believe, Dovey, but God can use this time in your life."

"I don't see how."

"We don't need to see how, but to trust that He can, and will. Perhaps God is pruning you, Dovey. In the gospel of John, Jesus tells us He prunes every branch that bears fruit, that it might bear more fruit. Whatever His plan, God works in our lives for great good—if we ask Him to. Do you pray, Dovey?"

"All th' time."

"May I ask how you're praying?"

"For God t' let Mama come home."

"I'm praying that God will reveal the mystery of your illness. But I don't see how lying here can help Him do it."

She burst into tears and turned toward the wall, her shoulders heaving with sobs.

"I have a plan," he said, at last. "Will you trust God to help me carry it out?"

"I reckon," she whispered.

"Will you?" he insisted.

She turned in the bed and faced him. "Yes," she said. "Yes!"

There would be no viewing. Uncle Billy would be buried in the town cemetery next to the plot reserved long ago for Miss Rose Watson, née Porter, by her long-deceased brother.

Betty Craig, God bless her, would care for Miss Rose until he figured out what else might be done, but Betty wouldn't last long, he could tell by her voice.

He called Hope House again, pleading.

"We're not miracle workers, Father."

He was wasting his time, and theirs, too. He asked to be put through to the chaplain.

"Scott, Tim Kavanagh. I need a miracle."

"Shoot."

"Uncle Billy's gone and Miss Rose can't live alone. She has no relatives. Isn't there a room . . . ?"

"I hear we're full up, Father."

"But Miss Rose is the sister of Willard Porter, who built the town museum! Miss Sadie loved Willard Porter until her death, and I know she'd want Miss Rose to have a room at Hope House." He was babbling like a brook.

"I hear you. I wish I could help. I'm really sorry, Father. I'll commit to pray about this, and you can count on it."

He was making people miserable, including himself.

He dialed Esther Cunningham, the tough, no-nonsense retired mayor who'd served the town for sixteen, maybe eighteen years. It was Esther who'd seen to it that Miss Rose and Uncle Billy had heating oil in their tank, and who'd negotiated a first-rate life-estate apartment in the Victorian-style mansion cum town museum across from the monument.

Esther Cunningham was an army tank, she was *Tyrannosaurus rex,* she was . . .

Esther would help him out.

"This is Ray Cunnin'ham, husband of Esther, father of four, gran'daddy of twenty-two, an' great-gran'daddy of more'n I can count. We're on th' road again, prob'ly doin' th' Oregon Trail as we speak. Leave a message at th' tone, an' get out there an' see America *yourself.*" *Beep.*

He thought Sammy's eyes beautiful, and full of expression.

"Thanks for your hard work, buddy. We're glad to have you as our chief gardener."

Sammy studied his paycheck; a mockingbird sang from the top branches of a pear tree.

"We're going to Mitford on Friday. I'm conducting a funeral and attending one. You could come along if there's something you'd like to do in town."

"I'd like t' shoot some pool."

"No pool in Mitford. You'll have to wait 'til we go to Wesley."

Sammy shrugged.

"That's a fine wage you've earned, we're proud of you." He shook the boy's calloused hand. "Well done!"

Sammy looked at the ground.

Father Tim realized again that he had no idea what to do with a boy who'd been held at gunpoint by his own father. He suddenly felt his heart as leaden as Sammy's appeared to be. "I'll be glad to hold your earnings for you, if you'd like. That's how Dooley got his first bicycle, by saving up. You could buy a used car or truck . . ."

"Maybe," said Sammy. He folded the check and put it in his shirt pocket.

Father Tim indicated the tiller. "Remember to run it at half throttle, not wide open, and go over the beds twice. Call me if you need me, I'll be in the library."

He spoke to Lloyd, who was working today from the scaffolding.

"I'd appreciate it if you'd help keep an eye on our boy while you're out here."

"None too happy, looks like."

Maybe, just maybe, things would be brighter for Sammy when he got his peas and potatoes in. And certainly things would change when Dooley came home.

Father Tim looked at the date on his watch. He was definitely counting the days.

The loss of Uncle Billy signaled the end of an era. But an era of what? Something like innocence, he thought, poring over the burial service.

Uncle Billy's rich deposit of memory had included a time when kith and kin went barefoot in summer and, if money was short, even in winter; when pies and cobblers were always made from scratch and berries were picked from the fields; when young boys set forth with a gun or a trap or a fishing pole and toted home a meal, proud as any man to provision the family table; when the late-night whistle of a train still stirred the imagination and haunted the soul . . .

He sat at the desk in the Meadowgate library

and considered the jokes Uncle Billy had diligently rounded up over the years, and told to one and all. Of the legions, he remembered only the census taker and gas stove jokes, the latter worthy, in his personal opinion, of the Clean Joke Hall of Fame, if there was such a thing.

It would certainly be an unusual addition to the 1928 prayer book office for the burial of the dead, but he was following his heart on this one.

He called Miss Rose and asked permission, not an easy task right there. Then he leafed through the Mitford phone book, jotting down numbers.

He felt the moist, quick breath on his face. Good grief! He sat up and looked at the clock.

Two in the morning.

"OK, OK, I'm coming," he whispered to Barnabas. Mighty unusual behavior . . .

He rolled out of bed and put on his shoes and threw on his robe and trooped down the stairs behind his obviously frantic dog.

When he opened the backdoor, Barnabas shot from the kitchen like a ball from a cannon, and vanished into the moonless night. He heard the occupants of the henhouse squawking to high heaven, and Willie's dogs baying from their kennel.

"Barnabas!" he shouted in his pulpit voice.

The farm dogs were awake and also wanting outside. So be it. He opened the door and let the pack loose.

More barking and baying as the whole caboodle vanished into the black ink of early morning.

He'd acted hastily by not putting his dog on a leash, and also by letting the rest of the canines run wild in the night.

Del's reportage had them pretty nervous these days; truth be told, he'd rather not know about the perils of country life. Ignorance is bliss! he thought, recalling one of his mother's favorite proverbs.

He poured his first coffee of the morning and sat at the kitchen table—he and Cynthia had precisely an hour and a half of calm until Lloyd and Buster showed up.

"Could have been something he ate, God forbid, on our walk in the pasture."

Cynthia looked contrite. "I have a confession to make."

"Your priest will hear it, my child."

"I gave him a dab of gravy last night with a bite of tenderloin."

"Aha! The truth will out, Kavanagh!"

She covered her face with her hands in mock fear and peered at him through her fingers.

"Small bite?" he asked. "Big bite?"

"Big bite. He's a big dog."

"You know he's supposed to have dry food only."

She uncovered her face. "Right. And you're supposed to have only *sugar-free* cherry pie."

"Cynthia, Cynthia . . ."

"Life is short, Timothy. For us, for dogs . . ."

"True enough. But . . ."

"We've denied him for weeks now, and he really wanted a bite. For old times' sake, you might say. I guess it was a little too much for his system. So, sue me."

"If it hadn't been for that forbidden act, he wouldn't have come home with this." He displayed the evidence. "Of course, I have no idea what to make of it."

"Then I'm forgiven?"

"Absolutely forgiven. But next time . . ."

"Next time?"

He laughed. "You take him out at two in the morning!"

Small blue and white checks on a scrap of lightweight cotton. Shirt material.

As Barnabas snored under the table, Father Tim examined again the torn patch of cloth which his good dog had delivered on returning from his moonless run.

What if he carried forth this foolish notion and no one laughed? Would that dishonor the man they'd come to honor?

"Psalm fifteen," he told the graveside gathering, "says 'the cheerful heart hath a continual feast.' And Proverbs seventeen twenty-two asserts that 'a merry heart doeth good like a medicine.'

"Indeed, one of the translations of that proverb reads 'a cheerful disposition is good for your health; gloom and doom leave you bonetired.'

"Bill Watson spent his life modeling a better way to live, a healthier way, really, by inviting us to share in a continual feast of laughter. Sadder even than the loss of this old friend is that most of us never really got it, never quite understood the sweet importance of this simple, yet profound ministry in which he faithfully persevered.

"Indeed, the quality I loved best about our good brother was his faithful perseverance.

"When the tide seemed to turn against loving, he loved anyway. When doing the wrong thing was far easier than doing the right thing, he did the right thing anyway. And when circumstances sought to prevail against laughter, he laughed anyway.

"I'm reminded of how an ardent cook loves us with her cooking or baking, just as Esther Bolick has loved so many with her orange marmalade cakes. In the same way, Uncle Billy loved us with his jokes. And oh, how he *relished* making us laugh, *prayed* to make us laugh! And we did.

"I hope you'll pitch in with me to remember Bill Watson with a few of his favorite jokes. We have wept and we will weep again over the loss of his warm and loyal friendship. But I know he's safe in the arms of our Lord, Jesus Christ, precisely where God promises that each of His children will be after death.

"This wondrous truth is something to joyfully celebrate. And I invite us to celebrate with laughter. May its glad music waft heavenward, expressing our heartfelt gratitude for the unique and tender gift of William . . . Benfield . . . Watson."

He nodded to Old Man Mueller, who, only a few years ago, had regularly sat on the Porter place lawn with Uncle Billy and watched cars circle the monument.

The elderly man stood in his ancient jacket and best trousers and cleared his throat and looked around at the forty other souls gathered under the tent on this unseasonably hot day.

"Feller went to a doctor and told 'im what all was wrong."

He sneezed, and dug a beleaguered handkerchief from his pants pocket.

"So, th' doctor give 'im a whole lot of *ad*vice about how t' git well." He proceeded to blow his nose with considerable diligence.

"In a little bit, th' feller started t' leave an' the' doctor says, 'Hold on! You ain't paid me f'r my *ad*vice.' Feller says, 'That's right, b'cause I ain't goin' t' *take* it!'"

Old Man Mueller sat down hard on the metal folding chair, under which his dog, Luther, was sleeping. A gentle breeze moved beneath the tent.

I've stepped in it now, thought Father Tim. Not a soul laughed—or for that matter, even smiled. He prayed silently as Percy Mosely rose and straightened the collar of his knit shirt.

Percy wished to the dickens he'd worn a

jacket and tie, it hadn't even occurred to him until he stood up here to make a fool of himself. But if he was going to be a fool, he wanted to be the best fool he could possibly be—for Uncle Billy's sake. "Put your heart in it!" Father Tim had said.

"A deputy sheriff caught a tourist drivin' too fast, don't you know. Well, sir, he pulled th' tourist over an' said, 'Where're you from?' Th' tourist said, 'Chicago.' 'Don't try pullin' that stuff on me,' said th' deputy. 'Your license plate says Illinoise!'"

Percy swayed slightly on his feet as a wave of sheer terror passed over him. Had he done it? Had he told the joke? His mind was a blank. He sat down.

In the back row, the mayor's secretary giggled, but glanced at the coffin and clapped her hand over her mouth. The Mitford postmaster, whose mother lived in Illinois, chuckled.

The vicar crossed himself.

Solemn as a judge, J. C. Hogan rose to his feet and wiped his perspiring forehead with a handkerchief. He wouldn't do this for just anybody, no way, but he'd do it for Uncle Billy. In his opinion, Uncle Billy was an out-and-out hero to have lived with that old crone for a hundred years.

The editor buttoned the suit jacket he'd just unbuttoned; if he was a drinking man, he'd have had a little shooter before this thing got rolling. And what was he supposed to do, anyway? Talk like Uncle Billy, or talk like himself? He decided to do a combo deal.

"Did you hear the one about the guy who hit his first golf ball and made a hole in one? Well, sir, he th'owed that club down an' stomped off, said, 'Shoot, they ain't nothin' *to* this game, I *quit!*'"

The postmaster laughed out loud. The mayor's secretary cackled like a laying hen. Avis Packard, seated in the corner by the tent pole, let go with what sounded like a guffaw.

The golfers in the crowd had been identified.

Exhausted, J.C. thumped into the metal chair.

The vicar felt a rivulet of sweat running down his back. And where was his own laughter? He had blabbed on and on about the consolations of laughter, and not a peep out of yours truly who'd concocted this notion in the first place.

Mule Skinner stood, nodded to the crowd, took a deep breath, and cleared his throat. This was his favorite Uncle Billy joke, hands down, and he was honored to tell it—if he could re-

member it. That was the trick. When he'd prac-
ticed it last night on Fancy, he'd left a gaping hole
in the middle that made the punch line go south.

"A ol' man and a ol' woman was settin' on th'
porch, don't you know."

Heads nodded. This was one of Uncle Billy's
classics.

"Th' ol' woman said, 'You know what I'd like
t' have?' Ol' man said, 'What's 'at?'

"She says, 'A big ol' bowl of vaniller ice
cream with choc'late sauce an' nuts on top!'"

Uncle Billy, himself, couldn't do it better!
thought the vicar.

"He says, 'By jing, I'll jis' go down t' th' store
an' git us some.' She says, 'You better write that
down or you'll fergit it!' He says, 'I ain't goin' t'
fergit it.'

"Went to th' store, come back a good bit
later with a paper sack. Hands it over, she looks
in there, sees two ham san'wiches."

Several people sat slightly forward on their
folding chairs.

"She lifted th' top off one of them
san'wiches, says, 'Dadgummit, I told you you'd
fergit! I wanted mustard on mine!'"

The whole company roared with laughter,
save Miss Rose, who sat stiff and frowning on
the front row.

"That was my favorite Uncle Billy joke!" someone exclaimed.

Coot Hendrick stood for a moment then sat back down. He didn't think he could go through with this. But he didn't want to show disrespect to Uncle Billy's memory.

He stood again, cleared his throat, scratched himself—and went for it.

"A farmer was haulin' manure, don't you know, an' 'is truck broke down in front of a mental institution. One of th' patients, he leaned over th' fence an' said, 'What're you goin' t' do with that manure?'

"Farmer said, 'I'm goin' t' put it on my strawberries.'

"Feller said, 'We might be crazy, but we put whipped cream on ours!'"

Bingo! Laughter all around!

On the front row, Lew Boyd slapped his leg, a type of response the vicar knew Uncle Billy always valued.

Thank You, Lord!

Dr. Hoppy Harper unfolded himself from the metal chair like a carpenter's ruler. He was the tallest one beneath the tent, which inspired a good deal of respect right off the bat.

The town doctor turned to those assembled.

"Uncle Billy told this joke quite a few years

ago, when he and Miss Rose came to dinner at Father Tim's rectory. I've never forgotten that evening, for lots of reasons, and especially because another of my favorite patients was then living—Miss Sadie Baxter."

More nodding of heads. A few murmurs. Miss Sadie Baxter!

"Uncle Billy, I hope I don't let you down."

Hoppy shoved his hands into the sport coat he was wearing over his green scrubs.

"A fella wanted to learn to sky dive . . . don't you know. He goes to this school and he takes a few weeks of training, and pretty soon, it comes time to make his jump.

"So he goes up in this little plane and bails out, and down he shoots like a ton of bricks. He gets down a ways . . . don't you know, and starts pulling on his cord, but nothing happens. He's really traveling now, still pulling that cord. Nothing. Switches over to his emergency cord, same thing—nothing happens; he's looking at the tree tops. All of a sudden, here comes this other guy shootin' up from the ground like a rocket. And the guy going down says, 'Hey buddy, d'you know anything about parachutes?' And the one coming up says, 'Afraid not; d'you know anything about gas stoves?'"

Laughter *and* applause. This would be a tough act to follow.

Father Tim waited for the laughter to subside and stepped forward.

"A census taker was makin' 'is rounds, don't you know."

A burst of laughter.

"I love this one!" Hessie Mayhew whispered to the mayor's secretary.

"Well, sir, he went up to a house an' knocked an' a woman come to th' door. He said, 'How many young'uns you got, an' what're their names?'

"Woman starts countin' on her fingers, don't you know, says, 'We got Jenny an' Penny, they're ten. We got Hester an' Lester, they're twelve. We got Billie an' Willie, they're fourteen . . .'

"Census taker says . . ."

A large knot rose suddenly in his throat. Uncle Billy felt so near, so present that the vicar was jarred profoundly. And what in heaven's name did the census taker *say*? His wits had deserted him; he was sinking like a stone.

Miss Rose stood, clutching a handbag made in 1946 of cork rounds from the caps of soda pop bottles.

"Th' census taker *says*," she proclaimed at the top of her lungs, "'D'you mean t' tell me you got twins *ever' time*?'

"An' th' woman says, 'Law, no, they was *hundreds* of times we didn't git *nothin'*!'"

Cleansed somehow in spirit, and feeling an unexpected sense of renewal, those assembled watched the coffin being lowered into place. It was a graveside procedure scarcely seen nowadays, and one that signaled an indisputable finality.

"Unto Almighty God we commend the soul of our brother, William Benfield Watson, and commit his body to the ground; earth to earth, ashes to ashes, dust to dust; in sure and certain hope of the Resurrection unto eternal life, through our Lord Jesus Christ . . ."

He'd always felt daunted by Rose Watson's countenance, for it bore so clearly the marks of her illness. Indeed, it appeared as if some deep and terrible rage had surfaced, and hardened there for all to witness.

She wore a black cocktail hat of uncertain antiquity, and a black suit he remembered from their days at Lord's Chapel. It was made memorable by its padded shoulders from the forties, and a lapel that had been largely eaten away by moths.

Betty Craig gripped Miss Rose's arm, looking spent but encouraged, as people delivered their condolences and departed the graveside.

"Miss Rose . . ."

He took the old woman's cold hands, feeling frozen as a mullet himself. Though he believed he was somehow responsible for her well-being, he hadn't a clue how to proceed.

She threw back her head and mowed him down with her fierce gaze. "I saved your bloomin' neck!" she squawked.

"Yes, you did! By heaven, you did!"

He was suddenly laughing at his own miserable ineptness, and at the same time, weeping for her loss. "And God bless you for it!"

He found himself doing the unthinkable—he was hugging Rose Watson and patting her on the back for a fare-thee-well.

"Timothy, there's a chicken at the back door!"

"Invite it in."

"I'm serious."

He walked to the screen door and looked out to the porch.

One of their Rhode Island Reds.

"The plot thickens," he said.

He showed the swatch of cloth to Sammy.

"Look what Barnabas brought home this morning at two-thirty."

He thought Sammy looked oddly pale. A muscle twitched in his jaw.

"W–what about it?"

"Here's what I'm thinking. When Barnabas went out to do his business, the poacher happened to be at the hen house . . . ."

"What's a poacher?"

"It's a British term for someone who trespasses on a property to hunt or fish, or steal game. So, Barnabas starts barking, the poacher starts running, and bingo! Barnabas catches up and nabs a piece of his shirt."

"If chickens are g–gettin' out on their own like th'-th'-th' one this mornin', there p–prob'ly ain't any poacher. Th' chickens're jis' somehow . . ."—Sammy shrugged—". . . f–flyin' th' coop."

"I believe the poacher dropped the chicken," said the vicar.

"Whatever," said Sammy.

Chilly tonight.

He put a match to the paper; the flame devoured it, and licked at the kindling. As Cynthia worked at the kitchen table, and Sammy watched TV in his room, he had a few calls to make.

The smell of popcorn wafted from the kitchen. An open fire and popcorn! Blessings galore, he thought . . .

"I need a favor. I understand how pressured you are, and this one, frankly, is huge."

"I know you, Father; you'd do it for me."

"Yes," he said.

"If you hadn't done me the greatest of favors, I wouldn't be the happiest of men. What do you need?"

Father Tim outlined the plan.

"I'll come in my scrubs; I'm hardly out of them these days."

"I'll meet you at noon—at the crossroads of Farmer and Bentley, in the parking lot at Kirby's Store. I'm in a red truck, considerably faded."

"I'm considerably faded, myself, but I'll see you then."

Lord, he prayed again, *reveal the mystery; let it be a mystery no more . . .*

"Hey, son. I'm missing you; just wanted to hear your voice."

Dooley had never warmed to such outpourings; nonetheless, Father Tim found it best to speak these things. The loss of loved ones always made him reflect . . .

"I'll be done with finals May tenth, and home on the eleventh."

"We're praying about your finals; don't worry, you can nail them. You'll never guess what I've been thinking. Remember the time we walked to Mitford School together—it was your first day. You went ahead of me, then thought twice about it and asked me to walk up ahead. You didn't want anybody to think a preacher was following you around."

Dooley cackled. "Yeah, well, I got over it."

At the sound of the laughter he loved, Father Tim's spirit lifted up. He would tell him about the money this summer. Maybe they'd trek out to the sheep pasture and sit on the big rock by the pond, or maybe they'd sit in the library— Dooley could have the leather wing chair for this auspicious occasion. Shoot, they might even haul around a few dirt roads in the new truck.

In any case, nearly two million dollars would be an astounding reality to grapple with.

Lord, he prayed, *pick the time and place for this important revelation, and thank You for so constructing his character that he might bear the responsibility with grace . . .*

CHAPTER FOURTEEN

Hungry and Imperfect

By four-thirty in the afternoon, peas, potatoes, onions, lettuce, and chard had been planted in the fresh-turned loam. Several rows sprouted red twigs wrung from a dogwood tree by the henhouse to give new pea vines something to climb.

At ten twenty-five in the evening, the rain began. It was a soft, steady rain that pattered on the tin roof of the farmhouse, and chimed in the gutters.

Father Tim listened to the music, contented. Every gardener's dream, he thought.

"Are you sleeping?" asked Cynthia.

"Listening to the rain."

"I've been thinking."

"That's scary."

"Very funny. I think we need Sunday School at Holy Trinity."

"I agree. Just haven't gotten there, yet."

"I'm volunteering to teach Sissie and Rooter."

"That's wonderful!" He was always thrilled when his wife volunteered in a church he was serving. "You'll be a great blessing to them, to all of us."

"And surely others will come."

"Surely. And even if they don't . . ."

"But I wish there was something for Sammy," she said. "He'd never stoop to attending Sunday School with a five- and a nine-year-old."

"Unless . . ." he said.

"Unless?"

"Unless he was your teaching assistant."

"How do you mean?"

"If there was something he could do with gardening to illustrate your teaching . . . I don't know . . . a seed, growth, the story of new life . . . new life in Jesus . . ."

"I like it," she said. "Give me a couple of weeks, let me think it all through."

He took her warm hand and kissed it and held it to his cheek. "Lord, thank You for sending Your daughter into this white field.

ThankYou for showing herYour perfect way to teach the love, mercy, and grace of Your Son. And help us become children, ourselves, eager to receiveYour instruction.Through Christ our Lord . . ."

"Amen."

"Thank you," he said to his deacon.

"Thank you back."

"For what?"

"For being willing to serve at Holy Trinity. It's my favorite of all your churches."

"Why?"

"Because it's so hungry and imperfect."

Hungry and imperfect."Yes," he said, smiling in the dark."Yes!"

He'd been in a pool hall or two when he was a kid, and they didn't look like places to cultivate desirable qualities of character.Then again, didn't the venerable English country house always have a billiards table? It did. And wasn't billiards a game for gentlemen? Generally speaking, it was.

Maybe if he just changed the terminology, and possibly his long-prejudiced attitude . . .

"Would it be possible for me to, umm, hang with you at the pool hall?"

He saw Sammy glance at his offending

tab collar. Like Dooley, Sammy wasn't thrilled with the idea of a priest following him around.

"I don't have anything else to do in Wesley and I thought . . ."

"OK, I guess."

Father Tim noticed that the scar on Sammy's face reddened, as it often did when he was uneasy.

"We'll drop over to Mitford; I need to check on a couple of people. Then we'll head to Wesley. Need anything for the garden?"

Sammy took a list from his jeans pocket; it was heavily penciled in capital letters.

"Thinking ahead! And I just remembered—we need to find you a haircut, buddyroe."

"I can c-cut it, m'self, if th' s-s-scissors are sharp. S-Saturday."

He was feeling proud, very proud, of Sammy Barlowe. But why was he afraid to trust that? Though he didn't want to admit it, he was waiting for the other shoe to drop.

He let Sammy out at the grease pit and parked the truck at the rear of Lew's building. J.C. wheeled in beside him in a Subaru van.

"How's it going?" he asked J.C.

Didn't look like it was going so well; J.C. appeared sleepless and red-eyed, and his pants were definitely on the baggy side.

"How's what goin'?" J.C. snapped.

"You and Adele, of course. Did you go to the station and turn yourself in?" That had been a great idea, even if he said so himself.

"No way would I do that dumb stunt."

"So, did you take her flowers?"

"No."

"Out to dinner?"

"No."

"Anything?"

"I tried."

"What happened when you tried?"

"I can't do that stuff. There's no way." Tears brimmed suddenly in J.C.'s eyes.

"Let's get in the truck and talk," said the vicar.

"What for?"

Because you can't stand out here bawling in the parking lot, he wanted to say.

J.C. caught onto the strap and hauled himself into the seat.

Father Tim closed his door and took a deep breath. "I've laid off you all these years, buddy, but I need to ask you something. Do you pray?"

J.C. gazed out the open window of the passenger side. "One time, a long time ago, a guy called you up and asked you to recite that prayer. You remember?"

He did remember, and had often wondered

who the caller was. Andrew Gregory had dropped by the rectory that day; Puny had served them tea. "That was before caller ID, so I never knew . . ."

"It was me. Disguising my voice."

Father Tim swallowed down the lump in his throat.

"I got to tell you . . ." J.C. drew out his battered handkerchief and blew his nose. "It made a difference, I felt . . . different after I prayed that prayer."

"Different better or . . . ?"

"Yeah. Better. For a long time. But I lost it. Let it slip away. For a while there, I was prayin' my head off, I was . . . I was, you might say . . . gettin' to know God for the first time. Then I met Adele, and . . ." J.C. shrugged. "And things changed. I guess I thought that was all I needed."

"Is it?"

"No offense to Adele, but . . . I guess not."

They sat for a time in silence. "That's all I've got to say." J.C. stuffed the handkerchief in his pocket. "And don't be preachin' me a dadgum sermon about it."

Father Tim grinned. "Good timing. This is my day off."

J.C. put his hand on the door handle.

"I have an idea," said Father Tim. "If you're interested."

"I might be."

"Maybe you've been trying to hold on to Adele on your own terms. And you can't do it; you said so yourself. You know what I think?"

"What?"

"Give it up. Let it go. Ask God to help you say the things you can't say . . . do the things you can't do . . . feel the emotions you can't feel."

J.C. gave him a cold look.

"That's not a sermon, buddy. That's not even a homily."

"Why would He want to help me do stuff I ought to be doing on my own?"

"Because He loves you."

"No way am I believin' that."

"I felt the same for years. Why would He want to do anything for me, a spiritual basket case? But here's the deal. You can trust that He loves you, and trust that He wants to do good things for you . . . because He promises that in His Word."

J.C. stared out the window.

"What do you have to lose by trusting Him?"

The *Muse* editor toyed with the handle on his antiquated briefcase.

"Seriously. What?"

"Nothing."

Twenty years of hanging with this sourpuss, twenty years of putting up with each other's peculiarities, twenty years of digging down, at last, to bedrock . . .

"Maybe it's too late," said J.C.

"It's never too late," said the vicar, meaning it.

As he entered the lobby of Hope House, he decided he wouldn't mention the money, unless asked. Though Louella could be forgetful, she'd been stubbornly mindful about the ninety one-hundred-dollar bills presumably hidden in the Plymouth Belvedere.

As he recalled, the bills had been stacked and bound with a rubber band. What kind of bulk would ninety bills create?

"I'll have to get back to you," the bank manager told him. "Nobody's ever asked me to measure money."

Louella was sleeping in her chair. A female cardinal helped herself at the bird feeder beyond the window.

Though he had no time to waste, he didn't want to wake her. But then, he didn't want to leave and miss this visit, either. He'd left Sammy at Lew Boyd's, where Harley had offered Sammy ten bucks to give him a hand with balancing the tires on a Dodge Dart.

He coughed. Louella dozed on. The TV, turned to mute, flashed images of a morning talk show.

He walked around the room with a heavy tread. Louella sighed in her sleep.

"Miss Louella," he intoned in his pulpit voice, "that's a mighty pretty dress you're wearing. Have you had your neighbor down the hall ordering off the Internet again?"

Louella opened her eyes and furrowed her brow. She adjusted her glasses and leaned forward. "Who's that?"

"It's me, Father Tim!"

"Honey . . ."

Having flatly refused to call him Father, Louella had long ago elected to call him honey.

"Yes, ma'am?"

"What you doin' 'bout Miss Sadie's money?"

He thumped onto the low stool that seemed his very own. "Everything I can, but we couldn't find it."

"Who's we? Who you tellin' 'bout this?"

"Andrew Gregory, who owns the car."

"You can't be talkin' 'bout big money aroun' folks!"

"We looked everywhere we could without tearing it apart. We looked in the glove department, umm, compartment; we lifted up the floor mats; we pulled out the seats . . ."

"Pulled out th' seats? Miss Sadie couldn't've pulled out no seats; she was a little bitty thing!"

"True! But my point is, we looked everywhere it was possible to look."

Louella appeared reflective. "Is money goin' up or is it goin' down?"

"Going down at the present moment," he said, having just spoken with Dooley's money man.

"Miss Sadie sure wouldn't like it if it was goin' up an' her nine thousan' was layin' someplace hid."

"Did Miss Sadie hide things . . . normally?"

"Did Miss Sadie *hide* things? Honey, she couldn't've found her little gray head if it wadn't screwed on tight! She hid her pocketbook ever' single night in case a bu'glar broke in. We'd git up ever'day, eat a bite, an' go huntin' for that pocketbook.

"I'd say, 'Miss Sadie, why don't you hide it in th' *same place* so we don' have t' go chasin' after it ever' mornin'?' She say, 'Then ever' body'd know where t' *look* for it!'

"An' 'er car keys! Lord have mercy, if we

didn't run aroun' like chickens wit' their heads cut off lookin' for them keys, she never knowed where she'd hid 'em."

"She hid her *keys*?" Keys that weren't hidden at all were hard enough to locate . . .

"If a bu'glar broke in, she say he'd want that high-dollar car, he'd be lookin' for them keys first thing. Then there was them high-dollar pills she was takin', she hide *them* in 'er shoes. Miss Sadie never th'owed away a pair of shoes, honey! She had forty, fifty pair of shoes in that big closet, an' ol' Louella never knowed which pair t' look in."

"Why did she hide her medicine?"

"Said th' bug'lar could sell 'er pills on th' street."

"Aha."

"She got that notion off a TV show. See this ol' gray head?"

"Yes, ma'am."

"My hair was black as coal 'til I come back t' live wit' Miss Sadie!"

Louella laughed heartily, and he joined in.

"I loved Miss Sadie better'n jam an' bread; she help raise me! But let me tell you, she was a *han'ful* t' keep up wit'.

"One time Miss Olivia sent a big box of choc'lates. Oohee, it was a nice box. I wanted to eat it up quick so it wouldn' go to th' bad, but

Miss Sadie, she want to ration it out. A little dab here, a little dab there, and no secon' helpin's!

"I say, 'Miss Sadie, what if Jesus come, an' we ain't eat up this candy—it would all go to waste!'

"She say, 'Louella, if Jesus come, you won't be studyin' no candy, no way.'"

Louella closed her eyes and shook her head, chuckling.

"One night I was thinkin' 'bout them choc'lates, this was 'fore we moved to Miss Olivia's house. We was still climbin' them steps at Fernbank ever' night; was it eighteen steps or twenty-two?"

"I believe it was twenty-two."

"You know it took us half th' night t' get up there—that's why we started sleepin' in th' kitchen!"

"I remember." They'd all had sweet times in that kitchen.

"Honey, I got out of my bed in that little sewin' room, an' down I went, slow as m'lasses so's not to make th' steps creak. Got down there, went to huntin' for that box an' couldn' find it. No, sir, that box was *hid*! That was th' first time Miss Sadie hid somethin' from *me*!

"Lord have mercy! Now I go t' start back up, an' I cain't *git* up! That was b'fore my knee operation. I say to m'self, I say, Louella, you done for now, Lord, you got t' help me!"

"Suspenseful!" he said.

"I was at th' bottom of th' steps, lookin' up an' prayin' an' these ol' bad eyes seen a little angel way up on th' landin'. A little angel, all in white!"

He scooted his stool closer.

"I say, 'Thank You, Lord, for sendin' a angel t' he'p me!' An' Miss Sadie say, 'You gon' *need* a angel t' he'p you if you been messin' in them choc'lates!'"

Louella burst into laughter; the cardinal departed the feeder.

"She was comin' down t' git in 'em, 'erself!

"She went an' got that box an' we set on th' steps an' eat ever' one. She say, 'Louella, I been thinkin'. We ain't goin' t' live forever, we best make tracks'; an' I say, 'Amen!'

"Whatever was in them choc'lates, th' good Lord used it t' git us movin'. Up we went like two little chil'ren, an' couldn't sleep a wink th' whole night! We lived upstairs two days, we was so wore out from bein' bad!"

"Where had she hidden the box?"

"I don' know, but she got out some little tool or other t' do th' job. Miss Sadie was handy with that ol' green toolbox."

"After she hid the money, did she come back to the house with the envelope?"

"Sure she did, Miss Sadie don't throw nothin' away! She use somethin' 'til it fall apart!"

"We'll keep looking, Louella. I promise we'll do our best."

"Th' thing I don' like is all this *we* b'iness. Miss Sadie's money is *private* b'iness!"

"Yes, ma'am," he said, respectful.

"You be prayin' what t' do wit' all that money when you find it."

He stood and kissed her cheek. "I'm praying," he said.

She patted his hand, and looked at him fondly. "Now see what you done, honey, you gone an' made me miss my mornin' show."

Bud's Billiards was empty except for someone who appeared to be the manager.

Sammy glanced at the sign on the wall, dug in his pocket for four ones, and laid the cash on the counter.

"Th' table in th' corner," said the manager.

They watched Sammy as he walked to the table. Father Tim remembered his craving, during the early years with Dooley, to hear Dooley laugh. He craved now to see Sammy lose the defeated stoop in his shoulders.

"You want a beer or anything?"

"I'm fine, thanks."

"I personally don't drink. There's some as drinks their b'iness down th' toilet."

"True enough."

"You 'is daddy?"

"A family friend." The vicar extended his hand. "His name is Sammy and I'm Father Kavanagh."

They shook hands.

"You ain't goin' t' b'lieve my name; nobody does."

"Try me."

"Bud Wyzer."

"No way."

"Some say I was named for that sign over th' bar."

"Truth is definitely stranger than fiction."

"We don't get many preachers in here."

Father Tim watched Sammy take a cue stick from the rack and examine it.

"I always liked preachers."

"You did?" Not everybody could say that, more's the pity.

"My great uncle was a preacher. Every summer, me'n' my brother went down to Uncle Amos's little farm in th' valley an' stayed 'til school started. Kep' up with 'is horses, fed 'is cows, done a little cookin' for 'im when Aunt Bess passed."

"What kind of cooking?"

"I took to cookin' when I was ten or twelve.

Mostly barbecue, cole slaw, fried chicken. Like that."

"Your basics," said the vicar.

"Right. Where d'you preach at?"

Father Tim watched Sammy hunker over the table and sight the cue ball. "A little church in the wildwood, you might say. Holy Trinity on Wilson's Ridge. Episcopal."

"I don' know about nothin' but Baptists. I guess th' rest is all pretty different."

"The key is relationship with Jesus Christ. If we get that right, the differences usually matter less than we like to think."

Sammy loosened his arm and wrist with a couple of practice strokes of the cue, then stroked the ball, hard. In the empty room, the loud and sudden cracking sound was startling.

"Good grief! What did he just do?"

"Broke th' rack."

"I'm sorry, we'll certainly replace it."

Bud hooted with laughter. "Don't worry, nothin's busted."

Father Tim adjusted his glasses. He was needing new lenses, big time, but he could see the look on Sammy's face.

Sammy Barlowe liked shooting pool better than planting peas.

"He's a slick little shooter," said Bud. "Got a nice stroke."

"I wouldn't know, never shot pool."

"You ought t' try. Whoa, look at that."

"What?"

"Put a little high left English on th' cue ball an' drove th' three ball in th' upper right corner. Th' cue banked off three rails an' dropped th' seven in th' lower right corner."

"Aha."

Sammy appeared completely focused, oblivious to anything except the table.

"Looks like he knows how to concentrate. Th' problem with most shooters is, they cain't keep their mind on th' table."

The cue ball cracked against the object ball and sent it into the upper right pocket.

"Pretty nice. How long's 'e been shootin'?"

"A few years is my guess. At a place down in Holding."

Bud leaned against the end of the bar, squinting toward Sammy's table.

Sammy banked the four ball off the rail and put it in the side pocket. Then he hunkered his tall frame over the rail, and with his right hand made an open bridge for the cue stick.

He studied the table intently and fired his shot.

"Blam!" said Bud. "Sonofagun."

"That t-t-table ain't no g-good," Sammy told Bud.

"I don't see it held you back any."

"It m-must be settin' on a slope. You ought t' level it."

"It don't bother most people. But here's your money back."

Sammy looked annoyed. "Plus you got a couple of bad d-dimples in th' s-slate."

"You want t' keep shootin', that table on th' left is as level as level can git."

The door opened and four customers blew in, one carrying a leather case under his arm.

"There goes th' neighborhood," Bud told the vicar.

"Th' kid in th' blue jacket is Dunn Crawford, th' vice chancellor's boy. He's a smart ass with a big mouth, an' th' only customer I've got that carries his own cue stick."

Father Tim felt mildly uneasy. The new customers had somehow changed the way the room felt.

"Dunn's buddies call 'im Hook. He's a hustler that goes after th' country boys. Reels 'em in like fish."

Father Tim watched Dunn light a cigarette and eye Sammy. Sammy never looked up. His cue ball cracked against the two ball but missed the mark.

"Rattled in the pocket," said Bud.

Greek, thought the vicar. Croatian!

He and Bud watched Dunn watching Sammy, while the other three in Dunn's crowd hassled about who had paid for the beer last time.

"I'll lay you money ol' Hook's goin' to hustle your boy."

"Should I let Sammy know?"

"In life, you're goin' t' git hustled, they ain't no way around it. Maybe he'll learn a good lesson. Th' way I look at it, this game's about a whole lot more than pool, that's what keeps it in'erestin'."

"All them boys is college-ruint." Bud lit a cigarette, took a long drag, and exhaled through his nose.

Dunn had warmed up with a couple of games of partners' eight ball, and walked over to Sammy's table.

"Haven't seen you in here before. You shoot pretty good."

"Th-thanks," said Sammy. "Not g-good enough t' have m' own s-stick."

"Birthday gift from my dad. I'm pretty lousy, really. Bet you could teach me some stuff."

"Here it comes," Bud said under his breath.

Dunn made a couple of random shots on Sammy's table and missed both.

"Look, since I don't have much time, let's play best two out of three games of nine ball. For . . ." Dunn lowered his voice.

Sammy shrugged. "I don't know."

"Come on."

Sammy shrugged again. "OK, I guess."

Dunn removed the striped balls, except for the nine, which he racked with the others. "Go ahead and break 'em up if you want to."

Sammy lined up his break and stroked hard.

The balls careened around the table; the seven rolled in.

"Got to catch th' phone," said Bud. "You're on your own."

Father Tim climbed onto the stool and drank bottled water. Sammy's scar was blazing as they finished the game.

"Who won?" he asked when Bud came back to the end of the bar.

"Your boy. That means he'll break again."

Sammy broke the rack.

"Pretty nice. Two balls on th' break shot, an' a good leave on th' one ball. He's makin' a very soft stroke here, yeah, great, sinks th' one. Okay, he's got an easy shot at th' five ball to th' upper corner . . ."

Sammy bent over the table, his chin just above the cue stick, and made his shot.

"Stroked th' ball too hard," said Bud. "Rattled in th' pocket."

Dunn's buddies quit their own game, and walked across to the table on the left. Father Tim saw the look on their faces as they watched Sammy. Not friendly.

Dunn aimed at the five and put it away.

"Where 'is cue ball's at don't give 'im much of a shot at the six ball." Bud ground out his cigarette and watched Dunn bend over the table. Dunn stroked the cue ball with reverse English off the rail, just behind the six ball.

"Oh, yeah! Caromed off th' six ball into th' nine, right in front of th' side pocket. Boom. Game's over."

"Hey, Bud!" yelled one of the players. "Four beers and a deck of Marlboros!"

"Who won?"

"Hook."

The vicar took out his billfold. "I'll have another bottle of water when you get to it. Make it a double."

Dunn broke with a shot that drove the one, six, and seven balls into the pockets. He lined up the two ball, stroked, and put it in the side pocket.

"Pretty slick," said Bud.

Dunn attempted to bank the three ball the length of the table, but missed.

Sammy had nothing between the cue ball and the three, but other balls blocked a direct shot to a pocket.

"Cheese gits bindin' right here," said Bud.

Father Tim figured he didn't have to know the game to identify the feeling in the room. Tense.

Sammy aimed and stroked the cue ball using upper-right-hand English. The cue ball barely touched the three ball, then rolled off the cushion with an angle that drove it onto the nine ball. The nine rolled toward the corner pocket, glanced off the eight ball, and fell into the lower corner pocket.

"Done," said Bud.

The vicar couldn't tell much from the faces of the pool players, including Sammy's.

"What happened?"

"Your boy whipped ol' Hook." Bud turned toward the bar so nobody could see the grin on his face.

"You want a little summer job, I'd like t' talk to you," Bud told Sammy.

"He has a job," said the vicar. "He's a very fine gardener."

On the way home, he could feel it coming.

"I'd like t' work f'r Bud."

"How do you think you'd get there?"

Long silence. Looking straight ahead, Sammy finally answered. "You could take me."

Father Tim restrained himself from out-and-out hilarity, and merely chuckled.

"I skinned t-twenty bucks off 'is butt."

What Lon Burtie had told him about Sammy's gambling in the Wesley pool hall had, until now, gone from Father Tim's memory.

"I didn't know gambling would be going on today, I'm pretty dumb about these things. You're a fine player, Sammy; Bud says you're a natural. It'd be great to see you play for the thrill of the game. Let the game itself be the payoff."

"I like hustlin'. I like it even b-better when s-s-some smart ass thinks he's hustlin' m-me."

"You have a good job with good pay. You

don't have to hustle to put food on the table or take care of your dad like you once did. Money always changes things. It looks to me like pool is a great game, and it deserves better than that."

They drove in silence for a couple of miles. He'd better lay it out right now, not tomorrow, not next week when Sammy wanted to go to Wesley again.

"Here's how it has to be. I'll drive you to shoot a little pool now and again, but only on one condition: No gambling."

They drove the rest of the way in silence.

"You should see him shoot pool. Blew everybody away. The owner offered him a job!" He wasn't ready to share the rest of the story.

"Say what we will about their upbringing," said Cynthia, "the young Barlowes have some amazing capabilities. Where is he?"

"In the garden, seeing if anything's sprouting. Who showed up today?"

"Lily."

"Thank goodness!"

"Violet is on the docket for tomorrow."

"You know they say Violet sings as she works."

Cynthia wrinkled her brow. "Continually, do you think?"

"Not sure."

"I've got to move my easel, Timothy. The kitchen is tourist season at the Acropolis; it's the Mall of America! I can't keep doing this, and yet—that's where the north light comes in."

"Shall we go home to Mitford?"

She rubbed her forehead. "Ugh, I've had a splitting headache all day."

"We can work it out," he said. "We could have you back in your studio, with everything pretty much in place, in two days."

"No, I'd rather find a way to do my work and let everyone else do theirs."

"Remember our retreat? We could have it tomorrow—and try to figure something out."

She smiled, cheered. "I'll bring the picnic basket."

"And I'll bring the blanket," he said.

When Violet arrived at eight o'clock, she wasn't wearing her cowgirl outfit, but something that resembled, however vaguely, an Austrian dirndl.

"Why, look here! An Alpine milkmaid!"

"I got it at a yard sale for three dollars!" she said, twirling around to give the full effect. "I also yodel."

"*Yodel?*"

She threw her head back and demonstrated. "Idaleetleodleladitee, yeodleladitee, yeodle-ladeeeee!"

"I'll be darned!" he said, blushing. "Umm, please don't do that in the house; my wife works in the kitchen."

"No problem!" she said. "Did you hear me on th' radio?"

"I didn't. But give us a heads-up next time, and we'll try to listen in. By the way, we have a cat named Violet. She's around here somewhere."

"I'm crazy about cats. Lily don't like 'em; she sneezes her brains out. Shooee, what's 'at *smell?*"

"Creosote. Wind blew down part of our chimney. We're working on it. Do you have a family, Violet?"

"Oh, no, sir, I'm barren like in th' Bible, an' my sweet husband died when he was thirty-five." She snapped her fingers. "Th' Lord took 'im just like that. Heart attack. It run in 'is fam'ly."

"I'm sorry."

"I ain't found *no*body as sweet as Tommy O'Grady. . . ."

"I'm sure."

Violet's face was bright with good humor. "But that's not t' say I ain't tryin'!"

"What do you think . . . so far?"

"I love that she wants to dry sheets on the line instead of in the dryer. But she *is* terribly vocal. When she was hanging the wash, it sounded exactly like she was . . . *yodeling.*" Cynthia appeared puzzled. "But surely not."

"Surely not."

He noted that their milkmaid had stopped on the path from the clothesline to the porch, and was watching the guineas career through the yard.

Father Tim's grin was stretching halfway around his head as he watched Lloyd watch Violet watch the guineas. "Lloyd," he said beneath his breath, "your eyes are out on stems."

Lloyd turned a fierce shade of pink. "Way out," he said, grinning back.

"It's a whole other world in here!"

Cynthia peered at the canopy of interlacing tree branches above the farm track. Light and shadow dappled the track, which was still recognizable beneath the leaf mold.

He knew at once an infilling peace. "Words-worthian!" he said, smitten. "A leafy glade! A vernal bower!"

At the foot of the bank to their left, the creek hurried on its journey to the New River.

Cynthia released a long breath. "I could sit down right here and be happy."

He sneaked a glance at his watch. In an hour and a half, he would need to talk to his lawyer about the adoption papers.

"I saw that," she said.

"Saw what?"

"You looked at your watch."

"I did. Force of habit."

"What a lovely little creek—why don't we pitch our camp here? I'm too famished to explore before lunch. And look, darling, this gives us a wonderful view of the sheep paddock."

Indeed, the view along the track opened out of the woods to the green meadow, with ewes and lambs grazing among the outcrop of rocks. Beyond the rocks, the fence line, and farther along, the rooftop of the farmhouse beneath a spreading oak.

Happy, he smoothed their intended place on the cushion of leaves and moss, and together they spread the quilt on a slope toward the creek.

She lay on the quilt and gazed up at the tracery of limbs against a blue sky. "Thank You, Lord!"

"Yes, thank You, Lord."

As he sat beside her, she turned her head and looked at him, content. "Churchill said, 'We're always getting ready to live, but never living.' We should have done this sooner."

"True enough. And then there's this one, by a good fellow named Henry Canby:

"'Live deep instead of fast.'"

Birds called throughout the copse of trees. "When the brick dust gets too thick, let's always remember to come here and do what Mr. Canby suggests."

He unwrapped their sandwiches. "We can handle that."

She picked something from the leaves. "A brown feather," she said, examining it. "Someday I'd love to do a book about how things look under a microscope. What might we see if I made a slide of it?" She twirled the feather between her thumb and forefinger. "What bird dropped it, do you suppose?"

"It's a chicken feather," he said.

Early afternoon sun filtered through the leaves above; they were light and shadow beneath.

He lay on his back beside her. "So what are we going to do about your work space?"

"Lloyd says we haven't seen anything yet, it's really going to get messy on Monday morning—they've been tiptoeing around the inevitable. Then there's Lily, of course, who must have the kitchen if she's going to cook, so we're looking at . . . chaos, to put it plainly."

"Sammy's room gets good light. Maybe, somehow . . ."

"I can't do that."

"Can we move you into the smokehouse? It has a window."

"Ugh. Lots of creepy crawlies in there, and spiders with legs as long as mine."

"Del would have them out of there in no time flat."

"No, sweetheart. Even with a window, too dark and confining."

"Here's a crazy thought . . ." he said.

"I love your crazy thoughts."

"The barn loft. The old hay doors open straight out to the north."

"The barn?" She was quiet for a time, thoughtful. "I don't know. But He knows. Could we pray about it?"

He took her hand.

"Father," he said, observing St. Paul's exhortation to be instant in prayer, "thank You for caring where Cynthia cultivates and expresses the wondrous gift You've given her. We're stumped, but You're not. Would You make it clear to us? We thank You in advance for Your wise and gracious guidance, and for Your boundless blessings in this life . . . for the trees above us, and the good earth beneath. For the people whose lives You intermingle with ours. For Sammy, who was lost and now is found. For Dooley, who's coming home . . ."

"And I thank You, Lord," prayed his wife, "for my patient and thoughtful husband, a treasure I never dreamed I'd be given."

He crossed himself. "In the name of our Lord and Savior, Jesus Christ . . ."

"Amen!" they said together.

"That feels better."

"Thanks for the kind words to the Boss."

She patted his hand; they listened for a while to the bleating of the lambs.

"I hope poor J.C. can step up to the plate, as you say; I'm sure he has all sorts of lovely feelings that need to get into general circulation."

"Feelings. There's the rub! It was all those scary feelings that held me back for so long. And then, standing at the wall that evening, I had the agonizing sense that I was losing you forever."

"I was thinking of leaving Mitford."

"What if I hadn't thrown myself at your feet? We would have missed everything. We would have missed this." The creek sang boldly; a junco called.

"Worse yet, we would have missed the sugar-free cherry tarts hidden under the table-cloth that we haven't unpacked."

"Aha!" he said, digging at once to the bottom of the basket.

Cynthia had trotted home to finish April and sketch May, and he'd stayed behind to check out what now appeared to be the track of long-ago hay wagons. He would take care of the papers before five.

He left the basket and blanket by the creek and trekked through the woods. Barnabas would love this . . .

As he rounded a turn in the overgrown trace, he was startled to see a shingled, one-story house standing in a clearing.

Had he somehow walked off the Owens' land and onto a neighbor's property? He didn't think so. The path had run here from the far side of the sheep paddock, well inside the property line marked by the state road . . .

A gutter rattled as a squirrel raced across the roof and fled onto a tree limb.

Might have been charming once, he thought. He walked toward the house, taking his time, inventorying the ruin of weather and neglect.

. . . A large pine tree across the broken ridge of the roof.

. . . Roof tiles missing and decking showing through; broken window panes; a shutter propped against the porch; the chain of a porch swing dislodged from its hinge on one side . . .

He didn't remember this house. When he and Hal had walked the property with the dogs a few years ago, they'd kept to the fields, and the stand of old hardwoods to the north.

Probably a tenant house, disused since Willie's little cottage was built in the fifties. His eyes roved the yard. A bale of rusted wire, discarded bottles, general rubbish.

With a good rehab and a coat of paint, exactly the sort of thing his wife would find intriguing. But she wouldn't be intrigued by the eerie feeling he got as he stepped onto the porch.

Beyond the patched screen, the door stood open.

There was a distinct sense of emptiness about the place, but just in case . . .

"Hello!"

In the two front rooms, ivy was growing through fissures in a west wall; thanks to the derelict roof, a large portion of flooring was rotted through. The kitchen had been stripped of cabinets and appliances; only a rusted sink remained and a fireplace half filled with ashes. A few sticks of wood had been thrown down next to the hearth; a wooden chair sat on cracked and peeling linoleum.

Curious, he took the stick that leaned against the chimneypiece and poked the sour-smelling ashes. A couple of crushed beer cans. A plastic top from a fast-food drink. Chicken bones.

He looked around the room and saw a narrow door—possibly a space that contained an ironing board—and opened it.

The small pantry retained only one of its shelves; on it were a fast-food drink cup, a pair of sunglasses with one lens missing, an unopened can of pork and beans, several dead bees, an open box of saltines, a half-roll of toilet paper, small packages of mustard, ketchup, salt, and pepper, and a beer opener. He took the cup down and peered into it. Dentures. Lowers. Not a pretty sight.

He shut the pantry door, leaving everything as he'd found it, and walked out to the porch, closing the screen door behind him.

His plan was to circle the house, but he stopped when he came to the derelict wood-shed, where he smelled a curious stench. He saw the fire pit first, then the large mound of feathers partially hidden beneath a slab of plywood.

In the farm library, illumined only by the glow of a computer screen, several e-mails queued up.

<Dear Father Tim,

<A stack of 90 $100 bills would be roughly two and a half inches high. Forgive lateness in getting back. Come and see us.

<Yrs sincerely,

<Kaye Abbott, Wesley National

•　•　•

<The good news is, I lost four pounds. The bad news is, Harold was right—it was all fluid.

<Love,

<Emma

• • •

<Timothy,

<Pray for your bishop. We're coming into the final sprint.

<Yours in Him Who loved us first,

<Stuart

• • •

<It's me again, Emma.

<I meant to tell you Esther is a wreck. Can you believe that all she wants to do is bake three-layer marmalades and give them away?

<She took one to Miss Rose, who I thought was her sworn enemy ever since she called Esther fat! And Old Man Mueller got one, it must have made his year. They say now she's baking one for Madge Thomas who couldn't bake one herself if somebody held a gun to her head, especially since she fell off a stool in her kitchen and broke her arm. Plus—plus they say she baked one for Nurse Herman before poor Gene was cold in his grave!!

<Esther is killing herself doing this fool thing. I mean have you ever baked a three-layer cake?

If I baked just one, they'd be checking me into Mitford Hospital on a gurney.

<Her friends want her to stop baking and start grieving. Since she will probably do what you say, e-mail me a note <u>telling her to stop</u> and I'll pass the word.

The vicar was hammering down on his Sunday morning toast when Sammy came in from the garden.

Sammy held forth an offering partially wrapped in newspaper.

"Asparagus!" crowed Cynthia.

"It's g-gittin' tall out there. I was j–jis' lookin' around in them ol' beds th' other side of th' f-fence, an' there it was."

"Roasted with olive oil and garlic, and spritzed with lemon—heaven! Thank you, Sammy."

"Lettuce might be in p-pretty soon, eight or ten days if we don't g-git a frost."

"I've been meaning to ask—what's your favorite thing to eat in the whole wide world?"

"Fries."

"Perfect! You've come to the right place. I'm doing a practice run Tuesday night."

Father Tim spread his allotted dab of no-sugar-added marmalade. "There's Irish in that boy somewhere."

Cynthia squinted at Sammy's home-style haircut, executed the night before.

"Short!" she said.

He shrugged; a light smile played at his mouth. "Won't have t' do it ag'in 'til th' t-taters come in."

Accompanied by his fourteen-year-old daughter, Sally, Hank Triplett thumped down on the epistle side, as did nine Millwrights. Though recovered from the worst, the Millwrights produced a veritable symphony of coughing for everyone's listening pleasure.

Lloyd Goodnight arrived with Buster, who, much against his will, had cleaned up considerably.

Miss Mary and Miss Martha brought a neighbor, Edna Swanson, who devoutly hoped that word of her visit to the Episcopalians wouldn't get around to the Methodists, where she'd been a member for thirty-odd years.

Though Miss Martha explained that the Methodists and Episcopalians had formerly been one Communion, anyway, this fact was much doubted by Edna, who knew a thing or two about local church history and had written a pamphlet on the subject that sold for fifty cents and helped support field missions.

Unaccustomed as most of the congregation was to the Anglican hymns, Sparkle Foster, who'd learned to read music in ninth grade, to-day felt sufficiently comfortable to sing out, loud and clear.

Father Tim pitched in with Sparkle, Lloyd gave it what-for, and Cynthia brought up the rear, doing her level best. Together with Agnes's confident but warbly soprano and Miss Martha's roof-raising mezzo, the melody of the opening hymn launched out upon the air above the gorge, mingling with the balmy May thermals enjoyed by fourteen Cooper's hawks.

> *"Thy beautiful care*
> *What tongue can recite?*
> *It breathes in the air,*
> *It shines in the night;*
> *It streams from the hills,*
> *It descends to the plain,*
> *And sweetly distills*
> *In the dew and the rain . . ."*

Some minutes after the service began, two

young children peered through the open front doors.

As the self-appointed greeter of latecomers, Miss Martha got up from the back row and went to see what was what.

"Well?" she demanded in a loud whisper.

The boy looked terrified, but courageous. "I'm Roy Dale; she's Gladys, th' baby. We heered you'uns got cake."

"Come in, come in, we'll see what we can do!"

As she herded them to her pew, Martha McKinney thanked God that Agnes had frozen the remains of last week's German chocolate . . .

Following the service and a brief tutorial on the rubrics, the vicar introduced Rooter Hicks. Rooter, he said, would demonstrate a way to communicate a simple greeting to Holy Trinity's crucifer, Clarence Merton, or to anyone without full hearing.

Rooter was seized by terror as he stood to make his demonstration. He was, in fact, struck dumb, and signed the greeting repeatedly before he at last recovered his voice.

"'Is here's how t' say *How y' doin', man*. Y'all are s'posed t' do it, too."

Father Tim mimicked Rooter's signing. "How are you doing, man," he said as he signed.

"Now, if we're going to get out of here at a reasonable hour . . ."—he glanced at his watch—". . . let's all pitch in and sign with Rooter."

At this exhortation, the congregation pitched in and signed with Rooter.

"Now you're talking!" said the vicar.

Fond of counting heads, Cynthia was pleased to report that attendance at Holy Trinity had shot to twenty-eight. Including their vicar, of course.

He was at first elated, then glum. Twenty-eight was more than half the capacity of their nave. What would they do if . . . ?

"Chairs in the aisle!" said his mind-reading deacon.

"Two services!" he said, astounded by the thought.

Cynthia threw up her hands. "Wait a minute; wait a minute. We're starting to mess around in the Lord's business."

He laughed, instantly relieved. "Thanks, Kavanagh. I was just cranking up to a full building program."

"If Roy Dale and Gladys come back, Sammy and I could have twelve in our Sunday School next week. Twelve! I'm sort of . . . nervous, really."

"Don't be. Have you talked to Sammy?"

"Not yet. Timing is everything. But I think he'll do it."

"Have you thought the lesson through?"

She gestured toward her heart. "It's kind of . . . soaking in there."

"And all the better for it!" he said.

He prayed for Esther Bolick, who was reeling with a hurt he could only dimly imagine.

Having known her for nearly twenty years, he came to a simple conclusion: Esther *is* grieving. And out of it was coming considerable good.

He hit "send."

<Let Esther bake.

CHAPTER FIFTEEN

Shady Grove

A blue plastic tent, occupying a large area around the mouth of the fireplace, had been erected to keep mortar dust and creosote from sifting into the room.

As anyone could see, it wasn't working.

The stuff continued to leak its way into the kitchen, living room, and dining room, and then turn the corner and drift along the hall to the library. The soot had a greasy base, which meant that wiping it off a surface had to be handled with some discretion.

Adding insult to injury, the pile of wet sand next to the back porch was slowly making its way into the house on the soles of Lloyd's and Buster's work boots. Then there was the issue of the kitchen table, which had to be jammed cheek by jowl with the stove, making it a nuisance to get the oven door open.

"How long?" he asked Lloyd, feeling desperate.

"Well, see, we're tearin' out y'r fireplace surround so we can get at th' old lintel and pull it out of there."

"That's so we can install y'r damper," said Buster.

"Aha."

"We'll be layin' y'r brick two wide up through th' throat," said Lloyd, "then pargin' up th' throat, which ain't easy."

"Rough," said Buster, shaking his head.

Lloyd removed his ball cap, hoping to clarify things. "See, pargin' th' throat from outside down is fine, but pargin' from inside up is harder, if you know what I mean . . ."

"How long?" His eyes were glazing over; he couldn't help it.

"I'm sorry about y'r two bushes," said Lloyd. "We'll sure be more careful."

"Yeah," said Buster.

This would be the third time of asking. "How *long*?"

Lloyd looked at Buster; Buster looked at Lloyd. They both looked at the vicar, and spoke in unison. "Three weeks?"

He couldn't help but notice the question mark at the end of what he'd hoped would be a declarative statement.

"Have you caught him in the act?"

He'd called the district attorney, whom he'd gotten to know during Dooley's encounter with the police a few years ago.

"Haven't even seen him. But my dog ripped a piece from his shirt, and he left some things in another house on the property."

"Is the property posted?"

"It is."

"How many chickens are you missing?"

"Seven. And I found the feathers and a fire pit."

"Did he cut down any trees for firewood?"

"Don't think so; didn't look for that. He probably picked up a few dead limbs around the place."

"What else do you know?"

"He left his lower dentures behind."

The DA laughed. "He'll be back."

"That's what I'm thinking. What kind of offenses do we have here?"

"Larceny. Second-degree trespassing. Cruelty to animals, which carries a class one misdemeanor. And if he cut down any trees or bushes for firewood, add a class two misdemeanor. Bottom line, if he has five or more convictions on his record, the judge could give him up to two hundred and forty days."

"Thanks," said Father Tim. "I'll keep in touch."

"Your guy's prob'ly over at Value Mart checkin' out the baby food aisle; you're OK for a while."

Very funny, thought the vicar.

Before his dash up to Wilson's Ridge, he found Willie mixing sweet feed for the cows. "Tell me about the house in the woods."

"About t' fall in, looks like."

"Know anything about who lived there?"

"Don' know. Miz Owen said their boy, John, used to write music over there b'fore he passed."

The Owens' son had died in his late teens of severe encephalitis; Marge and Hal had never been able to resolve that loss, and seldom talked about it.

"Ever notice anybody hanging around, using the path?"

"Nossir. I never went over but once, I don' hardly think about it bein' there."

Father Tim had long ago learned his lesson

about keeping the truth from his wife. In this case, however, he didn't see how the truth could possibly help matters. Evidence gave pretty good indication that the poacher would return—news that would make the whole household edgy.

He'd keep his eyes and ears open, keep the phone number of the sheriff's office handy and, of course, keep counting their chickens.

"Granny will hold your hand and Father Tim will pray for you," said Hoppy. "You can't get a better deal than that."

Dovey was stiff with fear. "OK," she whispered.

"The needle will go in with a question, and I believe it will come out with the answer."

Dovey flinched as the needle found its mark.

"I'm about t' pass plumb out," said Granny.

"Don't even think about it," said Hoppy.

When the vial filled with Dovey's dark blood, he removed the needle and flipped up the safety cap. "You're going to live," he said, applying a gauze pad to the insertion point.

"Is it over?"

"Not yet. I'll listen to your breathing and your heart with this." He put the stethoscope around his neck. "And I'll check your pulse, check your blood pressure, and probe your liver."

"How d' you probe m' liver?"

"Use my fingers to feel around . . . right here. Nothing serious."

"Do I need to hold 'er hand f'r that?" asked Granny.

"You're off duty, Nurse Meaders."

Dovey raised her head. "Can I have me a drink of water?"

"I'll git it," said Granny.

Hoppy helped his patient sit up on the side of the bed. "What are you going to do when you're up and around and feeling like a young woman again?"

"I don' know, I've near about f'rgot how it feels. Sing, I reckon."

"Breathe in and hold it. Do you sing? Let it out."

"Yessir."

"Breathe. Hold it. Let it out. Good."

He placed the diaphragm of the stethoscope over her heart, then moved it to her back.

"What're you'uns hearin' in there?" asked Granny, delivering the water.

Hoppy grinned. *"Ker-thump, ker-thump."*

After the examination, Hoppy sat in the chair by the bed, thoughtful, and watched

Dovey drink with obvious thirst from her transferware cup.

"OK, Dovey, how about this one?"

Mitford's Harvard-educated doctor began singing in what Father Tim remembered from his Lord's Chapel days as a darned good tenor.

> *"I went to see my Shady Grove*
> *Standing in the door*
> *Shoes and stockings in her hands,*
> *Little bare feet on the floor."*

As Hoppy headed into the chorus, Dovey joined him, harmonizing.

> *"Shady Grove, my little love,*
> *Shady Grove I say*
> *Shady Grove, my little love,*
> *I'm a-goin' away . . ."*

"Well done!" crowed Hoppy.

"Lord have mercy!" Granny was wide-eyed. "You best not tell Donny you done that!"

Hoppy stuck the stethoscope and blood sample in his bag. "What shouldn't she tell Donny?"

"Donny's been a-beggin' 'er t' sing, an' she ain't sang a note in I don' know when."

Hoppy packed the blood pressure cuff and zipped the bag. "It's our secret, Dovey. Father Tim will be in touch; we'll let you know what's what. God bless you, stay strong. And God bless you, Granny."

"Hit was good of y' t' come, Doc." Granny grinned, revealing pink gums. "Hit was good medicine f'r Dovey."

"Where in the world did you learn that song?" asked Father Tim, as they walked to their vehicles.

"I was a hippie for about fifteen minutes; everybody sang 'Shady Grove.'"

"You should get out more often," said the vicar.

Dear Paster Kavanagah,

Thank you for the nice letter you wrote to me. It was a comfort to hear about Dovey and Donny and little Sissie and to know the dogwoods was blooming good this year.

I done a terribul thing to my loved ones the way they have sufferd. I will never get over the shame of it but God has let me know I am forgiven even for this terribl crime. Jesus feels near to me every day. There are times when he helps me with my Bible study lesson in knowing how to catch the meaning. Yes sir thank you we could use more Bibles. Ten or eleven would be about right.

Thank you for caring about me and my family. I hope to see you one day. Pray for my children and little gran.
Ruby Luster
#10765L

He showed the letter to Cynthia. "Paul and Moses were murderers, Rahab was a prostitute, David was an adulterer. The list goes on."

"Which only proves, darling, what you're so fond of saying."

"Every saint has a past . . ." he said.

"And every sinner has a future."

He was taking a bag of greens to the chickens when he heard Sammy and his visiting brother and sister talking behind the smokehouse.

"You better not say 'ain't' aroun' Dooley," Poo warned.

"Why not?" asked Sammy.

"'Cause 'e don't like it, 'at's why. He says it makes people sound country."

"He says it makes people sound *stupid*," corrected Jessie.

"Whatever," said Poo. "I don' never say it around 'im n'more.

"Yeah," said Jessie, "but when he leaves, you jump up an' down an' holler, ain't, ain't, ain't, *ain't!*"

"I like t' say 'ain't,'" Poo confessed.

"If you don' say 'ain't,' what d'you say?" asked Sammy.

"'Is not,' 'are not.' Right, Jess?"

"Right," said Jessie.

Father Tim tossed the greens through the top wire. By the grace of God, he'd kept his mouth shut on this particular subject. Out of the mouths of babes . . .

"Dooley, he says 'yes, sir,' 'thank y',' 'please,' an' *all* 'at ol' stuff." Poo sounded affronted. "He learned it at school."

"Mama an' Buck makes me an' Poo say 'yes, sir' and 'yes, ma'am'; when you come t' live with us, you'll have t' say it, too."

"I ain't comin' t' live with you."

"Why ain't you?" asked Poo.

"'Cause I ain't."

"Don't then!" Jessie's voice was shrill. "We don't care if you do or not!"

Father Tim saw her round the corner of the smokehouse, head down. He tossed in the last of the greens and caught up as she stomped toward the porch.

"BLTs, lemonade, and apple pie with ice cream . . . coming up!" he said. "What do you think?"

"I think Sammy's a big, dumb creep."

<To: Vanita Bentley, *Mitford Muse*

<Holy Trinity Episcopal Church seeks the tax-deductible gift of an upright piano in good condition. Thank you in advance. 476-2394. Or write Fr Tim Kavanagh, PO Box 16, Farmer, NC 28611

<Vanita, let me know what I owe you. Run until further notice. Many thanks.

•   •   •

<Dear Fr Tim:

<You would owe us eleven dollars per week for this insertion. I can save you money if you'll let me have a go at it.

<Yrs sincerely,

<Vanita H. Bentley

•   •   •

<Do it.

<Yrs in Christ

•   •   •

<Dear Fr Tim:

**<Holy Trinity Episcopal Church seeks
upright piano good condition.
Tax-deductible. 476-2394.**
11 words

<Total: $4.00 per insertion.

<Yr copy had 31 words. Nobody writes
letters anymore, so may as well use phone
only.

<I got rid of thanking in advance as to
me personally it seems too over the top.
Hardly anybody says thank you anymore,
much less in advance. A big savings right
there!

< And—because of the hyphen, tax-deductible
is charged as one word, it's your lucky day!!!

<Of course, you could delete the name of the
church, and get copy down to 7 words. I love
classifieds!!!

<Pls advise

"But who'll *play* it?" asked his wife.

"Cynthia, Cynthia! If we provide it, somebody will come along who plays it. Mark my word."

"Consider it marked," she said.

"Sammy!" He knocked on the bedroom door. "What's going on?"

"Watchin' TV."

"I can't find anything to watch. What did you find?"

"Pool."

"May I come in?"

"Yeah."

"They have pool on TV?"

"Yeah."

He stood and gazed at the screen. Pool on TV!

"She's got to make a l-long sh–shot," said Sammy.

Women shooting pool! Amazing.

"May I watch with you?"

"Yeah." Sammy got up and removed a pile of unfolded laundry from the other chair.

"Thanks," said Father Tim, making himself comfortable.

Sammy's eyes were glued to the screen. "No problem."

Cynthia was beaming as she undressed for bed. "Sammy and I talked today."

"And?"

"And the Holy Spirit gave us a wonderful Sunday School lesson. I'm thrilled! We'll go over it with you later."

"No clues now?"

"We're still polishing."

"How did he feel about doing it?"

"I think he likes the idea."

A certain hope kindled in him.

"The kitchen was dreadful today," she said. "Maybe we should walk out to the barn after supper tomorrow. I can't imagine working there, really; it sounds romantic, but surely it wouldn't be. Aren't there mice in barns?"

"You could take Violet with you; let that girl do an honest day's work for a change!"

She turned back the spread and gave their down pillows a good wallop. "In any case, we're having my new and revised fries tomorrow night. Dooley comes home in four days, and with this one further experiment, I'm sure they'll be fabulous."

"If it ain't broke, Kavanagh . . ."

She ignored his wisdom, and crawled into

bed. "Burgers with blue cheese . . . and cole slaw, Puny's recipe."

"Count me in," he said, sitting on the side of the bed to remove his socks. "I'll be home in time to grate the cabbage."

The time had arrived to stop "drumming up business," as Lloyd called it, and get down to the fine particulars of ministering to their flock. Thus, today's round of Wilson's Ridge and environs would be the last for a while.

"Want to come?" he asked Barnabas.

Was the pope Catholic?

He and Barnabas were trotting to the truck when Lloyd hailed him.

"You asked me t' keep a' eye out for y'r boy."

"I did."

"He's been smokin' in th' barn. Thought you ought t' know that, bein' that's one way to lose a barn."

"You're sure about this?"

"I seen 'im light up a couple of times when he was walkin' over there. Then, too, I got a nose for it. Since I give it up twenty years ago, I can smell t'bacco smoke far as th' wind'll carry it."

"Thanks, Lloyd."

"I know smokin's off-limits around here; Buster sets in th' truck to smoke. It's awful hard to get good help, so I don't say nothin'. I hope that's all right."

What to do? Find Sammy and deal with it now? Or get up to Wilson's Ridge and talk to Sammy this evening? George Macdonald had put a fine point on it:

"You have a disagreeable duty to do at twelve o'clock. Do not blacken nine and ten and eleven, and all between, with the color of twelve . . ."

"Have you seen him this morning?"

"He's grubbin' manure out of th' henhouse. For y'r okra patch."

He was struck by this comment. How could he do what he had to do with a boy who was mucking chicken manure to satisfy a culinary whim of Timothy Kavanagh's?

"He's lucky to have you to kick 'is butt," said Lloyd. "I wish my daddy'd kicked mine; might of saved me a whole lot of grief."

Tough love is what they called it these days. But tough for who?

For both parties, it seemed to him.

He stopped on the path to the chicken house.

If he nailed Sammy for smoking, Sammy would know he'd been spied on. Who was doing the spying—Willie? Cynthia? Lloyd? Buster? He wouldn't be able to trust anyone at Meadowgate.

He'd give to Sammy Barlowe what God had given time and time again to Tim Kavanagh: grace.

He'd also ask God to keep the barn from burning down in the process.

He screeched into Jubal's yard and turned off the ignition.

"Stay," he said to Barnabas.

Jubal had seen him coming; as he walked toward the porch, the door opened.

"Jubal? It's Father Tim."

Suddenly, he heard his dog lumbering up behind him.

"No, Barnabas! Go back!" A scripture, a scripture! His mind was a blank.

"Lord God A'mighty!" Jubal Adderholt was brandishing a pistol and yelling at the top of his lungs.

"Don't shoot, Jubal! Don't shoot!"

Barnabas hit the porch with such force as to

rattle the windows. Standing on his hind legs and wagging his tail, he slammed his front paws onto Jubal's shoulders.

"Lord he'p me an' save me!" shouted the old man, staggering back.

"I am crucified with Christ!" pronounced the vicar. "Nevertheless I live! Yet not I, but Christ liveth in me . . ."

His dog sank slowly to all fours.

"And the life which I now live in the flesh, I live by the grace of the Son of God, who loved me and gave himself for me!" Father Tim's heart was pounding as he polished off the verse from Galatians 2:22.

Barnabas lay sprawled on the porch floor.

"I'm sorry, Jubal, please forgive us. My goodness, he hasn't done such a thing in *years*. It must be the squirrel tails. Are you all right? I think he likes you."

"*Likes* me? Hit's a good thing he didn' git 'is head blowed off."

"He's harmless, I promise. Just overly friendly."

"I was jis' startin' t' clean m' snake pistol when I seen ye drive up. What in th' nation do ye want with me, now? I cain't hardly git a minute's peace since you'uns opened up y'r church."

"Just stopping by to say hello, see how things are going."

"Set down." Jubal wagged his gun at the sofa, newly delivered from its winter tarpaulin.

He sat.

"Where's Miss Agnes at?"

"She's got a stiff knee."

Jubal looked petulant. "I reckon she's done f'rgot about me."

"Oh, no, she wouldn't forget about you, not by a long shot. How's th' squirrel business?"

"May's m' cut-off date, but hit's been s' cold, I'll be a-shootin' squirrel f'r another week or two."

"Your gun . . ."

"What about it?"

"It's, ah, pointing at me."

"They ain't nothin' in it, far as I know." Jubal aimed the pistol above his head and pulled the trigger. *Click.* "That's one empty chamber f'r ye."

The vicar bolted to his feet. "We've caused enough trouble for one day, we'll just be pushing on."

"Ye ain't got ary eggs, are ye?"

"No eggs today. Next time. I promise." That gun was waving around in his face for a fare-thee-well; he was out of here.

"Ye wouldn' be goin' by Miss Martha, would ye?"

"I would, I would. Directly by."

"I shot two squirrel this mornin' b'fore th' dew was off; they're done skinned out, nice an' meaty. I could send 'em with ye . . ."

"I'm sure Miss Martha wouldn't want to take food off your table."

"They's more where them come from."

"Well, then, I'll be glad to make a delivery!" Father Tim had suspected all along that a big heart beat beneath Jubal Adderholt's beard.

"Course ye know I'll be expectin' somethin' from Miss Martha."

"Aha."

"An' I'd be obliged if ye'd drop it off on y'r way back."

How he got himself in this mess, he couldn't figure. He had to haul out of there securing a poke of squirrels between his feet, with his dog going nuts in the passenger seat.

And, of course, Miss Martha wasn't at home.

He couldn't leave this particular offering stuck in the screen door like a morning newspaper. Indeed, today's high was predicted to be in the seventies, and what if the sisters didn't come home 'til the afternoon?

"Lord have mercy!" he said aloud, quoting Granny.

"I hate that y' found out about m' drinkin'. Sissie says she tol' you.

"Tells ever'thing, that young'un. I'd 'preciate it if you wouldn't preach me a sermon, I've done preached m'self half t' hell an' back.

"Ever'thing'll go along good for a while, then somethin' happens, I cain't even tell y' what it is. It's like goin' down th' road and all at once th' road jis' drops off a cliff. I see th' drop comin' but like a fool I keep walkin'.

"I want t' quit, I've prayed t' quit, I've tried t' quit, but I keep fallin' off th' cliff. An' besides th' worser thing of lettin' th' Lord down, I don' have time t' mess with alcohol, I got a b'iness t' run. Th' way things is goin' with havin' t' take care of Dovey an' Sissie, it's root hog or die."

Donny leaned his elbows on his knees and put his head in his hands.

"My daddy was th' worst sot you ever seen, an' you know what th' Ol' Testament says about th' sins of th' fathers. But I believe God t' be a merciful God, otherwise he wouldn've sent Jesus. I b'lieve th' sins of th' fathers runs in us like poison, but we're not bound. He was willin' t' die f'r us on th' cross so we wouldn't be bound, but set free."

Indeed, Donny had preached him a sermon;

one that Madelaine Kavanagh, his mother, would have called the gospel truth.

"Can I go on y'r rounds? Can I?" She stood on her tiptoes and held her arms out to him.

"Not today, Sissie." He bent down and picked her up. "Whoa, you're growing!"

"I ain't a baby n'more, that's why."

"I'm glad your mother's sleeping. How's she feeling?"

"She don't hardly sleep at night, she sleeps mostly in th' day."

His heart felt heavy against the child in his arms, against the things of the world in general.

"We'll look for at you at church on Sunday. We're having our first Sunday School, you know."

Sissie furrowed her brow. "Are they cake at Sunday School?"

"I'll see what I can do." He set her down, and squatted beside her. "May I pray for you, Sissie?"

She bowed her head; he placed his hand upon it.

"Father, I thank You for the marvel of Sissie Gleason. For her bright spirit, her inquisitive mind, her tender heart. Thank You for blessing her life above anything I could ask or think. Prepare a way for her, Lord, that she might become all You made her to be. In Jesus' name . . ."

Sissie squeezed her eyes shut. "An' Lord, please make Mama better, make Donny quit drinkin', bring Mamaw Ruby home, an' give us cheese dogs f'r supper t'night."

"Amen!" they said in unison.

He was feeling suddenly brighter.

While at the trailer, he'd parked in the shade, set the bag of squirrels under the truck, and made sure the windows were rolled high enough to contain his dog.

He looked at his watch as he pulled out of Donny's yard. He had no idea how long his cargo had sat in Jubal's kitchen before he picked it up forty-five minutes ago.

He applied his lead foot to the accelerator and hauled to Hank Triplett's store at the crossroads.

"Do you have a freezer I could put this bag in, and maybe pick it up later in the day?"

"What's in y'r bag?"

"Two squirrels. Dressed."

Hank pondered this. "Don't think that'd be too good. I mean they's ice cream san'wiches an' all in there."

"Right. Well." He smoked over the shelves and bought pretzels, chips, Snickers, assorted crackers, and a lump of what country stores call rat cheese. He also exchanged the paper bag for a plastic bag and dumped ice in on the contents, managing not to look.

"See you and Sally on Sunday, I hope."

"We'll be there," said Hank, looking pleased about it.

He knocked on five doors, only one of which was slammed in his face, but lacked courage to approach the sixth, which sat in the midst of a private junkyard. He also stuffed seven mailboxes, and posted flyers on nine telephone poles. On the way to the schoolhouse, he stopped to offer a ride to an elderly man who was walking along the right-hand side of the road in a pair of overalls and a battered hat.

He rolled the window down a few inches. "Need a lift?"

The old man looked up with alarm into the face of a black dog that seemed only slightly smaller than the truck, and turned and fled into the woods.

Clearly, Barnabas was not a good marketing tool.

"Agnes," he said, hurrying into the school-house, "would you mind if I put this bag in your freezer?"

"Of course not, Father. What's in it, may I ask?"

"There's the rub. Two squirrels, dressed out and ready to go in Miss Martha's pot, but she wasn't home."

Agnes burst into laughter. "You've been to see Jubal."

"Yes, and he asked about you. Said he reckoned you'd forgotten him."

"The old so-and-so. Who could ever forget Jubal Adderholt?"

"Not me!" he said, meaning it.

"How was your round?"

He stuffed the bag into the freezer and gave her a synopsis.

"I'll just put the kettle on for tea; I'm eager to hear your plan, Father."

He drew the papers from the large envelope and sat down at her table. "This will be a surprise even to Cynthia. So, please—keep it absolutely to yourself."

"Consider it done," she said, quoting her vicar.

On his way to Meadowgate, he gave it another go.

He tried the front door and went around to the back. As tight as Fort Knox.

He hoped nothing was wrong; the sisters were usually here except for grocery shopping days.

He schlepped the bag around to the front yard and got in the truck, noting that Barnabas had at last lost interest. What a blasted pickle.

"Stay!" he said in his pulpit voice.

The moment his foot hit the porch, Jubal's door opened.

"I been a-lookin' f'r ye."

"I expect so."

"What're ye totin'?"

He thought Jubal had a very expectant look on his face.

"Well, you see, Miss Martha wasn't home. I stopped by twice, and don't have a clue where she might be. Your squirrels have been on ice and in Miss Agnes's freezer, so I'm sure they're just fine." He handed off the bag, thankful to his very depths to be rid of the blasted thing.

Jubal opened the bag and eyed the contents suspiciously. "This ain't squirrel."

"It ain't? I mean . . ."

"Hit's . . . Lord he'p a monkey; what *is* it?"

The vicar peered into the bag. "You've got me."

"I send ye out with two fine squirrel an' back ye come with a pig in a poke!"

"Wait right there, Jubal."

He dashed to the truck and pulled the other bag from behind the driver's seat. The idea was, if Miss Martha had been home and wasn't prepared to send her own offering today, Jubal would still get a return on his investment.

Back he trotted to Jubal's porch. Lord help a monkey, indeed, seeing as how Timothy Kavanagh was the monkey. Sometimes, he'd like to just lie down and go *morte,* as Lew Boyd would say.

Lloyd and Buster were pulling out as he pulled in at four o'clock. Thanks be to God, their kitchen was free; he was weary in every bone.

"You're not going to believe this!" said his wife. She was beaming; she was glowing; she was electric.

"Come with me."

She grabbed him by the arm and away they

went along the hall and up the stairs and past Sammy's bedroom and around the corner to the green door. He was panting like a farm dog after a rabbit.

"Do you know where this door leads?" she asked.

"The attic, I seem to recall, though I've never been up there."

She opened the door and they ascended the narrow stairs until they came to a spacious, light-filled room with three north-facing windows and a smaller window to the west.

Silent, she took his hand as they wound themselves through the jumble of old furniture and dust-covered boxes, and stood at the large center window.

They looked down upon the mossy roof of the smokehouse and Sammy's emerging garden, then out to the barn with its red tin roof and away to green pastures dotted with cows, and up to blue mountains beyond.

Wordless, she drew him to the west window, to the view of ewes and lambs and Meadowgate's recalcitrant ram, and the great outcrop of rocks pushing forth from emerald grass.

"Beautiful beyond telling!" he said, moved.

"It needs only one thing more."

"Del!"

"Yes! Otherwise"—her eyes were bright with feeling—"it's heaven."

"Speaking of heaven," he said, "why am I too often surprised when God answers prayer?"

"How's May coming?" he asked, grating cabbage.

"My favorite. Want to see?"

She dried her hands and fetched the watercolor sketch. A lamb lay by the side of a ewe, smiling—as lambs are wont to do. Violet perched on a nearby rock, her green eyes wide with curiosity.

"Aha! My favorite, as well. Blast, but I'm proud of you! And Violet, also. A charmer, that girl."

"Thanks, sweetheart. Only seven more to go, and three months to finish."

"Sammy and I can take your things up to heaven after supper."

"Supper?" she said, grinning.

In some way he couldn't understand, *dinner* was becoming *supper* since they'd moved to the sticks.

After grating enough cabbage for a small regiment, he sat in the war zone, aka the kitchen, and stared unseeing at the blue tent.

His diligent wife was going about the business of getting their meal up and running.

She came to his chair and touched his shoulder. "What is it, sweetheart?"

"I'm feeling my age."

"Well, then, go and do something about it!"

"Like what?"

"Walk in the pasture with the dogs, zip down to the mailbox . . . get your heart racing."

"I've spent nearly seven decades getting my heart racing."

"How's your sugar?"

"Fine. I really want to just sit here and feel my age. Instead of, you know, denying the feeling."

His wife gave him an odd, but undeniably tolerant, look, and went back to the business at hand.

He guessed his own nose, like Lloyd's, was pretty sensitive. As he walked toward the garden to call Sammy in for supper, he smelled tobacco smoke on the spring air.

Sammy was sitting with his back against the picket fence, and was startled when Father Tim opened the gate. Sammy flicked the cigarette into the fence corner, where it landed among the rakes and shovels.

"Supper time," he said.

They were silent as they walked to the house. Did he talk with Sammy now and spoil Cynthia's dinner? No. But if he didn't talk with Sammy, the dinner was spoiled anyway—he felt his stomach in a veritable knot. Perhaps what was needed was time.

"We'll talk after we eat," said Father Tim. If nothing else, they'd have time to think about what they wanted to say to each other.

As he bowed his head to ask the blessing, he noted that Sammy's scar was aflame.

If he had such a scar, his would be aflame, also.

He decided to talk on what could loosely be called his own turf: the library. The leather chairs lent a certain authority that he might find lacking in himself when push came to shove.

"The day after you arrived, we talked about the rules."

"Yeah, but you said th' g-garden was all m-mine."

"I also said no smoking, and thought that should cover it."

"Yeah, but if it's all m-mine, then I ought t' be able t' do what I want t' d-do in there, I'm th' one w-workin' it."

"You're being paid to work, the rules come from the household that's taken you in."

"You t-tell me somethin', then it ain't t-true n'more."

The clock ticked on the mantle. A lamb bleated in the paddock. "You lived as an orphan for many years, Sammy. No mother, and a father who couldn't be a true father to you. In truth, you were father to him.

"Now you're living in a family. There's a oneness to family life—what one person does affects all the others. I know it's frustrating for you, you've been making your own rules for a long time."

"No smokin', no hustlin', no c-cussin', k-keep m' room clean. I can't d-do all that b-b-bull."

"Here's the deal about rules. They aren't meant to put you in a box; they're meant to give you freedom. Doesn't pool have rules? Can you ignore the rules and win the game?"

Sammy didn't respond. He jiggled his leg, anxious to be away from the inquisition.

"You have a secure roof over your head, three meals a day, a job you say you like, a paycheck, your own room, people who care about you. Does that mean anything to you?"

Sammy's jaw flexed; Father Tim sensed he was ready to bolt. He didn't want to push

Sammy too far—he had money in his pocket, and shoe leather for the road.

"Think on these things, son. And let's go up and get some rest. We can talk again tomorrow; we can always talk. One thing you can count on is that we can talk."

Sammy shot to his feet and headed for the library door. He stood for a moment with his hand on the knob, his eyes defiant. "I hate this p-place."

He opened the door and vanished down the hall and up the stairs.

Father Tim listened to the sound of Sammy's feet on the treads, as he'd often listened to Dooley's all those years ago.

It was painful to do what was right. There were times when he'd like to let things slide, go with the flow, call it a day, whatever.

His heart was a stone as he poked his own way upstairs.

He had no idea how he'd lived so many years without someone to talk with in bed. In his somewhat unsophisticated opinion, it was the apex of the common life.

Thankfully, the fries weren't mentioned. They'd tasted like cardboard, he thought, through no fault of the cook.

"He says he hates this place."

Cynthia sighed, rolled toward him, and laid her hand on his shoulder. "Poor Sammy. I guess you could say we're in over our heads."

"Way over," he said, disconsolate.

CHAPTER SIXTEEN

Cake

"Father Tim? Lew Boyd.

"I been meanin' to tell you that some rough-neck come by th' station lookin' for you. I told 'im you were livin' in th' boonies. Don't know who it was, 'e looked mighty low on th' food chain t' me. I give 'im directions t' where you're at.

"Let's see. I guess it was two, three weeks ago when he come by, maybe more, I don't know—time flies when you're balancin' front ends." *Beep.*

The call must have arrived in the library answering machine yesterday; he'd been too distracted to notice the blinking light when he talked with Sammy.

For years he'd had an odd fantasy that his childhood best friend, Tommy Noles, would come searching for him. He devoutly hoped, however, that Tommy, who'd vanished after college as into ether, wouldn't turn up looking "low on the food chain."

The character who showed up at Lew's was probably one of the several who'd passed through Mitford over the years, seeking a handout from the priest at Lord's Chapel. He'd kept a special cash fund labeled D&O, which only he and Emma knew to be Down and Out.

He hit the "message" button again.

"Father Tim? This is Betty Craig. I hate t' bother you, but pretty soon, there'll be nothin' left of me t' bother you *with*. Miss Rose throwed a pot lid at me, an' that's not th' half of it. Let me know if you've come up with anything, an' I hope t' hear back real quick." *Beep.*

He had no earthly idea what to do. If Esther Cunningham weren't out riding the range, she'd have this thing in the can. After sixteen years in office, Esther had thrown in the towel, otherwise he'd have voted for her 'til the cows came home. The only thing to do was stall for time; he'd call Betty and give her a pep talk, and next week, he'd bear down on this . . .

He glanced at the clock on the library mantel and noted that he was pacing the floor. This was no way to get his heart rate up. He felt oddly lost, anxious.

It was way too early for Sammy to be stirring. Cynthia was sleeping in 'til seven, having had a restless night. He'd already taken the dogs out and downed his toast and coffee. And, of course, he'd read the Morning Office and talked with the Lord, albeit in a dispirited sort of way, for his mind had dashed about like a terrier.

He continued pacing, pulling at his chin.

Sammy couldn't have been more than six or seven years old when Pauline deserted her children, taking Poo with her. Clyde Barlowe had made off with Sammy; Kenny had been traded by his mother for a gallon of whiskey to a stranger named Ed Sikes; Jessie, the baby, had been abducted by a dysfunctional cousin of Pauline's.

It was during this terrible upheaval that the eleven-year-old Dooley had come to live at the rectory. How he and Dooley had gotten through those early years was more than a mystery, it was a miracle. And now, Sammy . . .

He realized that Sammy probably had little or no memory of ever sitting down at a table for a family meal. Almost everything he was doing at Meadowgate would be, in one way or another, new to him.

With one possible exception. Truth be told, Sammy had been reasonably deft at keeping his room in a semblance of order, which had amazed both Cynthia and the Flower Girls. Very likely, this sense of order came naturally to him; plus, he'd been father to his father for years, and therefore seriously acquainted with responsibility. Lon Burtie once said Sammy's gambling in the pool hall helped put food on the table when Clyde drank up his disability check.

First thing this morning, he'd praise Sammy for the good job of keeping his room straight. He'd been meaning to mention that . . .

The wind was picking up, he could smell the noxious odor of creosote throughout the house. Cynthia sneezed; he sneezed . . . same old, same old. The chimney fiasco was a lesson in patience if ever there was one . . .

At precisely seven-thirty, Lloyd and Buster trooped in with buckets of wet mortar, looking apologetic.

"We'll try not to spill nothin' on y'r floors."

Buster nodded. "We'll try not to."

Willie trotted in their wake.

"Dozen," said Willie, who had bypassed the frills of a carton and used his hat.

Father Tim plucked the brown eggs from the hat and deposited them in the blue bowl. "So we're holding our own?"

"Yessir. Holdin' steady."

Maybe he'd been wrong, maybe the lowlife who'd robbed their henhouse had moved on, after all. A set of beat-up lowers and a can of beans were hardly an indication of serious housekeeping.

"It's Del!"

He positively shouted as he saw the blue van with the American flag decal wheel into the backyard. A Confederate flag waved from the antenna.

His wife's face lit up big-time. "I never dreamed I'd be thrilled to see Del—especially when I was expecting Lily."

"Full of surprises, those girls."

"Only one problem. Del doesn't cook or bake, and we need a cake for Sunday. Sissie's expecting it, and Roy Dale and Gladys . . ."

"Won't Lily be coming tomorrow?"

"I've been meaning to tell you, we're on our own tomorrow; Lily's doing a birthday party at the mayor's office in Wesley."

He considered this. "I don't suppose baking a cake would get my heart rate up?"

"Probably not. But it would be lovely of you to try it and see."

There he went again, opening his big mouth.

By eight-fifteen, they were en route to the attic, schlepping a vacuum cleaner, a broom, a dustpan, two easels, four boxes of art supplies, a box of art books, a stool, a basket of cleaning rags, an upholstered chair, a cat bed, two cat bowls, a ten-pound bag of cat food, a jug of drinking water, and a cat.

They bumped and thumped along the hall like so many Conestogas across Kansas.

He'd pitch in and haul one more load, then knock on Sammy's door. Maybe he'd run to Mitford today and take Sammy and his siblings to Sweet Stuff, and pick up cake ingredients while he was at it.

Chances were, Sammy was already awake. Even a teenager would have trouble sleeping through the move from hell to heaven.

The bed was loosely spread, there was an empty package of Camels in the trash basket, unfolded laundry sat in the chair . . .

From a cursory look in the closet, Sammy was wearing the black jeans, blue sweatshirt, and threadbare tennis shoes he'd arrived in.

Maybe Sammy had gotten up early, and walked out to the garden, or even to the barn, and all that was needed was to go and find him. He stood looking out the window, unseeing, then turned and went downstairs.

He and Willie searched the place, but to no avail.

Sammy was gone. His heart told him so.

"I saw his potatoes yesterday. They were so healthy and beautiful. And the lettuce . . ." His wife sat at her easel by the attic window, look-ing bereft.

"He'll be back," he said, trying to convince them both. "Gardeners always want to see their potatoes come in."

He sat in the upholstered chair they'd dragged up from the lower hall. He didn't want to ask this; he knew he wouldn't like the sound of it in the room. "Should we call the police?"

"I think we should give him a chance to come home," she said. "What if he just went to the woods to think things over? Or maybe he walked to Kirby's Store. The police seem a very serious piece of business at this point."

"I guess we shouldn't call Dooley . . ."

"Heavens, no!"

"Pray that we don't have to."

"I'm praying," she said.

"Want another cup of coffee?"

"It's a long trip to the kitchen."

"It'll get my heart rate up," he said, glad for something to do.

"Coming again soon?" he asked Del.

"If m' back don't go out." She was shifting the kitchen table away from the stove so she could open the door and clean the oven. She gave Lloyd and Buster a look they'd be grateful to have missed.

"Know anyone who sits with the elderly, does a little cooking, that sort of thing?"

"Th' trouble with elderly is, you don't *sit* with 'em, they keep you bobbin' up an' down like a jack in th' box."

"But do you know anyone?"

"Our mama's done that . . ."

"Terrific!"

"But now *she's* elderly. So, no, sir, I don' know n'body."

"I'm baking a cake today," he said, trying to sound upbeat.

Del had dropped to her knees and was getting on with it.

"Know anything about cake baking?" Baking a ham was one thing, but cake was another.

"Not a bloomin' thing, an' don't want t' learn. I knowed a woman who choked t' death on coconut cake. That done it f'r me right there. I only bake pie, now, an' as little of that as I can git by with."

He'd get no help around here.

He hadn't threatened or cajoled or demanded, he'd said what had to be said, and there was no turning back. He had spoken the truth in love, and that would have to be OK.

He prayed again for Sammy's safekeeping, and for God to lift the heaviness from both their hearts and give them wisdom.

Cynthia said she'd be waiting when Sammy came home, and in the meantime, Holy Trinity's vicar was to go and do something for himself that wasn't work related, something light and amusing and entirely brainless.

But he didn't know how to do that, he'd protested.

I'm sure you can come up with something, she'd said, gazing at him as if he were a four-year-old.

For one thing, he thought as he started the truck, he might drop in on Blake Eddistoe on his way to Mitford to get the cake ingredients. After all, they hadn't seen Blake in weeks, except to wave whenever they glimpsed him down at the kennels.

And then he would . . .

As he was trying to figure a further agenda, he forgot his mission and blew past the clinic and out the gate and onto the state road. The new wayside pulpit flashed by.

IF GOD IS YOUR CO-PILOT,
CHANGE SEATS.

And then he would . . .

Would what? He was brainless, all right, not to mention sick at heart.

It occurred to him that Sammy may have hitchhiked to Wesley. So maybe he should turn around and go home and call Bud Wyzer. But no, it was too early; the pool hall didn't open 'til one o'clock.

Out of the blue, the proverbial lightbulb switched on. He was amazed that he could come up with a sensible idea at a time like this.

"She's back there somewhere," said Judd Baker. "I've seen her with my own eyes this morning, she bought baking soda."

"Don't let me get out of here without ingredients for a cake," said the vicar. "And before I go, I'd be grateful to use your phone, into the bargain. Local call."

"No problem. What kind of cake? I'll be glad to pull your stuff together."

"Hadn't thought of what kind . . ." Blast. Now he had to figure what kind. "Don't have a clue. What do you think?"

"Can't go wrong with chocolate."

"Do it, and I'll appreciate it."

"Nuts in your frosting?"

"Whatever you say. Surprise me!" He'd be surprised, all right, if he could bake a cake that anybody would eat.

"Miss Lottie?"

He merely tapped on the door, not wishing

to startle her. When he got no answer, he knocked louder—Absalom's widowed sister may have trouble hearing.

The door opened and a stooped, white-haired woman peered out. "Miss Lottie! Father Tim Kavanagh, Absalom's old friend."

She looked at him curiously, then smiled in recognition.

"Is this a good time?"

"You'll have to speak up!" called Judd.

"Is this a good time, Miss Lottie?"

"Oh, yes, anytime is a good time for a friend of Absalom's." She stepped aside for him to pass into the sitting room.

He felt a stab of nostalgia. The room was more beautiful than he remembered, with a clematis vine grown over the small window like crochet work. The minuscule fireplace with its rock surround sat beneath a shelf of smoke-blackened cherry that displayed faded photographs of Greer's Store in its heyday, and a hand-colored portrait of Absalom as a young evangelist.

"I'm sorry to hear about your cat, Miss Lottie."

"Thomas gave me eighteen years of mousing and companionship. That should be enough for anybody, but I miss him, nonetheless."

Her hand trembled as she indicated Absalom's chair. Then she took the chair across from him, where she'd stationed herself for so many years as her brother's companion, confidante, nursemaid, and housekeeper.

"I've been hoping you would come," she said, lowering her eyes to her lap. "Absalom thought the world of you. You were always so kind to us, and thoughtful."

"Thank you, ma'am, but it was you and your brother who were kind to me. I did stop by recently; but I'm ashamed I haven't been here more often."

"Everyone's so busy," she said, as if bewildered by this truth.

"I hear you get out and about."

She nodded, smiling. "When I can."

"I miss Absalom. He was the best of the lot."

"Yes. He was." Always shy, she seemed shyer still. "I wanted to tell you how it grieves me to know I failed him."

"Good heavens! In what way, may I ask?"

"You know I was against his love for Sadie Baxter. All those years, I conspired against Sadie, and spoke meanly of her, for I didn't wish to lose my brother."

She raised her head and looked at him with frank, brown eyes. "As children, Absalom and I were as thick as thieves, as Mother used to say, and he was always tender to his little sister. Each summer, he climbed the cherry tree and brought me down a hatful of cherries."

"I always wanted a brother or sister," he said, as if thinking aloud.

"When my husband died after such a brief marriage, Absalom took me in. I didn't have to worry about anything at all. He depended on the Lord and I depended on Absalom." She pressed her hand to her forehead. "He was everything to me, and now it's too late."

"Too late for what, Miss Lottie?"

"To late to ask forgiveness of them both. I so regret not asking their forgiveness."

"I'm sure you've asked God's forgiveness."

"No," she said. "I never have. God was Absalom's territory. I let him handle such things for us both."

"Ah."

"I never understood God in the way Absalom did."

"What do you mean?"

"God seemed so near to Absalom, and so distant to me. I would go to my brother and say, 'Brother, will you pray for a good crop of potatoes this year?' And he would pray and the Lord would faithfully provide. When I prayed, it didn't seem to . . . work. So I quit. Long years ago."

She sounded wistful.

"It's never too late, Miss Lottie."

"For what, Father?"

"For the peace of His forgiveness."

A breeze stirred the clematis vine at the window, rearranging the pattern of light on the hearth rug.

"When we ask God to forgive us—and we must ask—the peace floods in. By emptying ourselves of the guilt and regret, we make room for His grace."

She sat looking at her hands, which were clasped tightly in her lap.

"Absalom was a man after God's own heart, and I have no doubt that He loved your brother mightily. But He loves you, too. Do you know that?"

"I don't know that . . . like I should. I never thought it important for me to know all those things about the Lord, if Absalom knew them. I believed my only task was to serve my brother, so he could serve the Almighty."

"Serving your brother was a great service to God. Look how fit you helped keep Absalom as he preached all those years to his little handfuls. Think of the souls that were saved in his long years of ministry, and the lives that were changed forever. You had something to do with that, Miss Lottie, something important."

Tears shone in her eyes.

"I miss him most after supper," she said, "when he'd tell me about his day out in the world."

"He sat right here, didn't he?"

"Yes, right there, for all those years. That was his spot to study the Word, and think on his sermons, and read. He wasn't school educated, you know."

"I know."

"He educated himself."

"That may be best, in the end." He leaned forward with his elbows on his knees. "If you ask, you still have a companion you can talk with every evening after supper."

She leaned her head to one side, pondering his meaning.

"The Spirit of God Himself, made known through Jesus Christ, will sit here with you. If that's something you might want."

She covered her face with her hands. "Oh, my gracious."

"What is it?"

"I can't even think such a thing. Why would He want to . . . to sit with me?" She looked at him, aghast.

"Miss Lottie, if you had a child, wouldn't you like to spend time with her in the evenings and go over the affairs of the day? Enjoy being together?"

"Oh, yes!" she said.

"You're God's child. You can tell Him everything, and ask Him anything. And think how grateful He'd be for your company."

She shook her head, dumbstruck.

"In the book of Revelation, we learn why He created us—it was for His pleasure. Indeed, He made us for Himself."

"Absalom used to say that—that He made us for Himself." A certain wonder softened her features.

"It isn't too late, Miss Lottie."

"Yes," she whispered. "Yes. It's time."

He left the sitting room with a feeling of elation.

"Chocolate cake mix, frosting in a can, walnuts," said Judd. "You got eggs?"

"I'll say!"

"You got sugar?"

"The whole nine yards, except for the basics here."

"There you go, then. Done deal."

"Many thanks." He dug in his pocket for his billfold. "May as well give me two of every-thing; we have a new Sunday School under way and the children are fond of cake." And wasn't Dooley coming home in no time flat? "Then again, make that three of everything. Are Miss Lottie's needs taken care of?"

"They are. Her brother left her in good shape."

"I'll be back now and then," he said. "May I use your phone?"

"On th' wall over there."

No, Cynthia told him, Sammy hadn't come home. He heard the anxiety in her voice.

He left Greer's Store with a sense of dread.

Cynthia was beaming as she handed him the manila envelope he'd waited for.

"Congratulations, darling."

They hugged, wordless.

They were the proud new parents of a hundred-and-sixty-pound boy.

Dear Father Tim,

The Mitford Muse kindly shared your address.

You won't remember me, but Frank and I

attended the nine o'clock at Lord's Chapel when we came up from Fort Lauderdale each summer.

Frank has passed on, and I am emptying our house, Overlook, just two doors from poor Edith Mallory's Clear Day. You would be so welcome to our piano! Frank played it at every single one of our parties for thirty years! Gershwin was his favorite, esp. "I've Got Rhythm!"

And while we're at it, could you use a nice card table and four chairs, a hall runner, an umbrella stand (very nice, only one dent), and a lamp made from the horns of a rinoscerous (sp?)?

I am downsizing.

Yours sincerely,

Marsha Ford

P.S. I hope all this would be tax deductible. One must think of these things. Anytime Tuesday would be convenient for you to pick everything up.

Dear Mrs. Ford,

Of course I remember you. You enjoyed wearing hats, a fashion which clergy are known to appreciate! And Frank was fond of giving out round tuits; I believe I still have mine.

We would be delighted to take the whole kit and caboodle and yes, indeed, all should be tax

*deductible. I will supply something on paper for
your records.*

*I know precisely where you are and shall be
there on Tuesday at eleven.*

*My sincerest condolences; Frank was a very
cheerful and upbeat fellow who made a difference in our midst.*

Yours in Him Who loved us first,
Fr Timothy Kavanagh †

The letter written, and his wife painting like
a maniac, he preheated their fastidiously clean
oven to 375, according to instructions.

There was a sense of waiting in the air,
something palpable; he was listening for a step
on the porch, a knock on the door, the ringing
of the phone; his shoulders were hitched up
around his ears.

He would try to forget what he was beginning
to think, and surrender his all to this cake . . .

He plucked three brown eggs from the blue
bowl and went about the exceedingly mysterious ritual that would result in laughter and
happiness on Wilson's Ridge.

"It's beautiful!" she said, meaning it.

He'd gone up to heaven and beseeched his

wife to come and see the common miracle he'd performed.

It sat on a cream-ware cake stand in the center of the pine table, and he was smitten with it.

"It worked," he said. "I can't believe it."

Even Buster and Lloyd had been impressed.

"But it took two hours," he lamented. "And that's out of a *box*. Think what it would take from scratch." He was mortified.

"Two hours' work," she pronounced, "will last a mere fifteen minutes at Holy Trinity."

He could hardly wait 'til Sunday.

"I can't be brave any longer," she said. The sun had just disappeared behind the mountain, and they sat, worn from waiting, in the old wicker chairs on the porch.

"I don't feel brave at all," he confessed. "Worried sick is more like it."

"Me, too."

"The police, then."

"Yes."

He rose from the chair; the enormous weight of his body astonished him.

Unconsciously, he shook his head all along the hall to the library. The prospect of a revolving blue light provoked in him a mixture of nausea and dread.

He prayed as he dialed.

Our Lord Emmanuel, thank You for living up to Your name and being with us . . .

He had walked out to the porch to wait for the county police when he heard the crunch of footsteps on the gravel. He knew at once . . .

Sammy ambled toward the porch, his tall, thin frame a silhouette in the dusky half-light.

"Hey."

"Hey, yourself. Where have you been?"

"Around."

"Around where?"

Sammy shrugged.

"Answer me, please."

Sammy sat down on the bottom step, his back to the vicar. "I spent th' n-night in th' b-barn."

"Come up to the porch. We'll talk face-to-face." He was giving it all he had to keep his voice calm.

Sammy took his time rising from the step and walking up to the porch.

"Sit down," said the vicar. "Tell me everything."

"They's snakes in y'r barn."

"Not that."

"I hitched t' Wesley this mornin'."

"Keep going."

"I waited 'til th' p-pool hall opened. B–Bud wadn't there."

Sammy jiggled his leg and looked at the floor.

"I'm waiting."

"I lost all m' m–money."

"All."

"Yeah."

"Yes, sir."

"Yes, sir. Dunn whipped my ass."

"You asked for it."

"Yeah."

"All your life there's been no one to care where you are or what you're doing. The minute you stepped foot on this place a few weeks ago, that changed. Now you have someone who cares very much where you are and what you're doing. You also have someone to report to—and that someone is me."

Silence.

"Listen carefully, and mark my words: This won't happen again."

Sammy shrugged.

"Did you hear what I said?"

"Yeah."

"Yes, sir. What did I say?"

"It w–won't happen ag'in."

He heard the wheels of the county car crunching on the gravel.

"It's the police. Walk out with me."

"W–what's happenin'?"

"Walk out with me."

Father Tim went down the steps and out to the parking area. He turned around and waited for Sammy, and they walked to the car as it wheeled in. He was thankful there was no flashing blue light.

An officer opened the driver's door and stepped out. His partner stepped out the other side.

"I'm Officer Justice; that's Officer Daley. This th' right place?"

"Father Tim Kavanagh." He shook hands with Justice. "It is the right place, and I owe you an apology. There's been a mistake."

"We were told somethin' about a missin' boy."

"Yes, well, he isn't missing at all. Standing right here in the flesh."

"Hey," Sammy croaked.

"You big, fat *bonehead*!" Cynthia punched Sammy on the arm. "Do that again and I'll clean your clock."

Sammy burst into laughter.

Cynthia laughed through her tears.

Father Tim felt the eighteen-wheeler roll off his shoulders.

"Anybody want a piece of cake?" he asked.

"Lily's doin' th' mayor's party; she does it ever' year an' they all love it! Course, if it was at night, like it used t' be, I'd sing, but they quit havin' it at night; said a little hanky panky got t' goin' on."

"Uh-oh." Violet was dressed in jeans and a T-shirt; he hardly recognized her. "Well! We didn't know anybody at all was coming today."

"Oh, yes, if one don't come, another'n does. When Lily said she was doin' th' mayor's party, I reckon she thought you *knowed* you'd git a replacement. We always give a replacement."

"Wonderful. Well! Do you bake, Violet?"

"Bake." She pondered this. "In what way?"

"Cakes."

"Lily bakes. I clean."

"Couldn't you bake *and* clean?"

"I wouldn't want to, t' tell th' truth. But what did you have in mind?"

"I baked a cake yesterday . . ."

"Git outta here! No way did y' do that!"

He saw Lloyd stick his head through the

opening in the blue tent, and smoke over their house help.

". . . and then, last night," said the vicar, "we had a sort of . . . celebration and Cynthia and Sammy ate most of it. So I need another one for Sunday." She seemed unmoved. "For the *children!*" he said, trying to close the deal.

She gave forth a moan. "OK, I'll do it f'r you an' Miss Cynthia. But jis' this once."

"Preheat the oven to three seventy-five," he said. "You can't just pop it in there, you have to wait 'til the oven heats."

"I ain't as dumb as a *rock*. I *have* baked a cake or two in my life; I jis' ain't made a *callin'* of it."

He remembered his life as a bachelor and how simple it had been.

Taking the red leash from the coatrack, he had a thought. When Sissie, Rooter, Sammy, Roy Dale, Gladys, and seven Millwrights got hold of that cake, it would be history. Sunday was a very special Sabbath, indeed, and wouldn't the adults be thrilled to find their own chocolate cake on the table at the end of the service?

He cleared his throat. "Violet?" he said.

He zoomed along the state road with Barnabas sitting stoically in the passenger seat, looking straight ahead. He had to get the papers notarized, pick up provisions at The Local, zip over to see Harley and Lew, then head back to the sticks, ASAP. His sermon was sitting in the library on the back burner and needed to be moved to the front.

He wanted to get it under wraps before Dooley arrived on Saturday night, probably a little worse for wear after driving an antediluvian Jeep all the way from Georgia.

He took a left on Lilac Road so he could run up to Church Hill and get a glimpse of the new paint color on Fernbank, now home to Andrew and Anna Gregory's three-star restaurant, Lucera.

He could barely glimpse the late Victorian Fernbank through the trees, but saw that it sparkled. The new paint appeared to be a pale yellow, which he hoped the former owner might view with approval from her post on high.

He swooped right onto Old Church Lane and, realizing that his good dog might need a pit stop, pulled alongside the curb at Baxter Park. "Just a quick one," he said, putting on the leash.

It was good being back in the park; it seemed years since he'd entered the leafy glade where he courted his wife and she courted him back.

He noted the patrol car parked beneath the

walnut tree. On occasion, an officer pulled into the park to check it out, though the worst, and possibly only, crime that ever occurred here was an attempted assault years ago on a Wesley college student.

Aha! The car was Adele Hogan's. Yes, indeed, brand spanking new and looking good. As he walked Barnabas to the bushes, he noticed that the heads of the two people in the front seat were very close together. In truth, they appeared to be . . .

. . . kissing.

He felt his blood turn to ice. He looked away and then looked again.

Yes! Kissing! Clear as day.

He gave the leash a yank and bolted from the park, his heart sick within him.

"Is it something you could do . . . gently?"

"I could take it down, but who'd put it back ag'in?" asked Harley. "An' come t' think of it, how could Miss Sadie have took down part of th' head liner and got it back t' look right? I don't b'lieve that's th' place t' go messin' around."

He hadn't yet checked with Andrew for permission to give the Plymouth a more thorough going-over. He wanted to see what Harley had to say first.

"Maybe she used a tool of some kind to hide this . . . thing."

"Wonder if she could of hid it under th' hood? Y' know that ol' car's got a Golden Commando V8 engine in it. Man, that thing was a stroker; it'd run like a scalded dog! Had y'r dual four-barrel carbs, had y'r special dual exhaust system . . ."

Father Tim checked his watch. "My hunch is, it's not under the hood. Miss Sadie wasn't an under-the-hood type."

"What're you lookin' f'r . . . exactly?"

"Something about this high, this wide, and this long." He made a series of gestures.

Harley appeared perplexed.

"Think about it, if you would. I'll check back. And Harley . . ."

"Yessir?"

"Don't mention this to anybody, please. Not a soul."

Harley nodded, sober. "You can bank on it, Rev'ren'."

He stepped inside where Lew was counting bills from the register.

"Hey, buddyroe," said the vicar.

"Hey, how's it goin'?"

"Good. Who do you think the character was who came looking for me?"

"Don't have a clue. Asked 'im 'is name; he didn't say nothin'. Just said he'd find you."

"Old? Young? Tall? Short?"

"Prob'ly late forties. Hard livin' on 'is face, so couldn't say for sure. Medium."

"Walking? Riding?"

"Walkin'."

"There but for the grace of God go us," he said.

CHAPTER SEVENTEEN

A Full House

The truckload from Meadowgate arrived early, trailed by the Jeep.

Last Sunday, Dooley had wrangled permission to sleep in, having pulled into Meadowgate at one a.m., "fried," as he said, from a week of exams and the long haul home.

This Sunday, Dooley wanted to see what his brother was up to at Holy Trinity. Though Sammy felt humiliated when Dooley learned of his involvement in Sunday School, Dooley's approval and interest had changed everything.

Toting his vestments in a dry-cleaning bag, Father Tim hurried into the church with Sammy, while Cynthia and Dooley lingered at the wall, admiring the swoop and glide of hawks above the gorge.

He was happy, instead, to admire their spinet piano, and the burgundy runner along the center aisle, and the four chairs folded and leaning against the rear wall in case of an overflow, and the card table in the narthex where the pew bulletins would greet one and all each Sunday. Sammy thumped several full egg cartons onto the table, along with a homemade tent card: *first come, first served,* and headed for the sacristy with the cake box.

Who needed a full choir and stained glass with riches such as these?

"You look divine," said his wife, who was helping him vest. "In a manner of speaking, of course!"

He noted that his scarlet chasuble and gold-embroidered stole made him feel splendid—yes, that was the word!—and full of hope. Indeed, their resident male cardinal was also vested for this glorious Whitsunday.

"Oh, and Timothy . . ."

"Yes?"

"John the Baptist."

"Already? I just had it cut."

"That was Lent. This is Pentecost."

If it wasn't one thing, it was two, as his grandmother had been fond of saying.

He was checking the altar that Agnes had prepared when someone trotted down the aisle. "Hey-y, Father!"

"Violet! My goodness, this is a pleasant surprise. Hey, yourself!" Violet was decked, to say the least.

"Lloyd said he'd give a dollar if I'd go t' church with 'im, so here I am! An' here's th' dollar." She waved it around for his inspection.

The vicar grinned. "I guess a dollar goes a long way, after all."

She gazed at the altar, the carved pulpit, the kneelers. "I ain't never been in a church like this, so y'all'll have t' s'cuse me if I step in it."

He laughed. "Not to worry. When the heart's right, it's impossible to do anything wrong."

"My gosh," she said, looking pleased, "that's a sermon right there."

Come, Holy Spirit, heav'nly Dove
With all thy quick'ning powers
Kindle a flame of sacred love
In these cold hearts of ours.

See how we trifle here below
Fond of these earthly toys
Our souls, how heavily they go
To reach eternal joys.

In vain we tune our formal songs
In vain we strive to rise
Hosannas languish on our tongues
And our devotion dies.

Come, Holy Spirit, heav'nly Dove
With all thy quick'ning powers
Come, shed abroad a Savior's love
And that shall kindle ours.

At the time of announcements, he looked out to his congregation with a certain gladness.

Given Sparkle's increasing confidence with their hymnbook, Miss Martha's flat-out volume, and Violet's impressive vocal skills, the a cappella singing at Holy Trinity had picked up.

Way up.

"Our Lord has given us yet another day of perfection, and we're going to do our part to savor every moment. After the offering, we'll process into the churchyard and have Holy Communion at the wall. Then, at the close of our service, we'll come back inside, finish up with chocolate cake . . ."—he liked the approving murmur that rippled through the nave—"and learn Rooter's new hand sign.

"Now. What's different today about Holy Trinity?"

Rooter's hand shot into the air.

"Rooter?"

"'At pianna."

"Yes, the piano! As you'll read in the bulletin, it's a gift from God—via a thoughtful and generous lady in Mitford. And now we need but one other gift from the One Who is, Himself, the Perfect Gift: we need someone to play it."

He looked at his parishioners; they looked at one another.

Much shaking of heads, followed by silence.

After a moment of sober introspection, Sparkle raised her hand.

Their vicar's grin spread ear-to-ear.

This morning, he'd seen three parishioners sign last week's greeting, *Peace be with you,* to Clarence.

"And also with you," Clarence had signed back. Good medicine for their amiable and gifted crucifer, he reckoned, and very good medicine for them all.

Father Tim figured his own hand-signing vocabulary consisted roughly of most of the alphabet, Rooter's installment of last Sunday, *How's your work coming along?, A thousand thanks, I love you,* and, of course, *How are you doing, man?*

Enough right there to found a civilization!

He walked to the church door, looking for Rooter to come in and give his weekly demonstration. He saw four young Millwrights seated on the wall; Rooter stood facing them, and appeared to be holding forth with some zeal.

"'Bout half of ever'body in 'is church has kilt somebody," he heard Rooter declaim.

The Millwrights were wide-eyed.

"Robert with th' tattoos on 'is arm? He kilt 'is own granpaw."

Mamie Millwright clapped both hands to her mouth.

"An' Sissie's granmaw? She shot Sissie's granpaw dead. *Blam!* Square in th' head. 'Is brains gushed out all over ever'thing."

Father Tim walked down the steps and crossed to the shady north corner of the church. "Rooter!" he said.

Rooter wheeled around, startled.

"Would you step over here, please?"

He sometimes felt as if he could soar over the gorge like the hawks. Standing with Cynthia and Dooley and Sammy as his parishioners filed through the church door and back to their lives above the clouds, he realized he was as eager as a child for all the Sundays to follow; Holy Trinity was his cake.

"Rooter, this is my son, Dooley Kavanagh." His heart seemed to swell, quite literally, as he spoke these words.

Rooter furrowed his brow and looked at Dooley. "How come if you 'n' Sammy are brothers, he ain't but one of y'all's daddy?"

"I don' see how he could be y'r *daddy*," said Roy Dale.

Dooley grinned. "Why not?"

"'E's too *old*."

The vicar winked at Dooley. No rest for the wicked, he thought, and the righteous don't need none.

Granny peered closely at Dooley, then at Father Tim. "He don't look much like y'r ownself."

"More hair," he said.

"See 'at bunion?" Granny pointed to her right foot, generously exposed by a bedroom slipper. "Hit'll be took off t'morrow. Lord have mercy, I'm skeered of th' knife! I'll be jumpin' out th' winder an' runnin' clear t' Ashe County."

Cynthia gave Granny a hug. "We'll be praying for you, Granny. And don't worry, you're going to be just fine."

"Agnes," he said, "what was in the bag I took from your freezer?"

"Wasn't it squirrels?"

"No, ma'am, I'm afraid the squirrels are still where I left them."

She laughed. "Which is where they'll stay 'til someone other than myself removes them!"

"Jubal couldn't identify what I took from the schoolhouse. I certainly apologize—and I'll be glad to replace it!"

"I have no earthly idea what it might be. The turtle Jeff Stokes brought us made the most delicious soup. And the frog legs . . . I believe Clarence fried them last week while I planted asters. Come to think of it, there was something his sales representative gave him, but I never saw what it was."

He didn't know if his culinary inclinations would ever catch up to those of his parish.

Each and every Millwright filed past with a wordless nod or hesitant smile. He found the entire family to be as shy as deer—a characteristic generously compensated for by Sparkle Foster.

"I used t' play th' piano at church," she confessed as she came through the line, "an' got s' wore out, I was kind of glad y'all didn't have one. Then when you called for somebody this mornin', I got this warm feelin', kind of like choc'late meltin' if you leave it in th' car when it's hot, an' I knew th' Lord wanted me to do it."

"And God bless you for it, Sparkle! It will make all the difference."

"Somebody'll have t' get me some sheet music. Y'all sing really diff'rent stuff."

"Consider it done!"

"An' tunin'," she said, "it'll need tunin'."

Miss Martha grasped his hand with both of hers and shook it mightily.

"Fine service, Father. Very fine."

"Very fine!" said Miss Mary.

"And thank you, Cynthia, for the new Sunday School. I've always said, if you don't go to Sunday School, you go home with *half* a load of bricks!"

Miss Mary nodded. "*Half* a load!"

"I really liked bein' with y'all," said Violet. "It's a good thing I can read music! Oh, an' I put th' dollar in th' plate."

"One of your better investments, I assure you. Bring her again and again, Lloyd."

Lloyd shook the vicar's hand, blushing furiously.

Father Tim liked to think that something in Robert Prichard might be lighter, freer. And yet, each time he looked into Robert's eyes, the darkness held fast, he couldn't find the light.

"Lead poisoning," he told Donny when they stopped by the trailer after church.

"She'll need to be at Mitford Hospital for at least three days, according to Dr. Harper. He wants her there first thing tomorrow morning, she's dangerously anemic and undernourished. They'll test her liver function; give her chelation therapy; start iron supplements; that sort of thing."

"It ain't depression?"

"Almost certainly some depression caused by her inability to be up and about. But no, depression isn't the main issue."

Donny kicked at a tree stump in the yard of the trailer. "How come they didn't find it th' other two times I took 'er?"

"Lead levels aren't always part of a fatigue workup."

A car sped along the gravel road, sending a flume of dust into the air.

"Any insurance?"

Donny gave him a hard look. "Lusters pay as they go."

"What about Sissie? Who . . . ?"

"Don' know who she'll stay with. I'll be cuttin' pines of a mornin' and runnin' 'em th'ough
th' mill of a e'nin'. Granny's goin' down th'
mountain to have a bunion took off t'morrow.
I'll figure out somethin'."

"Doctor Harper says Dovey can't come back
to the trailer for a while."

Donny glowered. "Why not?"

"The state environmental people need to
come in and check the pipes, and any other
potential lead sites. You and Sissie will need to
get out, too."

"F'r how long?"

"I don't know."

Donny uttered an oath. "Now I got t' git out
of m' own house?"

"I'll meet you at Mitford Hospital at seven in
the morning, help you get her checked in."

"I don' know whose goin' t' pay f'r all 'is mess."

"Tell you what," said the rector. "Let's pray
about it."

"Pray about it? I've prayed about th' whole
deal 'til I'm blue in th' face. He don't hear me
n'more."

Donny turned away and took a cigarette
from the pack in his shirt pocket and lit it with
a book match. He inhaled, and angrily flipped
the dead match into the bushes.

"You pray," he told the vicar.

They were headed toward Meadowgate with Sissie, a grocery bag stuffed with pajamas, a derelict toy bear, and a change of clothes. Dooley and Sammy drove ahead in the Jeep.

Father Tim glanced down at Sissie, who was looking glum. "Can you tell me what you learned today in Sunday School?"

Sissie kicked at the dashboard with the toe of a yellow shoe. "Sammy, he give us a seed apiece an' a little pot with dirt in it. I went off an' f'rgot mine."

"We'll give you another one. Did he say anything about the seed?"

"Cynthy, she said a seed's got t' git light . . . an' what else?"

"Water," said Cynthia. "And food."

"She said Jesus is all them things, an' when He lives in us, He makes us grow."

"Well done, Sissie. Have you ever watched a seed grow?"

"No."

"You will when you get to our house," said Cynthia. "Can you believe that the little seed we gave everyone this morning is really a very tall sunflower, as high as this truck?"

Sissie shook her head. "No."

"Me, neither," said the vicar.

"Sho-o-o!" Sissie looked around their dese-
crated kitchen and wrinkled her nose. "Hit
stinks in you'uns' house."

"M-might be y'r upper l-lip," said Sammy.

Father Tim crawled into bed and punched
up his pillow. As all beds were taken, Sissie
sprawled on the loveseat in their bedroom,
snoring beneath a quilt.

"A full house," he said, feeling both the weight
and the providence of such a circumstance.

His wife heaved a sigh. "I always wanted
children. But I never dreamed they'd all belong
to other people."

As he was leaving the house at a little after
six on Monday, he saw Willie trotting to the
porch in the dusky first light. He was toting his
hat and looking defeated.

"Took 'em out of th' nest yesterday evenin'.
Eleven."

"You counted the chickens?"

"Eleven."

"Blast. We lost one, then."

"Yessir. But didn't hear nothin' in th' night."

Willie shook his head. He was totally mystified, and plenty disgusted into the bargain. The whole thing was a dadgum aggravation.

He did all he could to assure Dovey, and promised to visit again on Tuesday. Afterward, he scooted to Dora Pugh's Hardware, jingling the bell above the door.

"I been lookin' for you in th' obituaries!" said Dora.

"Don't look there yet!"

"Have you heard about Coot Hendrick's new job?"

"Coot's *working?*" As far as he knew, Coot hadn't struck a lick at a snake in at least two decades.

"Has a hundred and seventy people under him."

"*What?*"

"Weed-eats th' town graveyard."

He laughed. "Ah, Dora, you're a sly one."

"I hear Bill Sprouse up at First Baptist cut his chin pretty bad while shavin', said he had his mind on his sermon."

"I'll be darned. Sorry to hear it."

"They say he should've kep' his mind on his chin and cut 'is sermon."

"You got me twice in a row!"

Dora cackled.

"What's your best deal on a garden spade?"

"You want a good garden spade or a sorry garden spade?"

"Better give me a good garden spade."

"Thirty-four ninety-five."

"Done," he said, reaching into his hip pocket.

He noted that Dora was smoking him over. "You've sure let your hair get long."

"Only around the collar," he said. "Nothing much happening on top."

It was definitely that time again.

He raced up Main Street and crossed to The Local, carrying the shovel.

"Avis, how's business?"

"Can't complain. How's yours?"

"Growing," he said, pulling out the grocery list. "We've got a crowd at the house—two strapping boys and a five-year-old. If you could put this together for me, I'll pick it up in a couple of hours."

"You need a U-Haul," said Avis, looking at the list. "I see Ol' Dooley's home—steak and p'tatoes." He scanned the list. "Nothin' on here for a little kid; better get you some peanut butter an' jelly."

"Brilliant! And while I'm thinking of it, add a couple of cake mixes. Chocolate."

"You heard th' one about th' guy who broke into th' dress store three nights in a row?"

"Haven't heard it."

"Told th' judge he picked out a dress for his wife an' had to exchange it two times."

Father Tim burst out laughing. He'd never known the poker-faced Avis Packard to tell a joke in the twenty years he'd known him. Miracles, he was glad to be reminded, happen all the time.

He had a few minutes to fill the tank and shoot the breeze, but no time for lunch.

Wheeling into Lew's, he realized he dreaded seeing J.C.

It wasn't his place to report what he'd stumbled upon, and yet, shouldn't J.C. know that his worst fear had come to pass? On the other hand, J.C. would find out soon enough—someone would surely spill the beans; carrying on in a patrol car wouldn't go unnoticed in Mitford, not by a long shot.

He thought the *Muse* editor looked . . . what? Tan? Slimmer?

And Percy, he observed, was definitely looking younger. "It's layin' up in bed 'til six o'clock," said Percy, who'd risen before five for more than forty years.

Mule, on the other hand, looked like he'd always looked which, in a world of change, was sort of comforting, thought Father Tim.

"You know how th' Presbyterians don't pay their preacher anything to speak of," said Mule.

That news had been on the street for years.

"Th' other night, somebody broke in through his bedroom window, and held a gun on 'im."

"Good grief!" said Father Tim.

"Told ol' Henry not to move; said he was huntin' for his money. Henry said, 'Let me get up an' turn on th' light, an' I'll hunt with you.'"

Father Tim hooted with laughter, as did the rest of the Turkey Club.

Percy unzipped his lunch bag. "I guess you heard about th' carrier pigeon that rolled in twelve hours late."

Nobody had heard it.

"Said it was such a nice day, it decided to walk."

J.C. rolled his eyes.

"What's going on?" asked Father Tim. "All of a sudden, Mitford is Joke City. I get jokes from Dora Pugh, a joke from Avis, of all people . . ."

"It's an Uncle Billy kind of thing," said Mule. "Holdin' on to th' tradition."

"Yeah," said Percy.

J.C. hauled a foil-wrapped lump from his briefcase. "Eat more fiber, tell more jokes. It's sort of a health deal that's goin' around."

"Speaking of health, looks like you're dropping a little weight."

"I blew off six pounds." J.C. peeled away the foil.

"And what's with the tan?"

"Yard work, buddyroe, yard work."

The fumes from J.C.'s lunch were killer. The vicar glanced at his watch.

"You heard about th' guy who was so short you could see his feet on his driver's license?" asked J.C.

Mule groaned.

"Th' same guy had his appendix out, it left a scar on his neck."

What an amazing outbreak, thought Father Tim, something like measles . . .

"You heard th' one about two guys who rented a boat to go fishin' on th' lake?" asked J.C.

"Haven't heard it," said Father Tim.

"Th' first day, they caught thirty fish."

"That's a joke right there," said Mule, who never caught anything to speak of.

"When they started back to shore, one

said . . ."—J.C. took an enormous bite of his sandwich—" 'Bettermarkisspotsowecancome-backt'morrow.' "

"What'd he say?" asked Percy.

"Don't talk with your mouth full, for Pete's sake." This was definitely one of Mule's personal peeves.

J.C. gulped. "So, next day when they were goin' to rent a boat, the guy said, 'Did you mark our spot?' Other one says, 'Yeah, I put a big X on the bottom of th' boat.' His buddy says, 'That was pretty stupid; what if we don't get the same boat this time?' "

J.C. burst into laughter, a sound something like ham sizzling in lard.

"Oh, *man.*" Another of Mule's personal peeves was people who laughed at their own jokes.

Watching J.C. hoot his head off, Father Tim felt a stab of pity. Innocence was always bliss. "Any news of Edith?"

"I hear she keeps sayin' th' same thing over an' over. God is, God is, like that."

He'd been right, thought the vicar. Edith was making a complete and full confession of His Being. There were miracles everywhere.

J.C. peered at Mule's lunch. "Mine's tuna fish on whole wheat. What's yours?"

"Ravioli." Mule stabbed his lunch with a plastic fork, which snapped in two. "Shoot a monkey, wait a minute. Maybe it's . . ." The realtor looked bewildered. "I don't know what it is."

"I'm out of here," said Father Tim.

"I don't know what to do," he told Betty Craig on the porch of the town museum.

"If you don't do *somethin'*, you'll be seein' me in Broughton next time."

"*That* bad?"

"If you only knew."

"Then tell me, so I'll know."

"But you don't want t' know."

Nor did he want to be the one to remove Rose Watson from the house her brother built, the home she'd loved and lived in nearly all her life. Further, he certainly didn't think much of the nursing home in Holding. And, as the only way to get into Hope House was for someone to die, he darn sure wasn't praying along that line.

Time. That's what he needed. Time, and the prayer that never fails.

"Father, I'll give you another week and after that, I'm done. I'm sorry, 'cause you've been

awful good to me, but I'm only human. I am
not a saint with a halo."

"Oh, yes you are, Betty!"

"An' don't go flatterin' me, now, 'cause it
won't work."

A week. To do the impossible.

On Tuesday morning, he figured he should
slip over to the house in the woods, check it
out, and get this thing behind them once and
for all.

There was no need to say anything to anybody here. Heaven knows, there was enough
going on at Meadowgate, including an impro-
vised kindergarten in the attic, where Sissie was
painting and coloring, and asking questions a
mile a minute.

While the boys were still sleeping, he'd go
over alone, see what was what, and if he needed
to involve the county police, Justice and his
partner looked like fellows who could take
care of business.

Then again, maybe he shouldn't go alone . . .

"Barnabas!" he said, taking down the red
leash. "How about a walk in the woods?"

As they neared the house, Barnabas growled.

Probably, he thought, because something was hanging from the light fixture on the porch.

He approached cautiously and saw that a couple of wire hangers contained a pair of beat-up khakis, stained briefs that washing hadn't improved, a pair of white socks, and a shirt.

A blue and white checked shirt.

He walked onto the porch and examined the sleeves. Someone had tried to close the gap in the left sleeve with an awkward go at stitchery. The clothes were still damp to the touch. Wash day at the house in the woods; the thought made his hair stand on end.

He would leave as quietly as he'd come, and return to the farmhouse at a clip; the phone number of the county police was on a notepad hard by the phone.

Suddenly, Barnabas dove off the porch, barking wildly, and raced around the side of the house. Father Tim ran after him.

A naked man cowered beside the woodshed as Barnabas stood a couple of yards away, barking in a booming baritone that echoed from the surrounding woods.

"Git this dog offa me!"

"You're on our property illegally, my dog's just doing his job." His heart was thundering.

He knew this face well, though he'd seen it only once. "And—he's got all day to do it."

Barnabas's incessant barking was punctuated by his low growl, not a pretty sound.

"I ain't doin' nothin' wrong, I'm jis' passin' through f'r a little warsh-up in y'r creek." The man hunkered over, trying to cover himself. "You cain't blame a God-fearin' man f'r usin' y'r creek."

"I could blame him for using my chickens."

"What chickens?"

"The ones you stole from our henhouse and cooked in your fire pit over there. Those chickens."

Barnabas stopped barking and settled into a low growl. The growl, thought the vicar, was even more alarming than the bark.

"I ain't stole no chickens . . ."

"Let's don't pretend. I know who you are; you know who I am, and I believe I know why you're here. Let's get down to it, or I'll let my dog run you out to the state road and all the way to Kirby's Store. After that, you're on your own."

"I been dog bit a time or two; I ain't skeered."

"Yes, but you ain't been bit by this dog."

"Let me git m' clothes on; I'll go away from

here. You'll not see me ag'in." He held up both hands. Father Tim noticed that his hands were trembling.

"Stick around awhile; we've got a lot to say to each other."

"I'm naked as a jaybird, f'r God's sake . . ."

"Living up to your name, then. I'm told you're known to the federal government as Jaybird Johnson, a name you stole from a man who died on one of your job sites."

"I don't know what y'r talkin' about." The one-eyed Clyde Barlowe, alias Jaybird Johnson, moved suddenly toward the rear of the wood-shed. Barnabas launched himself in that direction and nailed Clyde at the corner of the building. Standing only inches away, Barnabas snarled at their prey so fiercely that even the hair on Father Tim's neck stood up.

"Lord God have mercy!" shouted Clyde.

"Tell me about the mercy you showed your son, Sammy, when you held him at gunpoint."

"I don' know what y'r talkin' about."

"I see you call on God."

Clyde spit vehemently. "That's a manner of speakin', they ain't no such of a thing as God."

"Why don't I leave my dog with you while I go make a phone call to the county police? It takes roughly eight minutes to walk to the house, and ten or fifteen for the police to arrive. That would give you plenty of time to get better acquainted with my friend here. Let me formally introduce you—his name is Barnabas. Barnabas, this is Clyde Barlowe, the father of Dooley and Sammy, who never gave any of his children a moment's love or protection."

Clyde uttered an oath, and dropped to his haunches, his back to the woodshed. "I'll git y' f'r this, I'll git y' f'r stealin' m' boys. I never signed nothin' sayin' you could take m' boys."

Father Tim sat on a stump. Barnabas hadn't once taken his eyes off the target. "Good fellow, Barnabas, keep doing what you're doing. So, Clyde, tell me why you're here. And please—don't waste my time or yours, or I'll have to ask Barnabas to get to the heart of the matter."

"When Sammy run out on me, I knowed where he'd go, he'd go to them as stole m' other boy from me. So I hitched up t' Mitford an' they tol' me where you was at. I come on th' place off of th' state road an' seen this house. I was goin' t' git Sammy t' come back to 'is rightful home."

"Looks like you weren't in any hurry to contact Sammy."

"When I seen y'r henhouse, I figured they

won't no use t' let a pen of chickens go t' waste."

"So you planned to eat up the chickens and then come and get Sammy."

"Looked like a good plan t' me."

"Clyde, you need somebody to help you think things through."

"I know how t' take a hen off th' roost slick as grease. I can git by dogs, by donkeys, you name it."

Father Tim didn't know how he got by the guineas, but that was a story for another day.

"You've got a lot of offenses going here, including larceny. A judge could throw the book at you—something like two hundred and forty days."

Father Tim knew the anguish both boys had suffered over their father. If he called in the police, Timothy Kavanagh would have to testify in court; the court date could drag on; and Dooley and Sammy would be seriously affected, to say the least. Bottom line, the summer they'd all looked forward to would be ruined.

"Let a man git 'is britches on, f'r God's sake. That'd be th' Christian thing to do."

"Look at it this way, Clyde:

"I know where your trailer is.

"I know something you don't want the government to know.

"I have a patch of your shirt that I will use as evidence.

"My witness can easily get you two hundred and forty days behind bars.

"And—if push ever comes to shove—I will take the stand against you on Sammy's behalf. You don't have a chance."

The sun had moved from behind the oak tree. Clyde shaded his eyes with his hands.

"Here's what I'm telling you: You don't ever want to come back here."

Barnabas sat down, still eyeing Clyde.

"In case a judge ever needs to see it, I'm keeping the shirt. Get your britches on, and may God have mercy on your soul."

After escorting Clyde Barlowe to the state road, he walked back to the farmhouse, now trembling, himself.

CHAPTER EIGHTEEN

Wisely Measured

He told her everything.

Should he also tell the boys? She didn't think so. Any discussion of his father always upset Dooley, just as it did Sammy.

Clyde Barlowe had come and Clyde Barlowe had gone. They decided to leave it at that.

At breakfast on Wednesday, his wife looked like the wreck of the Hesperus.

"I'll take over tomorrow," he promised, "if you can handle Sissie one more day."

"But only one," she said. "Then I'll take her again on Friday. How's that?"

He'd long considered division of labor a highlight of the marital state.

"Lily! Is that you?"

"Already got m' apron on, an' ready t' roll."

"We have a couple of new faces since you were here. Sissie Gleason and our son, Dooley Kavanagh."

She thumped her jar of sweet tea on the table. "Didn't know you had kids."

"Just one. Got him last week."

"How old is 'e?" She pulled on her plastic mask.

"Twenty-one."

"That's th' way t' git 'em, all right. Fully growed."

"You don't have to wear the mask; Violet's in the attic these days, working with her mistress."

"Y' never know what a cat'll do; if she gits out of th' attic, she'll head straight f'r me, sure as you're born. What's on th' menu f'r t'day?"

"Lasagna. Mac and cheese. Lamb stew . . ."

"*Lamb stew?* Y'all ain't eatin' them innocent little things I seen in th' pasture?"

"Heavens, no." The very thought gave him a turn. "This is, umm, store-bought."

"Good! What else?"

"Raisin-oatmeal cookies. And two chocolate pies, one for the freezer. If that's not too much to ask."

"Lord help! I hope you don't have y'r cholesterol checked anytime soon."

"That menu's mostly for the young people. The old people of the house will have fruit salad and cottage cheese."

"You want me t' cut up th' fruit?"

"I'd be much obliged," he said.

"By th' way, I don't have a soul to send t'morrow; you'll have t' put up with me ag'in."

"Great!" He liked having a plan; he'd never been much on surprises. "And Lily . . ."

"Yes, sir?"

"Thank you for coming whenever you can, and for sending your charming sisters when you can't."

"You're welcome. Arbutus says she's ready to go back to work, so you might git her once in a while."

"Arbutus! Lives in a brick house with two screen porches?"

"An' married t' Junior Bentley," she said proudly.

He would fly up to Wilson's Ridge where, he'd just learned, not a Wilson remained. Then he'd trot to the hospital and see Dovey, run by to visit Puny, and dash home to help with Sissie.

At Hank's store, he bought two cantaloupes for Agnes and Clarence.

"They're from Georgia," said Hank. "Sweet as sugar. By th' way, Morris Millwright come in yesterday, tol' me they won't be back to church."

His heart sank. "I'm sorry to hear it. Why?"

"He heard a couple of people who go to church there killed somebody. Didn't think 'is kids should be around that kind of thing."

"I'll talk with Morris."

"I told him they wadn't but one of th' congregation who'd killed somebody, an' he'd served 'is time."

"Robert did serve time, but we may not know the whole truth. You're a good fellow, Hank. Thanks."

What to do, Lord? Robert Prichard would be dogged by this for the rest of his life, and now Holy Trinity had taken a blow for it, as well.

To get to Holy Trinity and the Mertons required a left turn out of the parking lot.

He prayed briefly, checked his watch—ten after nine—and turned right.

Someone had said that the school bus was situated at the foot of an embankment, beyond an outcrop of rock. Roughly two miles from

Hank's store, he saw the sign—FOGGY MOUNTAIN ROAD—and turned onto a narrow gravel track overtaken by weeds. He drove until he spied the faded orange roof of the bus, then parked and looked for a way down the bank.

The narrow footpath was well concealed, and worn circuitously along the steep decline to the bus.

Truth be told, he wouldn't have minded having Barnabas along on this deal.

"By y'r looks, I reckon y're a preacher."

"Father Kavanagh," he said, extending his hand.

His hand was ignored.

"Y' don' want t' come in; I done cooked collards. They stink s' bad I'll have t' burn th' place down. Let's set on m' deck; I poured that little *ce*ment slab m'self.

"Ain't it a nice e'enin'? Look at th' hawks a-wheelin' up yonder; I could watch hawks a-wheelin' all day if I didn' have a job of work t' do at th' cannin' fact'ry."

Fred slapped his right leg three times and hopped twice.

"Set down right here, I don't need no chair, I'll set on m' fist an' lean back on m' thumb."

Father Tim declined the offer.

"Git on away, Virgil, I ain't got time t' mess with dope heads, I got m' mama in' th' house, us young 'uns cain't fool with nobody as does dope.

"I mought as well tell y', Preacher, Fred Lynch never kilt Cleve Prichard; hit was 'is granboy that done it." Fred made a slashing gesture across his throat, and glared at his visitor.

"I never kilt nothin' more'n a 'coon, an' one time a serpent, but a man's got a right t' kill a serpent, like it says in th' Bible. When I was Holiness, I was bit handlin' a serpent, see that arm, th' whole thing turned black as tar an' th' swell never left it. I've charged cash money f'r people t' look on it; hit's good luck t' look on it . . ."

His host spun around three times, spit twice on the ground, and performed an odd jig.

> "Onesall, twosall
> Ziggesall zan
> Bob tail winnepeg
> Tinklum tan
> Harum Scarum
> Virgin Mary
> Cinklum Sanklum
> Warsh an' a buck!"

"Speakin' of rabbits, see that'n settin' in th' weeds yonder? Hush up! Don' say nothin'! We don' want t' scare 'im off. Hold it right there; don' move . . ."

Fred sidled to the open door of the bus and reached in.

"Hush up talkin', now, I cain't half think if people runs their mouth when I'm tryin' t' kill somethin' . . ."

The visit to the school bus sat on his stomach like bile.

He parked behind Holy Trinity, and made his way along the path to the schoolhouse. Beneath an overcast sky, the blue mountains had turned purple.

"Cantaloupes!" said Agnes. "We can't grow them in our rich soil. What a fine treat."

"From Georgia. I let Hank pick them out. And I brought the new knob and escutcheon for the sacristy door. Clarence said he'd install it for us."

She peered at him, concerned. "You seem ill."

"I'm all right." Those few minutes on the broken cement had left him enfeebled, somehow. "How's Clarence coming with his big order?"

"Very well. I do wish he had help, but of course, no one can carve for him; it would be like forging a signature."

"Would it be all right if I stopped in for a moment?"

"He'd like that. He's carving a family of black bear just now; it's his first bear family." Agnes poured boiling water from the kettle into the teapot. "I'm glad you made it ahead of the rain."

"Yes, and I'll be glad to see it. Sammy's certainly looking for it."

"We all are, but it will do my spinach no good; the rabbits have eaten every leaf."

There had been no rabbit at the school bus. In his rifle scope, Fred Lynch had sighted a patch of shriveled weeds, and blasted it to kingdom come. He'd then done a frantic, arm-waving, hollering dance that sent his caller beating a retreat up the bank.

He walked to one of the many bookcases in the large, paneled room with its enormous stone fireplace, and browsed her shelves. He felt the peace of this home flow into him.

"Come," she said, "let's sit on the porch."

As the rainstorm rolled east over the gorge, he drank his tea and they talked about where he'd been and what he'd seen. His visit to the school bus seemed to affect even Agnes. She sat still and pale in the porch chair, her puzzle close by on a small table.

"Enough of that!" he said, at last. The sassafras was having its way with him; he felt stronger as he trekked to the kitchen and grabbed a towel from the drawer and toted the stool to the porch.

"The same as last time?" she asked.

"Yes, ma'am, and I appreciate it."

"You know I don't feel equipped, Father, as I said before."

"Indeed, you are equipped! My wife thinks very highly of your work."

"Well, then!" she said.

Beyond the screened porch, every vernal leaf dripped with rain from the short, sudden cloudburst.

"Look!" He pointed with eagerness to the rainbow arching over the mountains. "That's what I want for our entire flock at Holy Trinity."

"May He fulfill that desire, Father."

"You know I feel guilty that I have but a year in this parish. Trekking off to Ireland seems selfish, if not entirely vainglorious."

"None of that, now. It's something you've promised yourself and Cynthia for a long time, and a promise is a promise. Think how often promises are made and never kept! Besides, I have a feeling you need the trip."

She snipped the hair overgrowing his collar, her hands steady.

"I do. But you know what they'll send you."

"What, for goodness' sake?"

"A callow youth, still wet behind the ears."

She laughed. "You can't scare me, Father."

"When will you tell the rest of your story?"

The snipping stopped for a moment. "Next time," she said. "Next time."

He looked down to the porch floor. A veritable bale of the stuff had been removed.

He found Dovey sleeping, and left a vase of three pink roses that he had picked up at Mitford Blossoms. He hurried on to The Local where he collected Cynthia's phone order, then zoomed by Lew's for a fill-up.

"You hear th' one about th' *po*lice pullin' th' woman f'r speedin'?" asked Lew.

"Haven't heard it." It was an epidemic!

"She come flyin' by 'im with 'er husband in th' car, *po*lice caught up to 'er, said, 'I'm writin' you a ticket, did you know you're doin' ninety-two?' She said, 'Sure I know it, it says so on that sign yonder.'

"He says, 'That's a highway sign, for gosh sake.' Husband's settin' there white as a sheet; police says, 'What's th' matter with him?'

"She says, 'We just come off of highway one-sixteen.'"

"Pretty funny."

"You ain't exactly bustin' a gut laughin'. I guess you heard about Miss Pattie . . ."

Miss Pattie was a legend in her own time. She'd been known to take a bath with her hat on, plant violets in her shoes, and once crawled out a window to the roof of her front porch, "stark," as Hessie Mayhew reported to one and all.

"What's Miss Pattie done now?"

"She died."

He grabbed his change and nearly knocked over the display of Red Man chewing tobacco as he blew out the door. He jumped in the truck, scratched off without meaning to, turned right on Main Street, hung a left on Lilac, and shot up the hill to Hope House.

Puny jiggled Timmy on one hip, and Tommy on the other. "Me an' Joe Joe thinks Timmy looks like 'is granpaw."

"Certainly not!"

"He does! Look at 'im. Little bald head, no

offense. An' look at 'is little nose. Ain't it jis' like yours?"

He felt his own nose while he peered at Timmy's. "Some resemblance."

"An' Tommy, he looks like 'is Granmaw Esther."

That was a fact. Put a pair of glasses and a wig on Tommy, and he'd be elected in a heartbeat. Mitford still hadn't gotten over losing Esther Cunningham as mayor.

"I've brought everyone a little something!" He began unpacking the shopping bag. "For you, Puny, a dozen eggs, fresh from the nest!"

"Great! Joe Joe eats two ever' mornin'."

"For these fine boys, a couple of books . . ."

"What kind of books're *those*?"

"This one's for Tommy, it's the writings of Mr. George Herbert, and this is for Timmy— Mr. William Wordsworth!"

"Are they any pictures in 'em?"

"No pictures."

"Jis' *words*?"

"Well, of course, they aren't to be enjoyed for several years yet. Sherlock Holmes said it's a great thing to start life with a small number of really good books that are your very own; I've inscribed each one on the flyleaf. And here's a couple of softballs . . ."

Puny looked mighty disappointed that her children's granpaw was so out of it where presents were concerned.

"Listen," he said, shaking one of the softballs. Something chimed inside; Timmy reached for it at once but couldn't grasp it; he batted it to the floor where it rolled under the sofa. The vicar dropped to his hands and knees, and searched it out.

"Oh, law, don't go pokin' around under there, I ain't dust-mopped in a month of Sundays."

"Not a problem!" he said, pulling himself up by a chair arm. "And of course, there's something for Sissy and Sassy . . ."

"You ought t' set down an' catch y'r breath."

Indeed, he felt as if he'd been spinning in a whirlwind since early morning. "Can't sit down; have to scurry. I know how the girls love books, here are the first four in the Boxcar Children series, I hope they don't have them already."

She studied the covers. "They don't! They'll be so glad t' git books from their granpaw; they read all you gave 'em f'r Christmas three or four times."

"Why don't you and Joe Joe pack up the whole brood and come out for supper one Friday?"

"When we go off from here, you never seen th' like of what we have t' haul—bottles, formula, diapers, sacks of this an' that, a change of clothes, books for th' girls, they read all th' time, Sissy's stuffed alligator . . ."

"Maybe in the fall, then—when they're older. We miss you."

"We miss you back. I hope Cynthy has some help out there on th' farm."

"My dear girl," he said, "it's taken three people to replace you."

"Maybe I'll come back t' work when th' kids have left home."

"Yes, but by then, there won't be anything left of *us*."

"Oh, phoo, you're goin' t' live t' be a hundred!"

"Not at the rate I'm going," he said.

He dumped the grocery bags on the pine table and went straight to the library phone.

"Betty? Father Tim. I have good news . . ."

"Thank th' Lord!"

". . . and some bad news."

"Oh, no. Give me th' bad first."

"Miss Pattie died."

"But I *loved* Miss Pattie!" wailed Betty. "I

nursed her at home for a whole month one time, and she's th' only patient I ever had who was actually *fun!*"

"Cynthia found her fun, as well. I hear she enjoyed taking a bath with her hat on."

"No, sir, that story is all wrong. She never wore a hat; but she did take a bath holdin' an *um*brella."

"Aha."

"Because the shower head dripped! I thought that made perfect good sense."

"Absolutely. Now, the good news. Miss Rose has a room at Hope House."

"Hallelu . . . oops, sorry. Since I know how she got it, I'd better watch my tongue."

"Good thinking," he said.

"Hey, Father, this is Connie at Hope House. Miss Louella sent for me this mornin' an' asked me to call you. She was in a strut; said you won't listen to her, but you'd listen to me. Why she picked me, I have no clue! I suppose it's because I work in the office, which always seems more, I don't know, *official*.

"Anyway, she wouldn't tell me what it was about, but she wanted me to ask you . . . where is that note, oh, here it is, you should see my desk, it's like a bomb went off. . . . *'What are you doin' about you-know-who's money?'*

"I said in case he don't know who you-know-who is, maybe she should be more specific. But she wadn't. Well, 'bye."

Beep.

"Teds and Cynthia! You must be out milking the sheep! It's your Yankee cousin, Katherine. Walter and I have done our darnedest to figure out when we might visit Meadowgate, but we're stumped!

"I've gone double duty at the nursing home; I love my dearlings, and then I've let the mayor's henchwoman talk me into chairing the big event in August for children with AIDS. Will you forgive us? You know we'd love to see you—but imagine the weeks we'll spend together in Ireland next year; you'll be sick of us all too soon!

"Which reminds me—Teds, what would you think of boarding with the lovely lady who made that luscious rhubarb tart? Or shall we go as the wind carries us? Loads to talk about!

"For now—hugs and kisses! And God bless!"

Beep.

"Father? Andrew Gregory.

"I've found someone to take on the job of restoring the Plymouth—for a very reasonable sum, it turns out! Thought I'd have the work done, and give the car to the town. We can use it in parades, and to add a touch of pomp to official mayoral activities. Long story short, I'm sending it down to Charleston in four or five days, the fellow has time to start the work now.

"Any interest in taking a final look?

"I'll wait to hear back. All best to you and Cynthia; oh, yes, and to Dooley. I have word he's become a Kavanagh. Congratulations to all."

Beep.

In faraway New Jersey, Walter took a sip of his after-dinner espresso. "Forget it, Cousin."

"Forget it?"

"Absolutely. Once a conviction has been obtained, the laws are very strict about overthrowing it. Further, there was never any evidence that pointed to Fred, and even if you pursued your hunch and something came of it, he'd be mentally incompetent to stand trial. No DA in his right mind would touch it."

He sighed. "I've always believed it's never too late."

"You're a priest, it's your job to believe that."

"You're a lawyer. I thought that was your job, as well."

Walter laughed. "Not this lawyer."

"You're right, of course. Well, sorry to hear you won't make it down this summer, but we understand; we have a house full, in any case. Dooley, his brother Sammy, and, temporarily, a five-year-old with the stamina of a freight train."

"Timothy, you are ever and a day taking in stray children. What a good fellow!"

"Can't help myself."

"To wrap up, Cousin, leave the poor, demented soul to his own devices. Unless there's something I don't know, you don't have the energy or years to chase a wild goose."

In truth, he was already chasing a wild goose, though of a far less serious nature—it was that blasted stack of hundred-dollar bills ostensibly buried in the deeps of a '58 Plymouth Belvedere.

"I c-could've c-c-cut y'r hair," Sammy said as he wolfed his lasagna.

"You could?"

"Yeah. You n-need a little more t-took off of th' sides."

Father Tim felt around up there; it seemed perfectly fine to him. "I do?"

"Yes, sir," said Dooley. "You do."

His wife was enjoying this way too much.

He'd like to shave his head as slick as a cue ball, and be done with the whole miserable business.

"That was a tough rack."

"Pretty hot shooter."

"She's th' champion sh-shooter in th' whole United S-states. Look how many b-b-balls she made on that break."

"*Man,*" said Dooley. "Could you do that?"

He stood at the upstairs linen cupboard, listening to the voices down the hall.

"I don' know. P-prob'ly not."

Sure you could, he thought. *Sure* you could!

Dooley had begun his summer internship at Hal's clinic, and Sammy was working, shirtless, in the garden. On the hottest, most humid day they'd had so far, he took Sissie for a lengthy and circuitous trek—out to the chicken house, down to the pond, up to the hay loft, and around by the cow pasture.

He'd been instructed to exhaust as much of her energy as possible, to prevent a repeat of last night's session. Unable to sleep, Sissie had climbed into their bed and talked a mile a minute until ten o'clock.

"It's sugar," Cynthia had announced at breakfast. "We can't give her anything sweet today. Fruit only."

"Raisins!" he said, being helpful. "Apples!"

"Silly me to show her where the cookie jar was. I've put it on top of the cabinet."

"Better hide the step stool," he cautioned.

After Lily's lunch, which utilized a considerable amount of Sammy's lettuce and peas, he announced nap time. Surely after a late bedtime and early rising, their young charge would sleep like a log . . .

As Sissie curled beneath an afghan on the library sofa, he scribbled in his quote journal.

If the trials of many years were gathered into one, he penned from an old book found on Marge's shelf, *they would overwhelm us; therefore, in pity to our little strength, He sends first one, and then another, then removes both, and lays on a third, heavier, perhaps, than either; but all is so wisely measured to our strength that the bruised reed is never broken. We do not enough look at our trials in this continuous and successive view. Each one is sent to teach us something, and altogether they have a lesson which is beyond the power of any to teach alone. H. E. Manning.*

He reread what he'd written. Wisely measured to our strength . . . amen and amen, Brother Manning, whoever you were . . .

His eyelids were drooping. He propped his head in his hands for a moment, then moved to the wing chair and thumped into it. A light breeze stirred through the open window. Bliss.

Sissie popped up from the pillow, looking urgent.

"How does Jesus git in us?"

"We ask Him in. When we do that, He comes and lives in our hearts."

She put her hand over her heart, furrowed her brow, and listened intently.

"What does 'e do in there all day?"

He heard the front screen door slap, and Dooley's footsteps along the hall to the library.

"Hey," said Dooley, going to the bookcase.

"Hey, yourself."

Dooley shook his head, disbelieving. "Unbelievable!"

"Blake?"

"You got it."

"Now what?"

"Bo's been having trouble with her neck; I noticed she can't bend it. Plus she hasn't been eating much, or moving around a lot."

"I thought it was probably the heat."

"No. She's in pain; I can feel the muscle spasms in her neck. And she's starting to drag her right hind foot. I'm sure she has a ruptured disk." Dooley located a book, took it down, and paged through it.

"What needs to be done?"

"Blake wants to call in a vet who does back and neck surgeries. Nobody around here does that anymore, we'd have to take her to Johnson City."

"Do you agree with Blake's idea?"

"No way. There's only a sixty-percent chance that surgery will work, and if it doesn't, she could need repeated surgeries."

"What are the options?"

"I think we should try acupuncture."

"Acupuncture? Isn't that kind of . . . out there?"

"Lots of vets are using acupuncture to manage pain. Along with that, we need to give her time; sometimes these things take care of themselves. Then, if that doesn't work, opiate drugs and steroids. Surgery would be a last resort."

In Hal's absence, Blake was definitely the boss. "Has Blake made up his mind?"

"He's going to call Hal and see what Hal says. But Hal will side with Blake."

"You're sure?"

"They think alike."

Dooley turned to Father Tim, looking fierce. "Blake is an arrogant, self-serving pain in the butt."

And you have to work with him all summer, thought Father Tim. *Lord, thanks in advance for wisely measuring this to his strength.*

With Sissie in tow, he made a run to visit Dovey, wheeling first into Lew Boyd's.

"Miss Sadie's car is going down to Charleston to be restored," he told Harley. "Could we comb over it again tomorrow?"

"What time would that be?"

"You tell me."

"Aroun' four I could do it. I got a awful job of work on Miz Mallory's Lincoln. Ed Coffey's bringin' it in at ten o'clock. They ain't kep' 'at car up like they should."

"I'll be here at four." Ed Coffey. Maybe he could learn Edith's latest prognosis.

"By the way, Harley . . ."

"Yes, sir?"

"If Cynthia and I had to raise another boy, could I count on you to help us out?"

Harley's toothless grin was wrapping around

to the back of his head. "You c'n count on me f'r anything, Rev'ren'."

Frankly, he wasn't sure he wanted to raise another boy; he didn't know if he could summon the strength. Even his indefatigable wife, though willing, had seemed daunted by the prospect. But what else was there to do?

At the sight of her mother, Sissie burst into tears and climbed onto the hospital bed, bawling. "When are we goin' home, Mama?"

"Soon, honey. Soon. Please don' cry." She smoothed the hair from Sissie's forehead. "Looky yonder, Donny brought m' plate an' cup an' all. Ain't' that nice? They won't let me use it, but I c'n look at it when I pray f'r Mamaw Ruby."

Father Tim took Dovey's hand. "Feeling stronger?"

"Maybe a little bit. I got up an' walked around th' room this mornin'."

Nurse Herman squished into One Fourteen on her lug-sole shoes.

"Mrs. Gleason, may I borrow your pitcher a minute?"

"Yes, ma'am, but please pick it up easy; th' handle's been broke off."

"*Two times,*" said Sissie, "but hit was pasted back."

Nurse Herman drew Father Tim into the hall, closed the door behind her, and held forth the pitcher.

"Here's your culprit," she said.

CHAPTER NINETEEN

Bingo

He stopped by Dora Pugh's for a mask, picking up an extra for Harley. The last time he rooted around in the Plymouth, the dust caused his sinuses to drain like spigots.

"Operatin' on somebody?" asked Dora.

"Operating on a car, actually."

"Takin' out th' drive shaft, I reckon."

Their hardware store owner was never at a loss for words.

"If we have to," he said, counting the correct change.

"Have you heard th' one about . . ."

"Next time!" He struck out for the door with his brown bag.

". . . th' fella who fell in a lens-grindin' machine an' made a spectacle of hisself?"

No rest for the wicked, he thought, charging up Main Street to the truck.

He saw a small gathering in front of Sweet Stuff. A good reminder! Cynthia had been craving Winnie's fig bars, which were, all things considered, relatively low cal. His wife would demolish a couple in no time flat.

He crossed Wisteria Lane, noting that the crowd appeared to be gathered around . . .

His heart hammered.

. . . around Edith Mallory . . .

. . . in her wheelchair.

As he approached, the Collar Button man was bending toward Edith, as if to hear what she was saying.

"Right, right." Appearing uncomfortable, he fled next door to his own shop.

Mitford's fire chief, Hamp Floyd, exited Sweet Stuff with a cake box, the bell jingling above the door.

"Miz Mallory! I declare!" Last September, Hamp Floyd had pulled out all the stops to save Edith's mansion on the ridge, but it had burned to the ground in spite of his effort.

Hamp leaned closer to Edith. "He is, ma'am, He certainly is!"

Winnie Ivey peered through the glass door of her shop to see what was going on, then came out to greet the woman who had tried without success to buy Sweet Stuff for a third of its value.

"Miz *Mall'ry*! Glad to see you on th' *street* again!"

Winnie extended her hand, and Edith took it. Father Tim was standing behind Edith and couldn't hear what she was saying, but it made Winnie smile. "Yes, ma'am," said Winnie. "Oh, yes, *ma'am*."

Ed Coffey stood patiently at the handlebars of the chair, gazing around the small gathering. He caught Father Tim's eye.

Father Tim had known Ed Coffey through some tough times; things had never been easy between them. He was surprised, and even moved, by the look in Ed's eyes—there was no anger or defiance as before, but a warmth he'd never seen. Ed nodded and gestured for him to step closer.

"Look here, Miz Mallory. It's Father Tim."

Ed eased the chair around.

Father Tim was struck by the frailty of his old and bitter nemesis; always a petite woman, she now appeared shriveled, even childlike. Yet her face was radiant.

"Tim . . . o . . . thy . . ." She scarcely spoke above a whisper.

"Edith."

"For . . . give . . . me."

"I did that long ago."

"God . . . is . . . good."

"Yes. Very good." He squatted beside the chair and took her hand and held it. Tears streamed, uncontrolled, down his cheeks.

"Thank . . . you."

"Thank you, Edith, for your witness. And thank God for His faithfulness."

She managed a smile from the left corner of her lips. "God . . . is . . . good," she said again. The large eyes, which had always alarmed him, shone with new light.

He watched Ed and Edith pass up the street, stopping to talk with everyone they met. It was some minutes before he realized his knees were weak and shaking, as if a terrible storm had passed and the sun had come forth at last.

He walked into the garden between Sweet Stuff and the Collar Button and sat on the bench, the brown paper bag in hand.

Bill Sprouse sat beside him with his dog, Buddy, on a leash. "A miracle, brother."

"It is."

"Lord bless 'er, she's puttin' the gospel truth into three little words. Tellin' everybody she sees."

Father Tim mopped his eyes with his handkerchief. The tears wouldn't stop; a dark weight, long carried, had been lifted.

"I know y'all went at it a time or two."

"More than a time or two."

"Old Scratch in a dress is what some called her. I love it when God reaches out and yanks up one of His bad young 'uns and holds 'em in His arms!"

"Like He did me," said the vicar, blowing his nose.

"Like He did me," said the preacher from First Baptist.

He and Harley pulled on their masks.

Andrew stood by, dressed to the nines in a cashmere jacket. Buttoned, noted the vicar. Still carrying a wooden spoon, Tony had taken a break from the Lucera kitchen, and thumped down on an ancient garden bench by the garage.

"What do you think, Harley?"

"Right off, let's git th' doors open an' let some air circ'late in there."

Andrew opened the rear left door; Tony opened the rear right door; he and Harley worked the front doors.

"Teamwork!" said Father Tim.

Harley stuck his head inside. "Been a mouse in here, looks like. An' I heerd snakes'll sometimes crawl up in a ol' car."

"Whoa, buddy; don't go there."

Tony brandished his spoon. "I'll take care of snake."

Father Tim laughed. "Good! Tony takes care of the snake; Harley takes care of the mouse."

"If a mouse jumps out, I'll be haulin' over th' county line. I never liked nothin' in th' rodent fam'ly." Harley got in, cautious, and sat in the passenger seat.

"Louella said Miss Sadie was handy with her toolbox. I can't imagine Miss Sadie handling a wrench or a drill. But maybe a screwdriver . . ." He sat on the backseat, eyeing the surroundings, trying to see things with a fresh eye.

"Top t' bottom is what you tol' me," said Harley. "So here we go ag'in." Harley poked the felt roof liner; dust baptized the interior.

When all was said and done, he still didn't know whether to take Louella's story seriously. Louella certainly believed it; but was it, perhaps, some fragment of an old dream? He felt like a sweaty, overweight fool pulling such a caper in front of Andrew Gregory, who, as ever, looked trim, cool, and dashing.

"I been readin' up on this deal," said Harley. "She's got it all—overdrive, power brakes, full-time power steerin', you name it." Harley continued to poke. "Prob'ly y'r worst problem's goin' t' be y'r power steerin', hit'll need rebuildin' . . ."

Poke, poke; dust, dust.

". . . an' y'r fuel tank'll mos' likely need replacin'."

"She'll look good on the street again," said Andrew. "Those tail fins will be a crowd pleaser."

"*Bello!*" said Tony.

"Hit'll be a jaw dropper, all right. Meantime, they ain't nothin' up here but roof an' linin'. Same as b'fore."

"What do you think about taking the door panels off?" asked Father Tim. "Looks like that could be done with a screwdriver."

"Wouldn' hurt." Harley got in the backseat and began unscrewing the right rear door panel.

Nothing but door-panel entrails and more dust.

"What do you think? Should we take off all the door panels? And what about the dash?"

"Do dash," said Tony, apparently having a delightful time. "Radio, clock, like that." He waved his spoon for emphasis.

"If 'at little woman took out 'er radio, I'll give y' a brand-new five-dollar bill. We start messin' around in th' dash, we'll be here 'til Christmas."

Needing a breath of fresh air, Father Tim suddenly stood, cracking his head on the dome light. "Dadgummit!" He staggered out the door, his hand to his scalp. Just as he thought— blood.

"Man!" he squawked, quoting Dooley.

"I'll bring alcohol and a Band-Aid!" said Andrew, looking concerned.

"I'll get!" Tony struck out for the house.

"Or would you rather come up to the kitchen, Father?"

"Oh, no, no. I'll be fine." He mopped his smarting cranium with a handkerchief. "Not a problem."

"Tell you what . . . ," said Harley.

"What?"

"I'm goin' t' take a look in that dome light y' jis' nailed. Hit's a whopper."

Harley unscrewed the dome light and trained his flashlight into the cavity. "I'll be a monkey's uncle!"

The men stooped down to peer in at Harley.

"You got bingo, Rev'ren'."

When he drove Harley back to Lew's, J.C. was pumping gas into his beat-up SUV.

J.C. threw up his hand, looking positively

sunny. Father Tim eased the farm truck to the other side of the gas island.

"So. What's going on?"

"Not too much."

"What's with the happy face? You look like the ice cream truck just stopped on your street."

"You're a meddlin' fool," said J.C.

"That's what they say."

"Have you heard th' one about . . . ?"

"No, and don't want to. I want to know what you know that I don't know."

J.C. cackled. "Maybe it's for me to know and you to find out."

"You're playing hardball with me, buddyroe."

"You get in my vehicle this time," said J.C.

Father Tim parked in the rear of the station, and stroked around front to the SUV, which J.C. had rolled to the side of the grease pit. He hopped into the passenger seat and slammed the door.

"You're not goin' to believe it, anyway," said the *Muse* editor.

"Try me."

"Things are fixed with Adele. Have been for a couple of weeks, but didn't see any reason to run tattlin' to you; you ain't my daddy."

"What happened?"

"She arrested me."

Father Tim whooped. "No kidding!"

"For . . . let's see, I got th' papers right here." J.C. ransacked his bulging briefcase.

"For being a cold-hearted, unemotional, self-indulgent, ah, hard-headed . . . *jerk,* " he read. "Oh, an' for jaywalkin'."

"Man. Threw the book at you."

"She busted me on Main Street; told me to get in the patrol car."

"What a woman."

"Drove me around. Read me the riot act."

"Whoa."

"You know what I said?"

"Not a clue."

"I said, you're right. And then I said . . ."

"What?" He was pretty much on the edge of his seat.

"I said I was sorry." J.C.'s face colored.

"Great! Good for you!" He suddenly remembered what he'd seen in Baxter Park; his unbounded delight turned sour.

J.C. grinned. "So . . . that's pretty much it."

"No, it isn't; there's more. Spit it out."

"Well, I mean, we like . . . drove somewhere. And you know, parked."

He'd take his chances. If the answer was no, he could cover things up.

"Under the tree in Baxter Park, by any chance?"

"How'd you know that?"

"I get around," he said. *Hallelujah!* "So, what kind of time do you have to do?"

"Six months of take-out."

"Take-out?"

"Take out th' garbage, take 'er out to dinner, pick up take-out at th' Ming Tree in Wesley . . ."

"She could have given you a lifetime sentence. You got off easy."

J.C. nodded, sober. "Real easy."

"Think you'll go straight after this?"

J.C. looked him in the eye. "With God's help. That's prob'ly th' only way."

"Amen," said the vicar, meaning it.

His adrenaline was pumping like an oil derrick as he came through the revolving door and along the carpeted hallway to Room Number One.

Louella was watering a gloxinia on her windowsill.

"Louella, Louella, Louella!" He threw up his arms as if delivering a speech from a balcony. "I have good news!"

She set the watering can down with a thump. "You foun' Miss Sadie's money!"

"Bingo!"

"*Thank* You, Jesus! Thank You, *Jesus*! An' thank Miss Sadie, I bet she put th' hidin' place in yo' head."

"In a manner of speaking," he said.

Hoppy ran his hand through his unruly hair.

"So there it was all the time. She was eating and drinking her own demise. As you know, Nurse Herman is the one who caught it."

Father Tim shook the hand of Mitford Hospital's director of nursing. "Very well done!"

"Like I said yesterday, I wouldn't know old dishes from pea turkey if my cousin hadn't been so sick with lead poisonin'. It was the same thing—she always ate and drank out of old transfer ware her grandma gave her in high school. She was treated for chronic fatigue syndrome for ten years before they figured it out!"

"I never thought about china containing lead," said the vicar.

"The worst amounts are mostly in stuff made before the seventies. Plus, my cousin *and* Miss Gleason really did a number on themselves— they used the dishes to microwave food!"

"Microwaving leaches out dangerous lead levels," said Hoppy. "And chips and cracks can be really lethal."

"Do they still have to get out of the trailer?"

"That's up to the state health crowd," said Hoppy. "They'll probably check the plumbing first thing—if there's a problem, it could be as simple as the hot-water cylinder. It contains a very high level of lead solder, which can deteriorate and turn to sludge. Pure poison."

"*And,*" said Nurse Herman, "Miss Gleason says she makes all her hot drinks with water from the hot tap!"

"When do you think she'll go home?"

"Monday," said Hoppy. "I'd let her go today, but don't want to take any chances. If she's here, I know she's eating. She'll improve on the chelation therapy, but it will definitely take time, and she'll have to check in again for liver function testing."

"What about the bill?" asked Father Tim. "There's no insurance, and she hasn't worked in some time. What's the usual procedure for . . ."

"I have a number you can call," said Hoppy. "Not sure what the result will be, but this is a nonprofit that's helped a lot of patients in her circumstances. Might work out. As for my bill, consider it paid."

Hoppy raised his hand against his old friend's protests.

"I've owed you a big one for a long time. Call it the chickens coming home to roost."

He told her everything, feeling a trifle like St. Nick flying in on his sleigh. Each time he dipped into the day's story bag, he brought forth yet another surprise for the wide-eyed kid in his spouse.

The money in the dome light (which he illustrated by displaying the cut on his head) . . .

The further unraveling of Dovey's curious mystery . . .

Edith's message to Mitford . . .

And then, the upbeat turn of events with Adele and J.C.

"Your go," he said, slurping down a glass of water.

"I could never top any of *that*," said his marveling wife.

"Say on."

"Hal didn't approve the surgery."

"Aha!"

"He didn't approve the acupuncture, either. He wants to wait a few days and see what happens. If the stiffness persists, they'll go to opiates and steroids."

"How does Dooley feel about this?"

"He thinks it's a fair compromise, though he believes acupuncture could alleviate the pain."

"Have things settled down between our resident vets?"

"According to Dooley, Hal made it clear that he wasn't siding with either viewpoint; it's simply what Hal would do if he were here. So, maybe that helped take the sting out."

"What if Hal's plan doesn't work?"

"Sounds like Blake will continue to stump for surgery, and Dooley for acupuncture."

"How did it go with Sissie?"

"Great news! I found the videos you bought for Jonathan in Whitecap; they came out from Mitford in a box of books! She watched *Babe* twice, and is seeing it again even as we speak."

"My kind of girl!"

"I saved *The Little Mermaid* for the two of you to watch tomorrow."

"A thousand thanks."

"So she ate an enormous lunch, and fell onto the library sofa where I thought she'd sleep as if drugged. But did she? Indeed not! She lay down for sixty seconds, then bobbed up again, full of questions.

"So, off we hied to the sheep paddock, where I got a moment's respite as she chased the lambs, which, as you know, can never be caught. Afterward, we paid a call on the henhouse and did Willie's job for him. I confess she was adorable; every egg was an amazement to her. I thought, aha, Sissie and Violet gathering eggs!"

"September?"

"October."

"Brilliant."

"By the way," he said, "whatever happened to your needlepoint plan?"

"The calendar."

"Of course."

She sighed. "A mere one out of three."

"Pretty good numbers," he said.

By eight o'clock, they had collapsed into bed, with Sissie snoring on the love seat and Barnabas snoring on the landing.

As for the rest of the household, Dooley and Sammy were eating pizza in Wesley and washing the Jeep. Lace was coming home tomorrow, and his boy couldn't hide his anticipation. He had tried, of course, but it wasn't working.

"'No disguise can long conceal love where it exists,'" Father Tim quoted aloud from La Rochefoucauld, "'or long feign it where it is lacking.' I committed that to memory when I was courting you."

"I thought I courted you." She kissed the bump on top of his head.

"Yes, well, the line did blur for a while."

"I love you more than ever," she said, patting his arm.

"I love you more than ever back." He patted hers.

"Please don't tell anybody we went to bed while it was still daylight."

He was fried. "They'll never hear it from me."

"Will you pray for us, dearest?"

He prayed the prayer attributed to St. Francis.

"Watch, O Lord, with those who wake, or watch, or weep tonight, and give Your angels and saints charge over those who sleep. Tend Your sick ones, O Lord Christ. Rest Your weary ones. Bless Your dying ones. Soothe Your suffering ones. Pity Your afflicted ones. Shield Your joyous ones. And all for Your love's sake."

"Amen," they said.

He took her hand and they lay quiet, the clock ticking on the mantel.

"I'm always moved by his petition to 'shield Your joyous ones,'" she said at last, "by his recognition that joy is a terribly fragile thing, and the Enemy is bent on stealing it from us. Such a wise thing to ask for."

She turned her head and gazed at her husband as if expecting a word from him, but he was sleeping.

After breakfast, he fished *The Little Mermaid* from the box, and settled Sissie in the parlor. He would do a lot of things in this world, but watching *The Little Mermaid* would never be one of them.

He set up his own camp in the library.

"Violet?"

"Who's this?"

"Father Tim. I have a great idea. Is this a good time?"

"Yessir. I love great ideas!"

"You're a fine singer."

"Thank you."

"And Sparkle doesn't do badly, herself."

"Oh, Sparkle's good, really good. I love 'er alto."

"I'm thinking we need a choir at Holy Trinity."

"A choir!"

"Yes. To help encourage the others to sing; so many are afraid to sing in church."

"They cain't read music, that's why; an' they never heard those ol' songs b'fore. I mean, you got a whole lot of Baptists in y'r bunch."

"True, true. In any case, a choir . . ."

"Beggin' your pardon, but I don't have *time* t' be in a choir. That's a big commitment I ain't ready to make."

"I hear you. What I was wondering is, could you just sit over by the piano during the service, and stand and sing with Sparkle every time we have a hymn? That way, our two best voices would be united."

"A choir of *two*?"

"Something like that, yes."

"You sing pretty good, yourself."

"I never thought so, but thank you."

"You could come an' stand with us. So, then we'd have three up front an' Miss Martha in back—she totally loses 'er key now an' ag'in but she's strong. An' I guess with *us* in th' front an' *her* in th' back, that'd . . . *hold up th' middle!*"

Violet giggled; his heart lifted. "Well said!"

A choir had to start somewhere.

<Dear Father Tim,

<The time is so close, I can't stand it!!!!!!

<Snickers is moping around like it's the end of the world, I could kick myself for taking my

suitcase out ahead of time, you know how dogs
are about suitcases, I should have waited til the
last minute, but who can wait til the last minute
to pack for a trip over an entire ocean?????

<Plus Harold is about to bust out crying. Can
you believe that a grown woman can't go off
on a little trip without sending the whole
household into <u>mourning</u>????

<I wish I hadn't said I'd do this and now it's too
late, my tickets can't be refunded because
they were so cheap. Like $400! Roundtrip!!!
But <u>no meal,</u> can you believe it??? Sandwiches
and pretzels! To cross an entire ocean!!!!

<I have finally made my peace with being as
big as a Buick. Harold has said a million times,
just go with the flow. Well, so I'm going with it.
I'm not even going to try to hold my stomach
in, who cares. I saw a magazine with English
women in it, and except for the royals who can
afford liposuction, they all look pretty much like
me. So, <u>no use to worry.</u> I know you would
approve of this.

<Sometimes I miss the old days when you and
I were squeezed into that little church office
like two hot dogs in a bun. It seems like things
were better then, more settled. Why do things

have to change all the time? Why can't they
stay the same???? Don't even bother to quote
me a carload of scripture verses on change, I
just want to stay mad about it for a while, OK?

<Well, lots of love. Please pray for me. I am a
basket case. The doctor has prescribed a pill
to take before I get on the plane. If it crashes,
I hope you will preach my funeral, haha.
Seriously, it will probably go down over the
ocean if it goes down, so there would only be a
memorial. But if it goes down on land and they
find the body, I would like to be buried in my
black-and-white polka dot with the white collar.

<Emma

He stepped down to the mailbox, then returned to the library, shutting the door against
the *chink, chink, chink* of the masons' trowels
in the kitchen chimney and the video in the
parlor.

Invitation to the annual barbecue of the elec-
trical co-op. Bill from The Local. Credit card
jive. Notice of a fish fry at Farmer's fire hall.

Dear Father Kavanagah,
Thank you for the Bibles. Everybody was so
happy to have one of their own. We are reading
in the gospel of John and studying where Jesus

says in chapter 14—If a man love me, He will keep my words and my Father will love him and We will come unto Him and make our abode with him.

It is a comfort to know that God hisself will come through these prison walls and set down with us in our cell which is our abode and be with each one of His incarcerated children. That is a thrilling thing and sometimes hard to believe but I have felt his presence and know it is true.

I don't hardly know if I should write this, but I have been working real hard to earn time off of my sentence. It looks like I might be coming home soon but I don't know yet so don't please say nothing to Donny or Dovey or nobody else. My crime was a Class B2 feleny, and I have kep a clean record during my time of incarceration and my sentence might could be cut from ten years to seven years.

I will appreciate it if you will pray for them to be able to do this. I will let you know. Please pray for Lucy in our Bible study she has a really bad heart and for Sue and Lonnie. Thank you and God bless you.

Sincerely,
Ruby Luster
#10765L

"So, what does 'e *do* in there all day? You f'rgot."

He leaned forward and put his elbows on his knees, so he could look into her inquisitive eyes. "He guides and directs us, and helps us make decisions, if we ask Him. He gives us a sense of belonging."

"What is belongin'?"

"Being important to someone, feeling at home somewhere. Because when He lives in our hearts, we belong to Him, and He is our home."

This was hard, he thought.

She placed her hand over her heart. "He ain't doin' nothin' but goin' *ka-bump, ka-bump.*"

"That's your heart pumping blood through your body so you can live and breathe and walk and talk and watch videos and eat peanut butter. God lives in our hearts as a spirit. We can tell Him everything, and ask Him anything. He wants to help us because He loves us."

"How come 'e loves us?"

"One reason is because He made us."

"I come out of m' mama's belly. She said her'n' m' daddy made me."

He took her hand. "Let's go up and see Cynthia," he said.

"Hey, Dad."

"Hey, son." He laid his book aside. "Sit down awhile."

Dooley sat in the window seat next to the library fireplace.

"Looks like your Jeep cleaned up pretty good."

Dooley shrugged.

"But you can't be hauling the beautiful Miss Lace Harper around in a Wrangler with a busted door. Tell you what. We hardly use the Mustang since we came out here. Why don't you drive it 'til your new truck comes in?"

"That'd be great. Really great." Dooley was beaming. "Thanks."

"It has a few idiosyncrasies; I'll have to show you."

"Sammy and I figured my truck comes in about the same time as his. He said he'll get potatoes, cherry tomatoes, squash, all kinds of stuff around mid-July. Very cool."

"I'm looking out for my first tomato sandwich. By the way, be careful coming home tonight; the roads are winding, as you know."

"Right."

"There's that hairpin curve just after the FARMER sign."

Dooley patted his foot.

"And that stretch by the old dairy farm—three people have . . ."

"Got it, Dad."

"So when will we see Lace?"

"I'm taking her for Mexican tonight in Wesley. Thought we'd eat with you all tomorrow night, if that's OK. She really likes it out here."

"Steak. Fries. Salad."

"No avocado."

"And chocolate pie, if memory serves me correctly."

"Right." Dooley grinned. "I took Sammy down to Holding yesterday, to his old pool hall. He's great. Really great. He said you saw him shoot a couple of games in Wesley."

"I did. And I've been looking around on the Internet at pro pool associations. Maybe there's a future for him in doing what he loves."

"When I'm working and have some money, I'm going to buy him a pool table. And, you know, get his teeth fixed."

"I mentioned that once; you'll have to hog-tie him to get him to the dentist. It'll take two or three strong men."

Dooley laughed.

"Of course, I'd like to see him get some education. But that will take more than two or three strong men. Remember what we went through to get you into prep school?"

"I was ballistic."

"To put it mildly."

"Do you think you and Cynthia could . . . you know, keep him?"

"We've talked about that. We're going to Ireland next year, but I'm sure we could work something out. The deal is, he must respect the rules of the house, and the people in it. Without that, there is no deal."

"Right." Dooley was reflective. "That's hard. He's really mad about a lot of stuff in his life."

"The option of living on his own, at his age, is not good. Does he know that?"

"He does. He didn't actually say it, but I think he's scared to do it. He left a couple of times before and got mixed up with some really rough guys. That's how he got the scar."

"I thought maybe that happened . . . at home."

Dooley's face grew hard. "Worse things happened at th' trailer."

"How's Bo?"

"Doing OK. I hate to see us waste time like this; she's . . ."

Better not go there, he thought. "How are you fixed for cash?"

"I have a few bucks. I don't get a check from the clinic 'til next Friday."

Father Tim stood and pulled out his wallet. He had to tell Dooley. And soon. He could hardly bear the burden of it any longer. But the time would have to be right; he was waiting for the go-ahead . . .

"Remember the first twenty I ever gave you?"

"It was my birthday."

"You said you weren't going to spend it, you were going to just walk around with it in your pocket." Where had the time gone? It seemed only yesterday . . . He gave Dooley five twenties. "Make it stretch, son."

"Yes, sir." Dooley folded the money and put it in the pocket of his khakis. "Thanks a lot."

Dooley headed for the door.

"Doctor Kavanagh."

Dooley hesitated a moment, then looked around, the light from the window gleaming on his red hair.

"We're proud of you."

He saw his boy try to speak, but it didn't work; he turned and fled along the hall.

On Saturday morning, he and Barnabas piled into the truck with the rhinoceros horn lamp, a stack of computer-generated pew bulletins, three dozen eggs, and a UPS package, and drove to Wilson's Ridge.

He tore open the package, unbaled the sheet music, and thumped it onto the piano bench. Sparkle would come early tomorrow and get things organized.

He sang the communion hymn as he went about the nave, straightening this, adjusting that.

"Just as I am, without one plea . . ."

He dipped his finger in the altar vases. Water. Agnes had been here.

"But that thy blood was shed for me . . ."

The Baptists among them would have no trouble with this one!

"And that thou bidd'st me come to thee . . ."

Someone sang the last line with him.

"O Lamb of God, I come, I come."

"Agnes! Good morning to you!"

Barnabas crawled from beneath the front pew, and lumbered up the aisle.

"Good morning, Father! Good morning, Barnabas! Clarence and I are just coming in with something for the altar vases."

She carried a basket of greenery and blooms

in her left hand, and managed her cane with the other. Clarence followed with a fistful of dried grapevines, hailing his vicar with a hand sign.

His love for his parish above the clouds flooded his heart with a sudden and startling force. He was in his place, as Wordsworth had enjoined him to be.

And he was content.

Grapevine spiraled up from the altar bouquets of cow parsnip, sweet Cicely, and mountain laurel; when Clarence left, they sat in the front pew, approving their labors.

"The tall white flower?" he asked.

"*Osmorbiza claytonii*. Sweet Cicely. The roots smell and taste like licorice, or anise. The species name, *claytonii,* honors John Clayton, who was an eighteenth-century botanist from Virginia."

"You know about all the flowers in these mountains?"

"Many, but never all! See the tall beauty that looks a bit like Queen Anne's lace? Cow parsnip, or *Heracleum lanatum*. You can cook and dry the roots and use it as a salt substitute. But one must never confuse it with water hemlock, which can be deadly."

"It's a jungle out there," he said. He gazed at the altar vases a moment longer, then turned to her. "Grace Monroe had taught Clarence to handle rare Staffordshire . . ."

She smiled. "You're certainly not troubled by forgetfulness, Father.

"We lived with Grace for eleven years; I'd gone to work at the Chicago Public Library. When he was six, I entered Clarence in a school for the deaf. Except for his woodworking lessons, he was miserable, so unhappy. He felt confined, somehow, and never free as a child should be. I was saving every penny I possibly could, and when Grace died, we came home to Wilson's Ridge and our schoolhouse.

"It was the most extraordinary transformation you can imagine. Clarence loved these mountains; it seemed the city had been but a dream. He flourished in every way—his color improved, his imagination took wing, he was happy. He learned the names of trees, and the grain of their wood, and carved his first bird when he was twelve years old."

"And you? How did you fare in coming home?"

"I told those who asked that Clarence's father had died before Clarence was born and that I'd resumed my maiden name. That's what

I told Clarence, also. I struggled with telling my son such a terrible lie. But it was best. It was best. I may be wrong, but I don't think anyone on the ridge knew the truth."

He heard their Pavarotti singing by the door.

"For many months, I sat each day in this very pew and prayed, never thinking much about the rain coming in, and the mice and the squirrels and the birds. Holy Trinity had been abandoned by the church, though oddly, never deconsecrated, and I felt I was simply borrowing, if you will, what was left of it.

"It was some time before God spoke to my heart, using the very words He'd spoken to St. Francis.

"'Rebuild my church,' He said, 'which, as you see, is in ruins.'

"I was still young then, and vigorous, and I began at once. In the beginning, my labor was a penance. For a time, it was a duty. Then—it became a joy.

"Soon, Clarence joined me and we did it together, as unto the Lord. It never occurred to us that we should ask money of anyone, or help of any kind. He had given us an assignment, a ministry; we did what we did in obedience to Him, it was a wonderful way to thank Him for all He'd done for us.

"Clarence's faith is deep, Father, perhaps far

deeper than mine. He absolutely blossomed as he repaired the roof and replaced the water-logged floorboards, and restored the altar railing. And indeed, God blessed his woodworking income in such a way that we no longer had to scrape and sacrifice for every nail—a blessing which we sometimes oddly regretted, I must say, for the scraping had been a blessing all its own.

"Thus we worked on, year after year. My father died and left his estate to me, though I can't say I deserved a penny of it. And then one day, Clarence and I began to pray that He would send someone to lead us, to draw us together again on the ridge—as a family.

"Many believe that seclusion of our sort is an offense, that we are to go out boldly, and serve Him in the great fray of the world. But these coves and hollows are a world, too, Father. And we're honored that He chose us to keep His church from falling to ruin—for such a time as this.

"That is my story." Agnes drew a long breath, and sighed with relief. "I know you must be grateful to have it end, but not so grateful as I to you, for having listened. You're the only one who has ever heard it through."

"He blessed with you a good-hearted and wonderful son. Out of what you experienced as wrong, He made right—as He always does."

"I suppose I should tell you who . . ."

"No," he said. "I know only that you attended the funeral of Cleveland Prichard."

She looked at him directly, with courage; her eyes were very blue.

"And that," he assured her, "is all we need ever say."

Jubal had stripped the winter tarpaulin from his derelict sofa and was sitting on the porch as Father Tim wheeled into the yard.

He parked the truck under a shade tree and gave Barnabas a leather chew for entertainment, then hopped down and collected a jar of tea and carton of eggs from behind the driver's seat.

Jubal threw up his hand. "Leave y'r animal in y'r vehicle!"

Father Tim heaved the lamp from the truck bed and set off for the porch. Even from a distance, he perceived an odd movement beneath Jubal's beard.

He thumped his plunder onto a bench. "Top of the day, Jubal!"

"What in th' nation . . . ?"

Jubal eyed the lamp with suspicion, if not downright disgust.

"It's a lamp! From the horn of a rhinoceros! I know how you like things from nature."

"Th' horn of a what?"

"A rhinoceros."

"I never seed nothin' like it; hit's ugly as homemade sin."

"Most sin is homemade, I'll grant you that, but this will give a cheering light in your place. Shall we step inside and plug it in?" He was personally pretty excited about his gift, albeit pass-along.

"Plug it in? I hain't got but two or three places f'r pluggin' in. M' hot plate's in one, m' shaver's in another'n . . ."

"Your shaver? But you don't shave."

"Hit's ready t' go if ever I git th' notion. Where's Miss Agnes at?"

"She sends her best wishes, and a jar of tea."

"She's done f'rgot me." Jubal looked bereft. "I hain't seed 'er in a coon's age."

"If you were in church on Sunday, you'd see her every week."

Jubal glared from beneath his bushy eyebrows. "Looky there! I knowed ye'd be a-tryin' t' hornswoggle me; I knowed it th' minute I laid eyes on ye!"

"I'm not trying any such thing, just stating fact. And here's the Brown Betties I promised."

Jubal opened the carton, looking suddenly pleased. "Well, set down, why don't ye? Don't keep a-standin' up, I declare, ye'd wear a man out."

The vicar sat on the other end of a Naugahyde sofa that had been generously patched with duct tape. "Jubal, what on earth is under your shirt?" Something was definitely moving around in there.

"Hit's m' whistlepig."

Whoa. He forced himself to remain seated.

Jubal pulled up his beard, put his hand inside his shirt, and withdrew a plump, brown groundhog with beady eyes and fossorial feet.

"I done took it in f'r a house pet; hit's a orphan."

"Does it bite?"

"Dern right; hit's wild, hain't it? A fox or coyote must've broke up its den. I been out a-lookin' f'r clover an' dandelion all mornin'. Livin' by y'rself hain't all roses . . . but it don't have t' be all thorns, neither." Jubal scratched the creature's head.

"He's a mighty lucky little fellow."

"Hit's a female."

"Aha. What's her name?"

"I been thinkin' I might call 'er Miss Agnes."

The vicar had a good laugh. "I'm sure she'd be honored."

"Who? M' pig or Miss Agnes?"

"Both, I'd say. So, Jubal, what was in the bag I brought over here?"

"Trotters. They was pretty good, if ye like 'at type of rations. I hain't eat trotters since I worked at th' sawmill."

He scratched his head. "I brought you . . . *trotters*?"

"You give 'em t' me out'n y'r own hand!"

"But what, exactly, *are* trotters?"

"Pigs' feet!" Jubal was plainly aggravated by such ignorance. "Lord he'p a monkey!"

Lord help a monkey, indeed. "Well, need to get moving pretty soon. Just wanted to say we're growing pretty fast up at Holy Trinity, and planning a homecoming at the end of October. Everybody's welcome. And maybe we can round up descendants of the people who went to church there in the early days. You'll have plenty of time to think about it, but we sure hope you'll join us."

"I cain't be settin' aroun' in a church house not believin' in Almighty God! Lightnin'd strike me dead as a doornail."

"You don't believe in God?"

"Nossir, I don't, an' if 'e ever comes messin' aroun' here, 'e'll be lookin' down th' barrel of m' pump gun."

"Well, then, I doubt you'll have any trouble from Him."

"An' don't ye f'rgit it," the old man warned.

He creaked up from the sofa. "Hope you'll enjoy the eggs, Jubal. I know how you like to stir up something on that fine stove of yours."

"I didn' cook a bite last e'enin'. Hank Triplett sent a plate from 'is mama; hit was loin of deer meat, with sweet taters an' a chunk of cornbread big as a man's hand."

"When you finished that good supper, did you believe there was a cook?"

Jubal studied the question for a moment, and put his groundhog back in his shirt. "You ain't tryin' t' trick me, are ye?"

"I'm not."

"Don't ye be tryin' t' trick me, or I'll set Miss Agnes on ye."

Father Tim laughed. "Which one?"

The groundhog poked its head through Jubal's white beard.

"This 'un!" said Jubal.

Sissie was helping Cynthia in the kitchen, and he had stolen into the library for a breather. Dooley should be leaving anytime to fetch Lace from Mitford.

He was standing at the bookcase when he heard his boy coming along the hall at a clip, probably to pick up the car keys.

Dooley stood before him as if frozen.

"What happened? You're white as a sheet."

"I called him a bad name. A really bad name."

"Who?"

"Blake."

"Why?"

"He argues about everything; I couldn't stand it any longer. I let him have it."

"Unbelievable." This was not good news.

"He's an arrogant, self-righteous . . ."

"That may be. But that's no excuse." He was disappointed in Dooley. Miss Sadie, dadgummit, don't look at me; he knows better.

"But I shouldn't have called him what I did. Actually, I wanted to punch 'im; I had to really hold back. But no matter how blind he is to the truth, I shouldn't have said what I said. Look, I'm sorry. I'll apologize to him, and I apologize to you, too. I know you hate this kind of stuff."

There. The boy had made a mistake and was apologizing to all concerned. Dooley was human, for heaven's sake, what was he waiting for? For his son to be canonized? It was time.

He let his breath out, like the long, slow release of air from a tire gone wrong.

"Let's sit down, son. Take the wing chair."

"That's yours."

"Not really. Right now, it's yours."

"You want me to sit down now or go and do what I have to do with Blake?"

"Do what you have to do with Blake, and get back here fast, I have something important to tell you." He could hardly wait another minute; the waiting was over. But where to start? He'd had this conversation a hundred times in his imagination . . .

He sat and prayed and stared out the window and scratched his dog behind the ears.

Dooley came back, looking relieved. "He took it pretty well; he knows he's hard to get along with. If he'd just listen . . ."

"How would you like to have your own practice when you finish school?"

Dooley sat down and glanced at his watch. "Unless somebody leaves me a million bucks . . ."

Dooley eyed him, grinning.

"Don't look at me, buddyroe. I am definitely not your man on that deal. How would you like to have the Meadowgate practice? Hal's retiring in five years, just one year short of when you get your degree."

"Meadowgate would be, like, a dream. It's perfect, it's everything I could ever want, but it'll take years to make enough money to . . ."

"What if you had the money to buy it?" Why was he asking these questions? Why couldn't he get on with it? He'd held on to his secret for so long, he was having trouble letting it go.

"Well, yes," said Dooley, "but I don't even know what Hal would sell it for. Probably, what do you think, half a million? I've done a little reading on that kind of thing, but . . ." Dooley looked suspicious, even anxious. "Why are we talking about this?"

"Since he's not planning to include the house and land, I'd guess less than half a million. Maybe three or four hundred thousand for the business and five acres. And if you wanted, Hal could be a consultant. But only if you wanted."

"Yeah, and I could fire Blake. Anyway, nice dream." Dooley checked his watch.

"Let me tell you about a dream Miss Sadie had. It was her dream to see one Dooley Barlowe be all he can be, to be all God made him to be. She believed in you."

Dooley's scalp prickled; the vicar's heart pounded.

"She left you what will soon be two million

dollars." He had wondered for years how the words would feel in his mouth.

There was a long silence. Dooley appeared to have lost his breath; Father Tim thought the boy might faint.

"Excuse me." Dooley stood and bolted from the library.

"You don't look so good," Father Tim said when Dooley returned. "What happened?"

"I puked."

"Understandable."

Dooley thumped into the wing chair, stupefied.

"What do you think?" asked Father Tim.

"I can't think. There's no way I can think. You aren't kidding me, are you?"

"I wouldn't kid about these numbers."

"It makes me sad that I can't thank her. I mean, why did she do it? I was just a scrawny little kid who cleaned out her attic and hauled her ashes. Why would she *do* it?"

"I can't make it any simpler. She believed in you."

"But why?"

"Maybe because the man she loved had been a boy like you—from the country, trying to make it on his own; smart, very smart, but without any resources whatsoever. It so happens that Willard Porter made it anyway, as you would, also. But she wanted you to have resources."

Tears brimmed in Dooley's eyes. "Man."

"You want to go out in the yard and holler—or anything?"

"I feel . . ." Dooley turned his gaze away.

"You feel?"

"Like I want to bust out cryin'."

"You can do that," he said. "I'll cry with you."

Cynthia knocked lightly and opened the door. "I can feel it. You know."

Dooley stood. "Yeah. Yes, ma'am."

"And the two of you are bawling about it?"

Father Tim nodded, wiping his eyes.

"You big dopes." She went to Dooley and hugged him and drew his head down and kissed his cheek. "Remember me in my old age."

Dooley cackled.

The air in the room released.

Father Tim put his handkerchief in his pocket.

A new era had begun.

CHAPTER TWENTY

A Living Fire

The preacher at Green Valley Baptist Church walked out to the road sign carrying a black box filled with metal letters. His dog, Malachi, trotted behind.

The preacher shaded his eyes and looked at the noon sky. After a dry June and July, the valley had experienced heavy September rains. Gulley washers! But since early October, they'd been steadily drying out again, and no indication of a drop to come.

To his mind, people were misguided to wait 'til a water shortage became a drought and showed up in the newspaper headlines. This Sunday, two days hence, he planned to insert a prayer for rain, even if some would count the petition premature.

He removed all the black sans serif letters from the sign and dropped them into their compartments in the metal box.

Though he'd planned to put up one thing, here he was fixing to put up another. *Exercise daily, walk with the Lord* was the message he'd had in mind. Then he'd gone and changed his mind, which he had every right to do, seeing as he'd prayed about it. This one would be more thoughtful, you might say, without a lick of humor in it. He'd get a fuss or two from somebody, but he always got a fuss or two from somebody.

He chuckled as he bent over the box, and selected an *L*.

"Malachi, are you still pretty good at spellin'?"

His dog did not reply.

"Writin' that last book of the Ol' Testament must have wore you out; you said all you had to say, looks like."

He dipped into the box and brought forth an *O*.

"I been meanin' to tell you that I especially noted what you set down in th' third chapter. 'Then they that feared th' Lord spoke often to one another: and the Lord hearkened and heard it, and a book of remembrances was written before him for them that feared the Lord, and that thought upon his name.'"

He selected a *V.*

"I'd like to think my name might make it into His book of remembrances; how about you?"

In a while, he wiped his perspiring face and stood back to see what he'd accomplished.

LOVE IS A

Malachi rolled on his side and slept; crickets sang in the dry grass.

A half mile up the road from Green Valley Baptist, collard, mustard, and turnip greens thrived among pumpkins, onions, and winter squash in Sammy Barlowe's garden. Working off water from the pond, a yellow sprinkler baptized its autumnal domain as an odor of rotted sheep manure rose in the vapor from mulched beds.

On Wilson's Ridge, Lloyd Goodnight and Clarence Merton were drilling holes for screws under the eaves of the church roof, to hang a painted banner for Sunday morning. The growl of the drill echoed off the surrounding woods; Agnes heard it from the schoolhouse, where she was polishing the brass altar vases.

In the nave, Cynthia Kavanagh, Dooley Kavanagh, Sammy Barlowe, Sparkle Foster, Rooter Hicks, the McKinney sisters, Clarence Merton, Lloyd Goodnight, and their vicar were in the final hours of Holy Trinity's first annual wax-off. The pulpit, the altar table, the altar railing, the four wooden folding chairs, and every pew were enduring a vigorous polish with beeswax.

"I hope nobody ever gets a notion to wax these *floors,*" said Miss Martha. "There ought to be a law against waxin' a church floor."

"There ought t' be a law," said Miss Mary.

"Bess Sawyer always sat in the back row at the Methodists, but one mornin' after the floors were waxed, she shot right by me and ended up at the pulpit. We thought Mr. Greer had given an altar call."

Clarence volunteered to unscrew the ceiling fixture, dump the bugs out, and hang it again; Rooter volunteered to hold the ladder while he did it. Everyone reckoned the bugs to be historic.

"I cain't do nothin' but set an' talk," said Granny, who had come for the social aspect of this affair. She had propped her foot, which still troubled her, on a kneeler.

Roy Dale and Gladys sat by her side, chewing bubblegum and watching the hive of activity. Granny gave them the once-over.

"You young 'uns're awful dirty. Y' better git a bath 'fore you come in here on Sunday."

"We warsh in th' waterfall."

"That's a good place t' do it. I've warshed in th' waterfall, m'self, a time or two. Are y' usin' soap, that's th' question?"

"We ain't got none."

"You ride with us when Mr. Goodnight takes me'n' Rooter home. I'll give y' a bar."

No comment.

"Say thank ye."

"Thank ye."

"Y'r mighty welcome."

"Hey, R-Rooter, what's y'r h-hand s-sign f'r Sunday?"

"I cain't show y', hit's a secret." Rooter appeared proud to be asked, and prouder still that he wasn't at liberty to reveal this information.

Father Tim set his wax container and rag on a pew and fiddled with the stove door. He opened it, then shut it; opened it, and shut it again. Cranky! he thought, as something so august was entitled to be. "They don't make 'em like this anymore," he said to whoever was in earshot.

A fellow from the valley had worked with Clarence for two days to reinstall the great iron behemoth, and Holy Trinity's vicar had stepped up to the plate and personally oiled it down, black as pitch from stem to stern. Then he and the installer and Clarence and Agnes had a cup of tea and enjoyed the test fire they'd built in its bulging fire box. They'd even walked outside to watch the hickory smoke roll from the chimney like exhaust from a locomotive. Snatched by a fall wind, it vanished above the gorge.

"Drawin' good," said the installer.

Father Tim had inhaled deeply, intoxicated by a fragrance that resonated back to his early childhood. Indeed, the old stove would be their thurible.

Cynthia rode home in the red pickup with Dooley and Sammy, each scented with beeswax; the vicar hung a left on the road by the creek, in the direction of Lambert.

"Hey, Dad."

"Hey, son. What's up?"

"We won't be coming out for dinner. Lace and I are taking Sammy and the kids for pizza and a movie."

"Too bad. You'll miss our okra stew."

"I'm really grievin' over that. Glad you're using your cell phone."

"Feels good to catch up with the rest of the world." He didn't mention that he used it primarily to talk with Dooley, and maybe four times in as many months to phone Cynthia when he was batting around Mitford.

"You and Sammy be careful coming home, you know that stretch by . . ."

"Right."

"Have we found out whether Lace will be with us for Christmas?"

"Yes, sir. The Harpers definitely have to go to Dallas for three days; she'd like to stay with us, if that's still OK."

"That's great. Better watch yourself in that red truck, I've seen a few police cars parked in the bushes on . . ."

"Got it, Dad."

"We love you, buddy."

"Love you back."

He stretched his legs, liking the warmth of the kitchen fire on what his father had called his sock feet.

Oh, the peace of a job well done—Holy Trinity was ready for the big event; they were polished to the nines. And, since he'd written his sermon on Wednesday, he'd gained the unfrayed liberty of Saturday.

"Now that your calendar's done, Kavanagh, why don't we find some trouble to get into tomorrow?"

"I haven't been in trouble for ages; I'd love that!"

"What sort of trouble would you prefer?"

"Maybe . . . something to do with antiques; I'd love a little table with a drawer to go by your chair at home. We could dash into Mitford, and see what Andrew has these days. Or, walking in the woods and listening to leaves crunch underfoot, and finding the waterfall Granny told us about."

"I'll arrange everything. Truck or car?"

"Truck."

"Morning, afternoon, or full day?"

"Full day."

"Lunch in a basket or in a restaurant?"

"In a basket."

"Consider it done. The okra smells good."

"It's all yours, darling."

His wife wouldn't touch stewed okra. He felt it his sworn duty to eat all that Sammy had planted and Lily had frozen—which was enough to last through March, if he was persistent.

Cynthia opened the oven door and checked the roasting chicken; the scent of rosemary and lemon infused the air. "You left Hope's letter for me to read, but if you'd read it aloud, that would be even better."

He went to the table where he'd left the letter.

"By the way, Timothy, you've been the cat that ate the canary for days on end; there are feathers in your mouth."

"Is that right?" He sat down and took the folded sheets from the blue envelope.

"I don't suppose there's any way I could finagle it out of you, this thing you have up your sleeve?"

He laughed. "You're quite right not to suppose it. 'Dear Father Tim and Cynthia . . .

"'When I asked the innkeeper for stationery, she told me that hardly anyone writes letters on their honeymoon. Yes, I said, but the people to whom I'm writing gave my husband and me the moon and the stars. That explains it, then, she said, and smiled.

"'Scott and I will never be able to fully express our gratitude, but we vow we shall try until kingdom come.

"'Our wedding was everything we wanted, and so very much more. The sweetness of Holy Trinity will remain always in our hearts, and the glory of the mountains, robed in their richest and most extraordinary colors, will never fade from memory.

"'I'm told that brides sometimes have no re-

call of what happened during the ceremony!
Yet I remember so vividly the way the church
smelled, like moss and beeswax, apples and
cedar. I can feel the carpet beneath my feet as I
came down the aisle, and Scott's hand on mine
as we knelt together. And we remember your
voice, Father, praying the simple prayer that
seems to cover all of life's goodness and grace:

"'Bless, O Lord, this ring, that he who gives
it and she who wears it may abide in Thy
peace, and continue in Thy favor, unto their
life's end, through Jesus Christ our Lord.

"'Afterward, we ate the cake you asked Esther
to bake for us—it was the grandest cake imaginable! And I love that we bundled into our coats
and went out to the wall with all those who are
dear to us, to marvel at the first blush of sunset
and drink champagne and laugh and weep and
laugh again. Then away we dashed, perfectly
astounded and happy that someone had actually
tied tin cans on our bumper!

"'Laura Ingalls Wilder said it is the sweet,
simple things of life that are the real ones, after all.

"'Our hearts are filled with gratitude for the
sweet and simple treasure of your generosity
and friendship. May you continue to abide in
His peace and favor.

" 'Scott and Hope

" 'P.S. We belatedly wish you a happy anniversary. I just realized it was eight years ago last month when I watched you do the same, very extraordinary thing!

" 'P.P.S. Vermont is enthralling.' "

"A very happy letter!" said his wife.

"I've been meaning to ask—did you notice that Hope's sister, Louise, shy as she is, seemed to get on with George Gaynor? And vice versa, I might add."

"I did notice, actually."

He grinned. "My goodness," he said.

<Dear Stuart,

<As you know, I've withdrawn small amounts from your special fund for Holy Trinity (for kneelers and whatnot), and recall that you said there's more to be had, if needed.

<It seems wise to confirm this with you (rather than trouble the new bishop), as I have an announcement to make on Sunday. I've envisioned a project that would dip quite seriously into the amount remaining. Could you let me hear, ASAP,

if this would have the blessing of the treasurer.

<Once again, the Great Hosanna of June was unforgettable. I failed to tell you what Cynthia said, that standing next to our new bishop, you appeared a veritable Tom Sawyer. I'm certain your time in the islands trimmed off another decade. In any case, you and all those associated with TGH gave us the most auspicious occasion in the recorded history of our diocese.

<May our Lord give you and Martha many years of health, happiness, and well-being.

<Will keep you posted, of course. You are ever in my prayers.

<Timothy

Nearly an hour before the service, he and Cynthia found people in the churchyard, bundled into their coats and jackets. Some were sitting on the wall; others strolled about, admiring the view.

He had smelled wood smoke when they got

out of the truck; he glanced up to make certain the banner was in place.

Holy Trinity Episcopal Church, est. 1899
Homecoming Day, October 28
Welcome one and all

It was nothing fancy, but if the curate wanted the trouble of an annual fete, this banner looked fit to outlast the Sphinx.

"Paul Taggart," said a jovial fellow, stepping forward to shake hands.

"Timothy Kavanagh. You must be kin to Al Taggart who bush hogs for the McKinney sisters."

"Same dog, diff'rent fleas. I'm from over at Lambert."

"We're glad to have you, Paul. My wife, Cynthia."

"Glad to meet you. My granmaw an' granpaw went to church here; I'd about forgot this old place. That's some of my cousins over yonder, an' my wife and kids."

"We'll just go in and get the preacher dolled up, and be right back," said the vicar.

"I pray we'll have enough food," Cynthia whispered, "much less enough places to sit."

The altar vases shone, the windows gleamed, the stove took the edge off the October chill.

Sprinting to the sacristy, they hailed Lloyd and Violet, who were about to set their food offerings on the table.

"'Nana puddin'!" announced Violet, looking as if she'd hung the moon. "'Nough f'r a army!"

"I brought m' baked beans," said Lloyd. "You want me t' start th' coffee after communion?"

He gave Lloyd a thumbs up.

Cynthia helped him draw the white alb over his head. "I've been meaning to tell you," he said. "You look wonderful in that dress."

"Thank you, Father. We aim to please." She buttoned his collar, and put the stole around his neck.

"I'm wild about you, Kavanagh."

She helped him pull on the green chasuble. "I'm wild about you back."

Smiling, she tied his cincture, smoothed his tousled hair with her hands, and gave him an approving blast of her sapphire eyes.

His heart rate was up. Way up.

How lovely is thy dwelling place
O Lord of hosts, to me!
My thirsty soul desires and longs
Within thy courts to be;
My very heart and flesh cry out,
O living God, for thee . . .

Leading the procession and wearing his new black robe with white cotta, Clarence Merton carried aloft the cross he'd carved from the wood of a fallen oak. Following him along the aisle were the choir—Violet O'Grady, Lloyd Goodnight, and Dooley Kavanagh—also wearing new robes.

> *Beside thine altars, gracious Lord,*
> *The swallows find a nest;*
> *How happy they who dwell with thee*
> *And praise thee without rest . . .*

Robed, sick as a cat with apprehension, and with his hair slicked down tight as a stocking cap, acolyte Rooter Hicks processed behind the choir.

> *They who go through the desert vale*
> *Will find it filled with springs,*
> *And they shall climb from height to height*
> *Till Zion's temple rings . . .*

Vicar Kavanagh bowed to the cross above the altar and joined the choir by the piano, singing as if his life depended on it.

He had welcomed the newcomers for a fare-thee-well, put forth a bit of church history, invited one and all to stay for their dinner on the grounds, and moved briskly onward.

In all his years as a priest, he had experienced few Sundays so richly promising, and so dauntingly filled, as today would be.

"Your pew bulletins were printed on Friday, well before I received some thrilling news, news that affects our entire parish—news that, indeed, causes the angels in heaven to rejoice.

"Add to that yet another evidence of God's favor to Holy Trinity, and I daresay your bulletin will be somewhat hard to follow."

He removed his glasses and looked out to his congregation; he felt a smile having its way with his face. "In short, be prepared for the best!"

Several of the congregation peered at their pew mates, wondering.

"In the fifth chapter of the book of James, we're exhorted to confess our sins, one to another. In the third chapter of the book of Matthew, we read, 'Then went out to him,' meaning John the Baptist, 'Jerusalem and all Judea, and all the region round about Jordan, and were baptized of him . . . confessing their sins.'

"I've always esteemed the idea of confession, and in my calling, one sees a good bit of it. But this notion of confessing our sins *one to another* is quite a different matter. Indeed, it involves something more than priest and supplicant; it means confessing to the community, within the fellowship of saints.

"When I left Holy Trinity on Friday, I was going home. But God pointed my truck in the opposite direction.

"I drove to see someone I've learned to love, as I've learned to love so many of you since coming to Wilson's Ridge.

"We had talked and visited several times, and I could see that his distance from God had made things uphill both ways. But I always hesitated to ask him one simple question.

"I didn't hesitate this time. I asked him if he would pray a simple prayer with me that would change everything."

His eyes roved the packed pews, and those seated in folding chairs that lined the aisle. There was Jubal. And all the Millwrights. And Robert and Dovey and Donny, and Ruby Luster holding Sissie on her lap . . .

"Now, the thought of having everything

changed in our lives is frightening. Even when the things that need changing are hard or brutal, some of us cling to them, anyway, because they're familiar. Indeed, our brother had clung . . . and it wasn't working.

"In our hymn this morning, we sang, 'They who go through the desert vale, or any parched and arid valley, will find it filled with springs.' When we choose to walk through the valley with Him, He will be our living water. He will not only sustain us, but give us the grace to move, as that beautiful hymn says, from height to height.

"In a moment, we will have a joyous baptizing, our first since Holy Trinity opened its doors again after forty years. As part of the service for Holy Baptism, our brother has asked if he might make his confession to all of us here today.

"Before I call him forward, I'd like to recite the simple prayer he prayed, similar to one I prayed myself . . . long after I left seminary.

"It's a prayer you, also, may choose to pray in the silence of your heart. And when you walk again through the parched valley, as you've so often done alone, He will be there to walk through it with you. And that's just the beginning of all that lies in store for those who believe on Him."

He bowed his head, as did most of the congregation.

"Thank You, God, for loving me. And for sending Your son to die for my sins. I sincerely repent of my sins, and receive Jesus Christ as my personal savior. Now, as Your child, I turn my entire life over to You.

"Amen.

"Robert Cleveland Prichard, will you come forward?"

Robert moved along the crowded aisle, trembling; his knees were water and his veins ice.

He stood by the pulpit and opened his mouth, but instead of words, tears came. For two days, that had been his worst fear. He turned away for a moment, then faced the people again.

"I'd like t' confess t' you . . . ," he said.

The very air in the nave was stilled. Robert raised his right hand.

". . . b'fore God . . . that I didn't do it."

Father Tim looked out to Miss Martha and Miss Mary, both of whom had forgotten to close their mouths. He saw Lace, riveted by what was taking place; and there was Agnes, pale as a moonflower . . .

"I cain't go into th' details of all th' stuff about m' granpaw, 'cause they's little young 'uns in here. But Friday e'enin' I done a thing with Father Tim that I guess I've wanted t' do, but didn't know how t' do. I give it all over t' Jesus Christ, like I should've done when m' buddy talked t' me about 'im in prison.

"All I can say is, it's good. It's good." Robert nodded, as if to himself. "I thank y'."

He gazed peaceably into the eyes of those seated in the nave.

Agnes Merton stood, and together with Dooley Kavanagh, presented the century-old basin to Father Tim, who poured creek water into it from a tin pitcher.

There was the sound of a log shifting in the firebox; something like a deep, collective sigh stirred among the pews.

My faith looks up to thee,
Thou Lamb of Calvary,
Savior divine!
Now hear me while I pray,
Take all my guilt away;
O let me from this day
Be wholly thine.

May thy rich grace impart
Strength to my fainting heart,

My zeal inspire;
As thou has died for me,
O may my love to thee
Pure, warm and changeless be
A living fire . . .

At the time of announcements, and with no suggestion of what was to come, Father Tim introduced Lloyd Goodnight and Clarence Merton.

The two men took their places by the pulpit.

Lloyd cleared his throat, blushed, and adjusted his shirt collar. He'd completely forgotten to check his fly, but it was too late, now.

"What it'll be is two stalls, one f'r ladies, one f'r men, four b' six each, with wash basins an' all."

He pulled a note from his pocket, studied it a moment, and once again addressed the congregation.

"Me an' Clarence will be y'r builders. We'll run a pipeline to th' spring, like th' ol' schoolhouse done. We'll have a tin roof an' a concrete slab, an' real good ventilation.

"We thank you."

The congregation stood as one, and applauded.

Rooter had pretty much felt his hair drying out by the end of the first hymn. He didn't know which way it might be shooting up since Granny chopped it off with a razor. But he couldn't think about that, he'd just gotten the signal from Father Tim and he had a job to do.

He stood as close to the vicar as he could, for protection—though he wasn't sure from what—and made the sign he'd learned this week from Clarence.

"Watch Rooter," said the vicar. Rooter made the sign, which involved three separate movements, three times. He was careful to do it slowly.

"Now it's our turn." Some got it right off the bat, others struggled.

"What are we saying here, Rooter?"

"God . . . loves . . . us!" shouted Rooter.

He hadn't meant to shout. His face felt hot as a poker.

"Amen!" said someone in the back row.

"I'm asking you to give that sign to someone today," said Father Tim. "And do it like you mean it, because He means it. Indeed, I would ask you to allow yourself . . . to really believe, from a deep place in your soul, that . . ."

His eyes searched the faces as he and Rooter signed.

"... God ... loves ... us.

"Amen."

"Amen!"

He nodded to Sparkle and the choir. Clarence took up the cross.

> *Blest be the tie that binds*
> *Our hearts in Christian love;*
> *The fellowship of kindred minds*
> *Is like to that above.*
>
> *Before our Father's throne*
> *We pour our ardent prayers;*
> *Our fears, our hopes, our aims are one,*
> *Our comforts and our cares.*
>
> *We share each other's woes,*
> *Our mutual burdens bear;*
> *And often for each other flows*
> *The sympathizing tear ...*

The rain began at dusk.

It quickly gathered force, and soon came down in sheets, filling dry creek beds and scattering cattle to the shelter of trees and run-in sheds.

In the downpour, anyone driving past Green Valley Baptist probably wouldn't have noticed the bold black letters of the sign by the road.

LOVE IS AN ACT OF ENDLESS FORGIVENESS

CHAPTER TWENTY-ONE

Let the Stable Still Astonish

They were piled in bed on the evening of the first Sunday in Advent, listening to Mozart and eating popcorn.

Violet was curled on the seat of the rocking chair; Barnabas was snoring on the rug by the bureau; a frigid wind howled around the farmhouse.

He noted that she'd been staring into space for some time, which could mean one, or even both, of two things. She was avidly relishing the Jupiter Symphony, or she was drumming up another book. He earnestly hoped the latter wasn't even a remote possibility, but he'd learned that once she began staring into space . . .

"A live Nativity scene," she said.

"For Holy Trinity?"

"For all of us. Right here at Meadowgate. In the kitchen. After the five o'clock mass on Christmas Eve."

"Tell me more."

"I'm starting to plan ahead, you see."

"Always a good thing."

"Dooley and Lace could be Mary and Joseph."

"Terrific."

"You could be a shepherd."

"I was a shepherd for your book *Mouse in the Manger*. I posed with that ridiculous tablecloth on my head, or whatever it was. Do I have to be a shepherd again?"

"But, Timothy, that's what you are—a shepherd!"

"Typecasting," he said.

He needed to do a little planning, himself.

He thumbed to the back of his quote book and started making notes.

First, he needed to drive to Mitford and pick up the Nativity scene he'd labored over for several months and presented to Cynthia last Christmas. He relished the thought of seeing it again, and the angel she'd made whole from smithereens.

Better get his order in at The Local, while he was at it. Chocolate truffles for the nurses at Hope House, as ever, and the crowd at the Children's Hospital in Wesley. And remind Avis to special order fresh oysters for his wife's dynamite oyster pie.

Something chocolate with nuts for Louella, and a rerun of last year's lipstick from the drugstore . . .

Gifts for the twins, already purchased and wrapped. Checkmark.

Sammy. Checkmark. He was personally enchanted by their gift for Sammy. It was a brilliant notion, if he did say so, himself.

Dooley. Waiting for the raincoat to arrive, and the silver key chain. Sweater back-ordered. He despised back orders.

He had no idea whether his flock would be able to gather for the Christmas Eve Mass at Holy Trinity. If it snowed, as some predicted it would, passage to the church could be limited and risky. *Give us Your grace to gather, Lord* . . .

The Grace to Gather, he scribbled. Sermon title.

And what would he give his helpmeet of eight years, his soul mate, his much better half?

Not a clue.

Last year, he had poured his very heart and soul, not to mention spleen, into restoring the twenty-odd derelict Nativity figures.

How could he top that?

It wasn't all roses with Sammy.

But then, he hadn't expected it to be.

Certainly, the almost-nightly phone talks with Dooley helped. No question.

The garden had helped.

His part-time job with Willie was helping.

And the trips to Bud Wyzer's pool hall were definitely beneficial, though Sammy resented the fact that he hung around, especially in his collar.

Agreeing that his presence at Bud's bar compromised Sammy's sense of independence, the vicar decided to bite the bullet and do something more than hang around.

Come January, he'd take up the game, himself.

Cynthia was dumbfounded. "Glory *be*!" she said.

Where his Yankee wife had learned such talk was beyond him.

"I thought you was p-prayin' f'r Kenny t' be f-found."

"I am. We are."

"He ain't showed up."

"Perhaps God has something else for Kenny's life. Something more important."

"Wh-what could be more important than b-bein' with . . ."

"Family?" Sammy had never used that word in the vicar's hearing. "I don't know. But God knows."

"M-maybe you need t' ch-change y'r prayer."

"I'm expecting God to send him, I believe God will send him, but in the end . . ."

"In th' end, what?"

"I continue to pray the prayer that never fails."

"Wh-what's it say, I f'rgit."

"Thy will be done. It's what our Lord prayed when He knew He was going to be crucified, it's . . ."

"An' s-see what happened?" Sammy looked deeply troubled. "It d-didn' work."

"So! We're hoping Dooley and Lace will be Mary and Joseph and of course, Father Tim will be a shepherd. You'll make a perfect wise man, and the costume will be lots of fun; I'll make it myself. We hope you'll do it; we really need you to do it!"

His wife was aware that this wouldn't be an easy casting job. "We'll give him everything he likes for dinner, and I'll use the word *need*. What can he say?"

"No," said Sammy.

"I've got a great idea."

They were sitting in the kitchen before a blazing fire. Lloyd had claimed the new chimney would draw better than it had in its heyday, and from the looks of things, he was right.

"We'll get our tree from the woods on the Thursday before Christmas. You, Dooley, Lace, Sammy, Willie, we'll all go out looking. How does that sound?"

He remembered how he and Peggy, his mother's housekeeper, had gone to the woods with a wagon and ax and chopped down what they had imagined to be a forty-foot cedar. It had been an immense accomplishment, even if the tree, as it turned out, reached only halfway to the ceiling.

"Straight from a Victorian postcard," said his wife. "And a perfect opportunity for hot chocolate in a thermos! I love it!"

"Cynthia, Cynthia, what don't you love?"

"Shopping malls at any time of year, especially now; flea shampoo that does nothing more than attract a new colony of fleas; and roasts that cost a fortune and cook out dry."

"When I ask you this question, you always have the answer on the tip of your tongue. How do you *do* that?"

"I don't know, I suppose it's just *in* there, waiting to get out."

"Where shall we put the tree?"

"On the window seat, don't you think? There's plenty of room. Of course, no one can see it from the road, which is a shame. I love to see Christmas trees shining in windows. But the kitchen is where we live."

"Done!" He went to the drawer by the stove and searched for the tape measure.

"Our boy will be rolling in tomorrow afternoon. What if I take us all to dinner at Lucera?"

"Umm," she said.

"Umm? You wouldn't like a fancy, overpriced dinner?"

"No, darling. And Dooley wouldn't, either, nor would Sammy, nor would you. But thanks."

"You're welcome."

He measured the depth of the window seat, and the height and width of the cubicle.

"Short and fat!"

His wife looked up from her book.

"Not you, Kavanagh."

He occasionally wandered through the house, gazing at the plaster Nativity scene.

While Mary and Joseph waited patiently on the window seat where the tree would be placed, the humble old shepherd and his flock resided in the library on the coffee table, and the wise men and their amusing camel had been appropriately placed "afar," in the parlor bookcase.

Unbeknownst to anyone but the vicar, the Child lay in a bureau drawer, swaddled in one of his undershirts.

It was no surprise that he'd been sent to Mitford on more than one occasion to haul back items for the holy days:

Old sheets for costumes, rope from Harley's vast supply of odds and ends, candles, wreath frames, ribbon, wrapping paper, gift boxes . . .

"Plunder!" he said, off-loading it all onto the kitchen table.

"Did you tell Willie we'll need straw?"

"Straw is easily come by, not to worry."

"I wish we could bring a lamb or two inside," she said, actually meaning it.

"Where are we going with this thing? You'll have me building the walls of Bethlehem as a backdrop."

"Wouldn't *that* be wonderful?" she said, looking interested.

When his wife wasn't doing a book or a wall calendar, she was a force to be reckoned with.

Two bowls of popcorn were making the rounds of their small soiree by the fire.

"I thought it would be lovely if we added something," announced their director. "Lace, will you read a poem for us on Christmas Eve?"

"I will!"

"Since our entire cast is assembled, save for a wise man, which is very hard to find these days, I was thinking it would be good if you read the poem to us tonight. Then, when we hear it again on Christmas Eve, it should have fresh depth and meaning for us all. What do you think?"

Lace took the book Cynthia proffered; her amber eyes scanned the poem.

She cleared her throat and took a deep breath, and began to read.

> *"Let the stable still astonish;*
> *Straw—dirt floor, dull eyes,*

Dusty flanks of donkeys, oxen;
Crumbling, crooked walls;
No bed to carry that pain,
And then, the child,
Rag-wrapped, laid to cry
In a trough.
Who would have chosen this?"

Father Tim watched the firelight cast shadows on the faces of his loved ones. The recovered Bo snored at his feet.

"Who would have said: 'Yes.
Let the God of all the heavens
And earth
Be born here, in this place'?
Who but the same God
Who stands in the darker, fouler rooms
of our hearts
and says, 'Yes.
let the God of Heaven and Earth
be born here—
in this place.'"

There was a thoughtful silence among them. The fire crackled.

"It d–don't rhyme," said Sammy.

"Not all poetry rhymes," said Father Tim. That was absolutely everything he knew about the subject. "Beautiful, Lace. You have the voice of an angel."

"Perhaps you could let everyone assemble around the manger, then you come into the room, read the poem, and take your place in the scene. What do you think?" Cynthia queried the cast.

"Brilliant!" said Father Tim.

"Sure," said Dooley.

"I like it," said Lace. "Should I just tuck the poem in my robe, afterward, and sit on the hay bale beside the manger?"

"Perfect!" said their director. "And Father Tim will kneel to Joseph's right—with Barnabas, of course. Timothy, do you have the shepherd's crook?"

"On top of the old cupboard, ready to roll."

"And then, we'll all sing 'Silent Night,' and Sammy will plug in the tree."

"What are you going to be?" Dooley asked Cynthia.

"I'll be the innkeeper."

"That's sort of a mean role—to have to say there's no room in the inn, sorry, go sleep in the stable."

"Business is business. If you're an inn and you're full up, well, then, there's no room. Just think of all those people swarming into town to pay their taxes, poor souls. And how many inns could there have been? Certainly not enough!"

"And who knew they would be turning away the King of Kings?" asked Lace.

"There's the rub!" said the vicar, getting into the spirit of things.

"Of course, there won't be any speaking," Cynthia advised the cast.

Dooley looked aghast. "Just . . . *silence*?"

"Yes. We'll use that time to look inside ourselves, to try and feel what they were feeling."

"How could we know what they were feeling?"

"How did Lee J. Cobb know what Willy Loman was feeling? He wasn't a salesman, he was an actor. Better still, how did John Gielgud know what Hamlet was feeling when he killed Claudius—Mr. Gielgud wasn't a murderer, he was an actor."

"She has a point," said Father Tim.

"Man!" said Dooley. "Do we have to do this? They say cows talk on Christmas Eve; I'd rather go to the barn and hear cows talk."

"I'll g-go with you," said Sammy.

"I have a question."

"I love questions."

They sat before a low fire in the kitchen. As the Harpers hadn't yet left for Dallas, where Hoppy's school chum would be having brain surgery, Dooley had taken Lace home. Sammy was watching a pool tournament on TV.

"Who'll be here to observe our living Nativity scene?"

"No one, I suppose." His wife was attempting to repair a hole in her favorite sweater. "Since you're celebrating Mass, I thought we'd have a quiet Christmas at home, just the five of us."

"It seems a lot of trouble to do it all for ourselves."

"It could be a very moving experience."

"Yes," he agreed, "it could be." But he didn't think that each and every member of this particular cast would get the hang of being moved. "Maybe we should have a few people in. A buffet or something. Willie? Harley?"

"You'd feel up to all that?"

"Definitely. Let's see, there's Blake Eddistoe without a relative to his name, though I believe there's a girlfriend in the picture. And if Harley comes, he could bring Hélène."

"Yes, and what about Lon Burtie? Sammy would like that."

"Good thinking!"

"I suppose Louella wouldn't want to come out at night. But we could ask."

"Absolutely!" he said. "Since she's who she is, I'm sure Hope House would bring her in their wheelchair van. And Miss Lottie, what would you think of inviting Miss Lottie?"

"Of course!" She studied the kitchen intently. "We could move the table to the corner by the window seat, which would open up the room, and rent folding chairs . . ."

He peered into the drawer of the small table at his elbow, and took out a notepad and pen.

He would make a list.

My dear Aunt,

I know you haven't heard from me in an eon but remember I told you once that neither time nor distance would ever diminish my affection for you? Though you may doubt it this sentiment remains decidedly true.

Africa is not for sissies not where I've been. After years of roaming the world I am as ready as anything to come "home" and rest my weary bones if only for a time. I am perilously on the verge of becoming an old reprobate. Perhaps I will settle down and have a great number of children—I hear they can be a solace in old age!

Could I possibly put up at your place until I get my bearings? Only for a few days I promise.

I know you're married again—I received your letter in the previous century am a blackguard for not responding sooner—and am thrilled to hear it's to a very decent sort of fellow (at last!).

Will be arriving in the states on 23 December and will draw up to your door on the following evening if that will not trouble you overmuch. Good heavens it just occurred to me that the 24th is Christmas Eve!

I shall bear gifts.

Following is my international cell phone number you may reach me at anytime. And if this awkwardly last-minute self-invite doesn't work for you, I shall fly on to another roost you mustn't worry not even for a moment.

Your loving and devoted albeit adopted nephew
David

She handed him the letter, beaming. "David never did enjoy using the comma."

When he finished reading David's letter, she handed him another before he could comment on the one he'd just read.

"When it rains, it pours," she said.

Dear Father and Mrs. Kavanagh:

Mother says she told you I will be making a new life in the mountains of North Carolina.

If it would not be inconvenient, I would greatly appreciate being able to spend a few nights with you at Meadowgate, beginning December 23, when I arrive in Charlotte. I would drive up and be there around four in the afternoon. I truly do not wish to trouble you in any way. I will happily take care of my own needs, as my years in foreign service have so well prepared me to do.

I will ring you on Monday next, and look forward to speaking with you. I know how very much Mother and Father treasure your friendship, and appreciate that you're watching over things in their absence. I have a pleasant memory, Father, of meeting you some years ago, and look forward to seeing you again.

Sincerely,

Annie Owen

"Where will we put them all?" he asked.

"My brain is in a spin. What do you think?"

He had no idea. Nor did he have any idea about what he was giving his wife for Christmas. He was in a pickle, big-time.

He picked up the list and smoked it over.

Cynthia
Dooley
Lace
Sammy
T.K.
Lon
Harley
Hélène
Willie
Blake
Laura
Louella
Miss Lottie

David, he wrote.
Annie . . .
Cards galore. Many forwarded from Mitford; one envelope bearing a note scribbled by the postmaster: *We owe you 32 cents. Merry Christmas, Jim.*

A postcard. That was refreshing. A Jersey cow in a meadow, with a banner reading WISCONSIN.

All is well with my soul, and pray same with yrs. Hope to see you in Mitford on Dec 24, my new territory brings me to western NC. I thank

God you lead me in that prayer on Thksgiving Day in Lord's Chapel. Your brother in Christ, Pete.

He picked up the notepad. *Pete,* he wrote.

It was two in the morning. He heard some sort of shuffling about in the room.

"Are you up?" he asked.

"Yes!" she whispered.

"What for?"

"The usual."

"Aha."

"I've been thinking."

"Scary."

"We need help."

"What sort of help?"

"Lily. And Del!"

"For Christmas Eve?"

"Yes, for heaven's sake, there'll be sixteen of us, and heaven only knows who we might bring home from church."

"Where are you?"

"Sitting in the rocker."

"Come back to bed. Go to sleep. It'll all work out. I promise."

"We'll need gallons of oysters."

"Willie said he would be a wise man."
That should be some consolation, right there.

<Dear Father Tim,

<After all this time, it just occurred to me who the Queen looks like. My Aunt Clara! Except the Queen dresses in hats and suits that match, and Aunt Clara never had the touch for matching anything.

<Seeing the Queen as she stepped into that car—just like we do, ordinary as you please—is just the best thing that ever happened to me. I'm so glad you taught me how to curtsy. Like I told you before, I curtsied anyway as they drove off, even though she didn't see it. I'm glad I did, she deserves all the respect she can get. Did you read yesterday's papers? I wonder if she takes an antidepressant to deal with all her family puts her through? They say she has something with gin in it at night.

<Esther is spending Christmas with her sisters. They refused to let her bake the cake for their family gathering. I think she was relieved, though she is taking a mince-meat pie.

<I'm in a jam.

<I have no idea what to give Harold. He doesn't like sweaters because they scratch.

Don't suggest a shirt; I don't iron. Don't suggest a tie; he never wears one, not even to church. The preacher doesn't wear one, either.

<I did have a few thoughts, but am undecided. If you were Harold, would you like:

<A nice mackintosh

<A nice book on World War II

<A nice belt for his sander

<Happy Advent to you and Cynthia. Glad you still like your new church.

<Love, Emma

If he were Harold . . .

If he were Harold, he'd be married to Emma. There was a thought to make what was left of his hair stand on end.

Good grief, now he was a consultant on gift giving—he who couldn't come up with a gift for the single most important person on his list.

<Mackintosh **and** sander belt, he typed. Life is short.

<Yours, Fr Tim

There were no nice books on war.

He couldn't wait any longer for it to drop down at his feet, already gift-wrapped. What he needed was a consultant.

"Katherine? It's Tim."

"Teds! How good to hear your voice! A blessed Advent."

"And to you and Walter. I'm fairly desperate . . . "

"A gift for Cynthia?"

"Yes. I'm vicar, now, as you know, of a mission church, and time slipped up on me. I keep drawing a blank."

"Pearls? She seems a pearl kind of girl to me."

"I don't know. Maybe a cross?" Quite suddenly, his mind was working. "I've never given her a really nice cross."

"This is so simple. Do you have a pen?"

"I have."

"Write down sapphires, they'll complement her gorgeous eyes. Platinum setting. Eighteen-inch chain. The jewelry department at Tiffany. Here's the number."

He scratched down the number. "Is this going to cost the moon?"

"Shameful that you'd ask! Merely the North Star, or possibly Orion, but not the moon."

Since their birthdays in June and July, he was seventy; Cynthia was sixty-four. They didn't have forever and a day.

"Done!" he said, feeling brighter. "I'm in your debt."

His teetotaling "cousin" laughed. "Buy me a ginger ale in an Irish pub."

Miss Martha had supervised the greening of the church this afternoon. The sharp, pungent odor of pine and cedar filled the nave; sticks of hardwood burned bright in the firebox.

"In the name of the Father . . ."

He crossed himself. ". . . and of the Son, and of the Holy Spirit. Amen.

"I wrote a sermon this week, but discovered something as I reflected upon it.

"It told us more than we need to know."

Someone chuckled. He could have some fun with that, but time was of the essence; a big snow was predicted for tonight.

"Well, Lord, I said, please give me what we do need to know. And He did.

"As many of you are aware, this pulpit was built and beautifully hand carved by one of our own—Clarence Merton. The church was not open when he did it; in fact, there was no earthly assurance that it would ever be open again.

"Yet Clarence chose to make this pulpit, anyway.

"Why would he do that? He did it to the glory of God.

"And then, a vandal broke in, and he took out a knife and began to do his own carving, right on this magnificent pulpit."

Someone gasped.

"For those of you who haven't seen that particular carving, it's right here." He leaned to his left and made a gesture toward the oak side-panel.

"I consider it to constitute the most profound sermon that could be preached from this or any other pulpit.

"'JC,' it reads, 'loves CM.'

"When Agnes and Clarence saw what had been done, they might have wept. But what did they do? They gave thanks.

"They might have felt it a sacrilege. But what did they do? They considered it a word from God.

"JC, Jesus Christ . . . loves CM, Clarence Merton."

A relieved murmur sounded among the congregants.

"The thrilling thing about this inscription is that it's filled with truth, not just for Clarence Merton, but for every one of us on this hallowed eve of His birth.

"In everything God has told us in His Word, He makes one thing very clear:

"He loves us.

"Not merely as a faceless world population, but one by one.

"J.C., Jesus Christ, loves you, Miss Martha. He loves you, Miss Mary. He loves you, Jubal.

"And you and you and you—individually, and by name. 'My sheep hear my voice,' He says, 'and I call them by name.'

"On this eve of His birth, some of you may still be asking the age-old question, Why was I born?

"In the book of Revelation, we're told that He made all things—that would include us!—for Himself. Why would He do that? For His pleasure, Scripture says.

"There's your answer. You were made by Him . . . and for Him, for His good pleasure.

"Selah! Think upon that.

"And why was *He* born?

"He came that we might have life. New life, in Him. What does this gift of new life in Him mean? In the weeks to come, we'll talk about

what it means, and how it has the power to re-
fine and strengthen and transform us, and deliver us out of darkness into light.

"Right now, Clarence has a gift for every
one in this room. And a wonderful gift it is."
He nodded to his crucifer. "Would you come
forward, Clarence?"

Clarence came forward, carrying a large, flat,
polished board.

He held it aloft for all to see.

"Oak," said the vicar. "White oak, the queen
of the forest.

"This is a place for us to carve our own inscription, like the one on the pulpit. The board
will be here every Sunday until Easter, and
whoever wishes to do it will get help from
Clarence, if needed. You don't even have to
bring your own knife, we have one. When
that's done, we'll hang the board on the wall
over there, where years later, others can see it,
and be reminded that He loves them, too."

He gazed a moment at the faces before him,
at those whom God had given into his hand.
Shine, Preacher! In thy place . . .

"For God so loved the world," he said, "that
He gave His only begotten Son, that who-
soever . . ."

Many of the congregants joined their voices

with his as they spoke the verse from the Gospel of John.

". . . believeth on Him should not perish, but have everlasting life.

"For this hour," he said, "that's all we need to know."

Silent night, holy night,
All is calm, all is bright
Round yon virgin mother and child,
Holy infant so tender and mild,
Sleep in heavenly peace,
Sleep in heavenly peace . . .

Silent night, holy night,
Son of God, love's pure light . . .

As the congregation and choir sang a hushed a cappella, he processed along the aisle behind Violet, Dooley, Lloyd, Rooter, and Clarence to the narthex.

He saw the wrapped box on the card table. Clarence was beaming. *For you,* Clarence signed, handing the gift to his vicar.

Sleep in heavenly peace,
Sleep in heavenly peace.

"Merry Christmas!" Lloyd shook his hand with a forceful grip.

"Merry Christmas, Lloyd, Violet."

"Lily'll have ever'thing in place when you git home," said Violet. "Y'all don't have t' lift a finger. Hope you like it, an' Merry Christmas!"

Agnes took his hand. "Joyeux Noël, Father!"

Rooter planted himself by the vicar's side, signing the message they'd learned at Homecoming. Not everyone had remembered. "F'r ever' three people I sign it to, hain't but one signs it back," he reported.

"Pretty good numbers," said Father Tim.

"Lord he'p a monkey," said Jubal, "they're callin' f'r eight t' ten inches." He pulled a faded wool cap over his head.

"Who's taking you home?"

"Donny, he's takin' me. I'm burnin' 'at horn lamp ye give me."

"I saw it in your window coming by. How's little Miss Agnes?"

The old man grinned. "A awful handful."

The vicar laughed. "She gets it honest," he said, putting his arm around Jubal.

"Was that a snowflake?" asked Lace. "It was! It was a snowflake!"

"We're out of here," said Father Tim.

The snow was falling thick and fast by the time they turned into the driveway at Meadowgate. The wreaths on the gateposts had a fine topping of snow, and the wipers had already pushed a good bit of it to either side of the windshield.

Everyone but Miss Lottie would be here tonight—she had chosen the cheer of her own fireside.

He saw Lon Burtie's and Harley's venerable pickup trucks, and the van from Hope House, its tires outfitted with chains. And there was Dooley's truck, which had gone ahead of them from Holy Trinity, and Lace's BMW, and an SUV, which would be Pete Jamison's . . .

Every window of the old farmhouse gleamed with light.

As he parked the farm truck, he saw headlights coming up the drive behind him. That would be Blake's van.

"Grand Central Station," he said, kissing his wife.

He left the motor running, eyeing the gift she held in her lap. "I confess I can't wait to see what Clarence gave me."

"What's wrong with right now?"

"Cynthia, Cynthia!" When it came to the business of when and when not to open a Christmas gift, his wife didn't share his more conservative conventions. "OK, Kavanagh. Go for it."

She untied the red ribbon and tore open the gift wrap, and chucked the whole caboodle to the floor.

"You lift the lid," she said.

He peered into the box by the light of the outdoor lamp; the wipers were still flinging snow off the windshield.

Bears. Black. Three, four, five of them. Two large, like the one he'd seen in Clarence's studio, and three small.

"Oh," she said.

He picked up one of the large carved bears and turned it in his hand, moved.

She read the card. "'Thank you for making us a family again. Merry Christmas, the Mertons.'"

He didn't think he should try to speak just then.

"You know, Timothy, you have a gift for doing that—for making people into a family again."

She took the bear, and placed it in the box and replaced the lid.

Then she smiled. "Let's go in where it's warm."

He removed the gift-wrapped cue stick from the top shelf of their closet and laid it atop the bureau with the other presents they would exchange. He then spread an afghan over the entire trove, a kind of tarp, as it were.

"Hey, Dad."

"Hey, son."

Dooley came into the room, pulling on Joseph's long coat.

"I'm only doin' this for you and Cynthia."

"I understand. And we appreciate it."

"There are tons of people down there. Are you . . . nervous?"

"Not a bit."

"Right. I forgot you stand up in front of people all the time and make a fool of yourself."

Dooley realized how he'd phrased that, and they both burst out laughing.

"Kenny . . ."

"What about him?"

"You know. I wish he could be here."

Kenny was the sibling to whom Dooley had been closest. "I believe he will be one day. I'm expecting it. Are you expecting it, like we talked about last Christmas?"

"Yes, sir. Sometimes. It comes and goes."

"I understand."

"They finally figured out what to do about the baby. It's a loaf of bread wrapped in Lace's blouse. The way the manger's sitting, you can't tell if it's real."

"Good show." He didn't know why this particular shepherd had to wear head gear; shepherds were poor; they let it all hang out.

"David's a nut case."

Father Tim laughed. "A very loveable nut case, I think."

"Right, I like him. And Annie—whoa. Really smart."

"Thanks for bunking in with your brother. And Lace is a champion to bunk in with Annie. David will end up on the library sofa, it appears."

"I hope he likes dogs," said Dooley. The farm dogs were especially fond of the library sofa. "Your, umm, head thing is slipping out of that noose thing."

"I can feel it going south; can you give me a hand?"

"Hey, man." Sammy came into the room in his wise man's getup. "This is th' dumbest thing I ever d-done."

Father Tim grinned. "You don't look like you've been on a camel for two years."

"Lace talked him into it," said Dooley.

Father Tim tied and knotted his rope sash. "Lace can talk people into most anything, would be my guess." He opened the bureau drawer and took out the plaster figure of the swaddled child.

"Sammy, just before you turn on the tree, would you place the Christ child in the manger?"

Sammy drew back. "Sh-shouldn't D-Dooley d-do that?"

"We'd like you to do it. Just handle it carefully and unwrap it before you set it on the window seat."

Sammy took the bundle. "I c-can hide it behind th' t-tree 'til time t' d-do it."

"Good thinking."

Dooley checked himself out in the mirror on the door. "The kitchen looks cool, Cynthia put straw all over the floor. Candles are burnin' everywhere, an' barn lanterns, there are like these huge shadows on the walls; they'll think they're really in a stable."

"Remember—what our director wants is for us to *feel* what we're doing, for it to be authentic. Let's try to make her happy, boys."

"I hope they's some c-cake left when we git through d-doin' 'is mess."

"Chill, Sammy." Dooley tightened the rope at his waist. "This ain't mess, this is th' real thing."

"You owe me f-fifty c-cents," said Sammy. "You said 'ain't.'"

The boys had gone ahead of him and were waiting in the hall with Lace and Willie and the innkeeper, as he came down the stairs.

He heard laughter in the kitchen, and music in the parlor, and felt his adrenaline getting up.

He was eager to tell Louella that, as they'd agreed, some of Miss Sadie's money had gone to help Dovey through a tough time, and five thousand had gone into a special fund for Holy Trinity scholarships. One day, maybe Rooter or Sissie . . .

Had he heard someone knocking?

It came again, twice.

Always room for one more, he thought.

He opened the front door, and saw a young man in snow-encrusted boots and a hooded jacket. The hood had slipped backward, revealing the snow in his hair, and the mole on his left cheek.

"Father Tim?"

He drew in his breath, and felt the stinging cold of it in his throat. "Come in," he said, hoarse with feeling. "Come in . . . where it's warm."

His hand trembled as he reached out to grasp the hand that reached for his. There was a kind of spark, something electric, as their palms met, flesh to flesh.

"We've been expecting you," he said.

Afterword

Father Tim lay on his back in a far corner of the sheep paddock, looking into the shining cumulus cloud that swelled above him in the bowl of heaven.

A bee thrummed in the clover; he drowsed, but did not sleep. Beyond the rocks, three ewes lay chewing their cud.

In all his years, he had never felt such peace, nor so much a part of everything that was and is and ever shall be, as if there were no distinction between his sun-warmed flesh and the sun-warmed earth beneath.

Since childhood, he had avoided lying in the grass, knowing only too well that spiders and beetles and worms lived there. Instead, he had discomfited himself in hardback chairs—and look what he had missed!

He closed his eyes, and laid a hand on his dog, who drowsed beside him. "Dogs are our link to paradise," Milan Kundera had said; he'd jotted it in his quote book. "To sit with a dog on a hillside on a glorious afternoon is to be back in Eden, where doing nothing was not boring, it was peace."

They had come to Meadowgate to collect a large box of books, left behind in the move on January 10. Indeed, it was nearly the last of the items on their to-do list before jaunting to Ireland in late June.

Though he needed to dash to the farmhouse and help Willie perform the heavy lifting, he felt no haste, no hurry, and none of the fret and care that had accompanied him all his days.

Go . . .

He seemed to hear in his imagination a distant voice from a distant past.

Go in new life . . .

The voice was oddly familiar, and he listened deep in his soul for what else it may say to him.

Go, the voice repeated . . .

. . . and be as the butterfly.

It was another voice, however, that caused him to sit up and take notice.

"Timothy-y-y!"

His wife was calling her truant laborer, but he was loath to end the mystery.

A red-tailed hawk cried; another answered. He shaded his eyes and looked up where they circled and dipped in utter freedom.

He stood, then, and brushed himself off and gazed at the impression made by his mortal flesh upon this patch of earth. It had been wondrous lying there where the grass had flattened beneath him, though he confessed that his heart had lifted up to hear Cynthia's voice, to know that somewhere, someone needed him.

"No rest for th' wicked," he said, quoting Uncle Billy, "an' th' righteous don't need none."

He trotted toward the farmhouse, Barnabas following in the path he made through the high, green grass of summer.

For more works by JAN KARON, look for the

JAN KARON books make perfect holiday gifts.

Also by Jan Karon from Puffin and Viking Children's Books: